THE PURSUIT OF JUSTICE

THE PURSUIT OF JUSTICE

A Novel

Ben Matthews

ISBN: 069239057X
ISBN 13: 9780692390573
Library of Congress Control Number: 2015903220
Rushton Press, Florence, SC

Dedication

She'll never admit it but I'm sure there were times my wife wished she had never suggested that I write a novel. This wouldn't have been possible without her faith and constant encouragement.

Acknowledgements

This is my first novel and it wouldn't have made it this far without the help of many people. Family and writing friends provided direction early on and the fine people at The Editorial Department, especially Jane Ryder and R.J. Cavanaugh, helped pull it all together.

There was movement outside Raymond Jackson's cubicle in the Horry County jail. He took a deep breath to calm his nerves but gagged on the bleach-filled air. There was an undertone of piss or vomit, but Ray didn't want to name it any more than he wanted to be there. *Hell, this wouldn't be happening at all if I hadn't screwed up. Most people would have been satisfied with the malpractice settlement. But no, they had to file a complaint with the Ethics Commission, too.*

The guard opened the door and Ray watched his new client shuffle in, avoiding the faded brown splotch on the speckled tile floor. This man was Ray's punishment. Ray had settled the ethics complaint by agreeing to take on three cases the public defender couldn't handle. *And, of course, the first is a murder case.*

The man was wiry, no more than five foot five or six. His hair was short, like a military recruit's. The tattoos began with a circle of barbed wire around his neck just above the orange collar of the county coveralls and extended out of his right sleeve to his wrist. On the left hand, the tattoos stretched into a half-glove encompassing his third and fourth fingers. He stood, staring at Ray like a charge of static electricity waiting for someone to touch him off, with only the hand and ankle cuffs to restrain him.

Michael "Bo" Heath held out his hands in a practiced motion for the guard to remove the cuffs. The guard lifted the keys and, with a glance, asked Ray's permission. Ray, leaning against the wall in the left corner of the tiny room, shook his head.

"Come on, man. I don't need cuffs," Bo said.

"You attacked your last attorney," Ray said.

"I didn't touch her. Just wanted to scare her so I could get a good attorney, not some girl just outta law school."

Ray nodded slightly. "Well, you got me now." He looked Bo up and down. *The poor idiot doesn't know he's made things worse. I've got less criminal experience than she does.* "You can sit." He was glad his voice hadn't cracked.

Bo sat in a plastic chair at the end of the table nearest the door.

Still standing, observing, Ray dismissed the guard with a wave. After the door closed, he was alone with his new client. *This shouldn't be too bad. The good news is he's probably guilty.* The police report appeared to be solid. And Bo certainly looked like he could be guilty. Ray hoped he could make a quick plea bargain and get back to his regular practice. That's what really needed his attention.

He adjusted his position against the wall and began. "My name is Ray Jackson. Tell me about Tonya Smalls."

Bo was watching him warily. "You got some ID?"

"You know who I am. You got the court order same as I did."

Bo reached across the table and pulled Ray's case file to him with his cuffed hands, watching for a reaction. Getting none, Bo opened the folder and pushed the pages around. "Ain't much here," he said.

"Not yet. I just got your case yesterday. What happened with Tonya?"

"I didn't kill her."

Ray crossed to the other corner of the room. "So you're innocent?"

"Yeah, I'm innocent. I wasn't even here." Bo shifted in the chair to follow Ray with his eyes.

"I don't believe you," Ray said, staring at Bo.

"Screw you. Besides, you have to believe me. You're my lawyer."

"No, I don't. I have to defend you." *Just to keep my license.* "And I can do a better job if you tell me the truth. It's confidential. I can't tell anyone or they could disbar me."

"Yeah, well, I didn't do it."

Ray stepped to the table to reclaim his folder, and Bo flicked it off the other side. The pages scattered, floating to the floor.

Ray stepped back, folded his arms across his chest and stared at his grinning client. He'd seen power plays before. He resumed his place against the wall, leaving the file on the floor, and waited. He was silent until Bo's grin faded. "You've been charged with the murder of Tonya Smalls, assault and battery of a high and aggravated nature, and criminal sexual conduct. That's like rape. You're facing life. Do you understand?"

"It's bullshit," Bo said, thrusting out his chin.

"Do you understand what you're facing?"

"I don't care. I'm not doing any time. I didn't do it. I wasn't here."

"That's what you told the police. Where were you?"

"I was working in Charleston."

Ray kicked a page out of the way and took a seat across from Bo. He opened his tablet and opened an app for notes. "What were you doing there? That's over an hour from here."

"Can you get me off?"

"Get you off? I thought you said you didn't do it."

Bo slapped the table with his fisted cuffs, startling Ray. "I didn't, but they think I did. Can you get me off?"

Ray dried the palm of his hand on his pants. He saw the guard checking through the window in the door. He took a breath and regained his composure. "I'm going to represent you to the best of my ability. What were you—"

"Best of your ability? What the ..." Bo tried to fling his arms open, but they were caught by the cuffs. He dropped his arms to the table and leaned forward. "Are you any good?"

"I am a very successful lawyer." That had been true before Ray's real estate practice crashed with the housing market.

"Shit. What does that mean? Can you win?"

"Before we decide whether to try your case or to seek a plea bargain ..."

"Plea bargain? Shit, man ..." Bo looked up at the ceiling. "How many murder cases you been on?"

Ray placed the stylus on his tablet. *I don't have to answer that. But maybe he'll open up if he knows the truth.* "This is my first."

"First?"

"I wouldn't have been appointed if the judge didn't believe I had the experience and skills to handle the case." *At least I hope that's true.*

"This is your first case. Damn!"

"It's my first murder case, not my first case."

"What other cases have you had?"

In truth, they didn't add up to much. After a brief stint with the solicitor's office right out of school, he joined his mother's firm. He had tried a couple of divorces with her, a few on his own and a DUI. *And I won that.* "Mr. Heath, we're here to discuss your case, not my pedigree. Tell me about ..."

"I want another lawyer."

Ray folded his arms across his chest. "Mr. Heath, I'm here because you pissed off the public defender's office. I don't think the judge will appoint another lawyer, but I'll be happy to make the request."

"You tell the judge I want another lawyer."

"He'll need a reason. What should I tell him?"

"You ain't never had a murder case."

"I'll ask, today. Now, can we discuss your case on the off chance that the judge doesn't give you a new lawyer?"

"Yeah, sure."

Ray looked at the blank page on his tablet and then back at Bo. "I read the police report. It isn't good." According to the report, Michael Heath had met Tonya Smalls, his former girlfriend, at a bar called the Three Door on a Saturday night in October. A witness saw them leave together. No one saw her again until her badly beaten body was found the following Thursday morning behind Palmetto Field. She had been raped and strangled. "We really should see what kind of plea bargain we can get."

"No deals."

"Mr. Heath ..." Ray took a breath. This wasn't going the way he'd planned. "Mr. Heath, you are facing life in prison. I saw the pictures of your hands, arms and face."

"So?" Bo shrugged, turning his palms up.

"Your hands are scarred and bruised. Your arms and face are scratched like you were in a fight."

"I was. I do MMA. Had a fight on that Friday. Beat the bastard bad."

"MMA?"

"Mixed martial arts. They call me Bo Master." He sat up proudly.

"All right. And there's a witness that saw you leaving a club with Tonya."

"Not true."

"If we can get a deal for ten years, that would be a lot better for us than life, wouldn't it?"

"Ain't no 'we' gonna serve the time. No deals."

"All right. Then I need to know what happened. Tell me why you were in Charleston."

Bo sat back and scratched his right wrist just under the cuff. "I need to get out. I don't like it in here."

"The sooner you answer some of my questions, the sooner I can get to work on getting you out of here. I'll check on the possibility of bail."

"Don't you know shit? They already set bail. It's too high."

"Mr. Heath, I just became your lawyer. I'll check on bail. Can you answer some of my questions? Tell me what you were doing in Charleston." *How hard can that be?*

"Check on bail? You ain't no good. I bet you can't get me a new lawyer, either." Bo pulled his arms up to his chest and looked at the wall.

"Mr. Heath, I don't think the judge will give you another attorney. I told you that I will ask, and I will. I'll go to the courthouse as soon as we're done here. But the chances are that you're stuck with me. So you can help or not." Ray waited until Bo faced him again. "Why were you in Charleston?"

Bo dropped his arms into his lap. After looking slowly around the room, he met Ray's eyes. "I was hanging sheetrock."

"Tell me about that."

"I work for Coastal Carolina Construction. Every Sunday morning around ten o'clock, Carlos—he's my boss—picks up me, Robert and Timmy and we go somewhere to work. We come back on Thursday evening most of the time. That's where I was when Tonya was killed."

"The police say you killed her after you left the club together Saturday night or Sunday morning."

"They didn't find her until Wednesday or Thursday."

"How long had you known Tonya Smalls?"

"Ever since she started dancing at the Stallion." Bo smiled and leaned back in his chair. "She didn't have the best body, but she knew how to turn you on."

"That's nice. How long ago was that?"

"'bout five or six years ago."

"Go on," Ray said. *We're finally getting somewhere.*

"I was working as a bouncer at the club and she started dancing there."

"Bouncer?"

"I'm not real big, but nobody messes with me twice," he said, flexing his upper body.

"Describe your relationship with Ms. Smalls."

"We hooked up for a while."

"What happened to your relationship?"

"I tried to get her to stop dancing. I didn't like all those men looking at her and stuff."

"Did she stop dancing?"

"No."

"Did you ever have sexual intercourse with her?"

"We was together for about a year."

Ray nodded. "When was the last time you had sex with Ms. Smalls?"

"Sometime last summer, maybe around July fourth, I guess." Bo shrugged.

"So you didn't have sex with her around the time she was last seen alive?"

"Not with Tonya." Bo sat up a little straighter.

"Were you with another woman on that Saturday?" *A solid alibi would be good.*

"No."

"All right, when did you and Ms. Smalls become 'just friends'?"

"When she moved over to the Men's Club. 'bout three years ago."

"The Men's Club?" Ray looked up from his notes.

"That's another strip club. You know, in North Myrtle Beach."

Ray knew because he passed Ye Olde Men's Club every day on the drive to his office. He used to take one of the bankers who referred business to his office to see the topless dancers every couple of months. *I might have seen Tonya Smalls dance. Hell, she might have given me a lap dance.* Ray made a note and clenched his teeth against an uprising of bile from his stomach. "When was the last time you saw Ms. Smalls?"

"Saturday, a few days before they arrested me."

"That would have been the day that she was killed?"

Bo leaned back in his chair and rolled his eyes. "I told you"—he was shaking his hands in front of him—"it was the day she went missing. They don't know exactly when she was killed. Coulda been Sunday, coulda been any day till they found her."

Ray stared at Bo, letting the room fill with silence. It wasn't intentional. His mind had wandered to another case. Another missing girl. And she was still missing. *Would knowing she was dead ease the pain?* He shook his head to regain focus and looked back at his notes. The police report didn't list the time of death. "So you saw her on the Saturday that she ... went missing?"

"Yeah, I was at the Three Door and she came in."

"The Three Door? Is that another men's club?"

"Just a bar."

"Did you speak to her?"

"Nah, she saw me but she ignored me. She been actin' that way for a while. I think she got a new boyfriend."

"Do you know his name?"

"Nah, she just been actin' like she's got a boyfriend."

"But you don't know?"

"I know how she been acting."

"Can you give me a name?" Ray said as if to a child.

"No."

Ray asked more questions, but Bo didn't have any more answers. He didn't know any addresses or phone numbers for the guys on his crew, and he didn't have any family in South Carolina. Finally Ray was out of questions.

"Mr. Heath, I'm going to talk to the solicitor. You are facing life in jail without parole with these three charges. He will probably offer a plea bargain sometime before we go to trial."

"I don't want no plea. I didn't do it."

Ray held up a hand to try to head off any eruption. "Mr. Heath, whether we accept a plea or not is up to you. But if we try this case and lose, you will spend the rest of your life in jail."

Bo's eyes dropped to the table. When he lifted his head again, the electricity was gone. "I am innocent," he said like a drunk at his first AA meeting. "I didn't do this. Not to Tonya."

Ray winced involuntarily. "Let's hope you don't have to say that to a jury." At least not without a lot more practice. Looking Bo in the eye as he shut off his tablet, he saw the first true emotion from his client. *Damn, what if he is innocent?*

Ray gathered the papers from the floor and stood up. "I'm going to see if the judge is still in. I'll let you know what he says about a new attorney."

2

Ray's phone rang as he unlocked his car. He checked the number, muted the ring and tossed the phone into the passenger seat as he got in. He didn't want to talk to his mortgage company. They wanted a payment and he didn't have it. *Things will pick up in January. At least I hope they will.*

Ray put the keys in the ignition and pounded the steering wheel. *If only I had been a little more careful, I wouldn't be in this mess. Careful, hell.* His mother had been dying. He got a little distracted and didn't take care of his practice like he should have. So he didn't return a few phone calls and missed a deadline? Or two. Did that make him a bad lawyer? No, but his real estate practice wasn't bouncing back with the market. He had some work to do to fix that. And now he had a new client. A nonpaying client. If he screwed this one up, malpractice coverage wouldn't help.

Ray cranked his car. Doubting that the judge would be in his office on the Friday afternoon before Christmas, he drove straight to the courthouse anyway. Maybe Judge King would feel a little holiday spirit and appoint someone else to represent Bo. *Fat chance, but I'm going to try.*

"Good afternoon," Ray said to the judge's secretary, "Would it be possible for me to see Judge King?"

"Today?"

"It's about a problem with a murder case."

"Well, Mr.—"

"Jackson, Ray Jackson."

"Jackson. He's already got an appointment after this one and he's trying to leave a little early today."

"I know, but I don't need much time."

9

"Can I make you an appointment for a week from Monday? That would be the thirtieth. He's out next week." She grabbed a sticky note and a pen. Her computer screen was black.

"I really need to see him today."

"I don't think that's possible."

"Can we ask?"

"You can ask when he comes out, but he really needs to leave."

Ray walked to the half-empty coffee pot. It wasn't very hot, but he poured a cup anyway. The powdered cream congealed on the top and refused to be stirred. He placed the cup in the bottom of the trash can so it wouldn't spill and took a seat on the new plump black leather couch.

Ray rehearsed his entire argument and checked the clock above the secretary's desk. Five minutes had passed. He reviewed the facts of Bo's case. *If time of death is an issue, I might be able to win this case.* But that was not why he was here. Ten more minutes passed before South Carolina Circuit Court Judge Leon M. King exited his office. The judge walked two attorneys to his door and wished them a merry Christmas. He looked at Ray and then at his secretary.

"Mr. Jackson would like to see you. He doesn't have an appointment."

"I only need a minute, Your Honor," Ray said standing.

"All right, but make it quick. I've got to go get a Christmas present for my wife." He motioned for Ray to enter his office like an impatient cop directing traffic.

"It's been a long time since I've seen you in this part of the courthouse, Mr. Jackson. What brings you here?" the judge said, looking like he had just noticed a bad odor. Ray suspected he knew the answer to his own question.

"Your Honor, I've been appointed to a murder case and my client wants another lawyer."

"Isn't this the guy that went after the PD?"

"Yes, sir."

"He's not getting another lawyer."

"Your Honor, I am not a trial lawyer. You know that. He is worried about my lack of experience."

"Come on, Mr. Jackson, it may have been a while, but didn't you start at the solicitor's office?" In South Carolina, prosecutors were called by the more archaic name of "solicitor."

"Yes, sir, but I didn't get to try any cases." A few months after joining the solicitor's office, Ray had taken an unauthorized leave of absence to search for his sister. Two months later, he was asked to resign.

"And you helped your mother try a few cases, didn't you? She was one of the best."

Delores Jackson, Ray's mother, had been one of the first "divorce bitches" on the Strand. She was proud of the nickname. "I might have been there, but she tried them."

"No doubt. We sure miss her."

"But that was all family-court work and I haven't been in a courtroom since. I'm a real estate attorney." He'd chosen real estate because it left him the time he wanted to continue his search.

"Well, Mr. Jackson, then this will be a learning experience. Isn't that why you signed up for the public defender's program?"

"Well, Your Honor ..." Ray looked at his feet. He didn't want to tell anyone why he was on the list. "I joined because ... because I'm trying to expand my practice. This is the first case I've gotten."

"I see," said Judge King, turning from his computer screen to stare at Ray over his reading glasses, which were perched at the end of his nose. "When the public defender conflicted out, your name came up. In fact, I think I had an e-mail suggesting that you be moved to the top of the list."

"Your Honor," Ray said with a sigh, "I would like to be relieved because of my inexperience in criminal law." He leaned forward, his hands involuntarily clasped like a parishioner seeking forgiveness.

Judge King sat up straight. "He knew what he was doing when he attacked the PD. He's trying to delay his trial. So I appointed you. You're his attorney."

"Yes, sir. It's just that—"

"Oh, you'll be fine." Judge King leaned back. "It's a simple murder case. Believe it or not, murder cases are the easiest to try. And it's not a death penalty case. You'll probably plead it anyway." He stood to dismiss Ray.

Ray remained seated, but his voice rose. "He is entitled to justice, and I don't believe he'll get it without an experienced trial attorney."

"Justice? Is that really what you're worried about? You can be sure that he'll get justice in my courtroom, and so will the victim and the victim's family. They're entitled to justice, too."

"Yes, Your Honor, it's—"

"But today, Mr. Heath is entitled to a lawyer. And I decided that you're the lawyer. So go get the case ready for trial. With the way real estate is moving, I know you have plenty of time to prepare. Now, is there anything else?"

Ray stood. "No, Your Honor. Thank you for seeing me."

"Maybe you can find an experienced friend to advise you on the case. Give you a few pointers."

"Yes, sir. I think I'll do that. One more thing, Your Honor—I need to get the bail reduced."

"You should probably have a preliminary hearing, too. Ask the solicitor to schedule that and we'll take up the bond then."

"Thank you again. Merry Christmas and happy New Year."

When Ray exited the judge's office, Nelson Patterson was leaning on his cane, talking to the judge's secretary. He was the local state senator, the leading partner in the most profitable law firm in Horry County and one of the best trial lawyers in the state. His silver head of hair was carefully groomed to give the false impression of a man who had gone prematurely gray. He shook the secretary's hand with both of his and started toward the judge's office. He stopped abruptly and stared at Ray. "What are you doing here? I didn't think you did trial work."

Ray had never really cared for Nelson, although he was an old friend of his mother's. "I don't usually, but I just got appointed to a murder case.

I was discussing the appointment with the judge." He took a step toward the door.

"Oh, that's right. It's not a death penalty case, is it?"

"No, thank God."

"Don't worry. You won't have to try it. Your guy will probably take a plea."

"The plea bargain system works well for the guilty and not as well for the innocent. My guy claims to be innocent."

"Don't we all? Call me if I can be of any help. Merry Christmas." He turned back to the secretary.

"He's on the phone with Judge Harrison," she said.

"Well, give him this and tell him I'll see him after the holidays," he said, shoving a bottle of red wine with a bow on top at her as Ray turned to leave.

"Wait up," Nelson called to Ray. "I'll walk with you."

Ray made a half-turn to the left and stopped. *Damn.* He put a smile on his face. Over Ray's objections, his mother had asked Nelson to help when she finally learned of the ethics complaint. Ray had spent more time caring for her than for the practice. And that cost his clients some money. Client neglect was the official charge, and the investigating attorney seemed ready to drop the entire matter with a warning because of Ray's mother's health. That is, until Nelson got involved. *He probably sent the e-mail to the judge, too.*

"Not that way," Nelson said, "this way." He threw his thumb toward a door marked "AUTHORIZED PERSONNEL ONLY." "We'll borrow the judge's elevator. Special privilege for the handicapped." He raised the prosthesis where his left foot should be. He lost it in some sort of boating accident years ago.

The door wasn't locked, and Nelson punched the "down" button with his cane. "So how are you doing?"

Ray's mother had died less than a month ago, the day after Thanksgiving. Although the stroke had happened over two years ago, she never returned to practice. Ray had farmed out a lot of her cases. Several had gone to Nelson at her suggestion. "I'm fine."

"I respected your mother. She was always kind to me. Outside of the courtroom, that is."

"She had no friends in the courtroom once a trial started. That was one thing I learned from her."

"She taught us all a lesson or two. So, how'd you get appointed?"

As if you don't know. "My guy attacked the public defender."

"Ooh, I heard about that one. Good client."

"Yeah," said Ray with a chuckle.

"Who's the investigating officer?"

"Jarrett Brown."

"He's good. He was hard-nosed before his daughter died a few years ago. But since"—Nelson rolled his eyes—"he lives for the job. You better look for a plea."

Ray didn't give a fuck about Jarrett Brown. Or his daughter. "My guy says he didn't do it and I think I've got a decent alibi."

"Is this the guy who strangled the stripper?"

"It is."

"Tony at the PD's office told me about it. Sounds pretty bad."

"Well, it's mine now."

"Do your homework and call me if I can help."

"Thank you."

Nelson stopped as they reached his new black Escalade. He looked around to see if anyone was near and, speaking a little softer said, "For what it's worth, I put in a good word with the Ethics Commission for you. I know you let a few things go because of your mother's condition."

Ray nodded and felt the blood rush to his cheeks.

"And I asked Leon to put you at the top of the list. That way you would get your required hours completed and be able to move on."

"Uh, thank you," Ray said.

"Don't mention it. I know it's been hard. I remember losing my parents. That's why I want you to come see me after the first. I've got some real estate work that I'd like to send your way—if you're interested?"

"Of course," said Ray. "Thank you." *I know I need it, but why would Nelson send it to me?*

Nelson thrust his hand out to Ray. "No, thank you, and merry Christmas."

"Merry Christmas and happy New Year to you." Ray walked to his car shaking his head. *I'm sure Nelson is only trying to help. How do I make him stop?*

3

———◆———

R ay's office phone stopped ringing before he could get the door unlocked. He kicked the door as soon as the sticky key released. *Damn, no message either.* He really needed some business. His cell phone began to ring almost immediately. It was Reverend Tim, his pastor. A cold drop of water ran down the back of his hand from his hair, still wet from his regular morning swim, as he put the phone to his ear. "Hi, Tim."

"Ray, we need you at the church now. SLED's here with a search warrant." SLED, the South Carolina Law Enforcement Division, was South Carolina's version of the FBI. "They just marched in and told everyone to step away from their computers."

"SLED? What do they want?" *I got the bingo reports in on time.*

"Financial records. They want all of our books for the last five years. Our new treasurer is in there with them, but she needs help. How fast can you get here?"

Ray had a mid-morning appointment in Conway. "Stay calm, I'm coming." The Reverend Tim Thomas was the pastor of Gethsemane Gospel Baptist Church. Ray had been the church attorney since becoming a member shortly after his sister disappeared. Reverend Tim had counseled Ray during that awful time and during his divorce. "Have you called Nelson?" Nelson Patterson was the long-standing chair of the church's Finance Committee.

"I called him first," Reverend Tim said. "He told me to call you since he was out of town and you prepared all of the bingo papers. He said he would try to find out what this is about."

"Don't answer any questions. I should be there in less than fifteen minutes." Ray grabbed his tablet and Bo Heath's file before heading for the door. His appointment was to see Bo to prepare for tomorrow's preliminary hearing. He probably wouldn't have time to come back to the office.

All five feet five inches of the Reverend Tim Thomas was pacing in the lobby of the church offices when Ray arrived. "There you are. They brought this." He shoved the search warrant at Ray as if it were burning his hands. He wiped a bead of perspiration from his temple near the receding edge of his jet-black hair and started toward the offices in the back. "Come on."

"Wait a second," Ray said. He unfolded the document and began to read. Looks right, b*ut what do I know? I've never seen one of these before.* "Is this for bingo or the Pro Life League?" Any kind of gambling, even church bingo, was highly scrutinized. And the South Carolina Pro Life League, Reverend Tim's aggressive political arm, had ruffled more than a few feathers in the past. There was even a rumored connection to the murder of an abortion doctor in Florida a few years ago.

"They didn't say."

When they stepped into the treasurer's office, Ray saw Jennifer Jones, his old girlfriend, standing against the beige wall watching two black-suited men work at the desk. *What is she doing here?* Ray's eyes engaged Jennifer's briefly, but he could read nothing there. He never could tell what she was thinking. She looked good. If she was going to be a problem, she would have to wait until SLED finished.

One of the men was sitting at the computer and conferring with the other, who was looking over his shoulder at the screen. A USB cable ran from the desktop Dell computer to a Mac sitting beside it. The agents looked up when Reverend Tim and Ray entered and then returned to their work without a word.

"Good morning, I'm Ray Jackson, the attorney for the church," he said. It seemed as good a start as any.

"Good morning," the one standing said. "I'm Agent Thompson and this is Agent Maroney. We're executing a search warrant for the financial records of the Gethsemane Gospel Baptist Church and related entities."

"Can you tell me why you need the records?"

"This is part of an ongoing investigation of certain criminal activities in the area," he said, acting as if he were revealing confidential information. The other agent's portable printer began to hum and everyone watched silently as it printed a multi-page document.

"I'm done," Agent Maroney said. He unplugged the cable and began to shut down the laptop.

"Who is the target of this investigation?"

"I can't say right now," Thompson said. "Here's a list of the documents we downloaded for your records and my card. Should we contact you when we're ready to take statements?"

"Sure," Ray said as he passed his card to the agent.

Ray's card went into Thompson's shirt pocket without a glance. "Thank you. We'll call your office. If you'll excuse us ..." He nodded at the door, which Ray was blocking because the office was so small.

Ray slid to his right to keep the agents from leaving. "What crimes are you investigating?"

"No one has been charged. This is a preliminary investigation."

"The warrant says 'financial crimes.' What is that? Fraud, embezzlement, tax evasion?"

"I can't comment, because this is an open investigation," Thompson said, shifting to his left foot.

"Come on, Agent"—Ray looked at the badge hanging from the man's coat pocket—"Thompson, you know who and what you're looking for. Tell me what's going on."

"All right. This is the most successful bingo operation in the state, by far. It also has the highest operating costs. When we looked at the quarterly reports, something smelled. We're going to tear those reports apart and compare them piece by piece to the records we have here. Then we'll be talking to anyone who prepared reports or worked on the accounting—including you, Mr. Jackson."

Ray resisted the urge to swallow. "When might that be?"

"You'll be hearing from us." He took a step closer to Ray and from that no-longer-polite distance said, "Now, please, step aside."

Ray met the slightly taller agent's stare and, still blocking the door, simply opened his hand because there was no room to extend it. "Let me know if I can be of any help. We intend to cooperate fully."

"Sure." Agent Thompson's eyes dropped to the hand, and his frown deepened. Then he shook the hand with the conviction of a politician rushing through a crowd. When he did, Ray slowly stepped aside and let the agents pass. Maroney rubbed the door frame with his shoulder, avoiding the proffered hand.

Ray turned to Reverend Tim, still smiling the grin he had pasted on for the agents. "Can we go to your office?"

"Sure," he replied with a nod. "Jennifer can show you the way. I'm going to stop by the break room and get a cup of coffee. Uh, I'm sorry. Ray, do you know Jennifer Jones, our new treasurer?"

Ray took a longer look at Jennifer. She was about his height, with green eyes that had captivated him not too long ago. Her brunette hair nearly reached her shoulders. She was obviously still making her seasonal trips to Atlanta or New York to keep her wardrobe and shoe closet up to date. Today she was showing off her carefully maintained figure in an expensive V-neck burgundy sweater and a hip-hugging black skirt with a modest side slit that stopped near her knees. There was a dress code at the church.

"We're old friends," Jennifer said before Ray could speak. She stepped over and, placing a hand on his arm, gave him a peck on the cheek. "It's been a while." She locked those green eyes on his.

Her perfume, one of his old favorites, attacked his memory. His hand found her waist but he didn't draw her closer. He didn't push her away either. He wasn't sure what to do. They had not spoken since their last date—or was it a fight?—just before his mother's stroke. She wanted a ring, and he didn't like the way she'd asked. When she finally answered one of his phone calls, she made it very clear that she never, ever wanted to see him again. She didn't even call to check on his mother after she got sick.

"Yes," Ray said after a few seconds. "Yes, it has."

"Would you, uh, old friends like coffee or a soft drink?" Reverend Tim said as his eyes darted from one to the other.

"We'll have coffee, please. Black," Jennifer said releasing Ray's arm. "Right?"

"Right."

The main offices of Gethsemane Gospel Baptist Church were located in what was still thought of as the "old' building. It had been the only building on the church property when Ray and his ex-wife joined. The concrete block structure had been remodeled after the new sanctuary was built almost ten years ago. Reverend Tim's office was in the new sanctuary building. The auditorium, which could seat five thousand guests, and a Sunday-school building had been added since Reverend Tim became pastor thirteen years earlier. The membership of the church had mushroomed because of his passionate right-to-life stance, which funded the growth of the church along with the highly successful bingo operation.

Jennifer took Ray out a side door. "This way."

"I remember," he said.

Jennifer reached out, took Ray's arm and began to walk. "I'm sorry about your mom. How are you doing?"

"I'm OK. How about you?"

"Fine. I had a relationship with a co-worker at my last job and it didn't end well. They never seem to end well for me, but you know that. Anyway, I needed a change of scenery and this was a perfect fit. But really, how are you? I haven't seen you out since your mom got sick."

You could have called. "I was taking care of her and really just haven't felt like it since she died."

"Our group is still hanging out at Fat Harold's. You should come out one night and have some fun."

"I'll think about it."

She frowned. "Don't think too hard. Here we are." Jennifer waved him through a door.

Reverend Tim's office was on the second floor in the back of the sanctuary building. His floor-to-ceiling window overlooked the prayer garden.

"Why don't we sit over here?" Jennifer indicated a seating area with a long plush couch and a couple of soft armchairs around a small coffee table that sat in front of a wall of books across from Reverend Tim's desk. It was where he liked do his counseling. Ray had spent a lot of time in these chairs. He had spent many hours talking to Tim after his sister, Brittany, disappeared, and he endured a painful session after the breakup with his ex-wife. Maybe he needed to find some time to talk about his mother.

"So, how's Kara?" Ray said, sitting in one of the chairs. Kara was Jennifer's pre-teen daughter.

"She's great. I talk to her a lot on Facebook." She took the chair next to Ray.

When she sat, Ray saw just how high the slit in her skirt went. "Still living with her dad in Greenville?" he managed.

"And his bitch wife."

"So how long have you been at the church?"

"A little over a month."

"How do you like it?"

"Certainly more exciting today."

"Yeah, what do you think they were looking for?"

"I don't know. They took all of our ledgers and reports for the past five years."

"Could you tell if they were interested in anything in particular, like bingo or the Pro Life League?"

"If it's bingo," Jennifer said, "I'll bet they are searching the records at Orion, too." Orion Management Group operated the bingo games for the church. For a significant percentage of the proceeds, Orion did most of the work. The church provided the license for the games, which was available only to nonprofit entities. The games had been lucrative before Orion took over, but the profits for the church, and for Orion, had soared under its care.

Reverend Tim walked in with the coffee just as Jennifer's cell phone rang. "It's John," she said. John DeHaven ran Orion. "SLED's been here, too," she said. "Let me put you on speaker. Reverend Tim and Ray Jackson are here." She touched the screen and put the phone on the coffee table.

"What did they take from you guys?" DeHaven said.

"Five years of financial records," Jennifer said, leaning forward slightly.

"Same here."

"Mr. DeHaven, this is Ray Jackson. Did they take all of your financial records or just those related to bingo?"

"Five years of everything."

"Do you know what they were looking for? They were not very forth-coming with us."

"One of the agents mentioned money laundering."

"That makes sense," Jennifer said. "We do handle a lot of cash."

"Jen," DeHaven said, "why don't you do a thorough review of all of the records? You can compare ours to the church and see if there is anything to worry about."

"Reverend Tim has already talked to Nelson. He's checking on his end, but we haven't heard back from him," Ray said.

"John, it's Tim. Tell your people to talk to no one. We need to keep this away from the press until we know what it is."

"No problem," DeHaven said. "Call me when you hear from Nelson." He hung up.

"Jennifer, can you print me a copy of everything they took?" Ray said. "Here's the list of files."

"I can, but it will take some time."

"We've got to go through it all."

"We could start now, if you like," Jennifer said with a brilliant smile.

"Unfortunately, I've got an appointment in Conway and I need to go." *She does look good, but I'm not going there until I know what she's after.*

"I'll call you when it's ready. I've still got your number," Jennifer said, running her hand through her hair. "Do you still have mine?"

"Yes," Ray said. "Yes, I do."

4

Ray and Bo were in the same cubicle at the jail again. It still smelled of disinfectant. This time Bo's handcuffs were off. Bo slouched into the chair at the end of the table. Ray took the opposite seat and opened his file.

"Mr. Heath, you know we have our preliminary hearing tomorrow."

"What about my bail?"

"We'll take that up, too. I think we have a reasonable chance of getting you out on bail. You don't have much of a record, and the state's case is pretty circumstantial. It seems to hinge on one witness, a Mr. Royal McKenzie who says he saw you and Ms. Smalls leave together."

"He's lying. He's the one that was with her."

"Did you see them leave?"

"No, but they was talking when I left."

"What time was that?"

"It musta been ten thirty or eleven. She was still there sitting at a table with Roy Mack. I had to go to work the next morning."

"Who is Roy Mack? Was he her boyfriend?" Ray wrote the name.

"Roy Mack? That's what we call 'Mr. Royal McKenzie,'" a smile broke out on Bo's face as he shook his head. "That son of a bitch. He ain't her boyfriend. He's supposed to be my friend. But he's turning on me. Why would he do that?"

"I don't know. Why would he do that?"

"I think he's the one who did Tonya."

"Really? Why?"

"She whored for him."

"How do you know that?" Ray underlined the name.

"She told me."

"Did you ever pay Tonya for sex?"

23

"No." Bo sat up straighter and gave Ray a sideways look. "I might give her some coke or something, but I didn't pay her for nothing."

"Does Roy Mack have any other girls?"

"I don't know—probably. He runs a club."

"A club?"

"Yeah, a strip club called the Pink Slipper."

Ray added that to his notes. "Have you ever had sex with anyone that might have been working for Roy Mack?"

"No," he answered with a sharp jerk of his head. "Why you cross-examinin' me?"

"I'm trying to learn what you know about Roy Mack."

"Why don't you go talk to him?"

"I've called him, but he hasn't returned my phone calls."

"No shit. He ain't going to call you back."

Ray circled the note he'd made. "Did Tonya use drugs a lot?"

"Not really. I smoked some marijuana and some crack with her a few times. Snorted some coke."

"Do you know if she was using any drugs when you saw her at the Three Door?"

"I don't know. I told you I didn't talk to her. She was ignoring me."

"Were you using any drugs that night?"

"No, I was broke."

"Who was with you at the Three Door?"

"Nobody. I was just getting a beer."

"Did you see anybody, talk to anyone?"

"Ricardo."

"What's Ricardo's last name?'

"Shit, man, I don't know. He's the bartender."

Ray made a note to talk to the bartender. "Who else was there that might have seen you leave without Tonya?"

"It was early. The place wasn't busy."

"But you said you left around eleven."

"Yeah, the Three Door don't get busy till midnight when other places close."

"But you didn't stay for that?"

"I was busted. I paid the rent and the electric bill. It took all my check. I got a beer and went home."

"How did you go home?"

"Same as I got there. I walked."

Ray paused and looked at his notes. "Did you talk to Roy Mack?"

"No. He must have come in after me. I didn't see him until Tonya was talking to him."

"What were they talking about?"

"How would I know?"

"I don't know. Do you?"

"No."

"Before you saw Tonya at the Three Door, when did you see her last?"

"I saw her at the church two, maybe three months before that."

"What happened there?"

"Nothing. She didn't talk to me then either. She don't pay me no attention when she got a new boyfriend. It's like she don't know me. People shouldn't do that."

"Shouldn't do what?"

"Ignore folks. It might make them mad or something."

"Did Tonya make you mad?"

"Yeah, it's not right to treat a friend like that. But I didn't do nothing."

Ray flipped through the pages in his file. Then he returned to his notes. "You said when we first talked that Carlos picked you up around ten on Sunday."

"Yeah."

"Do you remember what time he came on that Sunday?"

"Around ten."

"Was he a little early that morning, a little late?"

"It was around ten like always. What does it matter?"

"Because the coroner says she died sometime between 3 a.m. and 3 p.m. on Sunday."

"She wasn't found till Thursday."

"I know. Do you know how to get in touch with Carlos? The number I have doesn't work."

"That's the only one I got." Bo shrugged.

Ray leaned back in his chair. He looked at his client for a minute before returning to his notes. "Let me get some background on you. It could help when the judge considers your bail. What did you do before you hung sheetrock?"

"I worked at bingo."

"Bingo? Where was that?"

"That church out on 544." Bo jerked a thumb toward the coast.

"Gethsemane Gospel Baptist Church?" Ray asked even though he knew the answer.

"Yeah."

"That's where you saw Tonya. What was she doing there?"

"I don't know. Maybe she was playing."

"What were you doing there?"

"Working."

"As what?"

"Bouncer."

"The church needs a bouncer?"

"Yeah, for bingo. I watched the money. Even counted some nights. Bingo makes a lot of money."

No shit. "Before that, where did you work?"

"Bouncer at the Stallion."

"OK, we've been over that." Ray stood and started to gather his file. "I'm going to work on your case the rest of the afternoon. I'll see you tomorrow."

"You still gonna be a lawyer then?"

"What?" Ray stopped and stared at Bo.

"I heard you got in some trouble."

"Really?"

"It was on the Internet."

"It's nothing for you to worry about. It's over. It has nothing to do with your case."

"You better do good for me or ..." Bo shrugged and opened his hands in front of him.

"Or what?" Ray said. "You'll get me disbarred? Well, fuck you." He picked up his file. He walked to the door and called the guard. He took a half-step back into the room. "If you screw with me, you will spend the rest of your life in jail. If you want a chance of getting out of here at a decent age, you really need to help me make a deal."

"I don't want—"

"Shut it." *Stupid fuck.* "I'll see you tomorrow." He waited outside the cubicle until the guard came.

Ray fumed all the way back to his empty office. There was no one there, because he'd had to fire his secretary six months ago. He couldn't afford her. He was managing, barely, on what little business was coming in because he kept his expenses low.

Ray sat down and dropped the mail onto the middle of his desktop. The blinking phone showed that he had four voice mails. He pushed back from his desk and surveyed the office. There were some diplomas on the wall, a couple of prints depicting old fox hunts and a dusty trophy for a second-place finish in some charity captain's-choice golf event.

He looked at the mail. All bills. He picked up the envelope from the IRS. They wanted money, too. He put it down and hit the "play" button on the phone. He could sure use a new client.

Three of the voice mails were about past-due bills, including his mortgage, but the last one was from Nelson Patterson about the work they'd discussed before Christmas. He called him first. Trish, Nelson's administrative assistant, answered immediately.

"Thank you for calling so quickly. Let me see if the senator is available."

Nelson picked up in less than a minute. "I hear you've got a prelim in the morning."

"Yes, on the murder case."

"Let me know if I can be of any help, but that's not why I called. I wanted to ask if you would be interested in handling some foreclosure cases for one of our clients."

Ray hesitated for a microsecond before answering. It was not the kind of real estate business he was expecting. "Sure, I would be happy to."

"Five hundred a pop unless it's contested. OK with you?"

"How about seven fifty?"

"The best I can do is six."

"All right, that's good." It was still a little low, but he was desperate.

"Great, I'll put Trish back on the line and she can get you up to speed. Good luck with your murder case."

"Thanks, I really appreciate the referrals," Ray said to the music on hold.

Trish agreed to e-mail the preliminary information, and he promised to stop by her office later to get the supporting documents.

Ray was eating his homemade lunch, a peanut butter and jelly sandwich, when the e-mail arrived. Just like that he had five new cases. Three thousand dollars would pay a few bills, including his past-due mortgage. *And all I have to do is toss five families from their homes.* He moved his mouse to download the first case and stopped. He took another bite of his sandwich, but he was no longer hungry. He slammed the sandwich into the trash can. *I didn't go to law school for this. I don't have to do this.* He reached for the phone. He put his hand around the receiver but didn't pick it up. *I need the money. Fuck.* He marched to the coffee maker and refreshed his coffee. He went back to his desk and kicked his chair. *Shit, shit, shit, shit. Goddamn you, Nelson Patterson.* He sat. He stared at the screen for a few minutes, but the e-mail didn't go anywhere. "And Goddamn me," he said. Then he downloaded the first case.

5

The cold February air seeped around the large windows of the Horry County Courthouse and beat back the feeble attempts of the ancient heating system. Bo Heath was shivering in the chair next to Ray. Bo didn't have a coat to wear like the spectators and members of the press who filled the back of the room.

"Hey," Bo said. "I didn't think they could keep me cuffed in the court." He held up his shackled hands.

"I'll ask the court to remove them."

"It ain't right."

"You won't have them during trial because a juror might think you're guilty because you're restrained." Ray said as he emptied the contents of his briefcase onto the table. "But it's up to the judge today."

"Great."

No one in the history of Horry County had spent more time getting ready for a preliminary hearing. *And felt less prepared.* There was a manila folder, which had Bo's name hand-printed on the tab. It contained the police report and some notes from his meetings with Bo. Ray's nearly empty legal pad sat on top of a dog-eared copy of the Rules of Criminal Procedure. The new bright yellow "used" sticker was still on the spine of the book. Despite all the effort, the pad had only a few questions that he'd finally scribbled on it sometime after midnight. Ray shed his overcoat and offered it to Bo. He refused.

Ray watched as Harry Carson, the assistant solicitor assigned to convict Bo, entered the courtroom from the judge's area. Harry greeted the bailiff and a couple of the guards. He shared something that was apparently funny with the court reporter. Harry graciously accepted congratulations from another attorney for a recent death penalty conviction.

Harry finally noticed Ray and strolled over to the defense table, his hand extended. "I'm Harry Carson, and you must be Delores Jackson's son." Harry shook Ray's hand firmly. Harry had come to the solicitor's office from upstate a few months after Ray left. He was the number two assistant to the solicitor.

"Ray, please."

"Ray. Well, Ray, is there anything you need here? You've got some water?"

"No, I'm good."

"This shouldn't take long."

"Why don't you just agree to a reduction of bail and we'll waive the hearing?"

"What? You've got to be kidding. You should be talking about a plea." He glanced across Ray's shoulder at Bo. He increased his volume so that Bo was sure to hear. "We got our guy." His voice was high-pitched and had a bit of a nasal twang.

"He has an alibi."

"But there are some holes in it. We can discuss a plea later. All I've got to do today is show probable cause." Harry adjusted the band holding his straight gray hair in a ponytail. A loud knock came from the front of the room. "Looks like we're ready," he said. "Good luck."

"All rise," the clerk said. "The Circuit Court of South Carolina is now in session. The Honorable Leon King presiding."

"Be seated," Judge King said. "Mr. Carson, good morning. You have the first case?"

"Yes, sir, it is the State of South Carolina v. Michael Jordan Heath. We are scheduled for a preliminary hearing with a request for a reduction of bail."

"I want a new lawyer!" Bo Heath yelled from his chair. "I want a new lawyer, I want a new lawyer."

Ray grabbed Bo by the arm. "Be quiet."

"I want a new lawyer now!" Bo said louder.

Judge King banged the gavel. "Mr. Heath, you will be quiet or I'll have you removed from the courtroom."

"I want a new lawyer."

"Quiet," Judge King said with a forceful stare at Bo.

Two bailiffs moved to the defense table.

"I want—" Bo stopped when the largest bailiff put a hand on his shoulder and dug in with his beefy fingers. Bo winced and squirmed in his chair.

Judge King's face formed a smile, but there was no humor there. "That's better. Let's be clear, Mr. Heath. I will not tolerate any further interruptions from you. You will be removed from my courtroom and we will proceed without you. Do you understand?"

Bo nodded.

"Good. Now, I take it that you would like another new lawyer assigned to your case. Mr. Jackson is the second lawyer you've had appointed. You and I know what happened to the first. That's why you have Mr. Jackson. He has been practicing law for many years, and I'm sure that he will represent you to the best of his abilities. Your request is denied. Do you understand me?"

Bo glared at Judge King,

"Do you understand me?" the judge said again.

Bo nodded.

"Mr. Jackson, are you ready to proceed?" Judge King said.

"Yes, sir." It was too loud, almost a shout.

Startled, Judge King sat up. "Very well. Mr. Carson, you, uh, you may call your first witness."

Bo leaned over to Ray. "I'm screwed," he whispered. "Even the judge knows you're no good."

Captain Jarrett Brown, Harry Carson's first witness, stood erect like a flagpole to take the oath. His black suit looked as if it had just been pressed. As head of the homicide division of the Horry County Sheriff's Department, he'd conducted the investigation of this murder. And he interrogated Bo Heath after his arrest.

"The victim is Tonya Smalls," he said. "Her body was found between six and seven a.m. on October nineteenth behind Palmetto field. She had been beaten and strangled. Her body was naked below the waist, and the coroner indicates that she had intercourse shortly before her death."

Ray jumped to his feet and yelled "Objection!" so that he could be heard over the outburst of talking from the gallery, "The coroner's report is not in evidence."

"I'll have quiet in this courtroom." Judge King said, stopping the murmuring. "Now, Mr. Jackson, you are correct, and in a trial I would sustain your objection, but this is a preliminary hearing. The usual rules of evidence don't apply, because you have asked the state to show that they have probable cause to bring this case. We aren't deciding your client's guilt or innocence today, just whether or not the case should be allowed to proceed. And once we decide that, we'll move to the question of bail. Overruled."

Captain Brown continued. "The body was discovered by Hattie Barcous and Lucille Johnson during the course of their morning walk around the field. They sent a neighbor, Royal McKenzie, to investigate. Mrs. Barcous called nine-one-one."

"How did you determine that the defendant was involved?"

"We found skin beneath the victim's fingernails and cuts and scratches on the defendant's arms that were consistent with wounds inflicted by fingernails."

"I see. Does that skin match the defendant?"

"According to the SLED lab, the pigment is similar. The DNA is being tested now."

"You don't have the results of the DNA test yet?"

"No, sir."

"Is there anything else that led to the arrest of Mr. Heath?"

"A witness at the scene, Royal McKenzie."

"Do you recall what Mr. McKenzie told you?" Harry said.

Ray jumped to his feet, but Judge King cut him off. "Mr. Jackson, sit down. Hearsay is acceptable in a preliminary hearing. Go ahead, Captain Brown."

"He saw the defendant and the victim leave the Three Door together shortly before she disappeared."

"And what is the Three Door?"

"It's a bar."

"Do you have any other witnesses, Captain?"

"The bartender at the Three Door confirms that the victim and defendant were in the bar on Saturday night."

"That was Saturday night, but the body was found on Thursday morning, right?"

Ray started to rise to object to the leading question, but Judge King stared him back into his seat.

"Right," Brown said, seeing the silent exchange.

"What happened in between?"

"The victim was last seen alive at the Three Door with the defendant. She was reported missing by her grandmother on Sunday night. We have no reported activity between Sunday and the time the body was found."

"Did the coroner establish a time of death?"

"He did. The victim died between 3 a.m. and 3 p.m. Sunday. The window for the time of death is large because we're not sure when the body was dumped behind the field."

"Thank you, Captain Brown."

Harry turned to the bench. "That's all I have, Your Honor."

"Very well. Captain, you're excused. I find the state has—" Judge King stopped, seeing that Ray was standing. "Mr. Jackson?"

"May I examine the witness, Your Honor?"

"Mr. Jackson, that doesn't usually happen in preliminary hearings, but you may proceed."

Captain Brown was halfway across the courtroom.

"Captain, please return to the stand," Judge King said with a look at Ray. "I'm sure this won't take long."

"Captain Brown, Mr. Heath was arrested in Charleston, isn't that correct?" Ray said as he walked toward the witness stand like a tiger seeing his prey.

"Yes."

"That's where he was working, right?"

"Yes."

"And he had been there continuously since leaving Myrtle Beach around 10 a.m. on Sunday morning, correct?"

"That's what he says." Captain Brown, who had sat like a soldier at attention for the state's questioning was now leaning forward like a wrestler ready to fight.

Ray stepped up to the witness box and placed both hands on the rail. He leaned toward the witness. "But you don't have any evidence to contradict that, do you?"

"Mr. Jackson," Judge King said, "please step back from the stand."

"Yes, sir," he said.

"You may answer the question, Captain," the judge said.

"No, but he had time to commit the murder and dump the body before he left."

"Given the large window for the time of death, isn't it more likely that she was killed after Mr. Heath left town?"

"She died sometime during that 'window,' and I think it was on Sunday morning."

"But it could have been on Sunday afternoon, right?"

"According to the coroner."

"Do you have any evidence that she wasn't killed Sunday afternoon?"

"The defendant left town."

Laughter in the courtroom was silenced by a bang of the gavel. "Quiet."

"So you believe that the victim died early Sunday and that her body lay undetected behind Palmetto field until it was found on Thursday morning, right?"

"Or, more likely, he hid the body and came back to dump it."

"But your investigation shows that the defendant left town on Sunday morning and did not return until you brought him back on Thursday afternoon, right?"

"We could still find some evidence that he returned. We haven't talked to his co-workers yet."

Ray stepped toward the stand. "But you have no evidence today that the defendant returned to Myrtle Beach before Thursday, isn't that right, Captain Brown?"

"That's correct."

"And you don't know what the co-workers will say, do you?"

"No. We haven't talked to them."

"So, Captain, your investigation isn't complete, is it?" Ray took a half-step closer.

"Mr. Jackson, give the witness some room, please," said the judge.

Ray stepped back. "It's not complete, is it?"

"It's complete."

"But you just testified that there are some potential witnesses that you need to interview, didn't you?"

"I don't need to interview them. It might help, but it isn't necessary."

"Isn't necessary? So you're saying that finding the truth … isn't necessary?"

"Objection!" Harry flew out of his seat. "Argumentative!"

"Mr. Jackson"—Judge King was leaning over the bench—"please confine your questions to the facts of the case."

"Yes, sir. Thank you, sir. Captain, you haven't found the murder weapon, have you?"

"No, sir."

"And, as I understand your testimony, the victim was murdered somewhere other than behind Palmetto field. Is that correct?"

"We didn't find any evidence of a fight or struggle at the scene where her body was found, so she was probably dead when her body was placed behind the fence."

"But the fact remains that you don't know where she was killed, do you?" Ray inched closer.

"No, we don't."

"And if you could find the murder scene, there might be evidence directing you to the murderer, right?"

"To Mr. Heath, yes."

"Or to someone else, right?"

Captain Brown looked at Harry before answering, "I suppose that's possible."

"So although you say your investigation is complete, you haven't talked to some witnesses, found the murder weapon or the murder scene and any evidence that it contains, have you?"

"Not yet."

"That doesn't sound like a very good investigation, does it?"

Harry lifted slightly from his seat. "Argumentative."

"Sustained," the judge said. "Please keep your questions to the facts, Mr. Jackson."

Ray didn't acknowledge the ruling. Instead he took a half-step toward the witness and fired his next question. "The fact is, Captain Brown, that for a lead detective you can't ever seem to find a damn thing, can you?"

"Mr. Jackson." Judge King was half-standing.

"Are you just a lousy investigator?"

"Mr. Jackson." Judge King banged his gavel and stood up. "You will treat this court and this witness with respect or I will find you in contempt. Do you understand?"

"Yes, sir. I'm sorry, sir. I—"

"I believe that you are finished with this witness."

"But—"

"Mr. Jackson," Judge King said, still standing with the gavel tightly in his fist, "I don't think you have any more pertinent questions for this witness."

"Yes, sir." Ray trod back to his seat.

"You screwed that up," Bo said with a sneer.

"We have a history," Ray said.

"Do you have anything further?" Judge King asked Harry, who was still standing from the objection he'd never gotten to voice.

"No, sir. I believe that the state has met its burden."

"I agree, and it is so ordered," Judge King said. "Gentlemen, can we set a trial date for April?"

"Your Honor," Harry said, "there is DNA evidence that was collected at the scene. We do not have the reports yet but expect them soon. Could we have a June date? That would allow Mr. Jackson time to find an expert to examine the results."

"Is that suitable with you, Mr. Jackson?"

"Yes, sir."

"Now, as to a reduction of bail. Mr. Carson, what is your position?"

"Your Honor, we would oppose the reduction of bail because of the nature of the crime, the defendant's prior violent criminal record and the possibility that we will bring additional charges against the defendant for a second murder."

Ray was on his feet. "What second murder?"

"Have patience, Mr. Jackson. I'm sure Mr. Carson is going to tell us."

"Your Honor, the victim was pregnant, eight weeks pregnant, at the time of her death."

Ray jumped up again. "A fetus isn't viable at eight weeks."

"Please let him finish, Mr. Jackson."

"It can be if the mother is alive and carrying it," Harry said. "At least that's what the South Carolina Supreme Court says. Do you want the case citation?"

"Mr. Carson, will you be seeking the death penalty?" Judge King said.

"I apologize, Your Honor, but that has not been decided yet. The solicitor would like the results of the DNA testing before he decides. The paternity test has established that the fetus is not the child of the defendant."

"Mr. Jackson, unless you have something that will blow me away, I am not inclined to reduce bail for a defendant with a record that includes several assaults and that could be facing the death penalty."

"I believe that bail is appropriate considering the startling lack of evidence against Mr. Heath and the incomplete nature of the investigation. I would also point out that Mr. Heath is a longtime resident of Horry

County and that the assault charges were all minor incidents that arose out of his employment as a bouncer at various gentlemen's clubs."

"Thank you, Mr. Jackson. I am going to deny the motion to reduce bail and place the case on the trial calendar for the last week of June. Mr. Carson, before we take the next case, I'd like to see you and Mr. Jackson in my chambers."

Bo Heath glared at Ray. "Could you have made it any worse?"

"I'll talk to you later. Let me see what the judge wants."

"Now, Mr. Jackson," Judge King said, holding the door to his office.

Both attorneys entered the chambers, and the judge shut the door and turned to face Ray. "What was that all about?"

"I'm sorry, Your Honor. I got a little carried away, but I have worked with Detective Brown in the past—"

"It's Captain Brown," the judge said.

"Yes, sir, Captain Brown, and he didn't do a good job then either," Ray said, meeting the judge's glare.

Judge King broke the eye contact and walked to his desk and sat. "If it wasn't for your lack of experience, I would have found you in contempt."

"It's just that Detective—"

"I can still find you in contempt, Mr. Jackson."

"Yes, sir. I'm sorry, sir."

"Captain Brown is an excellent police officer who has served the people of the county for many years."

"I'm sure you're correct," Ray said with a shrug. *But I know of two investigations he screwed up, this one and my sister's.*

"You're damn right I am," the judge said, taking his feet again. He walked around his desk to stand beside Ray. "And, Mr. Jackson, I will not tolerate any more behavior of this sort. Is that clear?"

"Yes, sir."

"I'm going to ask Harry to make sure the police follow up on those witnesses, but you can talk to them, too. Watch yourself."

6

"I knowed there was something evil over there as soon as I opened my door that morning. The dogs was barkin' and actin' up and I had a chill come all over me. Then I saw Lillie Mae's grandchild."

Ray's chair wobbled. He tried to ignore the fact that one leg was shorter than the other three, because Mrs. Hattie Barcous was finally talking about the day she found Tonya Smalls's body. Mrs. Barcous, a widow who appeared to be in her late sixties, made the call to nine-one-one when the body was found. She lived alone, surviving on her Social Security, in a shotgun house on Avenue C across the street from Palmetto baseball field.

"What time of the day was this?" Ray said. His phone was on the kitchen table recording the conversation. The table was clean, but the walls and windows were grayed by years of smoke from the wood stove in the middle of the room.

"Lucille Johnson and I used to walk around the baseball field every morning about six thirty. She had just knocked on my door and I was goin' out to walk with her, so it had to be about that time." The call had been received by nine-one-one at six forty-four. "Would you like some more coffee?"

"No, thank you." The coffee was cool, but he didn't want to stop her. "Where did you find Tonya Smalls?"

"Behind the baseball field in the bushes." She pointed toward the front of the house.

"Would you tell me what happened that morning?"

"Well, I opened the door when Lucille knocked and I saw her. I didn't know it was Tonya. I asked Lucille did she see it and what she thought it was. She didn't know, but we didn't want to go over there, so we sent my neighbor, Roy Mack, to look. Roy Mack was just coming home from work and getting out of his car. And Roy went over there and then he come back and say to call nine-one-one, there's a dead woman over there. So I called nine-one-one and told them and the sheriff come out."

"How do you know Roy Mack?" Ray said.

"He's my neighbor, lives right there," she said, indicating the house to her left. Looking through a window with frilly curtains, Ray could see the faded green siding on the house he planned to visit in the day. "Is his full name Royal McKenzie?"

"Yes, I think so, but everybody call him Roy Mack."

"What do you know about him?"

"He's my neighbor." She shrugged. "He works nights, so I don't see him much, but he's always nice when I do."

"According to the police report, you and Mrs. Johnson walked around the ball field regularly."

"Every day except Saturday and Sunday. We have church and have to get ready." "Where do you go to church?"

"I'm a deaconess at St. Paul AME," she replied, straightening her back.

"So y'all have services on Saturday and Sunday?"

"No, sir, me and Lucille and some friends get on the bus for bingo over across town on Saturday mornings."

Ray was afraid he knew the answer, but his mother had taught him to ask anyway. "Where do you play bingo?"

"At that big church—what's its name? I got a card with the name on it over here. I won one hundred dollars Saturday three weeks ago."

"Congratulations." Ray wiped his forehead with his handkerchief. He was closest to the wood-burning stove that heated the house.

"Thank you, but that's nothing. Lillie Mae won twenty-five hundred dollars two weeks after her girl was killed."

"Wow, that's a lot of money."

"Nearly enough to pay the funeral bill. And you know what they did? Well, Lillie, she wins and she just starts cryin' and cryin' 'cause she needs the money so bad and the Lord just blessed her and give her twenty-five hundred dollars. And Lillie's so happy and so sad cause she misses Tonya and Tonya had come with us sometimes to play. Well, Reverend Tim, he come over to see what was goin' on. When Lucille tells him 'cause Lillie Mae's sobbin' too hard, Reverend Tim he stops the game. He prays for Lillie Mae and for Tonya and then he takes up a love offering for Lillie and the final expenses and there's enough to pay for the whole funeral. Now that's a man of God!" She clutched both hands to her chest and looked at the ceiling. Then she reached across the kitchen table and patted Ray on the hand. "God is good. Would you excuse me for a minute? I need to get a tissue."

When she returned, Ray said, "Where were you standing when you first saw Tonya's body?"

"Mr. Ray, I done told you. I was standin' at my front door."

"So you weren't actually on the field when you saw the body."

"Well, like I said, I didn't know it was Tonya, but me and Lucille could see somethin' over across the field and it was evil." She shook her head slowly.

"Did you walk around the field on the Monday before Tonya was found?"

"And Tuesday, and Wednesday and she wasn't there." She smiled. "How many more men are going to come ask the same questions?"

"How can you be so sure?"

"I seen her from the front step on Thursday. If I seen her from that far on Thursday, one of us woulda seen her when we walked right by the spot on one of them other days, don't you think?"

"Yes, ma'am." Ray checked his phone to be sure it was still recording. *Maybe they got the time of death wrong and Bo really didn't do it.* "Do you know Michael Heath? Some people call him 'Bo.'"

"I don't think so."

"Do you know why anyone would want to kill Tonya?"

"She was a pretty girl. She had some problems, but the men liked her. And I guess if one of her men got jealous or something, he might hurt her."

"What kind of problems did Tonya have?"

"She had a lot of man friends and Lillie told me that Tonya had done some drugs."

"Did Tonya have any children?"

"No, lord, she didn't have any children. That's a blessing. Lillie Mae wouldn't need that on her now."

If she'd known that Tonya was pregnant, that question would have let her say so. "That's about all the questions that I have. Thank you for your time. On the way out, can you show me where you were standing when you first saw her?"

Hattie led Ray to the wooden front door. It was solid except for three small windows across the top. The veneer had cracked at the bottom, and a couple of pieces had broken off. It sagged and added to the scratch on the floor as she dragged it open. When they were both on the top step she said, "She was right over there," and pointed to the outfield fence.

"That's a long way." Ray surveyed Palmetto field. Hattie lived on the third-base side of the complex. Directly across from her front door was the third-base dugout. A couple of sets of metal and wood bleachers, the kind with no backs, sat between the dugout and home plate. They were in pretty good shape, as was the entire facility. The grass had been mowed recently. The area around the field was littered with cups, cans and wrappers, the residue of last night's Little League games. "What could you see? Did you know what it was?"

"No, not exactly. But it did look like somebody or something pretty big was lying down behind the fence." A six–foot-high chain-link fence ran all the way around the field. Telephone poles supported chicken wire on top of the fence that ran from the end of one dugout behind home plate to the other dugout and was about thirty feet high. It reminded Ray of the field where he'd played Dixie Youth Baseball when he was a kid.

Ray could see right field clearly over the dugout from Hattie's front step. Live oaks and blackberry bushes were growing behind the outfield fence. "Would you like to walk over there with me?" he said.

"No, siree, me and Lillie haven't done our walking over there since."

Ray thanked Hattie and gave her a business card before he walked to the place where the body had been found. It had been about four months since Tonya's body was discovered here and he couldn't tell where she had lain. There was a fairly well-worn path that ran along the outside of the fence. It was only wide enough for one person. It was probably used for chasing balls that went over the fence.

Ray started for his car, smiling as the sun warmed his face. It was one of those great February days that brought the promise of spring. White clouds dotted the sky and the temperature was near seventy-five. Ray decided to walk to Lucille Johnson's house. Her home was on the corner after you crossed a side street. She wasn't home. He left his card stuck in her door with a note on the back asking her to call him. Then he returned to Royal McKenzie's residence. He reviewed his notes quickly before he climbed the concrete block steps.

7

Ray knocked on Royal McKenzie's door three times. He shifted his tablet to his right hand and then back to the left. He scanned the yard and looked across Palmetto Field. No one came to the door. If Royal McKenzie was home, he had heard. A car was in the dirt driveway, so someone was home. Unlike Hattie Barcous, Royal McKenzie had not responded to Ray's letter asking for an appointment. Ray rapped on the door again, harder. A well-groomed young man dressed in starched khakis and a fuchsia polo shirt slowly opened the door and then only enough to see who had disturbed him. The muscles in his arms were well-defined and his belt was cinched tight around a trim waist. He looked like a bodybuilder. The expression on his face seemed chosen to discourage the bravest salesman.

"What do you want?"

"I'm attorney Ray Jackson. Is Royal McKenzie in?" he said from the top step as he looked up through a screen door.

"He's asleep. He works nights," the man said. If they had been on the same level, Ray would have been taller, but the man was one step higher. Staring down from the interior of the house, he tried to use the height to intimidate Ray. "Come back later." He began to close the door.

"This concerns an important legal matter. When might be a good time to talk with him?"

"I don't know." He closed the door another inch.

"Well, what time does he usually get up in the afternoon?"

"It varies."

"Would you ask him to call me?" Ray slapped a business card against the screen door so that the man could read it.

The man paused and then opened the door just wide enough to reach out and take the card with his manicured hand. He read it slowly. "What kind of legal matter, Mr. Jackson?"

"It's about the body he found a few months ago."

"He already talked to the police."

A light wind disturbed the dead brown leaves that had gathered by the steps. It was getting cooler, and Ray adjusted his jacket. "I have a few questions. It won't take long."

"So, you're Bo Heath's attorney?"

"That's right. Do you know Bo?"

"No, I just heard Roy Mack talk about him."

"What did Roy Mack say?"

"He said Bo … He can tell you, if he wants to."

"It's pretty late. Why don't you let me in and I'll wait until he gets up."

"I'll give him your card." He gave Ray a nod and closed the door.

Ray heard the deadbolt turn. He smiled to himself as he returned to his car. *Roy Mack will talk to me. He's hiding something. There must be a hole in his testimony and it helps Bo.* He shook his head. He sounded just like his mother.

"Tonya was my youngest granddaughter," Lillie Mae Smalls began in answer to Ray's question. Her home, just a block and a half down the street from Royal McKenzie's, was clean and neat even though the furniture was well-used. Ray was sticking to the plastic-covered cushions of her couch while learning about the victim.

"She was a very pretty young lady," he said, reaching for a black-and-white school photo on the end table beside him.

"That's not Tonya. That's her mama, my third child, Bernice. Tonya looked just like her mother." Lillie carefully laid a framed photo of the winners of a beauty pageant in his hands. "That's Tonya," she said, pointing to the contestant smiling next to the queen.

Ray nodded.

"Life wasn't fair to Tonya," Lillie said. "Her mama was young when Tonya was born and she wasn't ready for no baby. She took off with some

45

man when she was nineteen and left me to raise Tonya. Last time I heard from her, five or six years ago, she was in New York. She hasn't ever come back to visit. The number I got for her is disconnected. It's like she just forgot us. She didn't even come for the funeral. She probably don't know that Tonya's gone." She paused and wiped her eyes with a wadded paper towel.

Ray nodded. He knew what it was like to have a family member disappear. *It's always with you.* "Was she in a lot of pageants?"

"No, that picture is from when she was first runner-up to the homecoming queen at Horry High School her senior year. When she was little, she always played at being a beauty queen or a model with her cousin Nettie."

"Really?" Ray added just to keep her going and to give him a second to bury the memory of Brittany as homecoming queen of the same school. *Same picture, different people.*

"They would put on beauty pageants and shows for me and her aunts. She was always in the choir at church or at school." Lillie reached into a drawer of the end table and handed him an album of photos of Tonya growing up. "When she was in the ninth grade, she even sang the national anthem before a basketball game. Sometimes, when she sang in church, she would bring tears to my eyes." Lillie dabbed her eyes again. "She even talked about trying out for American Idol once, but I think she knew that she wasn't quite good enough."

"How did she do in school?"

"Tonya was smart, but she didn't always try very hard. She never got her diploma. Then she got a job as a dancer at one of those strip clubs. I told her that was bad. But she wouldn't listen."

"Hattie Barcous told me that Tonya would go to play bingo at the church with you and some of your friends sometimes."

"Yeah, she went with us a few times. She didn't play a lot. She would talk with the guys that were running the bingo mostly." Lillie shifted forward in her chair like she was about to rise.

"Just a few more questions. Did she seem to have a special relationship with any of them?"

"No, not really. All of the men would want to talk to her, even Reverend Thomas."

"Do you remember who any of them were?"

"I never met them. They was just talking. I was playing my cards."

"Tell me about the last time you saw Tonya."

"It was the Friday before she was killed. She come by and I fixed her some fried chicken, rice and greens. She didn't eat much of it."

"What did y'all talk about?"

"Nothing really. Just talked."

"Did she tell you about any problems with her boyfriend?"

"No, I knew something was bothering her, but she didn't talk about it. I don't know what I'd a done if she did." Lillie glanced pointedly at a basket of laundry on the floor of her kitchen.

"I know you've been over this many times and I appreciate your patience, but did she mention any names?"

"No, I would have told you if she did."

"Do you know why anyone would want to kill her?"

"Some of the men she saw were real mean. Sometimes she would come by and she would have bruises on her arms. A couple of times, she had a black eye. You don't meet nice men at a strip club."

"That's true. Do you know any of their names?

"There was a Tom fella and somebody she call JD."

"Do you know their full names or where to find them?"

"No, I don't. It's been a while since they was around."

"If you remember anything about them, would you let me know?"

"Sure, but I doubt I'll think of anything. It's just what she told me."

"I understand. Do you know why anyone would want to kill her?"

"No. I asked the other policeman that. They said it was passion." She shrugged slightly.

"Has the coroner told you that Tonya was pregnant?"

"Yes, they did. She didn't need no child."

"Do you know who the father was?"

"Tonya didn't tell me about it, so I don't know. Something had been bothering her lately. I guess that was it. We didn't talk about it."

"Do you know Bo Heath?"

"Tonya didn't bring her men around me."

"Was he one of her men?"

"Well, I had heard her talk about him some. And they said he was."

"Who said that?"

"The other policeman. Are they going to electrocute him?"

"No, right now he's facing life in prison." Ray didn't remind her that he was defending Bo. "Do you think Bo Heath murdered Tonya?"

"That's what they say. They should fry him if he did it." She clenched both fists. "That's what the Bible says, eye for an eye, tooth for a tooth."

Old Testament justice. "And what if he didn't?"

"They said he did."

"Do you remember what Tonya said about Bo? How he treated her, anything like that?"

"She thought he was pretty nice. Not much to look at, not real smart. I remember her telling me that."

"Did she ever say that Bo had hit her or hurt her?"

"Do you fellas all ask the same questions? I done told the first fellow no, she never did say that he had hit her."

"Did you ever see her with bruises or other signs of injury?"

Lillie looked at the floor and then back at Ray. "It made me mad, but some men are that way."

"I know that this next question may be difficult for you, but I need to know. Did Tonya use drugs?"

"She was always dancing at the club or a party. She could have used drugs there, but she wasn't hooked on 'em or nothing."

"Where was she dancing last?"

"She wasn't. She had finally quit. She acted like she was gonna settle down a little. She had been going up to church where we go to bingo. She was doing some work with Reverend Tim Thomas himself. That's how she knew him at bingo. The church was paying her good. And she had moved out of the projects and into an apartment near the college. I think she had found a decent man."

"Do you know the name of that man?" She was shaking her head, so Ray continued. "Who might know his name? Did Tonya have a friend she talked to?"

"Her cousin Nettie. She and Nettie have been close since they were little girls. Nettie's five years older and she would come watch Tonya so I could do my work. They have been like sisters ever since."

"Do you have Nettie's number or know how I could reach her?"

"Are we about done? I've got some clothes to wash and some ironing to do."

"If you've got Nettie's number, I'll take that and go."

"Be right back," she said as she rose. She shuffled into the kitchen area and returned with a local phone number written on a scrap of paper towel.

Ray stood and took her hands in his. "Thank you for your time. Again, I am sorry for your loss."

"I don't mean to be rushing you out. I'm tired, and talking about Tonya just makes me miss her."

Ray understood that too well. "I don't have any more questions now. Thank you. You've been very kind and patient."

Lillie walked Ray to the door and hesitated before she opened it. "You know, I like you. You aren't like them others. You promise me, if it wasn't that Bo Heath that did this to Tonya, you'll find who did it."

"I will," he said. "Yes ma'am, I will."

———

8

Ray fumbled his ringing cell phone as he pulled away from Lillie Mae Smalls's house, nearly taking out her mailbox. He stopped in the middle of the street and recovered it from the passenger-side floorboard before it stopped ringing.

It was Nelson. "I think I know what the problem is," he said. "One of my sources says you screwed up the quarterly reports to the Department of Revenue."

"What? No way. Those—"

"Well, try them again," Nelson bellowed to someone in his office. "What did you put in those reports?"

"It's not the reports. It's the numbers behind them."

"That's not what my guy says. He's telling me that your name came up in a conversation he had with a friend at SLED. They are taking your reports apart and I need to know what's in them before they haul your ass off to Columbia. What are you doing to fix this?"

"The financial director is completing her review of everything SLED took." Ray moved to the edge of the road to let a car pass.

"Are you still screwing her? Is that why this got so messed up?"

"What?"

"Are you sleeping with Jennifer Jones?"

"No."

"Y'all dated for while, didn't you?"

"Sure, but what's—"

"Are you stupid? You've been sleeping with the financial director and that looks like collusion."

"It's been a couple of years—"

"Reverend Tim says y'all were really friendly."

"I hadn't seen her since Mom got sick until the day SLED came."

"Ray, I hope that's true, because I'm getting tired of covering for you. You had the mess while your mother was hospitalized and now this. If you screw one more thing up, I'm not going to be able to help you."

"My reports are correct."

"OK, but I want you to go over the records SLED took. Review them line by line and entry by entry. And make sure that you thoroughly examine every damn thing you filed with the Department of Revenue or anybody else for the last five years."

"Yes, sir."

"And all of the church's procedures, too."

"I'll tell Jennifer to do that."

"No, you're going to do it. You need to know this inside out. SLED is coming back, and when they do they'll be looking for someone to arrest, like you or your girlfriend."

"She's not my—"

"We're meeting at my office Monday morning at nine. You've got the whole weekend to go over the records. And that will give me time to talk to my contacts at SLED. I will find out what's really going on."

"Yes, sir," Ray said, but Nelson didn't hear it. The line was dead.

On the drive back to the office, he called Jennifer. "It's Ray."

"I know. I still recognize your voice."

"Yeah, well, how are you coming with the review of the records?"

"About halfway through. We should finish next week."

"I need to get a copy of everything SLED took. And I need it quick. Can you do that for me?"

"Sure, I'll have it in the morning. But you'll owe me a drink."

"That's probably not a good idea. Nelson just told me that SLED thinks you and I are still seeing each other. They think we're covering something up."

"That's ridiculous. We're just old friends."

"Yeah, well, call me when you've got the copies ready."

At the office, Ray found the quarterly reports and put them on his desk to take home. He did have some other work to do, for Nelson. He had two new foreclosure cases to file. He tried not to think of it as putting two more families on the street. After all, they were keeping his business alive and his mortgage current.

When he finally got home, Ray changed into some jeans and an old pullover shirt, tossed the reports onto the kitchen table, opened the refrigerator and grabbed a cold bottle of beer. Whiskers, his black cat who gets his name from his extra-long white whiskers, rubbed against his leg, ready to curl up with him on the couch for a back scratch and some TV. Ray closed the refrigerator door and stopped. He put the beer back unopened.

He picked up the cat and scratched its stomach. "Whiskers, sorry, buddy, but I've got some work to do. I'm going to play bingo." *Where better to review the procedures than at the church itself.* He added a Carolina baseball cap to his ensemble and was ready to go.

He put the cat out with an apologetic scratch behind the ears and started down Highway 17 toward Gethsemane Gospel Baptist Church. He drove past Broadway at The Beach, the water parks, restaurants and golf courses, miniature and full size, and wondered how a childhood game like bingo could compete with all this. But he knew. It was the draw of something for nothing, the good feeling you get when you win and the thrill of being envied and admired, even if only for a moment. And it was all for a charitable purpose.

Ray was a little disappointed when he arrived. He'd here earlier in the day and it looked pretty much the same. No flashing lights or neon told the world about the game. Just a roll-out sign with grass growing around the wheels lighted by two spotlights that said "Charity Bingo Game Tonight 7:00 p.m."

The atmosphere inside was similar to the slots area of a Vegas casino, full of the excitement of a nightclub at closing time just after the lights have been turned on. The people still wanted to play, but most of the mystery was gone. There were a few differences from a casino: the music was some sort of elevator-worthy Christian pop, there was no alcohol and the attendants were not scantily clad.

Ray had his choice of one card for three dollars or four cards for ten. He chose one card. He was given a ticket and told he would be brought a card as soon as the next game started. He picked a spot near the back of the room. It reminded him of a large law-school classroom with a half-circle of tiered rows and student desks bolted to the floor. He watched the crowd as the game drew to an end. Just two rows in front of him, a woman jumped to her feet and called "BINGO!" She started hopping in place and shouting, "Thank you, Jesus, thank you Jesus," while an attendant checked her card. When the attendant handed her a hundred dollars, she screamed another "Thank you, Jesus" and showed her winnings to the people sitting next to her. Then she waved one of her new twenties at an attendant and bought another round of cards. Shortly after that, an attractive young lady came down Ray's row with some cards.

"Hi, I'm Annette. What's your name?" she said as she took his ticket and gave him a card. Her dark brown eyes were enhanced by her creamy light brown skin.

"Hi, Annette, I'm Ray."

"Just one card, Ray? It's a lot more fun if you play two or three at a time." She fanned a handful of cards for him to choose from.

"Not right now. I haven't played in a while." That brought a beautiful smile to her face.

"Well, I'll be back to check on you. And we have sodas, water or iced tea as well as popcorn, nachos, hot dogs and an assortment of candy bars, if you need a drink or a snack."

Ray knew she was flirting just to sell more cards. He didn't mind at all. *Hell, it might just work tonight.* They played until there were three winners. Then the attendants swept the room offering more cards.

Ray bought another card and ordered an iced tea from Annette and watched her walk down the row. He was having a hard time getting excited about the game, it was so simple. Bingo was slightly more challenging than slots but a lot slower. The tension did begin to build if the game went on for a while without a winner, but that was about all it had to offer for Ray.

Annette returned with his tea after the second game. "How about two cards this time?"

That beer in Ray's fridge was beginning to call his name, but it was no match for Annette, who was wearing a red church T-shirt that revealed far more than the deacons had intended. "OK, I'll take two," he said. "Is it normally this busy on a Thursday?"

"Actually, it's a little slow for a Thursday. Is this your first time?"

"No, I was here for the very first bingo game. Reverend Tim stood in front of one of the Sunday-school rooms and pulled the numbers from a game set that a deacon had purchased at Walmart that same day."

"So you're a member of the church?"

"Yes, but I haven't been very regular. Are you a member?"

"No, I just work here. But I do come to some of the services. I'll be right back. I've got to check on some other players."

The first five numbers of the next game were already on the board, but Ray caught up quickly. He still needed B-3 when bingo was called. Ray was grabbing his cap when Annette came back.

"Where do you think you're going?" she said, her hands on her slender hips.

"I've had about all the excitement I can take."

"Well, you're going to have to endure a little more. Reverend Tim has sent you a free card for the next game."

I guess I'm playing one more. "That's great. Is he here? I didn't see him."

"He's been helping in the kitchen. He'll be out in a minute to visit with some of the players. How's your tea?" She smiled again.

"It's good." *I can manage another game as long as she's around.*

"Can I get you anything else?"

"No, I'm fine, thank you."

"I think there is something else you need." She leaned over and wrote her number on the back of his bingo card. Ray liked her perfume. "You better call me," she said softly so no one else could hear.

"I will," Ray promised. He took in her smile and watched her walk away. Then he looked at the number again. It seemed vaguely familiar.

Reverend Tim walked back to Ray's place in the room as the next game was finishing. "Ray, what brings you out to our game tonight? It's been a while, hasn't it?"

"I haven't been to a game in years. But with all that happened, I decided it was a good time to come out and see the bingo operations for myself."

"Glad to have you. Oh, look here, you had a winner. You missed B-12. You're obviously a little rusty."

Ray was not rusty. If he had called bingo, they would have taken his card. "I guess so," he said. "Could I get a tour of the operation?" He folded the card and put it in his pocket.

"Sure. Come with me."

They walked down front and passed through a side door and into a room with a small safe, a table and a couple of chairs. "This is where we reconcile the monies each night. In the safe we keep enough in reserve to pay the prizes."

He introduced Ray to the two men in the room. Like the rest of the workers, they were employees of Orion. They showed him the cash log and explained what they do after every session. As the cash came in, it was counted twice, bundled by denomination and logged into the system. At the end of the night, it was recounted and the deposit was prepared, and both men would sign the deposit slip. Ray didn't see any flaws in the system. They moved on to the kitchen. Two women and a man were preparing the drinks and food. Annette was waiting for an order.

"Should I save your seat, Ray?" Annette said as they walked in. "It's getting pretty full."

"I think I've had enough for one night." He watched her take the order into the bingo room. *Is tomorrow too soon to call?*

"She's nice to look at, isn't she?" Reverend Tim said.

Ray had to agree. "Can I ask you a question on another subject?"

"Sure."

"I have been appointed to represent a man who has been charged with murder. I was told that Tonya Smalls, the victim, used to work here at the church. Her grandmother thought that she might have had a boyfriend here. Did you know Tonya Smalls?"

"Tonya Smalls." Reverend Tim put his hand to his forehead and rubbed. "Tonya Smalls. I do recall a young lady of that name doing something around here earlier this year, I think. And you say that she was murdered. Oh, my. I'll ask my staff and let you know. If she was here, she must have left before … before she died."

"Her grandmother thought that she might have been employed here."

"Employed? No, I don't think so. She may have been a volunteer, if anything. I know all of our employees and most of our volunteers. I'll ask our volunteer coordinator and let you know."

Ray thanked Reverend Tim. He stopped at the exit and waited until he made eye contact with Annette and nodded good night. He was rewarded with another smile. The evening air was cool on his arms.

"Hi, Ray," Jennifer Jones called across the parking lot. "What are you doing here?"

"I haven't been to a bingo game in a while. It seemed like a good time to visit. And I could ask you the same thing," he said as he walked over to her car, a new red Camaro convertible.

"I'm making that copy of all of the documents taken by SLED that you wanted. Since it's your fault that I am working so late, why don't you buy me that drink and let's catch up a bit?"

He hesitated. "That would be great. Where to?"

"Fat Harold's?"

He followed Jennifer to one of their old haunts. She loved to Shag, and he wasn't half-bad. The Shag, a form of swing dance, was the state dance of South Carolina and was danced to beach music. Beach music had nothing to do with the Beach Boys but was the music of The Tams, The Drifters and The Embers. The music was heard around the world, but rarely was the dance seen outside of the Carolinas.

Fat Harold's was one block from the ocean and they arrived a little before nine. Its walls were decorated floor to ceiling with photos of Shaggers and beach music performers from years past. In fact, Jennifer and Ray were in the background of one or two. It was still a little early for the Thursday party crowd and the dance floors were empty, but the bar was filling up. During the spring and summer, the doors would be open and the dancing would be outside. Ray got a couple of Corona Lights with lime wedges from the bar and joined Jennifer at a table just a few steps from the dance floor. Her foot was tapping in time to the music playing on the jukebox.

She smiled. "Just like old times." And it was, almost. They had met at Fat Harold's and had been part of a regular crowd that was there three or four nights a week. Ray had stopped coming when they broke up.

It wasn't long before they were joined by a couple of their old friends. Sue and Cathy gave him a hug, Bob shook his hand with a firm grip and Mark slapped him on the back and gave him a fist bump. They caught up briefly until the band started. After a second beer, Jennifer asked Ray to dance.

"Are you seeing anyone?" she said as he took her hand to dance.

Ray spun Jennifer onto the sandy floor. *I'm going to pretend I didn't hear that.* Maybe she was just curious. He doubted it. *She wants to know if we still have a chance ... I don't think so.* They turned into an embrace. He felt all her familiar curves for four beats and then spun her out. It was nice to be back at Fat Harold's with her. And she did look good in her navy slacks that highlighted her trim waist. She had undone three buttons of her cream blouse and he could see the frills on her push-up bra when she spun. It aroused him as it always had.

The Shag was a partner dance and the moves came back to him pretty quickly. The music ended with Jennifer spinning into his embrace. She stayed there long enough to whisper in a slightly husky voice, "You've still got it."

The next song was an old favorite called "Turn Back the Hands of Time." They could dance to it, and later, he could probably take her home. They had been great in bed. He missed that, probably needed it, but he motioned to the table. He wasn't ready to follow the song's suggestion. Not yet, anyway. Besides, there was the issue with SLED.

He finished his beer quickly and leaned over to Jennifer. "I hate to dance and run, but I've got a lot do tomorrow." *That was lame.* "This was fun. Maybe we can do this again sometime." *Maybe not.*

Ray told the rest of the table good-bye and walked to his car. That beer was still in his fridge, but he put three fingers of Maker's Mark in a glass as soon as he got home. He mixed the bourbon with one cube of ice.

He plopped onto the couch and turned on *SportsCenter*. Whiskers pushed his head under Ray's hand. "Hey, buddy," Ray said as he began to scratch the cat's ears. "I've got you, don't I? And we just don't have time for a woman right now, do we?"

9

It was only nine fifteen on Friday morning and Ray had already worked through three years' worth of quarterly reports. He couldn't find anything unusual. *Damn. What does SLED see that I don't?* Nelson was probably right about Ray's being the focus of the investigation. He had signed all the reports. The ring of the office phone startled him. "Jackson Law Firm."

"You promised to call me."

He smiled as he fingered the unfolded bingo card sitting beside the reports on his desk. "Please accept my deepest apologies."

"I'll forgive you, this time." He could hear her smile. "Reverend Tim gave me your number. I asked him about you and he said that you are a nice single guy even if you are a lawyer and maybe I should call you. So I did."

"Would you like to join me for a cup of coffee?" Ray said. "There's a Starbucks not far from the church."

"That would be nice, but why don't we meet at Margaritaville tomorrow night about seven? I like the outside bar and the weather's nice."

"That's a much better idea."

In a happier mood, Ray tackled the last two years of bingo reports. If there was something suspicious about them, he just couldn't find it. Maybe it would show up in the records he was getting from Jennifer. He sent her a text and got an immediate reply to stop by around noon.

That gave him a few minutes. He grabbed Bo's file and made his daily call to Royal McKenzie. Roy Mack had answered once and clicked off as soon as Ray said his name. Today it went straight to voice mail. Ray didn't leave a message. By now, Roy Mack knew it was him and what he wanted. *Maybe I can wear him down.*

He flipped through the pages of the file. He had tried to contact every witness, with no luck, except for the bartender, who was certain that Bo and Tonya had left together. He reread his witness notes and came across the number for Tonya's cousin, Nettie. She wasn't really a witness, but maybe she knew who Tonya was seeing and who might be the father of her baby. He began to dial the number and stopped. He picked up the bingo card from his desk. The numbers were the same. "Damn," he said and popped his desk with his fist. *Can I date a witness?* He knew the answer to that. But it really wasn't a date. They were just meeting for drinks. And was she really a witness?

Around twelve, Ray sent Jennifer a text asking her to leave the records at the front desk, since he was running late. He arrived at the church shortly after twelve thirty. "Hi," he said to the receptionist. "Is Jennifer in?"

"Yes, she's expecting you."

"Great," he said. *Damn, I really wanted to miss her.*

"Do you know where her office is?"

"Yes," he said. "I do." And he walked down the hall.

"Here's a copy of the documents that SLED took." Jennifer handed him a USB flash drive. "I put each year in a separate file."

"Well, thanks. I've got to get to the courthouse and research some deeds. I'll see you later. Let me know if you find anything."

"I will. Ray, I had fun last night even though you ran off early. You should come join the crowd again sometime."

"I don't think that's a good idea. Not with what Nelson said."

"I don't know why you're worried about that. Nelson's just screwing with you."

"Maybe so, but let's get through this first." *Besides I've got a hot date tomorrow. That I will cancel as soon as I get back in the car.*

"Call me if you have questions about these."

"I'll do that. And thanks for getting these together."

Ray's cell phone rang while he was dialing Annette. His caller ID displayed a local number he didn't recognize, so he ignored it. When she didn't answer, Ray didn't leave a message. He tapped the button to return the missed call. *It might be a new client.*

"Horry Solicitor's Office," the woman said.

"This is Ray Jackson. Can I speak to Harry Carson?" He was the only one in that office who would call Ray.

Queen's "Bohemian Rhapsody" was the on-hold music. He listened to Freddie Mercury's murder confession until Harry answered.

"Mr. Jackson, I was leaving you a message on the other line," Harry said.

"I'm returning your call."

"We just got the DNA test results back from SLED."

"And?"

"Your client's DNA matches material that was removed from beneath the victim's fingernails. But he is not the father of the baby. It's just like I told you. He got jealous when Miss Smalls told him about the baby and he killed her."

Damn. Bo lied to me. He was with her on Saturday night like Roy Mack said. "That, uh, doesn't prove he killed her."

"Nice try, but the fingernail scrapings are defensive. She scratched him while he was strangling her. You've seen pictures of his hands and arms. They're all beat up."

"He's a construction worker and an MMA fighter. Of course he's got cuts."

"So if you're right, why did he lie about being with her if he's not guilty?"

"Because he was afraid of being accused of something he didn't do." *That was weak.* "Can I get a copy?"

"I was trying to fax it to your office, but I must have the wrong number."

Ray had canceled his separate fax number a few months ago. Now if you wanted to send him a fax, you had to call his office number and hope he had the machine on. He must have forgotten. "I'm on the way to Conway now. I can stop by your office and pick one up if that's not an inconvenience."

"That would be fine. I'll have it waiting for you."

Ray was standing in the door to Harry's office in less than twenty minutes. The office was actually of a decent size for a government worker. It just seemed small because the desk and the floor beside it were piled with case folders. Instead of a window, Harry had a single framed photograph on the wall. It was a copy of a scene from the Old West showing four men hanging from the gallows. It was called <u>Frontier Justice.</u>

Harry was facing the back wall, working at his computer, when Ray knocked. His chair squeaked as he spun around. He handed Ray a small stapled stack of paper. It looked official. "Here's the report from SLED," he said. "The front page is a summary. You can hire an expert to read the rest and explain it to you, but I'll save you the trouble. The victim scratched the hands of the man who was strangling her, leaving bits of his skin underneath her fingernails. The DNA from that skin matches your client."

Harry didn't offer Ray a seat, so Ray leaned against the door frame while he scanned the two-paragraph summary on the front page. "Harry, only one of the samples matched Mr. Heath and it was"—he looked for the word SLED had used—"degraded."

"So it wasn't in pristine condition. It had been outside since Saturday night or early Sunday morning. That doesn't change the fact that it matches the defendant."

"Did SLED match the other sample, the bodily fluid on the front of her blouse near her right shoulder, to anyone?"

"Yeah, your client. It's pretty clear that he had or tried to have sex with her near the time of her death."

"Or someone else did."

Harry shrugs. "It was your client."

"That's not what this report says."

"Yes it does."

Ray found the paragraph in the summary, stuck his finger on it and showed it to Harry. "No, it says here that the DNA has some characteristics similar to the defendant's. But it doesn't say it's a match. Obviously, I haven't read the entire report. Was SLED able to determine how old the DNA samples were?"

"No, I don't think that they can do that." Harry stood and took his jacket from the back of his chair. "Ray, I appreciate the zealous defense of your client, but let's face it—I've got your client's DNA under the victim's fingernails. I've got a probable match to your client for semen on her shirt and a witness who saw them leaving the Three Door together. I can probably offer a plea to twenty with no parole."

"That's the max. Why would he take that?"

Harry sighed. "It's not the max. I'll drop the second murder and the CSC. The max for all three would be forty-eight years. I'm offering twenty. And it takes the death penalty off the table. It's a hell of deal. You ought to take it."

Ray perused the report for a second before he stood up straight. "I'll talk to him."

"Wait." Harry leaned over and picked through a large stack of papers on the floor. He selected a thin sheaf of documents and handed it to Ray. "Here, these are the responses to your discovery request." Discovery was the process that required each side of a case to share information.

Ray thumbed through the papers. "That's all?"

"Yeah. It's a pretty simple case."

Saturday night, the weather was comfortable, with the temperature in the low eighties. There was some humidity, but it was Myrtle Beach. All in all, not a bad evening weather-wise. The outside bar at Margaritaville wasn't too crowded for a spring weekend. It was busy and there were no tables available, but Ray found two stools at the bar without much of a wait. He had arrived a little early because he knew the wait was often longer than thirty minutes, more for a table. He was seated on the far side of the bar and had a good view of the entrance. He ordered a bourbon and water. *How do I bring up Tonya and Bo?*

He spun his glass of mostly melted ice and wondered how long he could nurse his drink. He had been sitting there since six thirty. It was seven fifteen. *Where is she? If she doesn't get here in another fifteen minutes, I'll just leave. Maybe it's best if she doesn't come.* But Ray sat. Twenty-five minutes later he pushed his long-empty glass across the bar. As he looked for the bartender to get his check, he saw her come in. Ray was not the only guy who watched her cross the room. This was a different woman from the one he'd met at bingo. This one was wearing a spaghetti-strap top that showed the cleavage that was hardly noticeable at bingo and a skirt that showed off legs that were sculpted like a ballerina's. A sweater embraced her shoulders. She looked a little older than she had last night, late twenties, maybe thirty. *But who wants a twenty-two-year-old that you can't talk to?*

"Sorry I'm late," she said as she slid onto the stool beside him. "I'll have a Cosmo," she said to the suddenly attentive bartender. Then she turned and smiled at Ray. "I would have called, but I don't have your cell."

"I can fix that," he said and dialed her number. "There it is. How was bingo today?" Not the brilliant conversation starter he'd been hoping for.

"Awful. I hate that place. Sorry, don't let me start this off by dumping my day on you. But it's boring. I wish it were as exciting as the casino boat."

"I've never done that. I'm not much of a gambler. I'll have to try it sometime." He looked at his hands. Annette, there's something—"

She checked her watch. "I won a hundred dollars in chips, employee of the week or something." She reached over and grabbed his arm. "If we leave now I bet we could make the next sailing."

"There's something I need to tell you first."

"You can tell me on the way. Come on."

Ray paid the tab and they hurried to his car. He put the top down and turned north on Highway 17.

"Now, what did you want to tell me?" Annette said.

"Well," he said. He looked across the car. Her hair was blowing in the wind and she had pulled it back with her hands into a ponytail. She looked so innocent even though her smile had a bit of mischief in it. "It's nothing," he said, deciding not to ruin her night. Then he grinned and chuckled.

"What?" she said. "I don't have a rubber band."

"You are a beautiful woman," he said. *And it's just one date.*

They reached Little River and boarded the boat with about ten minutes to spare. She grabbed his arm and gave him a quick tour. She knew the bartenders at both bars and some of the waitresses. One of the waitresses offered her condolences about Tonya.

"That's my cousin," Annette said to Ray. "She died a few months ago."

"I'm sorry for your loss," he said. "What happened?"

"Not now. I'll tell you later. Let's play some blackjack."

They split the chips and took a seat at a five-dollar blackjack table. As soon as they reached international waters, the dealer began. On the first hand, Annette leaned over and put her hand on Ray's shoulder. "You must be good luck," she whispered in his ear and kissed him on the cheek. "Blackjack," she cried out, flipping the ace and jack of spades.

They didn't break the house, but they turned that hundred dollars into a little over a thousand. They won at blackjack, roulette and craps. Ray had never played craps, but he did what Annette did until he gained a little understanding and he was ahead when it was time to stop and go back into port. Gambling was a lot of fun when you were winning. They got a fresh drink and went out on the upper deck to cool off.

"Why don't we stand over there. It's out of the wind." He pointed to a corner that was in a darker spot of the deck. When they reached the spot, he put his arms around her waist. She turned to him and they kissed.

She put her arms around his neck and stared into his eyes. "I don't know when I've had so much fun," she said. Her kiss was a long, lingering confirmation. They kissed for a while and then stood quietly in the semi-dark holding one another until a voice from the speaker said it was time to prepare to disembark.

"Would you like to stop by my place for a nightcap? It's on the way." He ignored a claxon from his brain.

She took Ray's face in her hands and kissed him gently on the lips. "Ray, I never go home with a man on a first date." And then she kissed him again in a way that only made him want her more.

They cashed in their chips at the window and disembarked. After they got into his car, Annette laid her head on his shoulder and they drove quietly back to Margaritaville.

"Instead of a nightcap, how about a cup of coffee?" He pointed to a late-night diner. He was not ready for the night to be over. *I am going to have to tell Reverend Tim thank you.*

"I would like that."

The diner was near Margaritaville in the Broadway at the Beach center and only a few yards from where they'd left Annette's car. They sat on the same side of the booth. She held his hand, examining it inside hers.

"What kind of lawyer are you?" she said.

Oh, shit. "Real estate. I do closings for people who are buying or refinancing their home. Or at least that's what I used to do."

"So, what are you doing now?"

"Well, I'm representing the National Bank of Horry in some foreclosures and I'm doing some work for the church."

"That SLED thing. What's going on with that? Is it about bingo?"

"I really can't talk about it. I have a duty of confidentiality to my client." *Like that's the problem tonight.*

"Is it true, though? Did SLED just show up and tell everyone to back away from their computers? That's what I heard."

"I wasn't there, so I don't know how it happened, but I don't think it was quite like that. But that's about all I can tell you." It was also all he knew.

The waitress interrupted them to take their order. Ray ordered a plain coffee, Annette a latte, both decaf.

"So tell me about your cousin." He had to ask. *It's going to come up anyway.*

"They found her a week before Thanksgiving. She was missing for three days and we didn't know where she was, what she was doing, if she was all right. Then to get the call that she's been murdered …" Annette looked like she was about to cry.

He reached around her waist. "I understand." He tried to pull her closer.

"No, you don't." Annette turned her hips away so she could face him. "You can't know what it's like."

"My sister is still missing."

"Oh, no, Ray. How long?"

"Ten and a half years."

"That's awful."

"After a while it kinda goes numb. But it's always there waiting to burst to the surface with just the smallest reminder."

"Were you close?"

"Closer than most brothers and sisters. You see, Dad died fighting a fire when we were very young. Mom used the insurance money to go to law school. That and then her practice took a lot of time. Brittany— that's her name—and I only had each other. I helped her with homework while Mom worked. I remember algebra was tough. Then I went to college here at Coastal and lived at home. When I started law school in Columbia, Brittany enrolled at USC and we shared an apartment"—he stopped and pinched the top of his nose to stop the threatening tears— "for three years."

Annette took his hand.

"I'm sorry," he said. He forced a smile. "The memories have been fresh these last few weeks." *It's this damn case and Jarrett Brown.*

"It's all right." She slid closer and kissed him on the cheek. "Reverend Tim told me you lost your mother recently, too."

"Yeah, about the same time Ton—your, um, cousin was killed."

"I'm sure that has something to do with it."

"Probably. But"—he slid a paper napkin from the table and blew his nose—"sorry. Brittany and I had a fight just before she went missing." *Why am I telling her this?*

"About what?"

"It wasn't anything really. When I look back, it was a hard summer for her. She worked for Reverend Tim, but she didn't like that. She broke up with Freddie, her boyfriend. We all thought they would get married. Anyway, she was getting ready to start law school. The plan was for her to come back and we'd all practice together. But suddenly she changed her mind. She wasn't coming back. And she wouldn't say why." He blew his nose again.

"When's the last time you saw her?"

"It'll be eleven years in August. We had packed her car to go to school. Mom and I waved as she drove away. And no one has seen her since."

"The police?"

"They never found a trace of her, her car, anything. They quit looking after just a few weeks." *When they confirmed Freddie's alibi. Jarrett Brown never really searched for Brittany.* "I searched for months and months."

"Ray, I'm so sorry."

"OK, who had the latte?" said the waitress.

After she left, they each took a sip of their drinks. "Now, let's try this again," Ray said. "Tell me about Tonya."

"Not tonight. Maybe next time. Besides it's late and I have to work tomorrow."

"I'm sorry. I spoiled what had been a great evening."

"No, you didn't. I've had a really good time."

"Listening to me whine about my sister."

She bumped him gently with her shoulder. "We had fun on the boat, we've won some cash and we talked. It was a good time."

"Thank you."

"Can you walk me to my car?"

Ray paid the check. As they walked to the car, she took his hand and held it. At the car, she pulled him in for a kiss. It was long and suggestive.

"I enjoyed tonight," she said and kissed him again.

They kissed and held one another by her car in the brash parking-lot lights for several minutes. "If I don't go now," Ray said taking a breath, "I won't let you go all night."

She answered with another kiss while she pulled him even closer.

She was soft, tender and warm. But something didn't feel right. Ray couldn't label it. He wanted her, really wanted her. But he broke the embrace and stepped back. *I don't want pity sex ... No, that isn't it.* "Annette," he said, "this is probably a first, but, uh, you told me earlier that you don't go home with men on a first date and I, um, I'm going to respect that."

She dropped her head to the side just a little and looked at him askance. "Really?"

He nearly melted. "Yes, it's not you. It's just after all the talk about Brittany ..." But that wasn't it either.

"OK, I guess I understand," she said, a question still on her face. "Call me?"

"You can count on that," he said, opening the car door for her. *But she's still a witness.* Maybe that was it.

10

The receptionist ushered Ray into the small conference room at Nelson's office Monday morning just before nine. The man sitting at the head of the table was dressed like he was from the West, in a fitted shirt with blue jeans over boots. His ten-gallon hat was on the table. He had once been solidly built, but the former muscle now bulged against the seams of the shirt. His eyes didn't move from his cell phone when Ray entered.

"Good morning," Ray said to Reverend Tim, who was pouring a cup of coffee from the pot on the counter. The cowboy finally looked up. "I'm Ray Jackson." He extended his hand over the table.

The man stood about halfway up and shook Ray's hand. "John DeHaven." He sat and returned his attention to his phone.

Ray chose a mug that had the scales of justice embossed on the side and filled it. The coffee was hot. That was all it had going for it.

"Good morning," Nelson said as he walked into the room. He sat at the end of the table opposite DeHaven. Ray took a seat across from Reverend Tim. "Thanks for coming. Ray, this is John DeHaven. Have y'all met?" They nodded in unison.

"Good. I made some inquiries and discovered that SLED was able to get the search warrants based upon information obtained from a confidential informant."

"An informant? Where?" DeHaven said.

"I don't know, but my contact says that SLED believes that large sums of money are being laundered through the bingo operations of the church or Orion. And there may be more."

"Money laundering is bad enough. What else could there be? Taxes?" Reverend Tim said.

"I'm not sure, but if it were taxes, I think we would have heard from the Department of Revenue first," Nelson said.

"Did your contact mention the Right to Life League?" Reverend Tim said.

"No, I don't think we have a problem there. It appears to be limited to bingo."

"We don't have to worry about our books. They're clean," DeHaven said. "We should look for the informant. That's our issue."

"Don't we need to find who, if anyone, is laundering money through our accounts?" Ray said. "Who would have the ability to launder money through the operations?"

"If we can find the little shit that's working for SLED or what information they are giving them, we can deal with the problem, whatever it is," DeHaven said, leaning forward.

"Shouldn't we focus on reviewing our records?" Ray said, turning to Nelson. "Isn't that—"

"I'll check all of our employees. Maybe I can find the bastard," DeHaven said.

"Do you think they'll charge one of us?" Reverend Tim said.

"It's still just an investigation." Nelson said. "Besides, you're not involved in any money laundering, are you?"

Reverend Tim shook his head.

"Then there's no need to worry about what, if any, charges SLED is going to bring. John, Ray, I think you're both right. We have to find the informant so we can learn what they've given SLED, and we should complete the review of our records. Ray has already started on that. John, let me know if you identify any likely candidates. I will press my liaison at SLED for more information as well. Since the legislature is in session, I don't have the time to pursue this fully. Ray, will you be able to follow up with SLED if I give you a contact?"

"Sure."

"And I want you," Nelson said, pointing to Ray and John DeHaven, "to make sure the review of the information that was seized is completed.

I need to be made aware of any irregularities immediately. I'll decide what other steps should be taken and get back to you."

"John," Ray said, "I've already gotten a copy of the information seized by SLED from the church. Could you send me a set of the documents they took from you? A comparison might give us an idea of what SLED is looking for."

"We reconcile the books between the church and Orion monthly. If there were any problems, they would have been found long ago."

"Not if the transactions are being covered up," Ray said.

"There's nothing wrong with my books," DeHaven said.

"I'm not saying—"

"John will get you a copy, right?" Nelson said.

DeHaven stood and stared at Nelson. "Sure, I'll do that." He put on his cowboy hat. "I'll call you," he said with a glance at Ray. Then he looked at Nelson and nodded. "I've got to go." He didn't wait for a response. He just walked out.

Nelson stood and offered Reverend Tim a hand while patting him on the shoulder with the other. "Don't worry, Tim, we've got this under control. I'll let you know as things develop."

Ray shook Reverend Tim's hand as well.

"Ray," Nelson said after Reverend Tim had left, "if you have a minute, I can get you the contact information for my liaison at SLED, and there's another matter I'd like to discuss."

"Sure, I've got some time."

"Come on."

They walked back to Nelson's office, where Ray took a proffered chair while Nelson settled into the leather chair behind his cherry wood desk. Some years ago, the Patterson law firm had remodeled an old warehouse along the riverfront, and Nelson's office overlooked the river and the marina. The rough-hewn hardwood floors reveled in the morning sunlight. The wall and credenza behind him were decorated with awards and photographs picturing Nelson with a laundry list of state and national political figures.

"Damn, my foot is killing me today. They cut it off over twenty years ago and I can still feel it some days. It's weird."

"I'm sorry."

"I'm used to it. So, how is that murder case of yours coming along?"

"Fine. I'm still interviewing witnesses. He's got a pretty good alibi." Ray leaned forward in his chair. "Do you think SLED will find anything?"

"I don't think SLED is really looking for money laundering. That's just a pretense. I think they're fishing. It's a big cash business. They'll probably find some cash that wasn't properly reported and taxed. The taxes will be paid and that will be the end of it. At least it looks like you're off the hook."

"What about the informant?"

"Weasels aren't usually volunteers. We'll be able to neutralize their testimony, if it gets that far. Besides, John might be able to figure out who it is and that will help us determine what SLED knows and how to address it."

"That would be good."

"If you will follow up with my contact, we can probably make this thing go away without a lot of trouble."

"I am happy to do that."

"Are you billing the church for the time you spend on this case?"

"No, you know I always do the church's work pro bono."

"Yes, that's one reason I wanted to talk to you. This is outside the scope of the work usually required for the church. If you don't want to handle this, we can hire someone or you can bill the church for your time. We can probably arrange for you to represent Orion as well. Whichever you want."

"I would be happy to bill my time." *I really need the money.*

"As chair of the Bingo Committee, I authorize you to do that. I'll let DeHaven know that you are representing them as well."

"Thank you."

Nelson leaned forward. "That brings me to the real reason I wanted to talk with you. As you know, I'm running for reelection to my Senate seat. But you probably don't know that I am considering a run for higher office. I am going to hire someone to take on part of my workload here so that I can spend the time I need on those races. I've been impressed with the way you handled those foreclosures, and you seem to have a lot of the qualities that made your mother such a fine lawyer. So I wanted to ask you first. Would you be interested in discussing a more permanent arrangement?"

Not in a million years. "I would be happy to discuss that further," Ray said. He couldn't be rude. Nelson's referrals had been like a life jacket to a drowning man. They were probably the only reason his office was still open. And now Nelson was offering to pull Ray into the boat. *But I'm not going to join the firm.*

"There will be a variety of matters from my business practice that you would handle. The foreclosures will still be the bulk of work," Nelson said.

Does that mean he won't be sending the foreclosures to me if he gets someone else? "What kind of things would I be handling?" *I'll have to think about this. Hard.*

"A lot of contracts and letter-writing. But DeHaven always manages to send something interesting our way." Reading Ray's arched eyebrows, Nelson continued. "They own or manage nine strip clubs and one of the casino boats in addition to some other businesses and bingo. We help when a dancer gets in trouble or when there is an incident at one of the clubs. It breaks up the monotony of all those contracts."

"Sounds interesting."

"Besides, you might get some free entertainment as well."

"Do they own the Pink Slipper?" Ray said.

"I think so. Why?"

"One of my witnesses in that murder case works there. He has been avoiding me."

"Call John. He'll help you." Nelson hit his intercom button. "Trish, can you write down John DeHaven's cell phone number and give it to Mr. Jackson on his way out?" He didn't wait for her to respond before he turned back to Ray. "Let me put together a proposal for you. I'll include a buyout of your practice. Can we get together in a few days?"

That's fast.

They set a time.

"Thank you, Nelson," Ray said, standing.

Nelson rose from his desk and shuffled around to shake his hand. "I look forward to having you with us. By the way, I'm hosting a party on my boat in a couple of weeks. You should join us."

"That would be fun." *Not.*

Nelson walked over to his panoramic window and pointed at a forty-two-foot Bertram. "There she is, 'Pole Dancin'."

"She's pretty," Ray said. And she was lovely, floating lightly on the current with the sun playing in her rigging. The Bertram Company would have been happy to put its photograph on its website.

Ray picked up DeHaven's number on the way out. He started dialing as soon as he got into his car. He didn't get an answer and didn't leave a message since he was going to the jail and didn't know how long he would be there. He was going to give Bo the news about the DNA and the offer. He had the discovery responses and a couple of notes he had made. He was also bringing a photo of Bo's hands and a copy of the front and back of a business card.

Ray was better-prepared for his body search this time. A guard took his folder and asked him to spread his legs and hold out his arms. She was taller than Ray and thin like a model, with her hair pulled back into a tight bun. The severity highlighted the natural beauty of her face. The guard's lips were pursed and her eyes were narrowed. *I bet she has a hypnotizing smile.* Instead of using one of those wands, she frisked him thoroughly by hand.

"I bet you don't get this intimate on a first date," Ray said.

"No, sir. Turn around, please."

"Why don't you have X-ray machines?"

"I'm better." She picked up his folder and flipped through the pages.

"Follow me, please." She returned the folder and led him down the hall to an interview room, where he waited until they brought Bo.

After Bo was seated, Ray began. "We got the results of the DNA tests, Mr. Heath. SLED says that you match a sample taken from under her fingernails."

"It's not me."

Ray reached into his folder and dropped the photos of Bo's hands onto the table. "These are pictures of your hands taken when they arrested you. Can you explain the cuts and bruises?"

"I done told you. I had a fight Friday and I hang sheetrock. My hands are always beat up."

"Mr. Heath, if you don't tell me the truth, I can't do my job."

"It's not me."

"And they think the DNA in some bodily fluid on her shirt is yours, too. How is that possible if you haven't been with her in over a year?"

"I went home. I didn't do nothing with her. It's not me." Bo's face began to turn red.

"OK," Ray said, "then I'll find an expert to examine the report for us and see what they say. The second sample is not a clear match to you. It could be someone else. Who is Thomas Reed?"

"What?"

"Do you know a Thomas Reed?"

"No."

Ray reached into his folder again and pulled out the photocopy of the business card. "This business card for the Lamb's Bible Book Store in Skokie, Illinois, was found in Tonya's back pocket. On the other side is the name Thomas Reed."

"Don't know him."

"All right. I met with the solicitor to discuss the report, and he has offered a plea to one murder. He'll drop the other charges. If you take the plea, you would still get twenty years with no parole. If we don't take it, you're facing forty-eight and he could still go for the death penalty."

"No."

"I suggest that we offer to plead to the criminal sexual conduct charge and drop the others. That would have you out in eight years or less."

"No plea."

"Why don't you think about it for a while? There's no need to make a decision until after we get our expert's report. But you need to consider that if we don't make a plea, the solicitor will bring another murder charge for the death of the fetus, and if he does, you could face the death penalty. Do you understand?"

Bo's eyes circled the room before he answered. "No plea. I didn't do it."

"Is there anything I can do for you before I leave? Do you have any questions for me?"

Bo shook his head.

"I'm going to stop at the offices of Coastal Carolina Construction on the way back to my office. I am going to get the addresses for your co-workers. Is there anyone else I should be talking to?"

"Roy Mack."

No shit. "I'm working on that."

11

This time John DeHaven answered Ray's call on the second ring.

"How did you get this number?"

"Nelson gave it to me. He thought you might be able to help me with something." Ray opened the door to his car and sat down.

"Do you have an idea about the informant?"

"No, it's not about SLED's investigation. I need your help in reaching Royal McKenzie. I have called several times and been by his house."

"Roy Mack? Why do you need to talk to him?"

"He's a witness in a case I have."

"He works nights. Sleeps during the day. That's probably why you can't catch him."

"I have called at all hours. I think he's avoiding me." Ray cranked the car and pulled onto the highway.

"Maybe he doesn't want to talk to you."

"That's why I could use your help."

"What's the case about?"

"I am appointed to represent Michael Heath. He is—"

"Bo Heath? Roy Mack isn't going to talk about that."

"He's a witness and I—"

"Bo killed one of Roy Mack's girls."

"Allegedly."

"Yeah, you don't know Bo. He killed her."

"You know Mr. Heath?"

"They should fry the bastard."

"They have to prove him guilty first. And I don't think they can."

"He's guilty. Maybe you can get him off, but that doesn't mean he didn't do it. And don't expect Roy Mack to help Bo. Roy Mack takes care of his girls and anyone that tries to hurt them."

"I still need to talk to him."

"Good luck with that. You can try to catch him at the club, but if Roy Mack doesn't want to talk to you, you won't find him. You're just wasting your time, and I know you've got more important things to do. Why don't you forget about Roy Mack and help me find this damn informant."

"Ask Roy Mack to talk to me and then I can turn my full attention to SLED's investigation."

"You should be focusing on this case anyway. Let me know when you have something useful."

Ray continued driving toward Royal McKenzie's house. It was the middle of the day, when he should be home sleeping. But the driveway was empty. No one responded to Ray's knock. *Maybe DeHaven's right. Maybe I am wasting my time. Screw this. I don't have to talk to Royal McKenzie right now.* Ray took a business card from his case and wrote a note on the back before leaving it in the door. The note said, "Why are you afraid to talk to me?"

While he was out of the office, Ray decided to swing by Coastal Carolina Construction. He needed to speak to at least one of the construction crew members to tie down Bo's alibi. He hadn't been able to reach any of them. On the way, he tried the number on the business card and got the voice mail for the Tasker family, not Reed. He didn't leave a message.

It took only fifteen minutes to reach the office of Coastal Carolina Construction. It was located in the middle of a mixed industrial/business development. The area used to be home to a little bit of everything, advertising-agency offices, auto and truck repair, heavy equipment dealerships and light industrial manufacturing. But easily half the buildings were empty now. The area was also home to a couple of the raunchier strip clubs in Myrtle Beach. On the corner of the road, just a few hundred yards from

Coastal Carolina Construction, sat the Pink Slipper. It glistened like a pile of fresh dog shit on a newly mowed lawn.

The club was in one of those steel prefab buildings. It was painted the brown of rotting leaves. The window glass was painted, too. The half-circle awning over the front door was a color somewhere between pink and neon orange. A once-white high-heeled shoe was printed on the awning. An eighties-model car was in the lot, probably abandoned by an incapacitated patron. It didn't look like anyone was there. The marquee indicated that the club opened at seven. Ray wondered what time Roy Mack got in.

Coastal Carolina Construction was right behind the Pink Slipper. The construction office was in the end unit of a strip of offices. Two of the spaces in the building were occupied. Three were for rent. Walking to the door, Ray read the sign on the outside wall of the office. The line on the bottom of the sign said the construction company was a division of Orion Management Group.

"Can I help you?" a young woman asked like he was the first customer of the day.

"I hope so. I'm Ray Jackson. I am the attorney representing Michael Heath. Do you know Michael?"

"Yeah, he used to work here until he killed that girl."

"Allegedly. He was traveling out of town with your crew when the murder happened. I need to speak with them to prove that he was in Charleston the whole time. Can you help me find them?"

"I'll try."

"Thank you. When would be a good time to catch Carlos Rivera?"

"He doesn't work here anymore."

"How about the guys that were on his crew when Bo was working here?"

"Nope, they're not with us either."

"What happened to them?"

"We laid off the crew members right after Carlos quit," she said.

"When did he quit?"

"It was about a month before Christmas. I think he was going to Texas to see his family and try to find some work down there. Juan might have gone with him. I don't know what happened to Frank."

"Do you know how to get in touch with any of them?"

"I don't think I can give out that information."

"I really need to speak with them to help prove Bo's innocence."

"You don't think he did it?"

"How could he do it if he wasn't even in town?"

She thought about that for a few seconds and turned to a file cabinet against the back wall. After a brief search, she gave Ray three addresses and phone numbers. "Here's the last information that I have. Don't tell anyone I gave it to you."

"I won't. Thank you."

"I hope it helps."

"Oh, one more thing. Did Thomas Reed work for you?"

"That name doesn't ring a bell."

When he walked to his car, Ray saw that there was another car in the lot of the Pink Slipper. It was not the car that he had seen at Royal McKenzie's house, so he didn't stop. He could go to his office and come back and try to catch him at opening time. Roy Mack wouldn't be expecting that.

At his office, Ray opened Bo's file to add the new information about the construction crew. The phone numbers and addresses were the same ones he had in the file. Knowing it was useless, he tried the phone numbers again. This time there was one answer. The phone company told him that Carlos's number was no longer in service.

The clock on his computer said 4:21. Ray picked up a foreclosure file. Then he dropped it back on the pile. He pulled up his search engine and typed in "Thomas Reed Skokie Illinois." About midway through the second page of results was an old article about a Thomas Reed who was wanted on suspicion of rape. All the other hits were ads or related to people who didn't look like they could create reasonable doubt for Bo. He called the police department in Skokie to see if anyone there knew where Thomas Reed was. He learned that, while Thomas Reed was still wanted, no one particularly cared, since the investigating officer was no longer with the department. He finally got someone who promised to look for the file if he would fax a request.

Ray prepared and printed the fax. *This is a waste of time. They just told me that to get me off the phone.* But he faxed the request anyway.

With still a little more time to kill, Ray typed "Orion Management" into his search engine. The websites for various strip clubs and the casino boats showed up along with a couple of newspaper articles about the business. The articles were all Chamber of Commerce stuff, probably submitted by Orion. Further down was an article about an arrest at the Stallion. Some drunk had gotten out of hand. Not unexpected. He searched "John DeHaven" next and found an article from a local paper about the suspicious death of an employee. About five years ago, Cindy Martin, a dancer employed at one of the clubs managed by Orion, either jumped or fell overboard from a casino boat. She had not been missed until the boat returned to dock in Little River. The Coast Guard conducted a full-scale search. After two days, the crew of a private fishing boat found her body. The closest law enforcement boat was from North Carolina, and the crew took the body back to their home dock, where the Shallotte County Medical Examiner's Office claimed it. A note had not been found, but foul play was not suspected. The Horry County coroner surmised that Martin had been depressed about her pregnancy and committed suicide. DeHaven was quoted in the story. That was all, except that the Reverend Tim Thomas led the funeral service.

An article from a different paper revealed that Martin had worked at the same club as Tonya Smalls. Reverend Tim did Tonya's funeral, too. What kind of relationship did Martin have with Royal McKenzie? *One more question to ask him when I see him tonight.*

After reading an e-mail from Trish, Ray turned on his fax machine. It rang and began to print. He had a new foreclosure case.

The sun was dipping toward the horizon when he finished working on the new case. He adjusted his tie and headed for the Pink Slipper. *Here I come, Royal McKenzie.*

12

Ray was so eager to question Royal McKenzie that he arrived at the Pink Slipper ten minutes before it was scheduled to open. There were three cars in the parking lot now. He tried the front door but it was locked. When he knocked, no one answered. Ray walked around the building and found the back door, which was locked, too. He knocked firmly, with no response. He banged on it with his fist, and in less than a minute, he heard someone turn the deadbolt. The door opened and a large man filled the frame. Ray stepped back involuntarily. The man was six three or four and about three hundred pounds. His head was shaved and his bottom lip pierced with what looked like a fish hook—for a big fish. The man stared but he didn't speak.

"I'd like to see Royal McKenzie," Ray said.

"Come back at seven," the hulking figure said. He shut the door. He didn't slam it. The huge man must not have seen any need to emphasize his point. It was 6:55. Ray walked back to the front and waited. He hoped no one he knew drove by. The club finally opened at two minutes after seven.

"I'd like to see the manager," Ray said to the man sitting on the stool just inside the door. It was the same one he'd met at the back door.

"Ten dollars," was the reply. According to the sign, ten dollars was the cover charge from seven until nine. After nine, it was twenty.

"I'm not here for the show. I would just like to speak to the manager," Ray said. He had done the math. He needed every dollar unless he joined Nelson's firm.

"Hey, man, it costs ten dollars to get through this door. I don't care if all you want to do is take a piss. Ten dollars."

Ray tried a different tack. "Is Royal McKenzie here?"

"Ten dollars."

Ray gave him a ten. The man dropped the bill into a slot. "Enjoy the show," he said without the slightest bit of enthusiasm or sarcasm.

"Royal McKenzie?"

He pointed toward the entrance with his thumb.

When Ray opened the door, the music assaulted him. The club was sadder than he'd expected, a place of false promises and poor fantasies. The bar, for instance, was nothing more than a soda fountain station. The Pink Slipper was one of those totally nude places and therefore couldn't get a beer or liquor license in South Carolina. The patrons brought their own alcohol in a brown bag. The club sold "setups" at outrageous prices. For five bucks you could get half a glass of tap water or off-brand soda over ice in a flimsy plastic cup. Everything was painted black, with no decorations on the walls or tables. The lighting was muted except on the stage, and the place smelled of stale smoke and beer. The music was loud, with an occasional crackle in the system. The curtain on the stage, a small inverted *T*, was the only pink thing in the place, and that was only because it had faded from its original red. Along both side walls were series of curtained booths for patrons who wanted some more personal but legally limited entertainment. The club catered to the traveling man who didn't really want to cheat on his wife but wasn't comfortable enough with himself to be alone, as well as to the guy who couldn't find a woman and couldn't afford or was afraid to be with a real prostitute. The entertainers at the Pink Slipper didn't earn their money on the stage.

There was no one behind the bar. There was no one else in the room. Ray saw a door to the right of the stage and started for it.

"Where are you going, honey? The show's out here," a dancer said over the music. She was walking down the stage stairs wearing only a bustier. In the semi-dark, Ray couldn't guess her age, but it was apparent that she had been doing this for a while. He suspected that she needed the bustier to support her surgically inflated breasts.

"I'm looking for Royal McKenzie," he shouted.

Her smile and friendliness went into hiding. "He's not here, hon," she said. "I don't know if he's coming tonight. You can ask Dillon." She pointed to the friendly doorman.

"He's not very talkative," Ray said. "Isn't Roy Mack the manager?"

"Yeah, but he doesn't come in every night."

"Do you know Tonya Smalls?"

She walked over to Ray and took a lapel of his jacket between her fingers. She looked into his eyes. "What's your name, hon?"

"Ray."

"Well, Ray, my name is Angelina. A girl's got to make a living and I don't have time to stand around and answer your questions." Another dancer had come onto the stage. She was leaning against one of the poles watching Ray and Angelina to see if she needed to start dancing. "But if you want a lap dance, you can ask all the questions you want." When Ray hesitated, she said, "I knew Tonya and Tameka."

Tameka? "How much?"

He paid her and she led him to one of the side booths. She pulled the curtain closed.

"No offense, but I didn't come for the dance. I'll—"

"I took your money, I have to dance. Sit down." She gave a push on Ray's shoulders to help him into a low armchair. "Comfortable?"

Ray nodded, but he wasn't. Her chest fell when she removed the bustier. She leaned over the chair and began to grind, sending a breast swinging toward his face with mechanical precision. He sank as far into the chair as he could, but she just leaned over more. *This might be a bad idea.*

"Have you been working here long?"

"A while."

"How about Royal McKenzie, how long has he been here?"

"Longer than me."

"He's from Ohio, right?" Ray said, thinking about Thomas Reed.

"Hell, no. He was born in Charleston and proud of it."

"How did you know Tonya Smalls?" Ray tried to ignore the floppy missiles by focusing on her face.

"I danced with Tonya at the Stallion a few years ago."

"Did she ever dance here?"

"Here? No, honey, she was still too young and pretty. The guys that come here, they want something else." She arched her eyebrows invitingly.

Ray didn't bite. "Did you ever see her with Royal McKenzie? Did they date?"

She laughed. "Roy Mack is gay. That's why he's a good manager of a place like this. He leaves the girls alone."

"Well, do you know if he knew Tonya?"

"Roy hired her to work at the Stallion. He and Tony Evans hire the dancers for all the clubs."

"All the clubs?"

"Yeah, they run about half of them on the beach." She made a turn and continued to dance, waving her bottom in his face.

"Can you turn back around? I like your face." *How drunk or lonely do you have to be to find this enjoyable?* She shrugged and faced Ray again, still dancing. "Did you know Tonya's last boyfriend?"

"I haven't seen her in a couple of years, but I heard what happened to her. Is that why you want to talk to Roy Mack?"

"He found her body."

"Oh." She kept grinding.

"Do you know Bo Heath?"

"Yeah, he used to bounce at the Stallion."

"When was the last time you saw him?"

Her dancing slowed as she considered her answer. A breast grazed Ray's cheek. He flipped his head to the other side to dodge the next one.

"I don't think I've seen him since the last time I danced at the Stallion, about four years ago."

"Tell me about"—*what was the other name she said?*—"Tameka." He took a breast in each hand.

"Ooh, that's more like it. You can massage them if you want."

He didn't. He was just trying to keep them out of the way. "Tameka?"

"Somebody tried to rob her outside the club here. They strangled her."

"That's awful. When did that happen?"

"About two years ago, two and a half. Roy Mack found her body next to the dumpster out back."

"Did they find her killer?"

"No, she was just a dancer. The cops didn't care much about her."

"What was Tameka's last name?"

"I didn't know her that good. She was working a lot of private parties. I don't even know why she was here that night. She wasn't dancing."

"She wasn't dancing? How do you know that?"

She didn't answer because the privacy curtain was ripped open. "That's it, man. You're outta here." It was the doorman.

"Dillon, what you doing?" Angelina said.

He pushed her aside and grabbed Ray by the lapels and stood him up. "You are creating a disturbance," he said. "It's bothering all the other patrons."

"What?" Angelina said.

"I'll go," Ray said, holding up both hands. "No problem."

The doorman punched Ray in the stomach. He doubled over and collapsed into the chair.

"Hey," Angelina said, "that's my customer." She began to beat the doorman on the back. He didn't seem to notice.

The doorman jerked Ray out of the seat and tossed him out of the private box. Ray stumbled and fell, but he stood up quickly and was dusting himself off when the doorman hit him in the midsection again. Ray went backward, tripped over a chair leg and hit the edge of the stage. He threw an arm across the stage floor and didn't go all the way down. The blow hurt but not too badly. Ray was a swimmer and his abs were strong.

"Hey," Ray said, holding up one hand. "I'm going."

The doorman grabbed his hand and twisted it back.

"Ow!"

He turned Ray to the door, pinched his neck between his thumb and forefinger and marched him to the door. "Roy Mack said you ain't welcome here and you should stop harassin' him," he said. "You hear me?" He shook Ray.

"I hear you."

Dillon shoved Ray through the open door. Ray's shoe caught on the threshold and he landed on the concrete walk on his hands and knees.

Ray rolled over into a sitting position. He glared back at the dark mass of doorman. Ray's left knee was bleeding. But worse than that, his suit pants had a bloody tear. He really didn't want to buy a new suit. He couldn't *afford* to buy a new suit. He rose and tried not to limp to his car. *Fuck.* The headlights on the vehicle were smashed. As he walked around the car, he saw that all four tires were flat and that the taillights were shattered. He stared at the car for at least five minutes before he reached for his phone to call the police. *But what can they do? Nothing.* He called Roy Mack instead and left a message: "I need to talk to you ... about several things." Then he called a cab. He could get someone to get his car in the morning. At least he had some insurance.

13

Ray went straight home and jumped into a hot shower. Now he knew why Royal McKenzie had been avoiding him. *And I know how to make him pay for tonight.*

"Ladies and gentlemen of the jury," Ray began to imagine his closing argument as he scrubbed the residue of the Pink Slipper from his body, "the solicitor has failed to explain the connection between their star witness, Royal McKenzie, and the very similar murders of Tonya Smalls and Tameka"—he still didn't know her last name—"Somebody. Both ladies were strangled. Both were exotic dancers. Both worked for Royal McKenzie. And both of their bodies were found by—that's right—Royal McKenzie." He dragged the name out and pointed at the shower curtain. "Yet the police have never investigated Mr. McKenzie for either murder." *I need to get the police report for Tameka's murder.* "Could Royal McKenzie also be Thomas Reed? We don't know. Could he match the other sample of DNA? We don't know. Like so many other things the police have failed to do, he has not been tested." *Not bad. And a shot at Jarrett Brown. Two birds with one stone.*

He shut off the shower and grabbed a towel. No, Roy Mack was not Thomas Reed. He was born in South Carolina and had probably been here all his life. Besides, he was gay, or at least that's what Angelina said. *But I can still make the argument. No ethical issues to worry about there. It's reasonable doubt. Let the jury decide—if it gets that far.*

Ray threw on some short pants and a Braves T-shirt with the number ten on the back. Chipper Jones was still his favorite player. He fixed a bourbon and water for medicinal purposes. After all, his knee was still stinging. He sat down with his laptop and opened a search page.

His first few searches were useless, but when your search terms include *dancer*, *stripper* and *strangulation*, you should expect an interesting list of sites. He'd had enough filth for one night, so he navigated to the *Horry County Tribune* website and searched the archives of the local paper. *Bingo!* He shook his head. He found an article about the murder of a dancer named Tameka Shelley. Tameka Shelley had been assaulted and strangled two years ago, her body found beside a dumpster behind the Pink Slipper. She had not been raped. According to the police, Tameka had been one of the last to leave the club. Robbery was the suspected motive because her empty purse was found at the edge of the parking lot. Her wallet and keys were missing. The police were asking the public to call with any information. That meant that they had no leads. Royal McKenzie was not mentioned in the story, but all the other information matched what Angelina had said. Ray made a note to get the police and the coroner's records. They would tell him the extent of Royal McKenzie's involvement and whether he was a suspect.

Could he use this to get Roy Mack to answer the questions he needed to get answered? *Probably not.* But that didn't really matter. He could screw with Roy Mack and help Bo's case at the same time. Still, it might be useful to have the answers to a few questions. Ray didn't know what a pregnant Tonya had been doing at the Three Door. According to Bo, she'd talked to Royal McKenzie. Was she there to meet him? If so, why? What did Tonya talk to him about? Did she know something that would make Roy Mack kill her? What could she know? Does it have anything to do with Tameka?

Further down in the search results was Tameka Shelley's obituary. She was survived by her mother, who lived in Murrell's Inlet, and several half-brothers and half-sisters. There was no mention of a father. Ray did a search for her mother and couldn't find an address or phone number. He printed the article. If he stopped by the church where the funeral had been held, maybe someone there would be able to help him find her. Perhaps she could tell him about Tameka's relationship with Royal McKenzie.

Also in the search results was an article about the death of another dancer, Candi Brown. According to that article, she'd committed suicide.

Ray broadened his search and found articles relating to the deaths of six more dancers. Susan Joye, Mallory Barnes, Cindy Martin, Wendy Lane, Ashley Mason and Jacqueline Ervin had all died within the last ten years. That made nine dancers in ten years. That seemed like a lot.

Candi Brown had been found in her apartment almost eight years ago. The coroner ruled that she had committed suicide by hanging herself. There had been no note. According to the article, her manager found her after he had become concerned when she didn't report for work at the Pink Slipper. *Hmm …Was her manager Royal McKenzie?* And hanging is a form of strangulation. "Roy Mack's going to wish he talked to me," Ray said to Whiskers.

Ray knew about Cindy Martin's drowning. The deaths of the other dancers did not seem to have any possible connection to the deaths of Tonya or Tameka. None of them had been strangled. Only Ashley had worked at an Orion-managed club, and it wasn't the Pink Slipper or the Stallion Room. There was no mention of Royal McKenzie in any of the articles concerning her murder. Besides, the boyfriend had confessed to shooting her with his shotgun and was serving life in prison.

Ray navigated to the Horry County coroner's website, where, not surprisingly, no records were available to the general public. He prepared a subpoena for the coroner's file on Tameka Shelley and paused before adding Candi Brown and Cindy Martin to the document. Candi Brown and Cindy Martin hadn't been murdered, so Ray doubted they would help with Bo's case. *But you never know.* They were connected to Royal McKenzie and you couldn't have too much reasonable doubt. Besides, it might give Roy Mack something else to worry about.

He also prepared a subpoena for the sheriff's records for each case. He printed the subpoenas and put them in his briefcase. He would have them served tomorrow.

14

Ray served the subpoenas personally on Tuesday morning. It was faster and cheaper to do it himself. Nothing happened for two weeks, and then one day Nelson's assistant, Trish, called Ray's office at five before nine. First, she reminded Ray about his lunch meeting with Mr. Patterson. Then she asked if Ray would speak to Tony Evans, one of John DeHaven's employees, about an incident that had occurred at one of their clubs. Nelson didn't have time, because he was preparing for a legislative committee meeting, so Ray took Tony Evans's number. It appeared that Nelson was pretty confident that Ray would be joining the firm.

Ray called and left a message for Mr. Evans, who apparently wasn't too concerned about the problem. He had taken the day off to go fishing.

Ray arrived at DiMarco's on time and found that Nelson had already been seated. DiMarco's was like any other upscale Italian restaurant. Black-and-white photos of Italian landmarks decorated the faux-stucco walls. Behind Nelson, a photograph of the Leaning Tower of Pisa hung crooked. Full-size replicas of Michelangelo's *David* and *Pieta* guarded the entrance to the bar area.

After the meal arrived, Nelson turned to the purpose of the lunch. "Here's a draft proposal for you to join our firm." He pulled a paper-clipped document from his briefcase and handed it to Ray. "I think you will find it to your liking. I am offering you a reasonable base salary plus up to 10 percent of your billings as an annual bonus. We will purchase your existing practice and assume the lease of your present office. We need a presence where you are. We'll move you to the main office in Conway and probably put one of our young associates in your office for the time being. And you can bring your secretary if you want."

"That's a very attractive offer."

"Well, there is one condition. I need an answer in the next week. Things have changed a little. I have learned that one of my potential challengers for the governor's office is beginning to organize, and I need to get busy putting together my team. And if it's not right for you, I need to get someone else, pronto."

"I understand."

"I'm really hoping you're going to join us. The bank has been pleased with your work. They're ready to send us all of their foreclosure cases. But you do understand that I'll have to keep that in house if I have to hire someone else."

"Of course." *That's the dilemma. No referrals, no practice.*

"I don't say that as a threat, but it is a fact you need to consider."

"I've been thinking about it." *That's why I'll probably have to join you. Whether I like it or not.*

"Good. Between those and some of the other files I can give you, you'll have plenty to do. Read the proposal, send me any changes you want us to consider and we'll get this done. OK?"

"Thank you, Nelson. This looks good. Let me review it and I'll let you know something in a day or two." *It probably won't take that long. I'm behind on everything after buying four new tires and covering the deductible on my car.*

"Good. Call Trish and she can e-mail you a copy that you can edit. And one more thing: we'll take that murder case of yours and give it to Clint Williams. He does most of the firm's criminal work. That'll be one less headache for you. I look forward to having you on the team." Nelson glanced at his Rolex. "Stay and finish your meal. I've got a conference call with the Budget Committee in fifteen minutes. Before I go, did you hear anything from my contact at SLED about the investigation of the church and Orion?"

"There's really nothing to report. The investigating agents still aren't talking about the case. Your contact did confirm that SLED has an informant, but we knew that. Has John been able to figure out who it might be?"

"No, no luck there."

"One quick question. How do you want me to handle the fee for the Tony Evans matter you referred today?"

"You keep it. But take good care of Tony. He's one of John's right-hand men."

After Nelson left, Ray read the proposal and enjoyed a cup of rich Italian-roast coffee. Ray was impressed with the offer. It was better than expected, better than it had to be. The base salary was above average. Plus up to a 10 percent annual bonus and they were going to pay him for his practice. He could catch up on all his bills. He might be able to get a new car. *Or a boat.* He could bring Donna back to work. And he could give the murder case to someone else in the firm. *What else could I want?*

He savored a sip of the coffee. *Why me?* He took another sip. Nelson could get a recent grad for a lot less and without having to pay for a practice. *Who gives a shit? I'm going to take it.*

Considering dessert, Ray was startled when a sheaf of folded papers landed in his plate like the morning paper on the doorstep. "Hey," he said.

A bulky man in a wrinkled brown suit and a yellow speckled tie commandeered the seat vacated by Nelson. "Just what are you trying to do with these subpoenas?"

"Detective Brown, it's so nice to see you."

"It's Captain. Is this some stupid attempt to punish me for not finding your sister?"

Ray fished the papers from his plate and dropped them onto the table. "No," he said. *My sister?* "They are pertinent to the defense of a client."

"Bullshit. It's an attack on me because you think I screwed up your sister's investigation."

"Detec–Captain"—the man was agitated enough—"I really do need this for my case."

"I'm going to fight your subpoena."

"Really?" Ray took another sip of coffee. It was getting cool. "On what grounds?"

"It's a sham to punish me. Besides, the families don't want you opening old wounds so you can trick a jury into letting a guilty man go."

"A sham? I may not think you're a great investigator, but—"

"I found you today, didn't I?"

"Yes, you did." Ray nodded. "That's amazing."

"It's harder than you think." Brown sat back but didn't really relax. "I know you don't believe me, but I turned over every stone I could to find your sister."

"This isn't about my sister."

"How long did you search for her? Months and months. You even lost your job over it. And you didn't find anything, did you?"

Ray rearranged the napkin in his lap. He never found a trace. Not one. He could do without the reminder. He looked across the table. "Captain Brown, I'm trying to enjoy this fine coffee and I'm going to order some cheesecake. Is there anything else you want?"

"Yeah, I want you to withdraw this subpoena."

"I've told you, I'm not going to do that. It's part of my defense preparation." The waiter, dressed in black with a white apron, saw Ray's signal and took his order. A fidgeting Captain Brown declined the waiter's offer.

Brown leaned over the table as soon as the server had left. "This isn't about Michael Heath. We both know he's guilty."

Why is this so hard? "Captain, if you had done a thorough investigation, you might not be so damn sure."

"See, it comes right back to your sister."

"No, it's about your competence."

"That's why you're attacking me personally."

"What are you talking about? Did you screw up the investigations on these cases, too?"

The cheesecake arrived and the waiter refilled Ray's coffee. The captain simmered quietly while the waiter completed his task. Ray took a bite.

Captain Brown looked around the restaurant before lowering his voice. "Come on, Mr. Jackson, you know that Candi is—was my daughter. I can't tell you how painful it was to lose her, and now you want to open the file and make us live through it again. I know you want to get back at me, but think about my wife."

Ray had lifted a forkful of cheesecake but put it back without taking the bite. "Captain, I didn't know. I am sorry for your loss. But this isn't about you or my sister. I need to look at the files for Michael Heath. I don't know what's in them. I might not find anything, but there might be a connection between the cases, and I am going to look."

"You're full of shit. You have a murder case. My daughter wasn't murdered."

"I believe that there is one common element. It may lead to nothing, but I have to check. If it might help my client, I'm entitled to know."

Brown paused and cocked his head. "I knew your dad and mom in high school. We'd run into each other around town after that. Your dad was a brave man. When your sister went missing, I busted my ass because your mother didn't deserve two tragedies like that."

"You didn't find anything."

"Neither of us did, but we both looked very damned hard, didn't we?"

Ray dropped his head. "Yeah, I guess so."

"I reviewed your sister's case before I came over here. I check it every year. Bet you didn't know that. I guess I thought if there was something new, something to report, you might change your mind."

"I appreciate that."

"No, I don't think you do. You don't know what you got. You have something I wish I had. You have hope." He held up his hand against Ray's protest. "It may not be much, but it's still there. Hope that tomorrow or next week or someday, your sister will walk through the door with some crazy story and say, 'I'm back.'" He looked down at his hands. "I don't have that." He looked at Ray again. "My Candi, my baby girl, is gone. She's not coming back, ever. That's why I really need you to leave this alone."

Ray understood how Brown felt. Too well. "Captain, I'm sorry, but I can't do that. Now, I've got to get back to my office." *I have a proposal to sign. Besides, the cheesecake is grainy.*

Captain Brown stood and walked around the table to Ray. He placed one hand on the back of Ray's chair. "I've tried being nice." He placed the other hand on the table. "I've asked you politely." Then he leaned in close to Ray's face. "But you won't listen to reason. So you need to understand that you should leave my daughter out of this or you will regret it."

Ray met Brown's stare. "Captain," he said as calmly as he could manage, "it's time for you to leave or I'm going to call the sheriff. You won't like that." He wanted to reach for his coffee cup, but he was afraid his hand would shake.

"Don't make threats you can't back up. I never do."

Ray could smell the onions on Brown's breath. "I think we're done here." He put his napkin on the table, forcing Brown to stand. "But I do have one question for you. How did your daughter become a dancer for Royal McKenzie?"

Brown's face turned red and he clenched his fists. "That's none of your fucking business." He straightened his jacket, turned and marched out of the restaurant. He didn't look back.

15

"He wouldn't let go of her tit. So I hit him a couple of times," Tony Evans said. Mr. Evans, a vice president of Orion Management, was facing assault charges arising from an incident that had occurred at the Stallion Room. They were in Ray's office on a sunny Thursday morning.

"What happened next?" *Nelson was right. Some of these cases were certainly a lot more interesting.*

"She asked him to let go. I politely asked him to let her go back to work, but the customer wouldn't release her. So I helped him change his mind."

"According to the police report, you gave him two black eyes, broke his nose, bruised his right kidney and his genitals. He was in the hospital for four days. One witness says you repeatedly kicked him in the side and groin after he was knocked out and lying on the ground."

"Nobody messes with my girls. He learned that the hard way." Tony sat back and smiled. "I'll bet he pissed blood for a week."

Tony was about six foot one, tanned and in excellent shape. He had two prior convictions, a simple assault and a possession-of-marijuana charge, which he had escaped with small fines. In the assault case, which had occurred just last year, he had badly beaten another drunken patron and initially was charged with assault of a high and aggravated nature. The charge was dropped to simple assault. Tony Evans didn't play when he fought.

Sitting in the chair next to Tony was Susan Allen, the dancer involved in the matter. She was wearing a baggy gray sweat suit that hid her required nice figure. Her bleached blond hair was pulled back in a careless ponytail, a couple of strands hanging across her face. She was not wearing makeup.

"Susan," Ray said, "tell me what you remember."

"It must have been around two or two thirty and this guy, back in the VIP room, he asks for a lap dance, only he's drunker than most of them and wants a discount." She curled a loose strand of hair around her middle finger. "My manager, he won't let us do that. I should have known then that he was an asshole. He was dressed like he thought he was Leonardo DiCaprio or something. Anyway, he comes up with the money for the dance, and all through it I'm having to tell him to put his hands down. He's not supposed to touch, not too much, but the whole dance he's trying to grab my tits and my pussy. When I finished, he wanted me to dance longer. I told him that he had gotten what he had paid for, and that's when he grabbed my left tittie and wouldn't let go. I still got a bruise. See." She lifted her sweatshirt, revealed her surgically perfected breasts and pointed to the bruise. There wasn't much of one to see. Ray might have missed it had she not pointed to it.

Definitely a first for this office. "Have you sought medical attention for that?"

She snorted. "No."

"Did you swear out a warrant against him for assault?"

"Can I do that?"

"You can. But there is no money in it for you. Perhaps I can use the possibility to help Tony. Would that be all right?"

"Sure." She shrugged.

After they left, Ray prepared and mailed a letter of representation to the solicitor. Then he called Nelson and accepted the offer. His finances made it a no-brainer. *But it didn't have to be forever.* Nelson reluctantly agreed to allow Ray to keep Bo's case for the time being, but Ray could still ask for help whenever he needed it. Ray agreed to start a week from Monday.

Feeling somewhat financially secure, Ray called and retained Dr. Norman Green from a prominent university in Atlanta to examine the DNA evidence in Bo's case. He needed two experts, a forensic pathologist and a DNA expert like Dr. Green, but Ray couldn't afford two today. He was entitled to some reimbursement from the state for expenses, but it would pay for only one expert, and the retainer had to come out of his pocket. When he got the reimbursement, he'd hire the other one. He could ask the court to approve the expense and hope it was approved.

That evening, he was changing out of his suit when he saw the folded bingo card on his dresser. He picked it up and examined it. *I really need to ask her about Roy Mack. I've been putting it off too long.* He dialed.

"I thought you had forgotten about me," she said.

"You know better than that. I've had a lot on my plate."

"Or have you been spending your time with your girlfriend?"

"I don't have a girlfriend."

"Really? I heard you and that Jennifer Jones lady were together."

"Where did you hear that? We haven't dated in years."

"OK. Can you call me later? I'm at the church and I've got to go into work."

"Annette, I just wanted to ask—"

"Of course, I would love to. How about tomorrow night?"

"Tomorrow night?"

"You can pick me up at seven. Gotta go. Bye."

Ray pulled the phone from his ear and stared at it. He had a date he didn't want. *Not very much.* He remembered holding her warm soft body next to his and kissing her in the parking lot. *She's a witness and she doesn't know I'm representing Bo Heath.* He hit "redial," but it went straight to voice mail. *I'll call her tomorrow and straighten it out.* Somehow he didn't find the time.

Ray arrived at Annette's apartment at seven on the dot and rang the doorbell. She lived in a complex at the southern end of the Grand Strand. Many of the best restaurants along the Grand Strand were located in Murrell's Inlet about midway between her apartment and Ray's condo. He had reserved a table at one of his favorites. *Before we leave her place, I have to tell her this isn't a date.* He rang the bell.

She opened the door. Her smile was dazzling, her brown eyes dancing with excitement and her yellow sundress showed off her dancer's legs above matching high heels.

He forgot his plan. "You look lovely," he said and took her hand to help her to the car.

He hadn't chosen the restaurant because they served fresh seafood from the local boats—they all did that. He'd picked this place because the spring sunsets were beautiful from its deck overlooking the saltwater marsh. Their table was ready when they arrived. It was nestled under a palmetto tree and close to the water. A duo was playing pop and beach music. Ray saw a fishing boat in the channel heading for its dock.

Dinner was delicious. He had blackened grouper; she had the creek shrimp scampi. After dinner they moved to a table in the outside bar as the white clouds faded to pink in a perfect sunset. The conversation was enthralling to Ray and, apparently, to Annette. She played her hand all over his as they talked of little things like favorite foods and first kisses. Then they danced. They Shagged to a few songs, and when the music slowed they danced song after song, with Annette's head on Ray's shoulder. When the moon came out, they ventured onto the boardwalk that meandered along the marsh. They strolled with their arms around each other's waists. In a darker spot, they stopped and kissed.

Eventually they found themselves back at the bar. Ray was surprised when the lights in the bar came on.

"Is it midnight already?" Annette said.

Ray pulled out his phone. "Uh, no. It's actually two o'clock. I guess it's closing time." When they left Murrell's Inlet, Ray turned the car toward his condo.

"Where are we going?"

"My place."

She kissed his cheek and laid her head on his shoulder.

The first time was fast and delicious. They'd barely got into the condo. Later they moved to the bedroom and spent a little more time learning about each other. At some point they fell asleep cradled in each other's arms.

When Ray woke up Saturday morning, Annette was sitting on the end of the bed with a mug of coffee in her hand. She had on one of his dress shirts, unbuttoned. That was all.

"I found the coffee," she said, "but I don't know how you like yours, so I made it like mine, a little sugar and cream."

Steam was rising from the mug on the bedside table. "How about we shower and go get some breakfast?" Ray said.

"Maybe we can take a shower in a little while." She stood and let the shirt slide off her shoulders.

Ray got out of bed around midday when Whiskers jumped onto the bed and demanded to be fed. Most of the time, he loved his cat. "I'll be right back," he said.

With juice in two glasses, he returned to find Annette dressed.

"I'd like to stay longer, Ray, but I need to go. I always visit my grandmother on Saturday. She's getting older and I want to make sure she's got everything she needs."

"Mrs. Smalls?"

"Yes, how do you know my ..." Her voice trailed off.

"Sit down," he said, indicating the bed. "I, uh, need to tell you something."

Annette sat on the edge of the bed. Her knees were pressed tightly together. Her hands rested in her lap. "So, how do you know my grandmother?"

"Don't hate me, but I am representing Bo Heath."

"You're defending the man that murdered my cousin and you didn't tell me until now?"

"I ... uh ..."

"Were you trying to fuck me for information?" Her eyes were burning.

"No, no that's not it. I just couldn't ..." *Damn, she's beautiful.*

"And that story about your sister. Was it just bullshit to get me into bed?"

"No. God, no."

"Then what?"

"I should have told you."

"Damn right, you should have."

"I know and I'm sorry. This will sound lame but it's the truth. I was having too much fun with you. I really like being with you."

"So it's my fault?"

"No, no, that's not what I'm saying. I should have told you at Margaritaville. Right then. But …"

"I guess that's why you didn't bring me here on our first date."

"Well, yeah, I …"

"That's what Nana and I figured happened."

"What?"

"I was wondering when you were going to tell me."

"You knew."

"I talk to my grandmother every day. I knew the next day and I was pissed."

"That's fair."

"But Nana likes you. And after a day or so I realized that I like you, too, but you've got to be honest with me."

"You're right. I will."

"I don't want you to be like all the other men I know."

"You're certainly not like any other woman I know."

A small smile appeared. "The lawyer comes out. I'll bet you're great in a courtroom."

Ray stood. "Let me get dressed and I'll take you home. You can go check on your grandmother, and then I will apologize by taking you to dinner tonight."

"You think you can get out of this that easily?" She put out her hand, and Ray helped her stand.

He took her into his arms and, nose to nose, said softly, "No, I expect I'll have to work very hard to satisfy you."

"Hard is right," she said. They kissed and fell back onto the bed.

Makeup sex …

16

Ray stopped by his office after he'd taken Annette home and picked up Bo's file. At his condo, he dropped the paperwork onto the coffee table, turned on a ballgame and opened a beer. The Braves were stuck in a pitcher's duel with a division foe. Two hours later, Bo's file was still lying unopened on Ray's coffee table and the game still had no score. With an audible sigh that made Whiskers jump to his feet, Ray finally leaned over and opened the folder. But he couldn't concentrate. There were still questions he had to ask Annette.

Around seven fifteen, Annette called. "They've got me doing the count tonight, so I'm going to be late finishing. I'm kinda tired. I didn't get a lot of sleep last night."

He knew that. "Why don't we go grab a pizza or something quick when you're done and we'll make it an early night?"

"I should be through around ten."

Beach Pizza was the closest place to the church. A tourist spot, its tables were the wooden picnic kind. There were surfboards, plastic sand buckets and shovels stuck on the bright yellow walls. But the pizza was pretty good and the beer was cold. Because it was near closing time, the place was quiet. Even the XM rock station playing on the sound system was somewhat muted. Ray sat across from Annette.

"I'll bet we counted over fifty-thousand dollars tonight," Annette said. Her hair was tied back with a multicolored scarf.

Ray couldn't decide if she was more beautiful tonight in blue jeans and the church T-shirt than she'd been last night. "Really?" was all he could manage to say through a mouthful of pizza.

"Yeah," she said, cutting her pizza with a knife and fork. She gave him a look. "It's hot."

Ray just smiled.

"Where do those old ladies get that kind of cash?" she asked before taking a bite.

"There's a lot of money in bingo," he said. "It brings in millions each year, so that's not really a surprise."

"I understand that." She took a swallow of her beer. "But you've been there and those folks don't seem to have that much to spend. I mean, fifty-thousand in one night?"

"It *is* the weekend and the economy is getting a little better."

"Still."

"Annette, I've read the reports. I work on the license renewal every year. They make millions. And they give a lot back in prizes. How many people have you seen win a prize and spend the whole thing on more cards?"

"Yeah, I guess I didn't really think about that."

When the pizza was nearly gone, Ray went to the counter for two more beers and sat beside Annette. "Can I ask you a few questions about Tonya and Bo?"

"I guess. But I have a question first."

"OK."

"Should you date a witness in one of your cases?"

"Actually, I looked it up. I would not be allowed to date a material witness." *At least that's my interpretation.*

"Do you think I'm one of those?"

"Truthfully, I don't know, but I don't think so. You would have to be a witness that knows things that other witnesses don't. Answer a couple of questions and we'll find out. Were you with Tonya or Bo at the Three Door that night?"

"No. I hadn't talked to her in a couple of days."

"Do you know Royal McKenzie? Some people call him Roy Mack?"

"I've met him." Her voice caught slightly. "Tonya introduced me once a few years ago."

Ray ignored the feeling that she was lying. "You do know Bo Heath, right?"

"Yes, I know Bo. He killed Tonya." Her lips pursed.

"I know this is tough for you, but I'm not emotionally involved. It doesn't matter to me whether Bo is guilty or innocent. I have to represent him. That means I have to try to prove that he's not guilty if I can."

"I know."

"Besides, wouldn't you like to find Tonya's real killer?"

"It's Bo."

Ray took a breath. *Let's be patient.* "Why do you think he did it?"

"Tonya never could find a decent man. Of course, she didn't have a lot to choose from. Bo was a lot like all of the rest, not too bright, jealous with a violent side. He beat her a few times. Not too bad or he might have lost his job."

"How long ago was that?"

"Back when they were together. Three, four years ago."

"What was their relationship like after they broke up?"

"Tonya kept him on a string. She could call him any time and he'd come running like a dog. But sometimes she had a hard time keeping him away."

"Had you seen them together in the months before her murder?"

"She was at bingo a couple of times before he lost that job."

"Was she dating him then?"

"No. She was trying to avoid him."

"Why?"

"Bo had started talking to her after they hooked up one night over the summer. Tonya said she was lonely and called him. But after that he was being more trouble than usual."

"Was Tonya dating anyone else during the summer or fall?"

"No, she didn't have time."

"Why not?"

"Her boss had her doing a lot of parties."

"What kind of parties?"

"Really?" She turned to him and shook her head.

"So that's why she could afford a new apartment?"

"Yeah."

"Bo thinks she had a new boyfriend.'

"Well, he always thought that. You don't know how jealous he could be."

"But she didn't?"

"She would have told me about a new man. She didn't have one."

"Did you know she was pregnant?"

"It was just a few weeks."

"So you wouldn't know who the father was?"

"No." She turned up her beer and finished it.

"Would you like another?"

"Not now. Are we about done with this?"

"Just one more question. Do you think Royal McKenzie could have killed Tonya?"

"Could he? Sure. But he didn't."

"Why do you say that?"

"Roy Mack wouldn't strangle anybody. He might shoot 'em or cut 'em or beat 'em to death, but he wouldn't strangle 'em. That's just not his style."

Not his style? "What …"

"Excuse me, folks," a man in an apron dotted with tomato paste said, "We're closing."

Ray drove Annette back to her car. "Thank you for telling me about Tonya. I know that wasn't much fun."

Annette took his hand and smiled. "That's OK."

At her car they embraced and kissed. "Why don't we go to your place?" Ray said as he stroked her breast.

She took his hand away. "Ray, I want to," she said, "but I'm tired and I don't want this to be just about sex."

If there's a good response to that statement, Ray didn't know what it was. "How about lunch tomorrow?" He nibbled an ear. He had a great line to follow any answer.

She pushed him back. "I think you should take me to church in the morning. You might learn something."

Except that. "OK. What time?"

"You can pick me up at ten thirty."

It was a long ride home. But Ray was grinning.

Sunday morning, Ray made a few notes about his interview with Annette. He would try not to bring that up again. He put on his seersucker suit with the solid navy tie. *Not too bad.*

Annette was prettier than an Easter sunrise in a rose dress edged with lace. "Where are we going?" Ray asked.

"Gethsemane Gospel Baptist Church."

Ray didn't let Annette see him roll his eyes. He couldn't remember the last time he'd attended a service, much less one at Gethsemane Gospel Baptist. He told people it was because he didn't want to run into his ex-wife, but the truth was that he'd never been a fan of Reverend Tim's sermons.

The congregation filled the sanctuary. There were only a few seats left. The people in the crowed pews looked like an impressionist watercolor of a field of spring flowers. The pastel blues, yellows and greens of sundresses and pant suits set off by the blacks and navies of sport coats and suits mixed with white dress shirts dribbled with multicolored ties. They found a spot in the center of a pew near the back of the middle section.

After the offering had been taken, Reverend Tim walked slowly to the center of the stage. There was no podium. He carried a black bible in one hand. When he reached the center of the stage, he dropped his head and the entire sanctuary became silent. No one coughed. No one sneezed. After a moment, he looked up at the congregation.

"You've all read about it or heard about it on the news," he said so quietly that Ray could almost feel the sense of expectation building in those around him. "Earlier this week, a man in Arkansas took the law into his own hands. He killed a doctor in front of an abortion clinic. I cannot condone the actions of Gerald Edwards, but"—he seemed to somehow fix his gaze on the whole congregation—"I do understand why he acted. Let us take a moment of silence to pray for Mr. Edwards and his family." Reverend Tim bowed his head. Every head followed.

Ray was the last to drop his head. *Did he purposely omit the doctor and his family from the prayer?*

"I cannot approve of the actions of Mr. Edwards because he committed murder. Just as the doctor he killed committed murder, for abortion is nothing less than murder. But I understand the holy anger of Mr. Edwards. I understand his rage at the holocaust that continues unchecked around us. I understand his desire for justice."

A chorus of "Amen" rang from the congregation.

"Aside from taking the life of one of God's glorious creations, abortion is particularly revolting because most abortions are committed to cover up a previous sin. That's right, these people are so deep in sin that they commit murder to cover up the sins of fornication and adultery. Fornicators and adulterers, be warned: you are condemned to hell unless you repent. The Word of the Lord says that joining with another outside of wedlock is sin. Mortal sin."

Annette squeezed Ray's hand, acknowledging their complicity. Ray smiled. Guilt was not the emotion he felt.

Reverend Tim explained at length the evils of murder/abortion. Ray was bored, but most of the congregation seemed to hang on every word.

"This week again, I cried to God from my knees, 'Where is your justice, Lord?'" He glided back to the center of the stage. "Where is God's justice?" He paused. "Brothers and sisters, God's justice is coming. Vengeance is mine, says the Lord!" Then, in a voice just above a whisper, he ended, "Let all who would take the life of a defenseless child growing in its mother's womb be prepared to reap what they have sown. God in his justice will condemn them to everlasting hell." The spotlight lingered on Reverend Tim for thirty seconds before it faded. An associate pastor prayed and closed the service.

Ray and Annette left the church walking arm in arm, making plans for the afternoon.

"Ray, excuse me, Ray." An older gentleman was waving at them. "Can I speak with you a minute?"

"Sure, how are you doing? It's been a little while. It's nice to see you." Ray shook the man's hand warmly. "Mr. Fitch, this is Annette Murphy. Mr. Fitch used to be the treasurer for the church," he said to Annette.

"So nice to meet you," Fitch said. "Excuse us a minute." He seized Ray by the elbow and took him a few steps away.

"We sure miss you. How is—"

"Well, Ray, I heard about this investigation." Fitch looked around as if he was afraid of being overheard. "And I wondered if it had anything to do with that large payment right before bingo heated up?"

"I, uh, I'm afraid I don't know what you're talking about."

"Come on, everyone's talking about how SLED came and took a bunch of computer records. I called the new financial director. She's not returning my calls. I never liked her anyway."

"No, I mean, I don't know what payment you're referring to."

"Oh, like I said, this was before bingo really started making some money, Reverend Tim wrote a two hundred fifty-thousand dollar check to Nelson Patterson's firm and no one has ever told me what the check was for."

"That *is* a big check. Surely there's an explanation."

"I was told to put it down as legal services. I asked what kind of work and never got an answer. Never saw anything done either."

"Well, don't worry about it. SLED's search didn't go back that far."

"That's what Reverend Tim always said. 'Don't worry about it. Don't worry about it.' It's just odd."

"Tell you what, I'll look into it." *I might as well. I've got to go through all the books anyway.*

"It just never made any sense," Fitch said, shaking his head.

"Now you can let it go. I'll take care of it."

"Thank you." They shook hands again and Ray and Annette resumed their walk to the car.

Jennifer Jones stopped them just as they were entering the parking lot. "Ray, is that you? What are you doing here?"

"Jennifer, this is Annette Murphy. Annette, this is Jennifer Jones. Annette is trying to save me."

The women shook hands and gave each other a complete up and down. It was as if two fighters were meeting in the center of the ring.

"Good luck with that," Jennifer said. "I tried for a while, but he's a lawyer and he isn't going to change." Ray saw the look that passed between the women. Jennifer turned to Ray. "Call me. There's something I need to show you."

"About the church records?" Ray said. *She's not leaving me in that trap.* "Jennifer's the new financial director for the church," he said to Annette.

"Yes, there is something I found in the books," Jennifer said. "I'm not sure what it means, but you need to look at it. It was nice meeting you." She walked away.

"You told me that was over. Are you sure?"

"Yes, she is a part of my past. It's been over."

"Let's let the past take care of itself."

Ray liked that. A lot of women he knew would have grilled him about Jennifer. Jennifer would have been relentless. No wonder he liked this girl.

Ray and Annette drove to the beach and walked unaware of anyone else on the sand. Before long, the day was gone and Ray spent the night. Only once did he wonder what Jennifer had found.

17

As he passed the Myrtle Beach Fitness and Aquatic Center, Ray realized that his regular schedule might change if he kept seeing Annette. On a normal Monday morning, he would be inside swimming his laps. He'd begun swimming regularly years ago when he became certified to scuba-dive. Swimming was a great way to get the morning started, but it wasn't anywhere near as nice as waking up beside Annette.

Ray spent the morning trying to get organized for his move to Nelson Patterson's building, and he went to the church later in the afternoon to meet Jennifer. He was curious about what she'd found but dreaded her questions about Annette. *Am I more afraid of Jennifer's questions or the answers?*

Jennifer greeted him in the lobby looking like an advertisement for casual work clothes from one of the designer magazines. Her pastel green blouse accented her eyes. She gave him a gentle hug, which he returned a bit awkwardly. The scent of her perfume was too familiar.

"I've spent hours going through these books," Jennifer said after Ray had taken a seat in her office. "They are perfect. Bingo, the church and the Right to Life League."

"You said there was something you wanted me to see."

"It was nothing. I found the correcting entry."

Thanks for letting me know. "I saw Jonathon Fitch after church yesterday. You know Mr. Fitch, don't you?"

"I do. I had to coordinate the bingo books with him when I was at Orion. He could be a real pain in the neck."

"Well, he seems to be doing fine now. But he's very defensive that someone would question his books."

"They're not his books anymore."

"That's what I told him, but he asked me to check an entry from several years ago. Earlier than the period SLED took."

"And?" Jennifer said.

"I told him I'd look into it. I wonder if you can find it."

"He's just worried about himself. It's a waste of time."

"Probably. But I promised. It was a payment to the Patterson Law Firm."

"A payment to Nelson's firm? What's unusual about that? You know it's just some legal work or lobbying."

"The check was for two hundred fifty-thousand dollars."

"Really?" Jennifer's eyes went wide. "Just how long ago was this?"

"Before bingo became big. Ten or so years ago."

"Something that old shouldn't be in this system. But Fitch kept everything. It's probably why this system is so slow. I've really got to clean it up when I get the chance." She looked up at Ray. "Why don't you let me finish this and I'll check on it for you."

"Would you do a quick search for it now, please?"

Jennifer frowned but turned to her keyboard. She hit a few keys and a document appeared on the screen. "Here's an invoice for two hundred fifty-thousand dollars. It just says legal services."

Ray leaned over the desk to see the screen. He caught the scent of Jennifer's perfume again and it brought back a pleasant but unwanted memory. "I can't believe Fitch signed a check for two hundred fifty-thousand dollars without more explanation than that. Not Fitch."

"A check of that size requires the signatures of two church officials," Jennifer said.

"Have you a got a copy of the check in there?" Ray said, standing straight to add space.

"Probably." A few more clicks and both sides of the check appeared. "Reverend Tim and Nelson Patterson signed the check as chair of the Financial Committee."

"And Nelson endorsed the check for his firm," Ray said. "It's too much for legal fees." He sat down and rubbed his chin. "Maybe there was a case that Nelson settled for the church that was sensitive."

"Why don't you ask Reverend Tim?"

"Is he here?"

"He should be." She looked out her window at the parking lot. "His Cadillac is here."

"I'll go do that. I'm sure there's a reasonable explanation. Don't get up. I'll see you later."

Reverend Tim's door was open. He was engrossed in some work on his desk. Behind the pastor, a huge crucifix, more appropriate for a Catholic church, hung on the wall over a credenza decorated with snapshots cataloging Reverend Tim's time at the church.

"That was a great sermon yesterday," Ray said.

"Good afternoon. Thank you. Come on in." Reverend Tim stood and they shook hands over the desk. "Did you listen online or catch us on TV?"

"I was here."

"Here? Really?"

"Annette brought me. Thanks for encouraging her to call me."

"You came with Annette? Oh, great, great."

"I'm enjoying her company."

"I'm sure you are. Have a seat." Reverend Tim gestured toward a burgundy leather armchair.

"Actually, I just have a question for you. I wondered if you remember why the church paid Patterson Law Firm two hundred fifty-thousand dollars a little over ten years ago."

"Did SLED find that?" Reverend Tim said, stopping halfway into his seat.

"No, they didn't go back that far."

"So, we don't have worry about that, do we?" he said, settling in.

"It might lead to some answers about what SLED wants."

"Oh, I doubt that."

"Well, we should clear it up while we can. Why did the church pay Patterson Law Firm two hundred fifty-thousand dollars?"

"I don't remember too much about it, really."

"I'm the church's attorney and I'm joining Nelson's firm next week. You can tell me."

"Congratulations."

"Thank you." Ray waited for Reverend Tim to continue. He didn't. "Two hundred fifty-thousand dollars?"

"Oh, yes, someone was threatening a lawsuit and Nelson took care of it. Anyway, it's over."

"Do you recall what it was about?"

"It has been, what, ten years at least? No, I don't remember too much about it. Something about a property line. I'm sure it's not anything SLED would be interested in. Just forget about it. By the way, how is Bo Heath's case doing?"

"It's fine." Ray wasn't ready to change the subject. *I won't be blown off like Fitch.* "A property line?" *Why wasn't I involved in that? I do all of the church's real estate work.*

"It could have been a real mess, but Nelson handled it. Now, tell me about Bo. He is one of our members and I visited with him last week as part of our prison ministry. He said you were his lawyer. I didn't know you did that kind of law."

"I don't usually. I'm court-appointed."

"Well, good luck. Bo has struggled with his substance abuse problems and he has a short fuse. I wouldn't have thought that he would strangle someone, but you never know what a person might do under the influence of drugs. It's a sad waste of two lives."

"So you think he's guilty?"

"It seems pretty obvious, doesn't it? Jealous ex-boyfriend kills his pregnant ex-girlfriend. It's almost a cliché."

"I think he has a pretty good case."

"Well, just know that I'm praying for both of you."

"Did you find out if Tonya was a volunteer or employee?"

"Ray, I can't comment on whether she's been here or not. HIPAA laws are so strict."

"She was here for counseling?"

"I didn't say that. I'm not allowed to confirm or deny that we are counseling anyone at the Right to Life League."

"I see." She'd been getting counseling about her baby.

The pastor looked at his watch and stood up. "Unfortunately, I, uh, I have a family to visit. They lost a loved one today."

"I am sorry to hear that. Anyone I know?"

"No, I don't think so."

Ray reached out to shake the pastor's hand. "One more quick question. I understand Tonya was here during the summer." *Before she was pregnant.*

"Lots of people play our bingo games."

"That's true." *But, at least according to Lillie, not Tonya.*

That night, Annette joined Ray at his condo. He grilled steaks from a butcher shop. They were the first decent steaks he'd in a long time, and they turned out perfectly. After dinner, they walked to the back of the complex carrying glasses of cabernet and sat in the gazebo overlooking the Intracoastal Waterway. The moon was out. He had his arm around her shoulder as she nestled beside him.

They were enjoying the quiet with little bits of conversation, but Ray's mind was wandering. "Could I ask you a question about Tonya?"

"Sure," Annette said.

"Did you know that Tonya was getting counseling about her pregnancy?"

Annette sat up. "What? No way."

"Yes, I have it from a reliable source."

"She didn't want a baby."

"But you didn't know she was pregnant."

"No, but it wasn't her first time."

"Didn't know that."

"Yeah, you can't dance if you're pregnant."

"I guess not. But maybe it was her new boyfriend's child and she was ready to, um, settle down."

"She would have told me about a boyfriend."

"She hadn't told you she was pregnant. Maybe it was different this time."

"I can't see Tonya with a baby. No, didn't you say she saw Roy Mack?"

"At the Three Door."

"Well, that's why. He would send her to the doctor and take it out of her pay."

Ray hadn't thought of that. "What if she told him that she wanted to keep the baby?"

Annette laughed. "Right." She leaned over and kissed Ray. "Any more questions?"

"No." He needed answers. Whether she'd aborted the baby or kept it, neither provided a reason for Roy Mack to kill her. *And I really need a motive.*

Annette ran her hand across Ray's chest. She leaned in and whispered into his ear. "Have you ever made love out here?"

Not yet.

18

"You look happy this morning," Donna Pew said.

Ray's secretary was back. She would become an employee of the Patterson Law Firm on Monday, just like Ray. She had a new title as well, assistant office manager, which required her to run Ray's old office for the firm. Trish would help Ray in the Conway office.

"I feel good. It looks like things are finally getting better." It wasn't just the work. It was Thursday morning and Ray had a new boat picked out. He had already rented a slip on the waterway with easy access to the ocean. He was paying for it with the check for the sale of his practice. He could barely afford it after paying the IRS bill, his back mortgage and a few other bills. But the eighteen-foot inboard/outboard was in good shape for a seven-year-old boat, and it had a dive deck on the back. And, to top it off, Ray hadn't slept alone all week. *Life is definitely improving.*

"The coroner's office called and said that you could pick up the files you subpoenaed at two this afternoon, and you have an appointment with Nelson Patterson at two thirty."

"Thank you, Donna."

Ray still had not gotten any information from Illinois on Thomas Reed. He wondered if they had any DNA samples. That could be really useful. He called again. The officer he'd talked to before was busy, and his supervisor was out of the office. Ray got the fax number and left a message for both of them. He drafted a letter requesting the files and asking if there were any DNA samples. He faxed it and gave a copy to Donna to mail.

It took longer at the coroner's office than expected, but Ray got the files. He was going to have to follow up with the sheriff's office. Captain Brown was probably still blocking those. Ray shook his head. He was running late for his appointment with Nelson. *Here I am joining the most prestigious firm in Horry County and all I can think about are the three files I just got.* He called and found that Nelson was running late, too.

Ray arrived just before Nelson. After brief greetings, Nelson took him on a tour. "Ray, this will be your office." It was beside Trish's. Nelson's was on the opposite side of the hall across from Trish. They had already moved the furniture into the room. Ray liked his new desk. "Trish has your user name and setup information for the computer system. I'll turn you over to her in a few minutes. Let's step into my office."

Ray signed the agreement and Nelson handed him a check for his practice.

"Welcome aboard."

"Thank you. I'm excited," Ray said with a grin. *I can make this work.*

"We're glad to have you. Anything new with SLED's investigation?"

"No, we've been through what they subpoenaed and can't find anything out of order. Fitch did mention a settlement check from about ten years ago. Do you know what that was about?"

"Settlement check?"

"You settled a case for the church for two hundred fifty-thousand dollars."

"I heard you were asking about that. It's a confidential matter. But you're part of the firm now, so I guess I can tell you. Someone was threatening to sue Reverend Tim for slander. It would have been a mess for Reverend Tim and the church. I got it resolved."

"I had the impression that it involved a real estate issue," Ray said.

"No, it was slander. His sermons can get pretty fiery."

There was a knock on the open door. It was one of the firm's other attorneys.

"Ray, this is Clint Williams."

Clint looked to be about six foot three inches tall and had the build of a runner. He entered and extended his hand. "I just wanted to stop in and say welcome to the firm."

"Thank you," Ray said, accepting the solid handshake.

"Nelson says you've got a tough little murder case that you're having some trouble with."

"It's coming together."

"Let me take a look and we'll see if we can get Harry to make a deal, OK?"

"My client wants a trial and I think he's going to get one."

"Really?" Nelson said, eyes widened. "Why don't you let Clint review the file and see what he can do?"

"Sure."

"Well, here are the rest of the crew," Nelson said and began a round of introductions.

The other partners and attorneys came by to welcome Ray. He smiled and shook hands with everyone. He tried to enjoy the pleasantries, but he couldn't concentrate. *Either Nelson or Reverend Tim lied. What are they hiding?* Before Ray could ask about the check again, Nelson excused himself for a fundraising dinner in Columbia.

After everyone had returned to work, Ray tried out his massive cherry wood desk. It was shiny and smelled of fresh lemon polish. Trish brought Ray his log-on information, the alarm code and a key to the building. He was set. She gave him a tour of the building and introduced him to the staff.

"Mr. Patterson has given me a list of cases to give to you to review. I'll have them on your desk Monday."

"I'll be happy to get them if you'll give me the list. I need to learn my way around anyway."

"Thank you. It's in my desk."

He followed Trish to her office. "You're divorced, right?" she said. Ray nodded. "My divorce will be final in about a month. Do you think it's all right to date before your divorce is final? My attorney says no."

"Depends. Why are you getting a divorce?"

"I caught him with his girlfriend."

"Listen to your attorney. Even one date could hurt your case."

She pulled her face into an exaggerated frown. "Well, I've made it this far and it's only a month to go." Trish was lovely. Five foot seven or eight, blonde, blue eyes, early thirties. Ray realized that he might have been tempted to give different advice if it weren't for Annette. Trish gave him the list and pointed him toward the file room. He thought again about the files in his car. They would wait until evening. He didn't want to be interrupted when he started on them.

The file room had a lock on the door for privacy reasons, but Ray's key opened it. The low-ceilinged room was large and nearly full of metal cabinets. Only recently had the Patterson Law Firm begun storing executed documents as PDFs. There was an old computer on a small desk that was used only to look up file numbers. He noticed three large Rolodexes that were for files that predated the computer system. He found the first five on his list and then, while he was alone, did a search in the case manager for the church's mystery case. There were several files for the church—not surprising. But none with the right date. Ray searched the name "Tim Thomas." Nothing on the computer. There was one individual file listed on the Rolodex. It was nearly ten years old. That must be it. A clerk came in and Ray turned the Rolodex to another card. He said "Hi" and took his files back to his office. He felt like a spy, but all he was wanted was to clear it up. *And it bothers me that I can't seem to get a straight answer.*

Trish stopped him on his way back to the office. "Mr. Jackson, could you meet with a client while you are here today?"

"Sure. What's it about?"

"Someone who works at Orion has a possession charge. Normally, Clint Williams handles the criminal cases, but he just left for court and you handle those, don't you?"

"Sure. When will they be here?" It wouldn't be right to turn down a fee before he started with the firm. Besides, he could pass the file to Clint next week.

"She's in the lobby now. Shall I get her for you?"

"No, thanks, but I do need a file or intake form. And a legal pad."

The form, legal pad and an empty file were on his desk when he brought Macy Jansen into his office. She was about five foot five with a pale complexion and heavy dark mascara. There was a Chinese dragon tattoo on the inside of her right arm. The edge of another tattoo was visible in the *V* of her black blouse. As he recorded the basic information into the new file, he learned that Macy worked in the offices of Orion as an assistant bookkeeper and had been charged with simple possession of powder cocaine. Her prior record consisted only of a conviction for underage drinking.

"So, what happened?"

"Well, I was driving home from work the other night and a Garden City cop stopped me because he said the light over my license plate was out. He saw a baggie on my backseat and asked to see it. I told him it was trash, but he opened the door and took it out."

"What was in the bag?" The ticket, which she had given Ray, said "one plastic bag of cocaine, less than one ounce."

"It was some cocaine that Bobby had given me," she said. "It wasn't even mine."

"Bobby who?"

"Bobby Jones. He's a bartender at the Stallion Room and my boyfriend."

"And what do you mean that the cocaine wasn't yours?"

"I sold it to a friend. He was going to meet me at my apartment when I got home."

That's going to help. "Did you tell the officer that?"

"No, he just took me to the jail and I waited till Bobby came and bailed me out."

"Do you know where Bobby got the cocaine?"

"No, he didn't tell me that. He told me to be careful because it was so pure."

Well, maybe she wasn't quite as naive as she appeared. The policeman had questioned her further. She had been told to call the firm by one of Orion's managers, Ray's client Tony Evans.

Macy paid Ray's retainer in cash. Ray didn't ask where she'd gotten fifteen one hundred dollar bills. Ray told her he would call the solicitor and believed they could work this out for a small fine. She was smiling when she left.

After Macy was gone, Ray called Tony Evans. "I expect to hear something from your case soon," he said. "I was just calling to thank you for referring Ms. Jansen to our office and to let you know that I'm with the Patterson Law Firm now."

"Uh, you're welcome. Who was it again?"

"Macy Jansen."

"Yeah, right. Don't worry about it."

Ray hung up and prepared a draft of a letter of representation to send to the solicitor for Ms. Jansen. His desk phone rang.

"Tony Evans is on line three for you," the operator said.

Ray switched over. "Hello?"

"Yeah, about Macy. Did she say where she got the cocaine?"

"Tony, I can't discuss her case."

"Yeah, but we sent her over because we know you guys will take good care of her. It's just that if she got the cocaine from one of our clubs, it would be good if we knew about it."

"Like I said, I can't discuss her case. I have a duty of confidentiality."

"Sure, I know. But if I told you I thought she got it from Bobby, would you say I got it right?"

"Tony, I—"

"Look, we're your clients, too. I'm just trying to clear up a little problem here. If Bobby's dealing coke out of the Stallion, we can talk to him before this thing gets worse."

"I can't tell you. If something were to happen, like losing a job, I could be disbarred."

"Hey, I understand. But this is between you and me. No else one has to know. We just want to talk to him, that's all."

"That's all?"

"I promise."

There was a long silence before Ray said, "Talk to Bobby."

"Thank you. That's what I call being a good lawyer." Tony hung up.

Ray wasn't so sure. *But protecting your clients is about preventing problems as well as solving them, isn't it?*

He went back to the file room and retrieved the remainder of the files on his list. He looked for Reverend Tim's file, but it wasn't where it was supposed to be. Another secretary came in and Ray decided to take his stack back to his office. He would have plenty of time to search for the file later. Besides, he needed to look at the church files, too. He spent the rest of the afternoon making a few notes on the cases and organizing his new office. Leaving around four, he told Trish he would see her Monday. From his cell phone, he called Donna and told her she could reach him on the cell if she needed him. There was still time to kill before Annette got off around ten. There was plenty of time to review three coroner's reports.

Around nine, after studying the files carefully, Ray realized he needed some help. Only one name came to mind. *What the hell?* He called Captain Jarrett Brown. When Brown didn't answer, Ray left a message. "This is Ray Jackson. I got the files from the coroner and I found something curious. I'll be at the doughnut shop across from my Myrtle Beach office at eight thirty in the morning or you can call me back."

19

———⊷———

Ray hadn't chosen the doughnut shop because Jarrett Brown was a cop. He'd chosen it because it was across the street from his office, his old office now, and because he loved their sugar-glazed doughnuts. They also made a very good coffee.

Not that it mattered, but Brown was late. *Hell, he's probably not coming.* Sitting at a cozy two-person table along the glass wall, Ray checked the time on his phone. It was eight fifty. There was just enough time for a third doughnut. Ten of Ray's original dozen remained in the box on the table. He reached for one more.

Jarrett Brown hit the glass door so hard it shuddered. Everyone looked to see who was in such a hurry. Brown ignored them and scanned the room with his eyes until he found Ray. He marched across the room and confiscated the remaining chair. He placed his elbows on the table, crossed his arms and leaned in close, deliberately invading Ray's personal space. "I'm here," he said. "What you got?"

"Good morning." Ray sat back and put a huge smile on his face. "Would you like some coffee or a doughnut?" He pointed at the box. The whole place was filled with the irresistible smell of the sweet confection.

"I've had my coffee and breakfast."

I'm guessing some crusty dry toast. Probably wheat, at least something with no flavor. "I got the files from the coroner's office." Ray met Brown's laser stare. "And I'll promise not to use your daughter's case if you will answer a few questions for me."

"That's not worth a damn thing. I told you last time we talked the cases aren't related."

126

"Oh, there's a connection. If you had taken the time to look, you might have found quite a few similarities."

"That's bullshit."

"Then why did you go out of your way to scare me off? And why is someone delaying your office's response to my subpoena?"

"I don't know what you're talking about," Brown said with what must have usually passed for a grin. "You said you found something. Or is this just a trick so you could ask me more questions about my daughter?"

"Do you really believe that Candi committed suicide?"

Brown erupted to his feet, his chair scraping the floor like fingernails on a chalkboard. Everyone in the place turned to look and the room quieted. Brown planted two fists into the table and leaned down into Ray's face. With a tone just short of a shout, Brown said, "I didn't come here to talk about that."

"What do you remember about Cindy Martin's case?"

"You better tell me something I don't know or I'm walking."

"You know the Horry County Coroner decided that her death was accidental, ruling out suicide because a note was not found. But did you know the first medical examiner, the one in North Carolina, thought the circumstances were questionable, possibly indicating murder?"

"How would I know that and why do I care?" Brown said but he relaxed and crossed his arms on his chest. He swayed from foot to foot, nervous like a child with ADD being forced to wait.

"You investigated the case, but you don't remember seeing that, do you?"

Brown sat. "You got the file?" He took the folder and began to thumb through it. After a few minutes, he looked up. "Where's the report from the Shallotte medical examiner?"

"It's not in there. But the cover letter is. If you'll read it you'll see that he finds some evidence that may indicate murder, but without further examination he can't tell. He's suggesting that Horry County follow up on that angle. I don't think they did."

"What's there to investigate? She fell off the casino boat and drowned."

"I've been on that boat. It's hard to accidentally fall over a solid four-foot-high rail."

"She jumped."

"But you didn't find a note."

"Some people don't leave a note."

"But that's part of the problem. If it were clear that she jumped, then why does the other medical examiner consider murder? What did he find?"

"Probably nothing."

"Then why isn't it mentioned in the final report?"

"Because there wasn't anything to it." Brown looked at his wristwatch.

"You have to look at all of cases."

"No," Brown said, "I don't. Bo Heath murdered his ex-girlfriend. That's a crime of passion. Even if Cindy Martin was murdered, it's a different kind of murder. They're not the same. Tameka Shelley was killed in a robbery gone bad. They're not related."

"I see a connection."

"Of course you do. The brilliant lawyer on his first case found something everyone else missed."

"Roy Mack—"

"I know they all worked for Roy Mack. They were all strippers. It ain't relevant."

"There's more."

"I'm sure there is, but you're wasting my time." Brown stood.

"They were all pregnant."

"What?" Brown shook his head.

"All of these women were pregnant."

"What has that got to do with anything? Don't call me again"

"Wait a minute. I need the report and it'll take forever if I have to subpoena it."

"What? Shit." Brown rolled his eyes. "I don't believe this. You want me to get it for you." He dropped his chin to his chest. "You got balls," he said, looking up. "I'll give you that. But no way, no fucking way." He turned to leave. Then he reversed. "I'll make you a deal. If you'll leave me alone, and my daughter out of your case, I'll get the report for you."

"Can you do that?"

"Yeah, I know a deputy up there. He'll get it if I ask."

"Then it's a deal. Thank you."

"Don't thank me. I'm just helping you waste your time. Bo Heath killed that girl."

"I think I can prove he didn't."

"I know you do."

"Captain Brown, what if Cindy was murdered and Candi didn't commit suicide?"

Brown looked at the floor and took a breath. "Do you want the records or not?"

"I do." Ray nodded his head slowly.

"Then leave me and my daughter alone, OK?"

Ray raised his hands in surrender. "Fine, fine. I won't ask again."

Brown gave him a long hard stare to underline his point before he turned for the door.

Watching him leave, Ray knew he would never keep the promise he'd just made to Captain Brown. But surely the captain knew that, too.

20

Annette and Ray were lying in her bed on Saturday morning. Ray could have stayed there all day. He pulled her close. "I really like being with you," he said.

"I enjoy being with you, too."

"So, maybe next weekend we can cook out and I can introduce you to a few of my friends."

"That sounds like fun, but let's just take this a day at a time."

"What's wrong with meeting some of my friends?"

"Nothing. I just want you to be sure. I'm not your usual kind of girl."

"So?"

She rolled on top of him and began to kiss his chest. "So let's give it a little more time, OK?"

"OK." *We can talk about it tonight.*

Ray finally let Annette kick him out of the apartment around two and he went home. She had to work and Whiskers was going to disown him if he wasn't fed soon. The Braves were on and he was just stretching out on his couch with a cold beer when his cell phone rang.

"Ray, it's John DeHaven. Nelson told me the good news. Congratulations. And thanks for passing on that information to Tony. We have taken care of that issue."

"Glad I could help," Ray said. *Fuck, Tony promised not to tell anyone.*

"But that's not why I'm calling. We're going out on Nelson's boat tomorrow afternoon for a little party and Nelson asked me to invite you."

"That sounds like fun. Can I bring anything?"

"No, just meet us at the marina beside the casino boat about eleven. We'll have everything, including a couple of my dancers. By the way, how did you like Annette?"

"Annette?"

"Yeah, she used to dance in my clubs."

"Really?"

"Yeah. She's got some beautiful tits, doesn't she? Anyway Reverend Tim told me that you seemed interested in her, so I told her to call you and gave her some chips for the boat. She said you had a good time."

"We did." Ray sat up and put his elbows on his knees.

"She knows how to take care of my friends."

"Yes, she does."

"Good, we'll see you tomorrow."

"Tomorrow."

She answered her cell phone on the first ring. "Did you miss me already?"

"Didn't you tell me that Reverend Tim suggested that you call me?"

"Yes, I did. Why?"

"Well, John DeHaven just told me that he asked you to take care of me."

"He gave me some chips for us to play with, that's all."

"He said that you were a dancer and that you know how to take care of his friends. What does that mean?"

"It's nothing."

"Is it true?"

"Look, Ray, there are some things in my past that I'm trying to put behind me. We said that we would let the past take care of itself. I'm at work. Let's talk about this tonight, OK?"

"So you were a dancer and DeHaven asked you to take care of me?"

"You don't understand. You don't know what my life was like. I was broke and I got a job dancing at a club. I went to some parties and I survived. But I quit dancing and ..."

"Oh my God."

"Ray, let me explain. I'm not doing that anymore. You are special."

"I bet you say that to all your customers. Just how many of his friends have you taken care of?"

She paused. "Don't be an ass." There was a tremble in her voice. "I can explain, but I can't talk now. You should know that I always keep my professional and personal life separate. My gig with you was over when we got off the boat."

"Professional life? Is that what you call it?"

She hung up.

She played me for a fool. Ray banged his fist on kitchen counter. He pulled one of his favorite glasses off the bar. It was part of a set of four dark blue double Old-Fashioneds with a palmetto tree and a gorget engraved on the side like the state flag. They were a birthday gift from Jennifer. *Women, fuck 'em. Fuck 'em all.* He put a single cube of ice in it and added two fingers of bourbon. Then he added two more. At least Evan Williams was a reliable friend. Ray didn't answer when Annette called. He deleted the message without listening to it.

Despite his best intentions, the bourbon sat on the coffee table. *How can I be so stupid?* He went to the kitchen and looked in the refrigerator. Nothing there. *Come on, she's just a girl.* Back in the den, the game was still on. The Braves were losing. *Figures. Forget about her.* He walked back to the kitchen and put some food in Whiskers' half-full bowl. The phone rang. It was Annette again. *What does she want? Hasn't she done enough for one day?* He let it ring. No message this time. He walked outside and stood on his front step. *What am I doing out here? Damn, I need something to do.*

He called Jennifer. She seemed happy to hear from him and agreed to meet him at Fat Harold's.

Ray wasn't a lot of fun, although he tried. He danced, he drank—a lot. Jennifer refused all his invitations to spend the night. She made him drink a large glass of water and wait thirty minutes before she allowed him to drive home. He shouldn't have driven even after the water, but he made it to his condo without incident. He fell into his bed and passed out.

His aching head woke him Sunday morning. He was still in his polo shirt and khakis. He hadn't even taken off his socks. He found his way to the kitchen, took three pain relievers and had started back to bed when he remembered Nelson's boat trip. *God, I really shouldn't miss that.*

After a shower, he was cleaner but not feeling any better. He hoped the weather was nice. His stomach couldn't handle choppy water.

He stared into the mirror. *What should I do about Annette? Nothing.* But she'd given him a chance to explain about representing Bo. Maybe he should call her and give her a chance to explain. But what was there to explain? She had been screwing him because DeHaven asked her to. What he really needed to do was to call Jennifer and apologize. He'd been an ass last night.

His cell phone rang. Annette. Again. This time he answered. Clearly, he was not functioning at full capacity.

"Are you going out on John DeHaven's boat?"

"What?" Not the apology he expected and deserved.

"John DeHaven called this morning and invited me to a boat party today. He said that you were going. Is that true?"

"Yes—"

"God, you're stupid. What do you know about him?"

She was talking loudly and it made his head feel worse. "Slow down. Calm down. What are you talking about?"

"Let me in. I'm at your door."

"You're here?'

"Let me in. We need to talk."

He walked to the door as fast as his head would allow. *I don't need this crap. She should just go away and leave me alone.* He opened the door. "What are you doing here?"

"You look like shit. What did you do last night? Never mind. We're not going on any boat trip today." She slipped inside and made a phone call. "John, we're not going to make it. Ray's a little under the weather and I am going stay here and take care of him." She laughed, said something else and hung up. Then she turned to Ray. "Let me tell you about John DeHaven."

"If I didn't have such a bad hangover, I'd throw you out." He raised his cold soda as evidence.

"Sure you would. You got any coffee?"

Ray had made a pot, but he couldn't drink it. It was still warm. "In the kitchen."

She walked past him and got a cup. He followed her. She sat at the kitchen table, but he stood and leaned his head against the cool metal of the refrigerator. It helped a little.

"Why didn't you tell me you were doing work for John DeHaven?" Annette said.

"Why didn't you tell me you're a whore?"

"Don't be an asshole. I came to warn you about John DeHaven. You're a nice guy, and for some reason I like you. I wasn't paid to go out with you. Somehow John heard that I had given you my number and asked me to call you. He gave us the chips. That's all."

"I'll have to thank him."

"Ray, I'm not kidding, he's dangerous."

"Dangerous? Come on. He's a businessman."

"John is much more than a businessman. He's into drugs and prostitution."

"We've established that."

"You can be a shit if you want, but you should listen to me."

"I'm warned." *Now go.* "Besides, I'm not representing John DeHaven, just a couple of his employees."

She walked over to Ray and put her hand on his arm. "You are involved with him in bingo. Be careful." She gave him a gentle hug. He didn't resist. "I like you. I'm sorry." She pecked him on the cheek and walked out the front door.

He didn't try to stop her. He sat on the couch and put his head in his hands. *Maybe I should have stopped her. I like her. I really do. But this is too much. Just too much.*

Ray woke on the couch. He must have fallen asleep watching the game. A quick check of his phone told him the Braves had won. Feeling better but groggy, he headed out for a swim at the fitness center. Maybe that would clear his mind.

"Ladies and gentlemen of the jury," Ray said to himself as he made the turn for the first lap. He hadn't prepared a closing argument in years. His mother had always used her closing argument to help her frame a case. If you can deliver a convincing closing that is supported by the facts presented in your case, you will do well. If you don't have the facts, it can't be in the close. Ray's problem was that he could hear what Harry Carson was going to say in his closing argument.

Harry was going to talk about Bo's having been with the victim on Saturday night. That was a problem, but he could answer that with the uncertain time of death and Bo's alibi. Harry would talk about the DNA, but Ray wasn't too worried about that. His expert was excellent.

The real problem was motive. He could try to discredit Royal McKenzie with the other dancers. Harry would call all the facts about their deaths circumstantial. "It looks bad," he would say, "but there are legitimate reasons for Roy Mack to be there. The women worked for him. One was discovered behind his business and one near his home. Would a murderer as clever as the defense would have you believe leave his victims in those places? And I can tell you that Michael Heath had a motive when he raped, beat and killed Tonya Smalls. He was jealous. But can anyone tell me why Royal McKenzie would want these women dead?"

That's my problem.

21

———◆———

"**M**r. Jackson," the receptionist said through the intercom, "you have a Macy Jensen on Line 4. It sounds urgent." Despite hitting the snooze button twice, Ray had settled into his new office at the Patterson Law Firm a little before nine. He was feeling much better, at least physically.

"Thanks," he said and reached to punch the line button. *I'll bet the solicitor hasn't even gotten my letter of representation. Some clients have unreasonable expectations.* "Ray Jackson."

"He's dead! They cut his hands off. He's dead. He's—"

"Calm down, Macy, calm down and tell me slowly. Who's dead?"

"Bobby, they found Bobby on the beach washed up like a fish. He's dead."

"Bobby Jones?" *Oh shit— the bartender at the Stallion Room.*

"Yes, Bobby, my Bobby. They cut his hands off. Why would someone do that?"

"Easy." *What do I do?*

"He said they would kill him if they found out. And they did. And they cut off his hands. I didn't tell anyone, I didn't. I didn't tell anyone except you. And I had to tell you. You're my lawyer."

"Macy, take a deep breath. Get hold of yourself. Bobby must have been involved with some bad people. They probably already knew." *God, I hope that's true.* "What was he afraid that they would discover?"

"He was mad when he found out I told Tony about the possession charge. Scared and pissed off. He started pacing around the room. He said I shouldn't have done that. But I didn't tell Tony where I got the cocaine. I didn't. Are they going to kill me? What am I going to do?"

"Macy, why would they want to kill you? You haven't done anything." *But I did.*

"Bobby didn't do anything to them either and they killed him."

"Who killed him?" *Tony and DeHaven.*

"The police said Bobby must have been stealing from a gang or somebody like that 'cause of what they did to his hands. But Bobby was afraid of those people. He wouldn't steal from them. The coke came from his roommate. That's what he told me."

"Calm down, Macy. What people was Bobby afraid of?"

"I didn't tell them. I didn't."

"I know. It's all right."

"I didn't ... I ... Did you tell them? I only told you, and Tony sent me to you. You told them. Oh—my—God. You told them, didn't you? You killed him!" She was gone.

Ray hung up the phone. He put his face in his hands, but he kept hearing Tony Evans and John DeHaven telling him "thank you." *Oh shit.*

Ray was unable to focus on his foreclosure work or anything else, so he decided to visit Bo Heath. He needed to tell him about Dr. Green's report. At least that's the excuse he gave himself.

Ray met Bo in the same attorney's room where they'd first met. This time the cuffs came off. Bo had gained some weight in jail and actually looked healthier and happier than when Ray had first met him. He had a big smile that revealed a missing lower left tooth. They discussed his case and Ray told him about the report from Dr. Green.

"With Dr. Green's testimony, I think your case is strong."

"When will you get me out of here?"

"If you are acquitted at trial, you will get out, but all I said is that our case is strong. Roy Mack is still going to put you and Tonya together at the Three Door, and even though Dr. Green's evidence is a big help, the DNA still matches you."

"What about that other guy she was screwing?"

"You mean Thomas Reed?"

"Yeah, him."

"Again, that helps your case but it doesn't prove that you didn't do it. We can't find him, so all it shows is that someone else could have been with her. Bo, you need to think about a plea agreement. If we can get a deal for five years or less, I think you should take it."

"I done told you, no deals. Why are you pushing so hard for a plea? I didn't do nothing. Are you afraid of the judge or something?"

"Bo, here's what hurts you. Tonya was beaten. Badly. The solicitor will show pictures of that. Then he's going to show pictures taken of you at the time of your arrest. You have cuts and scratches on your arms and face."

"I had a fight."

"I know, I know, but it looks bad. The solicitor will argue that this was a crime of passion, jealousy. He will say she was pregnant by another man and you got mad and killed her. And then he'll wave those pictures in front of the jury. Despite all we have, you can lose. Bo, all I want you to do is think about it. You never know who or what a jury is going to believe. A trial is risky. You could wind up in jail for twenty years or more. Do you want that?"

"No, I want to get out now. No deals."

"It would help if we could find a member, any member, of your work crew. Do you have any idea where they are?"

"No."

"Do you know anybody who might be able to contact them?"

Bo looked at the table for a moment and then raised his head. "You could talk to Bobby. He was friends with Carlos and Juan."

"Do you know where I can find him?"

"He works over at the Stallion. Everybody knows him."

Ray leaned back in his chair. "He's a bartender, right?"

"Yeah, how did you know that?"

Ray decided to lie. "I just heard it on the news. A bartender from the Stallion named Bobby Jones was killed over the weekend. They found his body on the beach this morning."

Bo looked at the brick wall to his left. "Fuck." He turned to Ray. "They got to his girlfriend."

Ray locked eyes with Bo. "His girlfriend?"

"Yeah, she got caught with some stuff."

"Cocaine."

"Yeah." Bo cocked his head. "I told Bobby not to do that."

"Do what?"

"Take shit from them. That's why he's dead." He dropped his eyes to the table.

"Bo, did Bobby steal cocaine from someone."

"Bobby thought he was smarter than them. They don't play around. And now he knows."

"What does he know?"

"You don't mess with them."

"Who are you talking about?"

"Nobody. I'm not talking about nobody."

"Are you talking about Tony Evans or John DeHaven?"

Bo looked at Ray. The eye contact confirmed what Ray already knew. "No. Nobody," Bo said and then looked away.

"Is Roy Mack involved?"

"I'm talking about nobody. I want to go back to my cell."

When he left the jail, Ray actually thought about calling Annette. He needed someone to talk to. He missed his mother. He called Jennifer instead and began by apologizing for his behavior Saturday night.

"Why don't you take me to dinner and tell me what's going on?" she said. He hesitated and finally agreed. He just didn't feel like being alone at home.

The waiter had cleared the table and they were finishing a bottle of Riesling. The berry sweetness had been a nice match to the lemon sauce on their pan-fried flounder. At least that's what Jennifer said. Ray didn't remember tasting any of it.

"Did you hear about the body that washed up on the beach at Ocean Drive this morning?" she said.

"Yeah," he answered in a tone as flat as that beach.

"Ray, I am trying to have a conversation with you. All I get is one-word answers. You have been awful all night. We've had a nice meal, a bottle of wine and I have put up with your mood for the entire time thinking maybe you would come around. But you're still acting like a turd. What's bothering you?"

"I'm sorry. Bobby Jones, the body they found, is connected to a case that I have. And I guess it bothered me more than I thought."

"Now, how are you connected to a dead drug dealer?"

"I represent someone he gave drugs to."

"So because the guy that provided drugs to a client was murdered, you're in a bad mood?"

"It's a little more complicated than that."

"Why don't you explain it to me?"

"I can't say anymore—client confidentiality." He shrugged, wishing for the millionth time that he had said the same thing to Tony.

"Come on, Ray, you and I know that's not it. She dumped you. And you're not handling it very well. First Saturday and now tonight. You're a big boy, get over it. I'm sure she was fun, but you can do better than that. I thought she was a little trashy myself."

Ray fought his impulse to defend Annette. "Is it that obvious?" It was easier to let Jennifer believe what she wanted to believe whether it was true or not.

"I'm flattered that you called me. But you need to get over her before you call me again."

"I will do that. I promise. Thank you for understanding."

At home, Ray turned on the basketball game because the Braves had an off day. It was the professional semis or finals or something. He was lost. He put the NBA on only when he wanted to fall asleep, but it didn't work this time. Bobby and Annette kept him up most of the night. Or was it Tony Evans and Royal McKenzie?

22

Ray spent the rest of week trying to build a personal fortress of foreclosure cases. He had plenty of building material—Nelson had called on his friends and the cases had followed—but he still couldn't sleep. Bobby Jones and Annette kept breaching the walls.

He skipped his morning swim for a few days. That hadn't helped, but neither had his swim this morning. Now he sat in his favorite doughnut shop staring at his sugar-glazed breakfast, its toppings oozing onto a paper plate in front of him. He was just beginning to enjoy feeling sorry for himself when a large envelope landed with a thud in the middle of the table, spilling his coffee.

"Shit," he said as he jumped to his feet, narrowly avoiding the brown waterfall. "Watch what you're doing."

"Sorry," Jarrett Brown said with a minimal shrug. "But that's the Shallotte medical examiner's file on Cindy Martin."

Ray glared at Brown, who casually took a seat. Ray walked over to the counter and grabbed a fistful of napkins. He mopped the coffee and deposited the mess into a can, annoyed by the smirk on Brown's face.

"What's it say?" Ray removed the paperwork and started to fan through it.

"The photographs didn't copy too well." Brown reached over and pulled several pages from the stack. He tested for dampness before he spread them on the table. Ray recoiled, making a mental note for himself: *Don't ever ask to see the remains of someone who has drowned.*

"Notice the bruising on the neck. Here." Brown pointed because the marks were hard to see. "The M.E. couldn't explain those. And there are other unexplained bruises on her arms and legs. That's why he thought the death was questionable. But ..."

"So this indicates that someone tried to strangle her and she struggled and was thrown overboard, right?"

"Or she fell down somewhere before she fell off the boat. Or she got them trying to jump off the boat. There are a number of reasons she could have bruises. And they are all guesses."

"How do you explain the bruising around the neck?"

"She could have tried to hang herself and when that didn't work, she took the boat and jumped off. It doesn't look like a murder. It looks like a suicide."

"Does he indicate a cause of death?"

"Drowning. She was still breathing when she went into the water." Brown held up the flat of his palm so he could continue uninterrupted. "Even if you pretend that this is a murder, Royal McKenzie isn't implicated. I got a passenger and crew list as part of my investigation. He wasn't even on the boat." He stood and placed both hands palms down on the table and brought his face slowly close to Ray's like a truck backing to a loading dock. "I got the file you wanted. You struck out. Leave my daughter out of this."

"Another employee of Orion was strangled this week."

"So?" Brown stood straight.

"He stole cocaine."

"How the hell do you know that?"

"I have a duty of confidentiality. I can't tell you any more than that."

"What does your client know?" Brown looked like a hunting dog on the scent.

"My client is afraid." *If they haven't already killed her, too.* She wasn't answering Ray's calls.

"We can protect them. I need a statement."

"Do you have any leads?"

"Can I get a statement?"

"I'll ask, but I need to assure my client of their safety."

Brown put his hands on the back of a chair, turned his head to the right and then looked back to Ray. "We don't have much. The drug unit has known for some time that a group is smuggling drugs in from the Atlantic. They just don't know who it is. They don't think that the drugs are being processed locally. They seem to think that it's more of a wholesale operation. The uncut drugs are being sold across the Southeast and the buyer dilutes the drugs for sale on the street. The uncut drugs are smaller and easier to hide and therefore distribute. Even though he's dead, Bobby Jones is the first real lead they've had on that case this year. That's why I need that statement. Solve the murder, find the dealers."

"I'll do what I can. No promises. They are scared."

"They should be. Call me when they're ready to talk." Brown nodded then marched out the door.

Ray walked to the counter to refill his coffee. Maybe Tonya and Tameka had somehow gotten involved in the drug smuggling and become a threat. Maybe that was Roy Mack's motive. *How do I prove that? How do I help Brown catch Tony and DeHaven?*

Ray called Macy Jensen when he got to the office. No answer. He didn't leave a message. He asked Trish to hold all of his calls. He didn't want to be interrupted while he read the Shallotte County medical examiner's file on Cindy Martin.

As it turned out, he didn't find anything that Jarrett Brown hadn't already told him. He looked at the photographs again. *Why didn't I get photos from the Horry County Coroner?* One advantage of Ray's new location was that the county government center was a short walk away. He told Trish he wouldn't be gone long.

A matronly woman was sitting at a desk behind the counter at the coroner's office. She looked up. "Can I help you, honey?" she asked with a true Southern drawl.

"Yes, ma'am. I subpoenaed some records from this office and the files that I received didn't include any photographs."

"No, we don't give those out anymore."

"My subpoena directs the coroner to provide me with a complete copy of the file."

"Maybe you haven't heard, but there's been some budget cuts and it costs to have pictures reprinted."

"I will cover the cost, but I would like to see the photographs now."

"I don't know if I can do that."

"I have a subpoena for the records. It entitles me to inspect the records. That includes the photographs."

"I'll have to ask Coroner Rodgers first and he's not here."

"I have a subpoena. Do you know what that is?" He pulled the document out of his file and thrust it toward her.

She looked over her glasses at him without moving from her desk. "Of course I do, honey. He'll be back this afternoon. Why don't you call me then?" She smiled the sweet meaningless smile that all government workers smiled when they'd won a battle. She could and would do this all day.

"What time do you expect him?"

"If you will call me this afternoon, I'll tell you if we can order the pictures for you."

"Mrs. … Harper,"—there was a nameplate on her desk—"you don't understand. I want to inspect the photographs now."

"Why don't you leave me a copy of that and I will ask Coroner Rodgers."

She won. Ray left.

Back at the office, he tried Macy again. It went straight to voice mail. *I hope she's at work and has her phone off.* He started to call her work number but stopped. *I really don't want to talk to anyone at Orion. Not yet.*

Shortly before noon his cell phone rang. It was Jennifer.

"Has your mood improved yet?" she said.

"Yes, I'm feeling much better." *My attitude still sucks, but my life is usually easier when I tell you what you want to hear.*

"There's the monthly Shag contest at Fat Harold's tomorrow night. I know you're rusty, but I need a partner and we were always good together."

They *had* been good together. When they were dating, they entered the contest nearly every month. They had fun. One time they even won a free drink. "Yes, we were but I don't think we should date until this bingo investigation is over."

"This isn't a date."

She always wanted what she couldn't have. "Jennifer," he said, "I..." *What the hell—it beats drinking with Whiskers.* "If I pick you up about eight, we'll have some time to work out the rust." *Besides, I can ask her about DeHaven and bingo.* If Annette was right, that might be a way to get him.

At two, Ray was back at the coroner's office. Mrs. Harper was ready for him.

"I spoke to Coroner Rodgers and I have ordered the photographs for you. They should be here in about ten days. Back then we didn't have digital cameras."

"Thank you. Would it be possible to examine the photographs now?"

"I already put the files back in the cabinet."

"That's OK. I can wait while you get them."

She was back in barely more than a minute. "What's going on with these cases? Captain Brown came by this morning, too."

"Really? What did he want?" Ray thumbed through the first file until he found the shots of the neck.

"He saw you leave and he wanted to know what you were looking for and then I got him the files. He said to give you copies of what you wanted. I feel so sorry for him. He came and got Candi's file once before—did you know that was his daughter?—but he never opened it then either."

"He didn't look at his daughter's file?"

"No, it just sat on the counter the whole time. He just stared at it, never even touched it."

"Can I make a copy of a couple of these to use until mine come in?"

"I don't see why not. What are you looking for? Are y'all gonna reopen these cases?"

"It's just research."

"Research." She gave him a coy smile. "Sure."

Ray's cell phone rang while Mrs. Harper made copies. It was Jennifer, again. *Maybe I should have made an excuse for tomorrow.* "Hi, Jennifer."

"Ray, SLED wants me to come to Columbia to answer some questions."

"Did they send a subpoena?"

"No, they just called."

"Good. Don't worry, they probably just want to verify some of the numbers. I'll go with you if you would like."

"Would you? I'd feel a lot better if you were there."

"Of course I'll go. When is it?"

"They want me to come on the twenty-eighth."

"I'll put it on my calendar. You'll be fine. We've got plenty of time to prepare. I can't talk right now. I'll call you when I get back to the office. Don't worry about it."

There was a potential ethical problem. Ray was representing the church, Orion and now Jennifer in the same case. *But it's not really a conflict of interest as long as Jennifer hasn't done anything wrong.*

23

Grimly, Ray removed the stack of the copied autopsy photos from the plain brown envelope Mrs. Harper had given him. He breathed through his mouth as if he were trying to avoid smelling a foul odor. After finding the photographs of each victim's neck and head, he arranged them on his desk so he could compare similar views. Each girl had a set of marks on her neck. They ran nearly straight across the neck and had blue coloring, like a bruise. They all looked similar but not identical. The marks on Cindy Martin's neck were hard to see, because of the condition of her remains. Candi Brown was the only girl who had two sets of marks. One set looked like the marks on the other girls, and the second set ran diagonally from her chin toward her ears and were reddish in color, more like an abrasion. *Does this mean what I think it means?*

He needed someone knowledgeable to examine the photos. He reached for his phone and found the contact. *I bet Jarrett Brown will be thrilled to hear from me again.* There was no answer, so he left a message.

He tried Macy again. She answered on the third ring. He tried to hide his sigh of relief.

"Who is this?"

"Hi, it's Ray Jackson. We need to talk about your case. The sheriff's office wants to talk to you. And I think you should talk to them."

"It's about Bobby, isn't it?"

"They have a few questions about where you got your cocaine."

"Did you tell them I got it from Bobby? Is that how they found out?"

"I didn't tell them a thing." That was strictly true. He hadn't told the sheriff's office anything. "But they know about your relationship with

Bobby and that you were arrested for possession. They can put two and two together. They can help."

"You're the only one I told about Bobby. Who did you tell?"

"No one." Tony Evans knew Bobby was stealing as soon as Macy was arrested. Ray really wanted to believe that, but he didn't say it. "Do you know who did this to Bobby?"

"I'm moving away. I can't stay here."

"That won't help. The only way to stop this and be safe is to talk to the sheriff. The sheriff can protect you."

"You told the sheriff, didn't you? Oh my God. You aren't supposed to tell anyone what I tell you, are you? You killed him."

"I haven't told anyone anything." A simple lie persistently told may be doubted but is rarely discovered. Tony Evans and DeHaven weren't going to tell. Ray was sure of that. "It's just that as your attorney, I want you to know that if you have information about this murder, the sheriff's office can protect you."

"I don't know anything."

"Did Bobby say where he got the cocaine or anything about it?"

"I'm leaving. Where should I go? It doesn't matter."

"Macy, if you leave before we take care of the charges against you, a warrant could be issued, and if you were arrested anywhere else, you could be extradited and brought back here to face the charges." Ray knew that was unlikely. It was such a minor charge that the court would probably keep her bail money as a fine and that would be the end of it. But it could happen.

"Shit, I'll, uh, I'll call you in a few weeks."

"Who killed Bobby?" One of the things his mother had taught him was that sometimes you have to ask the question and wait silently until you get an answer. People don't like silence—they will fill the void. His phone was quiet. He wanted to ask if she was still there. He checked the screen and it was still connected. He waited.

"You know," she said softly, "he sent me to your office."

"And where did Bobby get the cocaine he gave you?"

"I don't know."

"Macy."

"I don't know. He didn't tell me."

"Did Bobby do any special work for Tony?" He was tired of dancing around the name.

"They go deep-sea fishing every Wednesday."

"Deep-sea fishing? Really?" *Tony Evans doesn't seem like a fisherman.* "Where do they go fishing?"

"I don't know. It don't matter, they never caught any fish."

"Macy, can you come to the office now?"

"Why?"

"I think you should talk to the sheriff."

"I'm not giving a statement. I told you I'm leaving town. I'll call you from … somewhere. I got to go."

"Wait, Macy. Let's talk before you do that."

She didn't answer.

"Macy, the sheriff can protect you." She was no longer on the phone. Ray surprised himself by offering a silent prayer for her safety.

The conversation left him with more questions. If Tony had strangled Bobby, had he had anything to do with the deaths of the dancers? Did he murder the girls with Royal McKenzie? Or did Tony kill and Roy Mack cover up? Was Tony on the boat with Cindy Martin? Why would they kill the dancers? Drug smuggling? That didn't fit. Ray went back to the photos on his desk. He stared at them for nearly an hour. He still didn't know why these girls had died.

He did know that it was nearly six o'clock when he left the office after spending another fruitless hour looking at the autopsy photos from every angle. He didn't know when he'd decided that he needed a drink, though, but finding himself at the bar at Fat Harold's, he ordered a double bourbon and water. Water on the side. He missed the mini-bottle. A good drink needed more than one ounce of alcohol, but South Carolina had eliminated the one-and-a-half-ounce mini in favor of free pour. That was why he ordered a double. He wanted to taste his bourbon. The drink went down well. The second was just as good.

It wasn't long before he was recognized by a few of his old crowd and joined them at a table next to the dance floor. Jennifer arrived about an hour later. She was the second woman he took to the floor to Shag, and she didn't give him the chance to dance with anyone else after that. They soon gained their old rhythm, or perhaps the bourbon just made it seem that way. Perhaps he was lonely, perhaps he was a little drunk and simply fell into an old habit. Whatever the case, she took him to her place and showed him a couple of things that she had learned since they were last together.

Around two a.m., Ray woke up. He was still in Jennifer's bed. He thought about going home but knew she would be pissed if he weren't there in the morning. He didn't want to have to deal with that. He missed Annette. She never felt the need to possess him.

Jarrett Brown called at 7:55 Friday morning. Ray put the mug of coffee that Jennifer had insisted he take on the dash of the car because it was too big for the cup holder. *Jennifer drinks better coffee than Annette. I really need to stop comparing them.*

"I looked at the photos. You got nothing."

"Really? They looked pretty similar to me."

"They would to an amateur."

"Can I meet you so that you can show me?"

"Am I going to get that statement?"

"Is it possible that cocaine is being smuggled from the ocean on fishing boats?

"What do you know?"

"I know that I need to understand some photos."

"Understand this: the cases aren't related."

"Can I get a copy of the list of people on the boat with Cindy?"

"Royal McKenzie is not on that list."

"Can I get a copy?"

"The case is closed."

"Can you explain why Candi has two sets of marks around her neck?"

"Fuck you."

"Have you even looked at Candi's file?" He didn't answer—he wasn't there.

Ray needed to get off the phone anyway. There was coffee all over the dash of his convertible.

24

Friday night Jennifer and Ray placed third in the dance contest. It was their best finish ever. It was a good night, and though tempted, he avoided a repeat of Thursday night and went home alone.

On Saturday afternoon, Jennifer came to his place. They sat around the battered old kitchen table. The round oak pedestal model that Ray had borrowed from his mother's attic after his divorce was the same one he had grown up with. He pulled up the spreadsheets on his laptop. Jennifer slid a chair beside him and they began to review the bingo financials. *Just like Brittany and I used to study at this table.*

After two hours of reviewing accounting entries, they were tired. "Why don't we take a break? How about a beer?" Ray said.

"Sure, something light?"

"Yeah." He grabbed a two bottles from the refrigerator and returned to his seat. "There's nothing obviously wrong with these books. So that means SLED must be looking for money laundering, right?"

"That's my guess," Jennifer said.

"Who's in a position to do that? John DeHaven?" *Might as well throw it out there.*

"Almost anyone who has access to the accounting programs, including John."

"That means Reverend Tim, you and maybe me, right? Anyone else?"

"Tony Evans could do it, but I don't think he's good enough with the programs to hide it."

"What about Nelson?"

"I don't think he has access."

"Is there anyone else at Orion that has the ability and opportunity?"

"A couple of girls that work in accounting, but I don't see that."

"And it's not us, is it?"

"Of course not."

"So our suspects are DeHaven and Reverend Tim."

"Yeah, but I don't think it's either one of them."

"No? So SLED's wrong?"

"I don't see anything out of place," she said, waving a hand at Ray's laptop.

"But SLED wants to ask you questions about the books. Why do you think that is?"

"I think they're fishing."

"Could be. Could be they have something from an informant."

"But we don't know what that is."

Ray took a sip of his beer. "If it's money laundering, money is entering the system somewhere and exiting as an apparently legitimate payment later, right?"

"Sure," Jennifer said with another wave of her hand. "It has to come in through the bingo games."

The mention of bingo brought back the memory of meeting Annette. Ray shook his head. "Any idea how that happens?"

"No. All I get are the deposit slips."

"Who makes the deposits?"

"I don't know. The slips are e-mailed to me every day."

"By?"

"Are you enjoying this cross-examination? I've got to go the ladies room." She got up.

"The e-mails come from someone at Orion. And they pay all the expenses, too," he said to her back.

"Yep," Jennifer said as she left the room.

And that means DeHaven. "We need Orion's books," Ray said when Jennifer returned.

"Don't you have them?"

"DeHaven was supposed to send them to me, but he never did." *Wonder why.*

"I guess we're at a stopping place. Why don't we go to the store? I'll get what I need to make my famous beef bourguignon and a bottle of decent wine. We can stay in and watch a movie or something," Jennifer said with suggestive smile.

Her beef was to die for and Ray wanted to see what else she knew about Orion, so he agreed. He could send her home any time.

Monday morning, Ray called John DeHaven. He needed a copy of Orion's books. He left a message. He left a message for Nelson, too. Nelson was attending the state legislative session in Columbia.

Ray called his forensic pathologist. He didn't want to spend the money, but he needed to widen the time-of-death window so he could show that Bo hadn't had the opportunity to kill Tonya. *But Roy Mack did.*

Martha Sturn was a New Yorker who had worked with that state's forensic pathology unit for nearly twenty years. She had been involved with several major cases in New York City. One of her last cases had led to the conviction of a police officer. Ray's background research hinted that that case had spurred her early retirement.

Ray was encouraged after their conversation. She assured him that there were circumstances that could significantly change the time of death. He added her to his witness list and notified Harry Carson.

He still hadn't heard from DeHaven or Nelson. He'd left messages for both of them on Tuesday and Wednesday. Thursday afternoon, when Nelson returned to the office, Ray was the first one to greet him.

"Jennifer Jones has a statement at SLED next week. I need Orion's books," Ray said, standing between the leather chairs in front of Nelson's desk.

"John assures me there's nothing out of place."

"I need them to properly prep Ms. Jones."

"You're not fucking her again, are you?"

"What? No."

"Good. I'm really interested to see if SLED arrests her after the statement."

"You think she's involved?"

"She knows both sets of books. She was the main bingo accountant at Orion before she went to the church. Of course she's involved. She's the only one who could manage it."

Why hasn't she told me that? "Another reason that I need to see those books."

"I'll talk to John again and let you know. And would you ask Trish to step in when you leave?"

Ray called Jennifer as soon as he closed his office door.

"I was wondering when you would call," she said. "I really enjoyed our weekend." She had stayed the night Saturday.

"What was your job at Orion?"

"I worked in accounting."

"For bingo."

"Yeah."

"Were you going to tell me that?"

"I thought you knew."

"Well, I didn't. Nelson just told me that he thinks you're the one laundering money."

"That's ridiculous."

"No, it's serious. We need to discuss this."

"OK. Why don't you come by my house tonight?"

"I'm not sure that's a good idea."

"Your condo then?"

"What's wrong with my office?"

"I'm tied up all afternoon today and tomorrow. The nonprofit tax returns for the church and the Right to Life League are due."

"I'll grab a pizza and see you at your house around seven?" It was easier to leave than to make her go. He learned that the last time.

She called around six. She was exhausted and they postponed their meeting until Saturday afternoon. But the meeting turned out to be useless anyway. Jennifer didn't remember anything out of the ordinary with Orion's books. Ray refused her invitation to go dancing and left her home after less than an hour. They didn't meet again.

25

Ray was standing at Annette's front door, unannounced. It was 1 p.m. Tuesday. He had thought about flowers but decided against it.

"What do you want?" She opened the door only halfway.

Maybe flowers would have helped after all. "I, uh …"

"Well?"

"I'd like to talk to you."

"Really?"

"I don't know. Maybe you shouldn't. But I would like to talk about what happened between us. I owe you an apology."

"You can apologize right there."

"Have you had any lunch? I'm going to the food court at the mall. You can ride with me or meet me there, whatever you prefer." Ray made a half-turn toward his car and paused. He didn't think this would be easy.

"Wait. Come in. I've got to change." Ray entered. It was like walking into a refrigerator, and her air conditioner had nothing to do with it. Annette was ready in less than fifteen minutes. She'd changed from old jeans and a T-shirt to a nice pair of slacks and a matching spaghetti-strap top. She had put on some makeup and pulled her hair back with a white scarf. She looked good, very good. Ray put his hands into his pockets to keep himself from touching her.

"Let's go," she said.

She ordered some lo mein from the local Chinese place. He got a fried chicken sandwich from a national chain. "How have you been?" he asked.

"What do you want?"

"I didn't handle the information that I received from you very well. In fact, I believe I acted rather poorly and unfairly. I am sorry. I have missed seeing you. I would like to spend some time with you again."

"Ray, I don't know." She watched her chopsticks. "I don't fit with you and your life. My past is bad, it's dirty, and you don't need to deal with that."

"I can handle that. I have a past, too."

"Ray, I started dancing while I was in college. I had a full ride. But I needed money to live on. The scholarship only paid for school. My grades dropped because I was working nights and I lost the scholarship. I dropped out. I got hooked on cocaine. Three years ago, I was arrested for prostitution and possession. I was sentenced to the state hospital to dry out. It worked for me. I've been clean for over two years."

"That's not so bad. I sent Bobby Jones to his death."

"What? What are you talking about?"

Ray told her about Macy and his conversation with Tony Evans. "I am responsible for the death of Bobby Jones, and Macy Jenkins is missing. I might as well have killed them myself."

"It's not your fault. You were just trying to help a client. You couldn't know that they would kill him."

"I keep telling myself that. But ..." He slid his food to the side and leaned forward. "I didn't plan to tell you that. I'm sorry. It's just that we both have pasts that we're not proud of. I was hoping—"

"Ray, I've slept with people you work with. I don't know what I was thinking when I let you see me after that first date, but it won't work."

Ray knew she was probably right. Before he could say so, she said "Besides, if you are going to work with Nelson Patterson and John DeHaven, I'm not sure I want to be with you. I'm trying to get away from them. I wish you would stay away, too."

"I work for Nelson, not John DeHaven."

"John couldn't do what he does without Nelson Patterson. I don't trust either of them, and while you work there, I can't trust you."

"Come on, Annette, Nelson's just DeHaven's attorney. I don't work for DeHaven."

"You know better than that."

"Al right, I'll admit that I've got some suspicions about Nelson, but I'm being careful."

"And didn't you just tell me that Tony Evans is your client?"

"Well, that was before—"

"You don't know what they're like."

"I know now. I can't leave the firm—I might learn something useful. Something that will put DeHaven away."

"I can't be part of that." She dropped her voice and leaned toward Ray. "John would kill me if he knew what I know."

"Now that's an exaggeration," he said.

"Ray," she said and patted his hand. She sat back and looked around. "You're just not part of my world."

"What do you know?"

"Ray, I can't tell you."

"But if you share with me, maybe we can work together to get DeHaven."

"I'm already taking care of that."

Now it was Ray's turn to lean in. "What do you mean? What are you doing?"

She looked around the room again. "Just leave it at that."

"You know you can trust me." He crossed his arms and rested them on the table. "Tell me what you know." And he waited.

After what seemed like ten minutes, Annette bent across the table and in little more than a whisper said, "I know all that money we count every night doesn't come from bingo."

"How would you know that?"

"I've been working at bingo for over a year. Most nights I help count the money, you know that. And there's always a stack of money in the safe when we come in."

"The reserve for the prizes."

"It's too much. Way too much."

"Do you count the players, too?"

She looked into Ray's eyes with a question on her face. "Sometimes."

"Annette, you are playing a dangerous game, you know that."

"I don't have a choice."

"You do know that after they arrest someone, SLED is going to put your name on a witness list and that will be filed with the court."

"I still have a little time but I've got to work quickly so that SLED will arrest him."

"You don't want to be around here when that witness list comes out."

"I know."

"Have you discovered where the money comes from?"

"No, but it's not bingo money."

"Are you sure?"

"The people playing bingo pay in small bills. I see fives, tens and twenties all the time. Once a week or so someone will pay with a fifty or a hundred, but when we do the count, at least half the total is in hundreds. And that happens every night."

"And you don't know where it comes from?"

"It's in the safe with the rest of the money when I come in to do the count. I don't know who puts it there."

"What can I do to help you?"

"You can leave me alone. I don't want to see you or be seen with you."

Ray stared at his sandwich. He hadn't taken more than a bite. Now it was cold. "I'm not going to eat this." Annette wasn't eating either. He balled his sandwich into a napkin and grabbed his plastic tray. "Let's go."

At her door, he tried again. He wasn't sure why. "Annette, neither one of us is perfect. Think about—"

"I'm seeing someone else."

"Oh. OK, good."

"It's better if you stay away from me. You don't need to be seeing someone like me." She didn't slam the door, but she did turn the deadbolt. Ray told himself she did it out of habit. She'd always turned the deadbolt when he left before. But this time it felt like the door had been welded shut, and he could almost smell the ozone.

When he got back to the office, Ray had a screen full of messages. Among them was one from Harry Carson. He returned the others first and answered some e-mail. The smell of rain that the blackening thunderclouds were bringing was in the air when he returned Harry's call. It had gotten darker outside.

"Ray, I've got good news and bad news."

"What's the bad news?" *Can't make this day any worse.* "The solicitor has refused my request to turn this case into a death penalty case. The county can't afford the extra expense. I guess there is a price on justice."

That's not so bad. "What's the good news?"

"Your case is on the roster for trial during the week of the twenty-fourth."

"I'll be ready."

"I hear you've got a serial-killer defense. That should be interesting."

Thank you, Jarrett. "What day should I tell my expert to be here?"

"You know that your hired gun has never testified on behalf of a victim." A bolt of lightning flashed, followed by a roll of thunder.

"A murder victim or a victim of shoddy police work?"

"Good one. Since you haven't responded to my suggestion that you make me an offer, I'm still willing to recommend twenty years if your man will plead guilty to one count of murder."

That was still not much of an offer. Bo was facing up to twenty years on each murder and seven on the criminal sexual conduct. If convicted, the judge could order that the sentences be served one after the other, but more often than not, multiple sentences run at the same time. Multiple convictions do affect your parole date, though. All that Harry was really offering is an earlier chance at parole.

"He didn't take that offer before—I doubt he'll take it now. When should I have my expert in town?"

"I'll put it on the calendar for Tuesday the twenty-fifth. We can try this in a day, day and a half, don't you think?"

Three weeks from today. "Sure."

After talking to Harry, Ray waited for the storm to pass before he left for the jail. Visiting hours ended at five, but attorneys were not limited by that schedule. When he got there, he told Bo about his conversation with Harry Carson and gave him an honest evaluation of his case.

"I put our chances of winning at 60 percent. We could offer to plead to something else. We could offer a plea to manslaughter or the sex charge. You'd serve less than five years, including time served for that."

"I don't want a deal. I didn't do it," Bo said with his fists clenched.

"That's not the issue. The issue is that there is a risk that you will be convicted of murder and serve twenty years or more. Is taking five years better than risking twenty or more?"

"No. No deal."

"All right, I'll be back in a few days to begin final preparations for your trial. We will need to practice your testimony."

"I'm ready to testify. I'm good at that."

He was wrong, very wrong. Ray knew he would be a terrible witness. But was a terrible witness better than no witness at all?

26

At 7 a.m., Ray rang Jennifer's doorbell. He would get her through the statement to SLED and then he could focus on Bo's case. He hadn't gotten the books from Orion and hadn't found anything on DeHaven. He'd have to worry about that later.

She opened the door. "I'm almost ready," she said.

"Good morning!" he said. The bags under her eyes showed she had hardly slept.

"What's good about it?" She did an about-face and headed to the back of the house. "I can't find my eyeliner."

"Hurry up, we need to hit the road." Ray dreaded the trip, too, but not because of SLED. They were taking the same road Brittany would have used to go to Columbia. He knew it very well. He had stopped at every little convenience store, gas station and farm supply on the route asking questions and leaving fliers.

He heard a crash of breaking glass. "Shit, shit, shit," Jennifer said.

Fifteen minutes later, after Jennifer had changed clothes, they finally left her house. The three-hour drive was quiet. She was nervous and she worked on her nails for nearly the entire ride. Ray was preoccupied, too. They knew the bingo books backward and forward. He still felt unprepared. *Does SLED know something or are they just hoping to get Jennifer to make a mistake?* He felt like he had in high school when he studied the wrong chapter for the history test.

The headquarters of the State Law Enforcement Division shared an old building with the South Carolina Children's Museum in Columbia, the state capital. Few visitors confused the banner- and balloon-festooned museum entrance with the entrance to SLED, whose door was marked only by a functional white sign with square black lettering. Ray directed Jennifer to a seat in the cramped waiting room and gave their names and information to the receptionist.

After a thirty-minute wait that Ray was sure was intended to heighten Jennifer's anxiety, a receptionist escorted them to an interview room. A single microphone was on the conference table, along with a plastic pitcher of water and a small stack of Styrofoam cups. The table and chairs were the only furniture in the room. There was no art on the off-white walls and no window.

"We're being recorded," Ray said, pointing to a camera globe in a corner of the room.

"No," said their escort. "It's just a security camera."

Ray didn't believe her, because she directed them to sit on the right side of the table, which gave the camera a better view of Jennifer's face, and his. He moved Jennifer to the other side of the table as soon as they were alone. It was something his mother would have done.

"What's taking so long?" Jennifer asked after they'd waited another fifteen minutes.

"They are just trying to make you nervous. Take a couple of deep breaths. Remember, take a deliberate breath after each question. That will calm you down, let you compose your answer and give me the chance to object if necessary. We'll be fine." He poured her a cup of water. "Sip on this."

Nearly twenty minutes later, Agent Thompson came into the room.

"Sorry for the delay. Agent Maroney and the assistant AG are on the way. It should only be a few more minutes."

"Thanks for letting us know," Ray said. Assistant Attorney General? That was not good but not totally unexpected. *If they are close to bringing some charges against someone, they would want to be sure the right questions were asked. And answered.*

Twenty two minutes later—Ray checked the time on his phone—Agent Maroney and Thompson entered the room again. A young lawyer was with them.

"I apologize for keeping you waiting," said Maroney. "This is Kristen Coxe, with the attorney general's office." Thompson, who would do the questioning, sat across from Jennifer. Ms. Coxe sat beside him. Maroney was on Ray's right at the end of the table. The room was full.

"Mrs. Jones," Thompson said, "you have not been charged with a crime. You are here to give a voluntary statement. Nevertheless, I am required to read you your Miranda rights." He pulled a card from his pocket and read them aloud. "Do you understand your rights?"

"Yes, I do"

"This document confirms that you have been read your rights and that you understand them." Ray reviewed it and Jennifer signed it.

The questioning began by confirming Jennifer's position with the church and her familiarity with the records.

"Where were you employed before you began working for the church?"

"Orion Management Group. I was the account manager in charge of the bingo operations."

Ray knew she'd worked the bingo books for Orion but had not heard that title before. *That's the kind of thing she should have told me.* His stomach pinged his brain as he wondered what else she hadn't told him.

"Before Orion?"

"I had a bookkeeping business at home while my daughter was in school."

"And you received a degree in accounting from USC?"

"Yes."

"*Magna cum laude*, very nice."

"Thank you."

"But no CPA?"

"I got married and then my daughter came. I guess I just never got the time."

"At Orion, did you supervise any employees?"

"Just one. Macy Jansen helped me."

"Please describe your relationship with John DeHaven."

"He was my employer and boss at Orion Management."

"Wasn't there a personal relationship?"

Jennifer took a quick look at Ray before answering. "Yes, I dated John for about a year. We stopped seeing each other in January of this year. The position at the church became available shortly after the relationship ended. We decided it would be best if I moved on. I started at the church in January."

Another detail she omitted. "I'm going to object to further questions about Ms. Jones's personal life," Ray said. "That's not what we're here for." He tried to look bored, but he felt the tightness in his jaw. He had trusted Jennifer to tell him the truth. *I know better than that. I should have pushed her harder.*

"Noted," Thompson said, "but the questions are relevant to our conversation. What role did John DeHaven play in securing the position for you?"

"One day he stopped at my desk and told me the church had an opening for financial director. I thought that it was a good move and it was an increase in pay. He talked to Reverend Tim Thomas for me and I got the job."

"And by 'dating,' you mean that you and Mr. DeHaven were lovers, right?"

Jennifer dropped her head. Then she looked at Ray with a Mickey Mouse grin.

"Objection," Ray said. He saw Thompson smirk. *Damn. He knows I'm sleeping with my client and that she hid her relationship with DeHaven from me.*

"Right, Ms. Jones?" Thompson said.

"Don't answer that," Ray said, putting a hand on Jennifer's arm.

Thompson smiled. He didn't need an answer. He knew.

They sat in silence for a moment. Then Thompson turned a page in his notes. "Ms. Jones …"

"Excuse me." Ray stood up. "I hate to do this, but all that coffee we had in the car—which way is the gentlemen's room?" He didn't need to go to the gentlemen's room. He needed a break to sort this out. *It's bad enough when a client doesn't tell you pertinent information. It's worse when the other side knows it.*

"Down the hall to the left," Thompson said to Ray's back. "We are taking a five-minute break," he said into the microphone.

Ray was returning to the conference room when "Is that Ray Jackson?" boomed from behind him. He turned around to find the extended hand of Bubba McHenry. Ray grabbed the hand and got an embrace as well.

"How are you Ray?" Bubba was the attorney general of South Carolina, the highest elected law enforcement official in the state. Bubba had been a year ahead of Ray at the University of South Carolina School Of Law. They had gotten to know one another while working for the *USC Law Review*. It was rumored that he had plans to run for the governor's office in two years. Ray believed the rumors, and he wasn't going tell Nelson who he was supporting.

"I'm coming to your part of the woods in a few weeks to meet with some kin and friends. Why don't you join us?" Bubba talked like that. He was from a small upstate county.

"That would be great."

"Have you ever shot clays? We're going to do some shooting in Georgetown after the meeting. You'll love it. Someone from my office will call—Donna, isn't it?—with the details." A successful politician never forgets a name. "By the way, what's a dirt lawyer like you doing here?"

When Ray told him, the gregarious politician was replaced by the lawyer charged with keeping South Carolina safe. He knew the case. He knew all the important ones. That concerned Ray.

"What's your involvement in the case?"

"I'm just here with the church's financial director."

"That's all?"

"Yeah. Why?"

"Well, some people have observed that you've been part of the church gambling operations since they started."

"I just do the annual reports."

"Yeah, but some are wondering how a real estate lawyer in a housing crash can afford a convertible BMW and a new boat."

"The BMW is six years old, and I got a good deal on a used boat."

"They are also asking about your long-term relationship with the financial director."

"Are you telling me I'm a suspect?"

"Just be careful," Bubba said as they parted.

Ray stopped outside the interview-room door and took a deep breath. He needed to focus on Jennifer's interview. He opened the door and asked for a minute with his client. Maroney and Thompson looked at Ms. Coxe, who agreed. The three of them left the room.

As soon as the door closed, Ray checked to make sure the recorder was off and put his hand over the microphone. He didn't know if that really worked—he'd only seen it done on TV—but it couldn't hurt. He turned to Jennifer, careful to keep his back to the camera.

"Don't you think it might have been helpful to tell me that you were in charge of bingo for Orion and that you and John DeHaven were lovers?"

"Well, I—"

"You are an insider at both places that are being investigated. Have the books been altered in any way?"

"You know they haven't," Jennifer said with a pout.

"Do I? After what you just revealed, I don't know what I know. Is there anything else you need to tell me about your work at Orion or your relationship with John?"

"No."

"It's hard for me to protect you if you don't tell me everything."

"I've told you everything."

Ray stared at her for a few seconds, trying to determine if that was the truth.

"I think you're overreacting. You know I dated other people after we—"

"John DeHaven is a major player in this investigation."

"Why don't you like John? What has he done to you?" She turned her back to him.

I can't tell you that. "It's just that I think he's the most likely candidate to launder money."

"My personal life doesn't have anything to do with that," Jennifer said over her shoulder.

"Unless it involves DeHaven."

"Well, I don't see how." She turned to face Ray. "I haven't done anything wrong and neither has John."

Someone, probably Thompson, knocked on the door.

"One more minute," Ray said to the door. "Is there anything else I should know about you, DeHaven and Orion?"

"Nothing."

He stared at her for a long second, and she looked away. Then he opened the door.

Thompson resumed by presenting a spreadsheet that showed the amount of the daily deposit and how it was divided between Orion and the church for a long series of dates. It also had a column for attendance.

"We don't keep attendance for the games, so I don't know how many players there were on any night. We count the number of cards sold," Jennifer said.

Thompson spent the next forty-five minutes confirming the numbers on his spreadsheet, except for attendance. The attendance information had to be coming from Annette.

"Can you explain why the weekly deposit never drops below $150,000 while the number of players varies from as low as 513 during Thanksgiving week in November to over 7,500 during some of the weeks in the summer?"

"I—I don't know how—"

"I object!" Ray was louder than necessary in the small room. Thompson actually leaned back. "She has already testified that the church doesn't keep attendance." He found a proper tone. "Perhaps you can rephrase."

"Can 513 players play $157,210 worth of cards during a week in which only three sessions were offered?"

"Objection. Mr. Thompson. I am instructing my client not to answer questions involving attendance. Where did you get those numbers anyway?"

He ignored Ray's question. "Turning now to the time you were employed with Orion Management, can you explain why this company"—he pointed to a name on a different spreadsheet—"received these payments?" He gave Jennifer the paper with a list of payments that were cross-referenced to Orion's books. "It looks like the company is receiving between three and ten thousand dollars every month. Sometimes there was one invoice in a month and sometimes two."

"They provide some management services. I paid them from their invoice."

"What do they do for Orion?'

"I don't know. My job was to pay the invoice."

"Weren't you curious?"

"Not really. I had enough to do without worrying about that."

He took her through the same set of questions and answers for a number of other companies.

"Mr. Thompson," Ray interrupted, "I think that we have established that Ms. Jones paid the invoices that were presented to Orion. Is there a point to this?"

"How did you pay these invoices?"

"It depends. Some vendors wanted a check, some I paid electronically."

"By 'electronically,' you mean by wire?"

"I guess."

"Did it concern you that you were wiring the funds for these companies to an account at a bank in the Cayman Islands?"

"I didn't know where it was. I just put the account number into a form and sent it to our bank."

"Who signed the form?"

"I did. I signed most of the checks, too."

"But you did know that all of the funds were being wired to the same offshore bank?"

"No. I didn't pay any attention to anything like that. I just paid the bills. That was my job."

"Did you have the authority to pay all the invoices yourself, or did they have to be approved?"

"Usually the manager or supervisor who authorized the work would sign the invoice. Then John DeHaven or Tony Evans is supposed to initial it so that I would know that I could pay it."

"Supposed to?"

"They weren't always real good about it."

"Then how would you know to pay the invoice?"

"Usually I would go to John's office and he would hand me a stack and tell me to pay them."

"Who authorized the payment of the invoices for these companies?"

"John DeHaven, I guess."

"Did he sign or initial the invoices?"

"I don't know. I would have to see them."

"Do you think Mr. DeHaven or Mr. Evans initialed any of these invoices?"

"No, probably not. But they told me to pay them."

"Mrs. Jones," Kristen Coxe said, handing a paper to Ray, "this is a subpoena for your personal financial records that are in your possession. Please have that to us within ten days. And here is a copy of the subpoena being served on your banks and your stockbroker that we executed electronically this morning." Ray took the documents.

Agent Thompson continued. "Would you please explain where the money came from that allowed you to pay for a new forty-two thousand dollar car last year?"

"Don't answer that," Ray said to Jennifer. "I object. This statement is only to cover matters concerning the bingo finances. We are not prepared to answer questions concerning personal finances."

"Where did you get the sixty-three thousand dollars that you invested in your brokerage account over the last eleven months?"

"This is over. Don't answer that. Unless you have some more questions in the area of church or bingo finances, we're going to leave."

"Would you excuse us for a minute?" Attorney Coxe said. The three of them rose to exit the room.

"No, I think we're done for today," Ray said. He took Jennifer by the arm and they stood to leave. Thompson blocked the door. *If they arrest her, it will be now.*

"We only have a few more questions. It won't take long," Ms. Coxe said and joined Thompson at the door.

"No more questions today. We're going to leave now."

"Mr. Jackson, we will have more questions for your client once we have her bank accounts," she said, pointing at him and nearly touching his chest.

"I am sure you will." He was just as sure that Jennifer should not answer them. *At least not until she answers them for me.* Jennifer needed to leave while she still could.

"Your client's cooperation with our investigation might serve her well," Ms. Coxe said.

"I'll discuss that with my client and get back to you."

"We'll give you a few minutes," Ms. Coxe said. She motioned for the agents to leave the room.

"No, we'll talk about it in the car—unless you are bringing charges today," Ray said. The words hung in the air for what seemed like an eternity.

"Perhaps we should discuss that," Ms. Coxe said, opening the door. She walked out, turned and held the door for Ray.

Ray hesitated. He didn't want to leave Jennifer alone with Thompson and Maroney, but if he could prevent her arrest today, he needed to do that. He left the room.

Ms. Coxe closed the door. "We have enough evidence to arrest your client today."

"But you want to get John DeHaven."

"Will she help us?"

"Total immunity from prosecution?"

"That will depend on how she performs."

"What do you want?"

"Right now, documents. Signed invoices, deposit slips, anything that will help us prove his involvement."

"You've already got her testimony."

"You know as well as I do that's only her word against his. We need more than that."

Ray nodded. He knew what they wanted. "We'll get it. Let's put it on paper."

"I'm not promising anything until I see what she can produce."

"I need something. She's not going to help you without some concrete promises."

"Mr. Jackson, this isn't a negotiation. Unless she agrees to help us, I'm going to step back into the room and have her arrested. All I can promise is that, depending upon the quality of her participation, I'll consider some form of immunity."

Ray put out his hand. "We have a deal. Let me tell her."

27

As soon as she was in the car, Jennifer started crying. "I'm not turning on John."

"Goddamn it, Jennifer, if you don't help SLED, you're going to jail.

"Ray, let me explain."

"I barely got you out of there. They were ready to arrest you."

"All I did was what I was told to do. I don't think there's anything wrong with that."

"Really? You're sure? Because you just told SLED that you wired hundreds of thousands of dollars to an offshore bank based on questionable invoices that were not approved according to company procedure. And you got significant unexplained income at the same time. It looks like you did something."

"I just did my job."

"Come on, you're not that naïve."

"Well, I did ask John about it, but he said it was legal."

"And you believed him?"

"Of course."

"How much money do you think you sent to those companies a month?"

"At least a hundred thousand dollars, usually more."

"Every month?"

"Yeah."

"So more than a million a year?"

"Easily, closer to two."

"And every one was just under the reportable limit?"

"I just paid the invoice."

"And you didn't see a problem with that?"

"No, the church was getting their part. Everybody was getting paid like I was told."

"Including you, and it sounds like a lot of money. Where did that come from?"

"John gave me some money every now and again."

"Can you tell me why he would do that?"

"John's a generous man."

"A generous man? Come on. I don't think anyone is going to believe that he just gave you the money for nothing." *Or just for sleeping with him. You're not that good.* "A jury will believe that you were involved in a money laundering scheme or something illegal unless we can give a better reason. When was the last time you took any money from him?"

"He gave me ten thousand dollars last month."

"Last month. For what?"

"He said he wanted to be sure that I had everything I needed."

"Did he give you a check?"

"No, it's always in cash. He says it is easier that way."

Ray learned that not long after Jennifer and John had become lovers, she accepted twelve thousand dollars from him for the down payment on a new car.

"I told him I didn't want it. But he insisted."

The next month she accepted thirty thousand so she could pay off the car. He continued to give her between ten and fifteen thousand dollars every month since. She had not reported it on her tax returns.

"They were gifts," she said.

She had put a lot of the money in the stock market. Most of it was gone. A significant sum had been spent on shopping trips to New York and Atlanta. She couldn't remember how much.

"John's a nice guy. He couldn't be involved in anything wrong," she said.

"Really? Where does he get all that money?" *It is amazing what people can't see when they don't want to see.*

"Orion has a lot of successful businesses and he gets a percentage of the profit. Besides the clubs, John has a casino boat, the bingo contract and a construction company. And he charters several fishing boats. People judge him unfairly because of the kind of clubs he manages. You don't know him like I do."

I know him well enough. "You just promised to help SLED with the case in exchange for immunity from prosecution." *Well, a consideration of immunity.*

"You made me do it. I'm not helping them. Besides, I haven't done anything wrong," she said with a flick of her head.

"They think that you have. People don't spend over a thousand dollars on bingo in a week."

"They could. Besides, how do they know how many people were playing? We count the number of cards sold, not players."

"We believe that SLED has an informant that is giving them some information about the bingo games. Why doesn't the church keep attendance?"

Jennifer pulled down the visor and opened the mirror. She began to check her makeup. "The number of cards sold per day is a better measure of the success of the game than attendance," she said. "It is closely related to the number of players but better reflects multi-card players and the effectiveness of our resales. It wouldn't surprise me if the number of cards per player increased during the winter, because business on the strand is slow and people don't have as much to do. In the summer, we've got tourists who are just trying it out. They don't play multiple cards as often as our regulars." The answer sounded rehearsed, like a high school actor reading her lines.

"That makes some sense, but I don't think it's enough."

"It's solid accounting."

Except that John DeHaven was giving Jennifer thousands of dollars a month for nothing or for reasons she wouldn't reveal and a lot of money was being wired to the Cayman Islands every month from the bingo proceeds. And somebody killed Bobby Jones. *And Macy Jenkins is in danger. I need to stop DeHaven.* "Then it won't hurt to help SLED."

"They don't need any help. The books are perfect. Why don't you like John?"

"This isn't about DeHaven. It's about you. SLED is going to charge you if you break your promise."

"They won't. Why don't you believe me?"

"That's the problem—I do believe you. That's why you'll be arrested."

"No, you don't. You think I'm guilty."

"No, I think DeHaven set you up."

"See, it *is* John." She crossed her arms and turned to the window.

"He's the one that has you wiring money offshore and he's the one who is giving you all of this cash. If it's not DeHaven, who is it?"

She didn't respond. She just stared out the window.

They rode in silence for a few minutes.

"One thing more," Ray said. "Don't talk to anyone about your statement today."

"If you don't want me to talk to John, why don't you just say so?"

"I think it would be best not to talk to anyone, especially DeHaven, until we know what SLED is going to do. I'm just trying to protect you."

"I can talk to anyone I like." She turned emphatically to the window.

That was the end of the conversation. They didn't exchange a single word for the next two hours.

When they arrived at her house, Ray put his hand on her arm. "I'm sorry if I was hard on you. But I'm just trying to take care of you."

"Well, I can take care of myself," she said as she jerked her arm away. She opened the door and turned to get out and then looked back. "I'm sorry, Ray, I know you're trying to help. I'm tired. I'll call you tomorrow." She got out and walked to her front door without looking back.

Ray stopped at a drive-in on the way to his condo. Annette popped back into his head. *I need to get over her. Or maybe I need to call her.*

At home, with burger in hand, Ray pulled up the bingo numbers on his laptop. Card sales tracked the gross receipts exactly. It wouldn't be hard to change the number of cards sold to match the deposit. It was simple math. It might not be as easy to match income to attendance, though. He knew that SLED had attendance figures and that they knew Jennifer received a lot of money that was unaccounted for and had not been reported on her tax returns. Add some potential tax charges to this mess. What else did they have? They had Jennifer's signature authorizing millions in wires to an offshore bank. They wanted to know where the money was coming from. They wanted John DeHaven.

Ray poured himself a shot of his favorite single-barrel bourbon neat. He took a sip and smiled. *Now I know how to get DeHaven for the Bobby Jones mess.* All he had to do was persuade Jennifer to work with SLED. Maybe she would be more reasonable in the morning. *Or maybe she's in the middle of it.*

28

Ray's head was pounding like it did when he had a hangover, but he hadn't drunk much last night. He hadn't sleep much either. He spent most of the night staring into the dark, rehearsing his argument to persuade Jennifer to help SLED. He called her on the way to the office.

"SLED is going to arrest you if you don't help them. Sooner than later."

"I'm not worried about that. I talked to John last night. I'll be all right."

"Didn't I tell you not to talk to anyone? Jennifer, SLED is going to bring charges against you, serious charges."

"They can't prove I did anything wrong."

"I wouldn't be so sure."

"John said it would be all right and I believe him. I'll be fine."

"Is John your attorney or am I?"

"I know what I'm doing."

"Jennifer, listen to me. Who is wiring millions of dollars offshore?"

"Orion is, and it's perfectly legal to do business with companies in other countries."

"Apparently, SLED thinks they can prove that this business isn't legal."

"John says it is."

"He is using you to protect himself."

"You know, Ray, I'm getting tired of this. I trust John and I'm not going to betray him. Bye."

She hung up. Ray's headache was worse. The coffee wasn't helping. He grabbed the bottle of ibuprophen from the glove box and took two. Then he took two more.

"Good morning, Nelson," Ray said as he passed his senior partner's office on the way to his own.

"Ray, there you are. I've been waiting for you. Come in."

The top button on Nelson's white business shirt was undone and his navy and red striped tie loosened, a sure sign that he had been working for a couple of hours already. It was only twenty-five minutes after eight.

"John talked to Ms. Jones last night and told me what she said. Did she really wire Orion's money to the Caymans?"

"Yes, with DeHaven's approval."

"John says he didn't know anything about it. He trusted her. He's going through his books again without her help this time. I have already called SLED and we're going to arrange for John to give them a statement. What else did she say?"

Since Jennifer had talked to DeHaven, Ray recapped her statement for Nelson. He was very interested when Ray told him about the wires and the invoices. And about the money that John had given Jennifer. Ray felt as if he were betraying a confidence. But Nelson wasn't surprised by any of it. He had heard it all from John.

"Did she really say that John is giving her ten to fifteen thousand dollars a month in cash just because he's a nice guy?" Nelson asked.

"That's what she told me. I didn't let SLED go into her personal finances."

"Does she really think that anyone will believe that?"

"Nelson, I don't know. First we need to see if the invoices are legitimate. If they are, that clears up a lot of the problem."

"John's going through the invoices now, but we both know that it's unlikely they are. John had never heard of some of the names she told him."

"It seems clear that someone is laundering money through the bingo games, but I don't think Jennifer Jones is doing it. Besides, it has continued since she left Orion and took the job at the church."

"She could have an accomplice."

"No, it's bigger than that."

"What makes you think that?"

"If SLED's attendance numbers are right, then it's someone at Orion. They are running at least a hundred thousand dollars a week through the games. I think Jennifer is being set up."

"John tells me that Ms. Jones is very savvy. She has a degree in accounting. She might very well be capable of running a scheme like this. You might be too close to her to see the truth."

"I find it hard to believe—"

"She has all she needs: control of the books and signature authority over the bank account. It was better when she moved to the church because she could control both sets of books. I'm sorry—I know that she is a friend of yours. Of course John, Orion and the church will have to cooperate with SLED. John thinks that there was another girl in the Orion office, Macy Jansen, working with Ms. Jones. She gave her notice last week and has left town. Isn't she a client of yours, too?"

"Just a cocaine possession charge," Ray says. *Damn, DeHaven's good. He's using this situation to deal with his potential problem with Macy.*

"Well, she's got more trouble now. Anyway, you can probably make a deal for Ms. Jones if she will tell SLED where she's getting the money and who she's sending it to."

"I don't think Jennifer realizes how much trouble she's in. If John's going to testify against her, I have a conflict of interest. I did get her to sign a conflict disclosure before we went to Columbia."

"I don't think you have to worry about that. I'm taking John to see SLED this week. We'll clear this up as far as the church and Orion are concerned. Once they're out of it, there's no real conflict. I got John to sign a waiver, too. You can continue to represent her if you think that's wise."

"I'll think about it."

"Well, again, I'm sorry for her, but at least we'll get this all behind us. Let me know if there's anyone I can speak to on her behalf when the time comes."

"Nelson, SLED had attendance figures for nearly every night." *From Annette.* "The church doesn't keep attendance. That information had to come from their informant. I don't know what else they have."

"Well, I don't think we have to worry about that now. We know who's responsible."

Ray left and walked to his office. *How can I turn this against John DeHaven?* The simple truth was that without Jennifer's help, he couldn't. Maybe she would finally see when SLED charged her, but he didn't think so. He didn't know why, but she wasn't going to turn on DeHaven. He pulled a new file from the stack Trish had left on his desk. The foreclosure business wasn't slowing down much. *Whose home can I take today?*

Thursday morning, Nelson was back. As always, he was in his office when Ray arrived.

"How did it go?" Ray asked from the doorway.

"We spent over six hours digging through Orion's books with SLED. Ms. Jones has been laundering money for over five years," Nelson says.

"Why didn't John catch it earlier?"

"Would you believe that he's in love with her and he trusted her?"

"No."

"Neither would I, but SLED bought it. He was brilliant," Nelson said with a big grin. "He even told them that he didn't want to press charges against her."

"Really?"

"They ate it up. I'm afraid your girl's going to spend a little time in jail."

"Have they been able to find any of the money?"

"No. It was transferred to seven different accounts in the Caymans and quickly dispersed from there. I don't think SLED will ever be able to trace it. And I don't think they care. They're happy they've solved the case."

"I'd better call Jennifer. I expect SLED will be charging her today." Ray turned to leave.

"And Macy Jansen as an accessory."

"Have they found her?"

"Not yet. John said she hasn't shown up for work since about the time that SLED asked Jennifer to come to Columbia. Her roommate told him that she left town. No one seems to know where she went. They'll find her."

I hope they don't. I hope she's safe and far away from here. "Thanks for the update."

"One more thing. Are you involved in any of this?"

"What?"

"Your name came up during John's questioning. How long have you been involved with Ms. Jones?"

"I'm not involved with her."

"It's bad enough that you're screwing a client, don't lie to me."

"We used to date—years ago. You know that." *Stubborn denial is difficult to defeat.*

"Well, John thinks you might be working with her."

"That's ridiculous."

"I reminded him of the good work you've already done for him. But you know if I believed him, I'd have to report you to the Ethics Commission and you would lose your license. So stop screwing her or get her another attorney. Your choice. OK?"

"I'm not seeing her, but if it will make you feel better, I'll see that she gets another lawyer."

Ray walked to his office trying to decide if Nelson knew about Bobby Jones. Suddenly his breakfast wasn't sitting on his stomach so well.

Jennifer was not home and she didn't answer her cell. Ray left messages on both phones. After lunch, he was checking his e-mail when his intercom buzzed.

He punched the button. "Yes."

"Assistant Attorney General Kristen Coxe is on Line 3."

Ray switched to the line, hoping she wasn't calling to ask for his statement.

"Mr. Jackson, you know we've been given a voluntary statement by Mr. DeHaven?"

"Yes, I heard about it."

"Does your client have anything we can use?"

"Not yet. She needs a little more time."

"I'm afraid we don't have that. Obviously, we'll consider anything she can provide, but we are going to charge Jennifer Jones with money laundering, fraud, conspiracy and tax evasion. Will she turn herself in?"

"Will you be reasonable on bail?"

"We're talking millions of dollars here. Most of that was wired overseas. Bail is going to have to be substantial. We don't know how much money she has. It would be very easy to run."

"What's substantial?"

"Half a million."

"Let me talk to her. I'm sure we can work something out."

"You know that I am ready to help her if she will help me."

"She's a pawn. I don't think she knows much more than she has already told you."

"Mr. Jackson, if you know anyone else who can help, we would be willing to listen and might be able to offer some immunity."

"John DeHaven is who you should be after."

"If that's so, Ms. Jones—or someone—needs to prove it to me. We don't have anything solid on Mr. DeHaven, but our case against your client is very strong. He was very convincing when he gave his statement."

"He's lying."

"Do you know something that would incriminate him?"

"Me, no. Just what my client has said."

"Well, if you change your mind, I'm willing to listen."

"Ms. Coxe, I'll talk to my client and let you know."

Ray tried Jennifer again. This time she answered on the first ring.

"Jennifer, John DeHaven gave his statement to SLED yesterday."

"Yeah, I know."

"Of course you do. Do you know that he said that it was all you? That he didn't know anything about it."

"That's not what he told me."

"Well, he did. I just got a call from the attorney general's office. They are preparing to charge you with money laundering, fraud, conspiracy and tax evasion."

"John said everything would be fine."

"It will be for him. But you are going to be charged and arrested. Jennifer, you could spend a lot of time in jail if you don't tell SLED what really happened."

"I'm not going to jail."

"Someone is, and the only way to protect yourself is to help SLED find who laundered all that money."

"I've told them all I know."

"Then think harder."

"You don't believe me. You think I'm guilty."

"I don't know what you did, but the facts don't look good. You got a lot of cash from DeHaven, which he denies, and you approved the deposits and authorized the wire transfers of several million dollars overseas to nonexistent companies. I'd say that is a problem."

"I just paid the invoices like I was told. There's nothing wrong with that."

"John is making it look like there is. That's why you need to help SLED."

"You're not listening to me."

"I'm not listening to you. You're not listening to me. You're facing at least ten years in jail, probably more, and you won't do anything about it."

"I told you, I haven't done anything wrong."

"That's not the point." Ray paused. "They want you to turn yourself in. I need to call them back today. I think we can agree on bail so that you don't spend any time in jail now."

"I'm not turning myself in. I didn't do anything except what John told me."

"I know that. We need to tell SLED. What else did John do?"

"He told me to pay the invoices. That's all."

"Think Jennifer. Where did the money come from? How was he involved?"

"The money came from bingo."

"Jennifer, damn it. You slept with the man for nearly a year. Surely you know that's not true."

"You think I'm guilty."

"My God. Open your eyes. DeHaven set you up for these charges. He's involved in drugs and murder. What did—"

"Now that's ridiculous. Just because John runs a few strip clubs doesn't make him a criminal."

"Do you remember Bobby Jones?"

"Bobby Jones?"

"Yeah, his body washed up on the beach a few months back. Both hands had been cut off."

"I remember. He was dating one of the girls I used to work with in Orion's office. What about him?"

"I discovered that Bobby was stealing from DeHaven and I told him. I shouldn't have, but I did. DeHaven thanked me. Then he told me the problem had been handled two days before the body was found."

"So now you're saying John's a murderer? It's just a coincidence."

"What about all the money he gave you? Where do you think that came from?"

"It was part of his monthly bonus from the clubs. That's what he said."

"And you believe him?"

"Yes, I do. Ray, I appreciate all you've done for me, but I think I need to get another attorney."

"That might be wise." *Maybe someone else can talk some sense into you.* "Carolyn O'Reilly is good. I'll set up an appointment for you to see her."

"Don't bother. I can call her myself. Maybe she'll believe me. Can you text me her number?"

"I'll send it to you now."

There was a pause. "Ray," she said quietly, "don't worry about me. I'll be all right."

"I hope so. Be honest with Carolyn. She can work with SLED."

On Friday morning, Jennifer met Ray at his office. They had an appointment to meet SLED Agent Maroney and Assistant Attorney General Kristen Coxe at the Sheriff's Department. Jennifer had retained Carolyn O'Reilly to handle her case. She was able to reach an agreement with SLED on bail so that Jennifer wouldn't be going to jail today. Unfortunately, Carolyn was in court with a case in another county, so Ray was handling the formalities.

"Are you all right?"

"I'll be fine. How long will this take?"

"Most of the morning. You have to be formally arrested, all the paperwork has to be completed and then we'll go over to the courthouse and have a preliminary hearing. That's where we'll plead not guilty and bail will be set. After that, a little more paperwork and you'll be released."

"I don't want to go to jail."

"Are you going to work with SLED?"

"Carolyn is working on that. But I mean today. Are they going to put me in a jail cell?"

"Probably for thirty minutes or so. Just while things are being processed."

"Don't let them do that."

"Jennifer, I can ask, but that's all I can do. Once you turn yourself in, you're in their custody until bail is met. It is all arranged, but some of the paperwork can't be done until the judge rules on it. They will likely put you in a cell while some of the forms are being completed."

"I thought we already did the paperwork. I signed over my house yesterday."

"We've done all that we can do beforehand. There is some that can't be done until you actually go over there and turn yourself in. We have to have a hearing, and that will be whenever the judge has time in his schedule today. We have all agreed upon the three hundred thousand dollar bail, but the judge has to formally set the bail and sign the order. I know you're anxious. It's a little early, but we could walk over now."

"No, I need to freshen my makeup. Where's the ladies room?"

She returned in less than ten minutes. "I'm ready now," she said.

Ray grabbed her file and a legal pad and started toward the door, but Jennifer threw her arms around his neck. He kept his arms at his sides. "I'm sorry, Ray. I've been such a bitch since we went to Columbia, and you were right the whole time. I'll make it up to you tonight, if you want."

"I don't think that's a good idea. Besides, I thought you were going to Columbia to stay with your mother."

She leaned back, still holding him, "I don't have to go today."

"I think it would be best."

She let go of him. "You're still mad at me. I understand. I'll call you when I get back."

Ray decided to deal with it then. "Let's go," he said.

29

"Amazing," Ray said as he hung up the phone. The attorney for the man whom Tony Evans assaulted had just offered to drop all charges if the dancer, Susan Allen, would drop the charges she'd brought against him. Not only that, but the victim would drop his six-figure personal injury suit, too. The attorney didn't give a reason and Ray didn't want to know.

After trying the number that he had for Ms. Allen without success, Ray called Orion. He didn't want to talk to Tony, but he couldn't see a way around it. He was sure Tony knew how to find her.

"Tony's taken the day off to go fishing," the receptionist said.

"Really? Well, it's a beautiful day for it. Do you know where he's heading?"

"He's going deep-sea fishing. We were looking at wave conditions on my computer." She sounded young and cute. No doubt Tony liked looking at the computer with her.

"Is he going out to the Gulf Stream?" The Gulf Stream, a current of warm water running north into the Atlantic from the Gulf of Mexico, was about seventy-five miles off the coast from Little River.

"I love it when my boyfriend takes me to the Gulf Stream. There are a lot of fish out there."

"But it's a long way. Is that where Tony said he was going?"

"No, we were looking at the buoy on the five-mile reef." Ray knew that reef. He did some training dives there. "Last time I went to the gulf, I caught a thirty-seven pound grouper," she said.

"Wow, I'll bet that was some good eating." They talked about her boyfriend and fishing for a few more minutes until she got another call. Ray didn't leave a message.

One good thing about doing foreclosures was that there were rarely any client appointments, just a few hearings. You could usually schedule several of those at a time and never on Friday. Ray checked his calendar. There was nothing on it that couldn't wait. He hit a button on the intercom. "Trish, I'm going to the Myrtle Beach office. I need to spend a little time on Bo Heath's case. You know, I might just work from home. It would be great if I wasn't bothered for the rest of the day. You can find me on my cell if anything important comes up."

He stopped at a sporting goods outlet on Highway 17.

"I would like to see your best set of binoculars and some fishing rods," he told the teenager in a light blue polo with the company logo screen printed where the pocket would be. Ray had bought his boat for skiing, tubing and, hopefully, some scuba diving. *But today I'm going fishing.*

The clerk brought two sets of binoculars and Ray chose the Minoltas that were barely larger than his hands. He also chose two fishing rods with open reels and two fishing rigs with double silver spoons. A silver spoon was simply a hook with a shiny metal plate attached. When you pulled a silver spoon behind a boat, it spun in the water and the reflected sunlight made it look like a minnow. Ray might not have been much of a fisherman, but he *had* been fishing before.

"Whatcha going after?" the clerk asked.

"Mackerel." Ray covered his lie with a huge grin. He hoped to catch a much bigger fish than that. His rough idea was to troll for mackerel around the reef while looking for Tony. It wasn't much of a plan, but he hoped something better would come to him once he got out there.

"I hear they've been hitting pretty good," the clerk said. "Good luck."

At his condo, Ray changed into shorts and a T-shirt. He filled a cooler with a six-pack of beer and ice. *Who fishes without cold beer?* He loaded the cooler into the boat and went back for his mask, snorkel, fins and a swimsuit. He grabbed the box that held his pneumatic spear gun, too. Forty-five minutes later, the boat was full of no-ethanol gas and he was on the way to the five-mile reef.

There were three other boats on the reef when he got there around midday, all about the size of his. Tony Evans was not on any of them. Ray checked twice. He prepped the fishing lines, got the spoons into the water and started trolling around the reef. He hooked a Spanish mackerel in the first ten minutes, and as he unhooked the toothy fish, he realized he didn't have a place to put it. After a moment's hesitation, he put it in the cooler with the beer.

It must be my lucky day. Actually having caught a fish will add credibility to my story if I need it. He caught four more over the next hour and a half, his best day of fishing ever, and was joined by five other boats of fishermen. Now there was more fish than beer in his cooler, but there was still no sign of Tony.

By five o'clock, the fish had quit biting. The other boats were long gone, and Ray was alone on the reef. He threw out the anchor to save gas and held a rod for show. The beer wasn't for show, though, and while the next-to-last can was a little fishy, it was still cool and went down pretty easy in the late-afternoon heat. *If Tony's not here by the time I finish the last one, I'm heading in.*

A long, steamy half-hour later, Ray was going to the cooler for the last beer when he saw a shrimp boat coming up from the south. He scanned the deck with his binoculars but didn't see anyone he knew. The captain was going wide to keep his nets off the reef and was going to pass about a thousand yards seaside of Ray's boat. Ray forgot the beer and put the rod back into its holder and began to pull in his anchor, planning a slow trolling pursuit even though he didn't know if it was the right boat. It was something to do and he was bored.

The shrimp boat was going so slowly that Ray had to begin the pursuit by turning away from it. The shrimp boat slowed as it neared the buoy marking the north end of the reef and began to take in its nets. That was unusual. Ray put his boat into neutral and began to reel in one of the rods, pretending to have a fish. When he paused to scan the shrimper with the binoculars again, he saw that another member of the crew had come on deck. He was standing in the door of the pilot house and appeared to be speaking into a radio handset. It was Tony Evans.

Ray reached the south end of the reef and made a wide turn toward the shrimper. The shrimper came to a stop near the buoy. Several of the crew members started working with something on the far side of the boat, and Ray saw a disturbance in the water, as if something large had been dropped into the ocean. But he hadn't seen them drop anything, and he couldn't see what it was. The boat was blocking his view and he was afraid that if he stared too hard, he would be noticed. Knowing Tony, he didn't want that. Then two of the crew members stepped over the side of the shrimper, but they were still visible. Ray could see their heads over the bulwark. They had to be standing in another boat or on what they'd dropped over the side. He knew another boat was not beside them—he would have seen it approach. A few minutes after going over the side of the shrimper, the crew members began handing boxes into the boat. They looked like the heavy cardboard boxes used to ship frozen seafood. The boxes were passed from hand to hand and loaded into the holds. Ray estimated that about fifty boxes were loaded onto the shrimper.

Tony turned away from supervising the work to scan the sea. Ray hid the binoculars behind his back and realized he might have gotten too close. He turned away and began to troll in the other direction. The loading process took less than ten minutes, and Ray decided to keep moving away. He couldn't discover the contents of the boxes without getting on the shrimper, and he couldn't think of a safe way to do that. *But it's got to be cocaine, pure cocaine.* Like the cocaine Macy got from Bobby Jones.

Ray continued to troll the south end of the reef until the shrimper began to move again. He started toward the north as the shrimper looped around the inland side of the reef heading south. *Where did those boxes come from? Did they scoop them up in their nets? Were they attached to the buoy and sitting on the reef? If it was another boat, where did the boat go? Where did it come from?* Ray felt a lot better when one of the crew members gave him a friendly wave as they passed on opposite sides of the reef. The shrimper was nearly out of sight when he got to the buoy. He looked over the side but couldn't see anything. He pulled in his fishing lines, which had done their job. He tethered the boat to the buoy and grabbed his mask and fins. Maybe they'd left some evidence behind.

Standing on the dive deck, he checked his spear gun. It was loaded and on "safe" for his entry. He stepped off holding his mask. The water was cool but stung his new sunburn. On the other dives he had made out of Little River, silt had limited the visibility to about fifty to sixty feet. Today, the water was crystal clear and the visibility was close to one hundred feet. He made a circle around his boat and the buoy on the surface, breathing deeply through his snorkel, but he didn't see anything except a few fish. A silver barracuda hovered just at the edge of visibility. His sharp teeth looked dangerous, but Ray knew it was not a threat. He released the safety on the spear gun anyway and swam to the buoy and took three deep breaths. He wished he had a tank so he could take his time and examine the entire length of the buoy chain. He dived, pulling himself along the chain. *I'll go as deep as I can. I hope I'll know what I'm looking for when I see it.*

He was about twenty-five feet deep when, just off the reef to his left, a sudden movement startled him. He fired his spear gun at a huge dark shape, but the spear clunked off the side of it. Ray had to surface. He took two quick breaths and dived again. Going as deep as he could as fast as he could, he swam in the direction of the object until he was close enough to see the blades of a single screw slowly churning bubbles as it drove a mini-sub out to sea.

He climbed back into his boat and pulled in his spear, scanning the ocean to be sure that the shrimper had not returned. He was alone. A mini-sub. *No wonder they haven't been seen.* He dried off and headed for the dock, cruising at a leisurely pace because he didn't want to catch up to Tony. His next task was to find who owned the shrimp boat. There should be plenty of information online. Her name was Caroline.

The setting sun colored the cirrus clouds the same pink as the saltwater taffy the Ohio tourists loved to eat. It amazed Ray that they would eat that stuff but wouldn't try a boiled peanut. *Now that's a delicacy.* He wished he had a bag right then. He finished the final beer as he made the last turn on the waterway toward the marina where he kept his boat. It was warm but he didn't care. His new plan called for a shower and some lotion. Then a little work online. The shower probably wouldn't be too comfortable with his sunburn, but that's what the lotion was for.

Ray throttled back in the no-wake zone where the gaming boats docked. They were beginning to board for the evening cruise. He saw Tony Evans exit a building next to the casino-boat office and speak to the driver of a Coastal Carolina Construction van. Ray ducked behind the center console. It wasn't much, but it was all there was. After the van driver headed off, Tony walked to the casino-boat offices. Marching like a Nazi and not looking around, he appeared to be on a mission. Ray said a silent prayer of thanks because Tony didn't look out into the waterway. Ray did not see the Caroline at any of the docks.

The building that Tony was leaving was an old commercial boat repair shop. It was nothing more than an enclosed pole barn over water. Ray examined the two huge weather- and water-worn barn doors of the shop that faced the waterway as he went slowly past. They were large enough to admit the Caroline for repairs or undisturbed unloading. A gap between the doors near the bottom was too small to see through, but a fresh stain of diesel fuel trailed from inside.

Ray reached the end of the no-wake zone and sped up. His dock wasn't far. He could check it out on the way home. But was he going to find anything? Her cargo had probably already been unloaded into the van. Besides, he really didn't want to bump into Tony. *No. I've done enough for one day. Let's head for home and that shower.*

30

Ray wanted to call Jarrett Brown as soon as his boat was tied off, but he resisted. He stowed his equipment in its place and wiped down the seats and upholstery. He had an idea and he couldn't think of anyone else to help. *What the hell?*

He called, and Brown answered on the first ring.

"What do you want?"

"I have something on the Bobby Jones murder." Ray cradled the phone on his shoulder and began walking to his car with his catch.

There was a pause. Ray heard a door close.

"Go on," Brown said.

Ray told Brown what he had seen. "They're in the repair dock now."

"So, you want to me to get a search warrant?"

"Exactly," Ray said as he put his cooler in the trunk of his car.

"Did you see any drugs?"

"I told you I saw boxes. I didn't see what's in them, but I'm sure they're full of cocaine. Bobby Jones used to go fishing with Tony Evans. He must have skimmed a little unloading the boat."

"So you saw a shrimp boat unloading boxes of frozen fish that they got from a submarine, right?"

"I told you I think they're smuggling drugs." Ray got into his car and fired up the air conditioner.

"The difference between being a lawyer and a cop is that I actually have to have facts. It's called evidence. I don't get to make up some story."

"You know it's true."

"A submarine? Give me a break. And I suppose you can tie all of this back to Royal McKenzie and your fantasy about him killing all those girls.

Tell you what, why don't you come into the department Monday morning and I'll let you give your statement to one of the drug guys? I don't do drugs. I'm sure they'll want to hear this. We'll see if your story fits anything they've got going. Maybe that will lead me to Bobby Jones's murderer. Probably not. Thanks for calling."

"Wait a minute. This is huge." But Brown was not there. "Shit." Ray put his car into "drive." "Shit," he said again, too busy fuming at Brown to enjoy the air conditioning.

Just a mile from his marina, Ray saw the sign for the casino boat. The nightly cruise was departing in a few minutes. *I'm not going in there. It's getting dark and they've moved the stuff by now.* "I'm so tired I'm talking to myself," he muttered. But it wouldn't hurt to stop for a minute, and he could blend in with the crowd boarding the casino boat. *I'll just make sure the Caroline's in the dock and go home.* He found a parking spot at the back of the lot. A weak economy sure didn't seem to be slowing down the gamblers. He sat in the car for a moment before taking a deep breath and getting out. A few people were in line to purchase tickets for the boat. According to the clock over the window, it was leaving in eleven minutes.

The ticket window and gangplank area were brightly lighted by spotlights and several arrays of decorative flashing lights. It looked more like a country fair than Vegas. He had to cross in front of the ticket windows to reach the repair-dock door that he'd seen Tony exit. He walked along the edge of the light until he reached the far side of the area, and he stayed in the long shadows of the buildings until he reached the door. The top half of the door was a checkerboard of windowpanes. He cupped his hands around his eyes and tried to see through the glass, but it was too dark inside to see anything. It was like looking out your bedroom window trying to see what was making a noise outside during a midnight storm. He tried the doorknob, but it was locked. No surprise. He walked around the inland side of the shop and found several tall stacks of boxes like those he'd seen being loaded onto Caroline. He reached for one.

"Can I help you?"

"I was just looking for a bathroom before I got on the casino boat," he said, turning around. Ray could barely make out the shape of the solid black man who was holding the beam of a flashlight in his face. Ray put a hand up to block the light that was blinding him.

"There are facilities on the boat. It's this way." The man gestured with the light.

"What's going on, Roy Mack?" called a voice from the gangplank. Ray could just make out Tony Evans walking his way.

"Just a gambler looking for the men's room."

"Hi, Tony." Ray stuck out his hand and they shook. "And Mr. McKenzie, I've been trying to find you." Ray offered him a hand. "I'm Ray Jackson." Roy Mack took a step back.

"Mr. Jackson, what are you doing out here?" Tony said.

"I was trying to find a men's room before I got my ticket. I guess I can get my ticket and find the men's room on board. Good to see you. Mr. McKenzie, can we talk a minute?"

"What about?"

"Mr. Jackson, they are about to pull the gangplank up. You need to board," Tony said.

"Tonya Smalls's murder."

"I don't want to talk to you," Royal McKenzie said. "You need me?" he said to Tony.

"No, I got this," Tony said.

Royal turned toward the office.

"Come on, Mr. Jackson."

"You know, on second thought, I've had a long day. I haven't gotten a ticket yet. I'll go another night." Ray took a couple of steps toward the parking lot.

Tony blocked the way. "You don't need a ticket tonight. It's on the house. Come on." He guided Ray to the gangplank and they boarded.

Ray went straight to the men's room to support his story and tried to clean up a little. He looked worse than he'd thought. He was red with sunburn, and his shirt was fouled with fish scales. He found the gift shop and purchased a Day-Glo green T-shirt that read "My life is Craps" and changed into that. It didn't help his appearance much, but at least it didn't smell. He did, though.

Ray got a hundred dollars from one of the ATMs and found a seat at the five-dollar blackjack table. He had done well there with Annette. The waitress brought him a watered-down bourbon, and in barely more than an hour, he lost all his cash. He decided to take a break and went out on the deck to get some fresh air. He found a spot near the bow and leaned on the chest-high rail. *Cindy Martin didn't accidentally fall over this.* A full moon shone over the two- to three-foot waves.

"Nice shirt. Are you winning?" Tony Evans said. He appeared at Ray's right shoulder smoking a cigar.

Ray wondered if he suspected something. "Not much luck tonight. I'm taking a break and then I'll try something else."

"I hear the craps table is paying pretty well," Tony said with a flick of his cigar. "Did you have any luck this afternoon?"

"What?"

"Did you catch anything? You saw me. I waved as we were going in. I was on the shrimp boat."

"Oh, that was you? I didn't recognize you. I got a few Spanish mackerel."

"You should be careful fishing in the ocean alone like that. It can be dangerous."

"My buddy bombed on me at the last minute. But it's a new boat. I had to try it out."

"First I see you on the reef and then you're hanging around our dock. Some people might think you were spying on them. But you wouldn't do that would you? I figure you're a good guy since you gave me that tip. We knew we had a little problem, but your tip—that helped us clear that up. Thank you."

"Well, I, uh, sure."

"So are you following me?"

"No, my girlfriend is out town, so I took the opportunity to go fishing. I didn't have anything else to do, so I decided to try my luck out here."

Tony nodded. "You keep your boat at Captain John's Marina, right?"

"I do. Say, have you seen Macy Jansen? I need to discuss her case, and I haven't been able to get in touch with her."

"I haven't seen her since right after her boyfriend died," Tony said, flicking some cigar ash over the rail.

Maybe she got away. "Let you know if you hear from her. I would like to talk to her."

"I hear SLED is looking for her, too, but I don't think we'll see her again," Tony said. "I think she's gone for good." He pointed at the nearly full moon with his cigar. "Nice moon tonight."

"Sure is."

"It's a big damn ocean, isn't it? If you drop something in it way out here, no one's going to find it." He turned to Ray with a big grin and took a long drag on his cigar.

Is that a threat or did he just tell me that he killed Macy, too? "Well, I need to try to get my money back before we head in."

"Good luck with that."

Ray went to the men's room and threw up. He wasn't seasick. He took another hundred dollars from the ATM and a drink from the waitress. He finished the bourbon before he made it to the craps table. After taking a seat, he placed the minimum bet and ordered another drink. You can't drink if you aren't gambling, and Ray wanted to drink.

At midnight, Ray disembarked more sober than he'd intended, because the drinks were so weak. He got into the car and it stank of fish. He didn't look in the mirror as he put the top down, because he didn't want to see his condition. All he wanted was a shower and his bed. *Maybe I'm tired enough to sleep tonight.* He pulled into his development to find that some damn weekend rental had taken his parking spot, and he had to park two buildings down. Lugging his smelly cooler and gear to the front door, he saw someone standing in the shadows by his front door. He was momentarily relieved to recognize Jennifer.

"What are you doing here?" he said.

"I'm back from Mom's. It was so suffocating. We had a fight and I left. I needed someone to talk to. I missed you." She took a half-step toward him and then back. She looked him up and down. "Where have you been? You stink."

"Fishing and the casino boat."

"Like that?"

"It's a long story."

"Well, I brought a peace offering." She held up a bottle of his favorite single-barrel bourbon. "But it doesn't look like you want any company."

"No, come on in. Just been a long day. I've got to clean up a little."

"Well, if you're too tired, I understand."

"No, I'm not tired." He forced a smile to his face. "Actually, it's good to see you." Even Jennifer was better than being alone. *And I'm probably not going to sleep anyway.*

Jennifer was sitting on his bed when he got out of the shower and walked into his room. She smiled at his manhood. She had a double Old-Fashioned glass, one of the blue ones, in one hand and a white wine in the other.

"I helped myself. Here. Bourbon and a splash of water. I'll be out here when you get dressed."

Ray joined her on the couch a few minutes later. She had put on some Sinatra. She slid over next to him and he put an arm around her shoulder as much out of habit as anything. She rested her head on his chest and told him about her travails with her mother. He recounted his day of fishing and gambling. But he didn't tell her about the shrimp boat or Macy.

"Ray." Jennifer was shaking him gently. "You were snoring. Why don't we get in the bed? Come on."

She sat up. He didn't. He didn't want to move.

"Ray, I bought you something else." Jennifer pulled a lacy black negligee from her purse and held it up for him to see through. "I got this in Atlanta."

"When were you in Atlanta?"

"I went shopping when I had all I could stand of my mother."

"You went shopping?"

"What's wrong with that?"

"Nothing. I'm sorry. I'm tired." Ray didn't need any more conflict.

"Well, if you're not in the mood, you can enjoy it in the morning. Get up."

"Go change. I'll be right there."

She leaned over and kissed him. "You're coming?"

"Be right there. I just want to check the doors." She went to the bedroom, and Ray went to find the box on the back of the top shelf on the coat closet. That's where he kept his gun.

The gun was a German WWII Luger. Ray's uncle had gotten it while he was stationed in Germany when he was in the Air Force in the early sixties. Ray was named after his uncle and the Luger was left to him when his uncle died of lung cancer twenty three years ago. Ray had taken it out of its lockbox only once since he got it. During his divorce, he had taken it to an indoor shooting range. He wanted to try it out, but the handgun was in such poor condition that the range manager would not allow him to fire it. No intruder would know that, though.

Ray turned off the light when he entered the bedroom. Jennifer was asleep and he didn't want her to see the gun. He went back out to the living room, grabbed a pillow from his armchair and tossed it onto one end of the couch. He lay down and put the gun under the pillow. He didn't think he'd sleep, but somehow he did.

31

"**G**ood morning," Jennifer said as she walked into the kitchen around ten. She was wearing Ray's white terry-cloth robe. She pushed Whiskers off the counter so she could reach the coffee maker. "You look like shit." She pulled a mug from the cabinet and filled it.

"Thanks. Didn't sleep much. Just needed to do a little research." Ray had woken up an hour ago with Tony Evans on his mind and had been at his computer since. His research into the Caroline was proving to be difficult. The Caroline was nominally owned by a corporation in Florida, which was owned by a corporation in Nevada, which was owned by a Delaware corporation. The trail ended there. The only common thread was that Nelson Patterson was the official contact listed for all three corporations.

"It's Saturday. Can't it wait?" Jennifer said.

"I had a new thought and I really need to check it out." He held his empty coffee cup toward her.

She stared at it for a second before she took the pot to the table. She kicked an attention-seeking Whiskers away from her foot and looked at the screen over Ray's shoulder. "What are you looking at?"

"It's just a list of contributors to Nelson Patterson's campaign fund." While searching unsuccessfully for the ownership of the Delaware corporation, Ray had found a news story listing it as a contributor to Nelson's political action committee. That led to the discovery that all three companies had consistently made campaign contributions to Nelson. Significant contributions. But he knew Jennifer wouldn't care about that.

"What case is that for?" she said.

"It's just some background work for a, uh, contract case."

She took a sip of her coffee and made a face. "Ugh. This coffee is cold." She walked over and put her cup in the microwave.

"I didn't know you supported Nelson," Ray said.

"I don't. I hate politics. They're all a bunch of crooks. I'm not even registered to vote."

Ray found her name on the list and pointed. "Well, according to this you gave his campaign twenty-five hundred dollars in January. And the same amount last year."

"That's not right," Jennifer said. "My name shouldn't be on that list." She crossed the room to look at the screen. The fluffy robe gaped open as she leaned over and revealed a bare breast. "Oops," she said, catching Ray's stare, "I guess I forgot to put on a nightgown. Maybe I should put one on now." She started backing toward the bedroom and began to take the robe off in a striptease. She dropped it to the floor and, naked, said, "Well, aren't you coming?"

Ray stood. He could make love to her. She wasn't his client anymore. *Not that that stopped me before.* "I'm not in the mood," he said. "Sorry." He shrugged.

"What's wrong with you?"

"I'm tired and I, uh, need to finish this."

"God, you're an asshole." She picked up the robe and put it back on. She picked up the untouched *Myrtle Beach Herald* and took it to the couch.

Ray put on a fresh pot of coffee and returned to the list of contributors. *If Jennifer didn't make the contribution, who did?* He printed a hard copy because he sometimes just liked to work with paper.

"Could DeHaven have made a contribution to Nelson for you?" Ray said as the printer started.

"Don't start with John again."

Ray ignored the comment. "Come look at this."

She walked over.

Among the individuals on the list of contributors in January of that year were the Reverend Tim Thomas and Tony Evans. Royal McKenzie was there, too, along with a few prominent Horry County citizens. There were also a number of names Ray didn't recognize. "Do you know any of these people?"

"I doubt it. Why don't you put that up and do something with me?"

"It won't take long if you'll help."

She rolled her eyes and looked at the page Ray was holding. "He's a bartender on the casino boat." She pointed at a name near the top of the list. "She's a waitress at a club. She's a stripper. So is she." Jennifer sat, pouting.

"They all made the maximum contribution. Do you think that any of these people would give twenty-five hundred dollars to Nelson's campaign, or did it come from somewhere else like yours?"

"So you think John contributed for all of these people?"

"It had to come from somewhere."

She sat up, displaying her breast again. When Ray didn't react, she leaned over and ran her hand down his thigh. "Can't this wait?" she whispered into his ear.

Ray was fixated on the list. Jennifer must have seen what he was looking at because she jerked the list from his hands. "Isn't this your ex-girlfriend? Annette Murphy? Maybe John made a contribution for her, too." She tossed the list at him, scattering the pages over the coffee table and onto the floor.

"She's an employee like you and the others," Ray said as he gathered the pages. Then he stopped and dropped to his knees. He knew the first name on the top of the last page. The name was Tonya Smalls. Ray also knew that Tonya hadn't made a contribution in January. She was dead.

"What's wrong?"

"Tonya Smalls is on the list."

"That's not strange. She's a stripper."

"It's just that—"

"Since we're talking about strippers, why is your Annette on the witness list in my case?" Jennifer's hands were on her hips. The robe had fallen off, but she didn't seem to notice.

Damn. "When did that come out?"

"My lawyer called me yesterday morning. Her best guess is that she is SLED's informant."

"Did you tell DeHaven?"

"No, I haven't talked to him since I got charged."

Ray picked up his cell phone and punched the speed dial for Annette. He wanted to know she was safe. He wanted her to know that SLED had revealed her name. Jennifer would live with it or not. He didn't care what Jennifer did.

"Who are you calling?"

"I want to see if Annette donated to Nelson. And I'll ask if she's the informant while I have her on the phone."

"You still have her number on speed dial?"

He ignored that. Jennifer watched him like a bird on its nest watches a cat. And Ray was the cat. "Annette, hey, it's Ray. ... Good morning to you. Fine. Can I ask you two quick questions? Have you ever donated money to Nelson Patterson's campaign? ... I didn't think so. ... You are on a list of contributors, twenty-five hundred this year and last. ... And did you know that you are on SLED's witness list for Jennifer Jones's case? ... Yesterday. ... I'm sorry I can't really talk now. Yes, go visit a friend for a few days. We'll talk later."

"I can't believe you called her."

"She didn't give Nelson any money either."

"You son of a bitch, you call your old girlfriend while I'm standing right here. God, you're such an asshole."

"Calm down. It's—"

"Calm down. You want me to calm down. I'm not your little stripper. I won't put up with your shit." She marched to the bedroom and slammed the door.

That was a classic Jennifer power play. He had seen it too many times. The last time she'd tried one with Ray, she wanted a diamond ring. They broke up because he wouldn't give in. *And I was in love with her then. Or so I thought.*

Jennifer came out of the bedroom after thirty minutes or so. She had dressed and put on some makeup. "Are you going to apologize to me?" she said.

"I haven't done anything to apologize for."

"You son of a bitch!"

Ray walked to the front door and quietly took everything she hurled at him. She finally sputtered to an end.

"I should have stayed with John. He's a better man than you'll ever be."

"He set you up to go to jail."

"Fuck you."

She marched out the front door, which Ray was holding open. And then he closed it behind her. Permanently.

32

Ray called Annette three times in the next thirty minutes. All three went straight to voice mail. He left a message the third time. After a quick shower, he tried again and, getting no answer, headed for her apartment.

Standing at her front door, Ray had a sense of déjà vu. When she answered the door, her hair and body wrapped in a towel, Ray couldn't find any words. He was momentarily disoriented by a rush of emotions almost like being stung by a jellyfish.

Annette glared at him for a moment. "What are you doing here?"

"You didn't answer your phone. I was worried. You should have left town already."

She gave him an exaggerated frown. "I will." She glanced back into the apartment. "I'm taking a hot bath."

"You know who you're dealing with. You should go."

"They have a deputy riding by every thirty minutes. I'm fine." She took a half-step back and began to close the door. "Thank you for checking."

Ray took a step toward the door. "I could—"

"No, you can't. I'm fine. Good-bye." She closed the door.

Ray stood on the step for a minute or two. He reached for the doorbell again but didn't push it. A Horry County sheriff's cruiser pulled into the complex and Ray decided it was time to leave.

The cruiser stopped behind Ray's car. The deputy got out.

"Sir, can I see some ID?"

Ray handed over his driver's license without complaint. He was glad they were on the job.

"What's this about, Officer?"

"Routine, Mr. Jackson. We've had some complaints and we're just checking. What are you doing here?"

"I'm an attorney and I know you're watching Ms. Murphy. I was checking on her, too."

The officer gave him a hard look. He returned the license. "You have a good day, Mr. Jackson."

"Thank you," Ray said as the officer walked away.

A bleary-eyed Ray didn't think about putting the top down for his drive to work on Monday morning. It was already eighty degrees and the humidity was so high that he was perspiring just from walking to the car. "Love Those Myrtle Beach Days," a beach music classic, was playing on the radio. *Yeah, right.*

With Bo Heath's trial only two weeks away, Ray had cleared his calendar for the day to make sure that everything was ready. But he couldn't focus. His head was a shooting gallery of ricocheting questions and dead ends. He kept hearing Tony say, "It's a big ocean. If you drop something in it, no one's going to find it." *Is Macy dead? Is Annette safe? What do I do with the information about Nelson?* Brown had laughed at the submarine.

The only thing Ray accomplished all morning was to accept an invitation to join Bubba McHenry in Georgetown for breakfast and to shoot clays on Saturday. Maybe Bubba could help.

Returning from an early lunch, Ray found a message from Deputy Daniel Ross of the Sheriff's Department on his desk. Ray didn't know who that was, but he returned the call and left a message for the deputy. *Just what I need, a time-wasting game of phone tag.* He flipped through the file again, trying to prepare for his meeting with Bo to go over his testimony, but Tony, Annette and Nelson kept interfering. He gave up and was loading his briefcase when Deputy Ross called back.

"Captain Brown told me that you saw a submarine over the weekend," the deputy said.

"I didn't think he believed me."

"I would like to know more about what you saw."

"I am on my way out to an appointment. Could we talk later?"

"When will you be back? I would like to talk to you today."

"I expect to be out all afternoon. I could stop by around five."

"That'll work. I'll see you then. Just ask the desk sergeant to page me."

The parking lot of the jail was about half-full, but the waiting room was nearly empty. "I would like to see Michael Heath," he told the guard at the desk.

"He has a visitor. I'll send you back as soon as she leaves."

Great. Should I make the whole day a waste or do I come back tomorrow? He checked the time on his phone, but before he could decide, Annette walked into the waiting room from the visiting area. Ray clipped his phone back in the holder and decided that Bo wasn't going anywhere.

"Let's find a place to talk." Ray said as he took her arm. He wasn't taking a "no" this time.

"You OK?" she said.

"Yeah, fine."

She gave him a worried look but left the jail with him. He found a bar in a strip mall called Murphy's Law. There were a few people already winding down from another Monday on the job and it was barely three o'clock. Ray ordered a couple of beers and they settled into a stained plywood booth near the back. She sat next to him on the bench.

"Why did you come to visit Bo?"

"I was saying good-bye."

"To Bo—I don't understand.'

"I felt I owed him an apology for thinking that he killed Tonya. Not believing him. I told him I missed Tonya. That I had not been very good to her the last few years and maybe I could have helped her. " She retrieved a tissue from her purse and wiped her eyes. She studied her beer but did not touch it.

"You should have left days ago."

"I know. But I'm leaving today. Anyway, Bo said his trial is coming up soon."

Ray paused. "Two weeks."

"Well, I know you're going to win."

"It's a decent case. I still don't have a motive for Roy Mack."

"That's OK. You convinced me, you'll convince the jury." She shifted in her seat and wiped her eyes again. "So, how have you been?"

"Fine. Busy with work. Getting ready for Bo's trial." Ray saw no need to burden her with his guilt about Macy or his fishing trip.

"Well, I've got to go. SLED has arranged a place for me out of town."

"That's the least they could do. What can I do to help you?"

"Nothing. I've just got to get my suitcase from my apartment."

"Let me go get it. I'll bring it to you."

"Don't be ridiculous. I'll be fine. Can you take me back to my car now?"

They left. The beers were untouched.

At the jail, she gave him a tight hug. "I'm going to miss you," she said.

Ray didn't want to let her go. "You'll be back here in no time. Call me to let me know you're safe."

"I will." She kissed his cheek. She got into her car and drove away.

Ray watched until she turned onto the highway. *I really am going to miss her. Maybe we can begin again when this is over.* But he knew that wouldn't happen.

Ray walked through the case with Bo. More like sleepwalked. His mind was still on Annette. Bo's practice testimony was awful. He came across like a late-night infomercial salesman pushing the latest miracle weight-loss gadget.

"Try not to smile so big. This is serious," Ray said.

But Bo didn't get it. He turned into the used car salesman whose face was a false frozen smile because he was afraid of the camera or bored.

"I don't think we should worry anymore with your testimony. Our case is strong enough without it." Ray closed the case file. "We can discredit

Roy Mack's testimony, and our DNA evidence is strong. And our patholo-gist will help your alibi. I don't think you should testify."

Bo nodded but didn't answer.

Ray checked the time when he got into the car to return to the office. He had thirty minutes or so before Deputy Ross was expecting to see him. *Maybe I can get a couple of letters written for paying clients.* He logged in to look for one of his files, and there in the file directory staring at him was a folder labeled "Nelson's Campaigns." It could have been there the whole time, but he had never noticed it. It hadn't been important before. Ray clicked on the icon. A spreadsheet opened. There were numbered files for each of Nelson's campaigns apparently in the law firm's file room. He went to the file room and located the cabinet in the back corner of the room. It was locked. He glanced around for a key but didn't see one. He'd search for it when he got back. It had to be nearby. He didn't have time to look at the files anyway. He was due at the sheriff's office.

Jarrett Brown answered the page for Deputy Ross. He escorted Ray to an interrogation room. "This is Deputy Daniel Ross. He's in the drug unit. He actually thought there might be something to your story."

Ray told Deputy Ross about seeing the Caroline. And about the sub-marine. Somehow the deputy got the impression that Ray had seen it all by accident. They went through it several times. Deputy Ross wanted every detail.

"That's an amazing story," he said. "Thanks."

"What happened to Royal McKenzie?" Jarrett Brown said. "I thought he was your guy?"

"I was fishing, I saw something strange and I was curious." Ray forgot to mention the part where he was looking around the repair dock and met Roy Mack.

"This is the first report of drug smugglers' using a submarine in South Carolina," Ross said. "DEA has reported their use on the west coast and in the gulf. Try to curb that curiosity. It might get you hurt. But we'll check it out. Thanks for coming in." He rose from his seat, nodded at Jarrett and left.

"Now, what were you really doing out there?"

"Fishing."

"Fishing, my ass."

"I caught five Spanish. You should come with me sometime."

Jarrett Brown just glared. He was letting the silence build until Ray talked.

But Ray knew that trick and changed the subject. "Can you explain the two different-colored marks on Candi's neck?"

Brown's nostrils flared as he sucked in a deep breath. And then another one. "Leave that alone."

"I've got a trial in two weeks. I know you haven't looked at Candi's file. I understand that—"

"You don't understand a damn thing."

"Captain Brown, if you want to keep the pictures out of the courtroom and the papers, you need to look at them and tell me what you see. You've got my number." Ray stood and walked out, expecting to be stopped before he got to the door. But Brown let him go.

33

Ray expected that no one would be at the office when he returned from the Sheriff's Department, but he was wrong. A van was in the parking lot, and the cleaning crew was vacuuming the halls. He couldn't search for a key to Nelson's campaign file cabinet while they were working, but he could search for the case that Nelson had settled for the church.

The printed list of cases involving the church wasn't long. As he walked to the file room, a crew member asked if they could clean Ray's office. He nodded and wondered if they had a key to Nelson's office. Nelson always locked his office when he left. Ray pulled each file and flipped through the pages of a few until his office was clean. He took the remaining files to his desk and listened while the crew worked its way down the hall. They skipped Nelson's office.

Ray returned to the church cases and found a file involving a settlement. In that case there had been a relatively minor issue with the architect of one of the buildings. The architect reduced his fee by five thousand dollars. None of the files dealt with a settlement paid by the church.

The crew was still working, so Ray searched the firm network for Tim Thomas. There was only one case, but it fit the time frame for the payment by the church. In a few seconds, he was standing in front of the file cabinet thumbing through the file tabs. The file was not where it should be, though, and he double-checked that he had the correct number. He went through the drawer file by file. He inverted the numbers and searched a different drawer. No file.

An alarm beeped, signaling that a door had been opened. It beeped again. The cleaning crew was done. Ray walked quickly to Trish's office because that's where the key would be. *Unless it's in Nelson's office or he keeps it on his key ring.* He went directly to her desk and jerked her middle desk drawer. He pulled it completely out and dumped the contents onto the floor. The alarm beeped again, and Ray sat down with the empty drawer in his lap. *It's just the cleaning crew. I don't have to explain anything to them.* When the alarm beeped again, he went to the window and watched until the van left.

Ray squatted and started refilling the drawer. He found a file-cabinet key and a door key. *That was easy. The cabinet key and Nelson's office key.* He put the drawer back and wondered, briefly, if Trish would say anything, because he was sure she would notice. Back in the file room, he tried the key. It didn't turn the lock. He wiggled it and tried again. No luck.

When he took the key back to Trish's office he saw the two-drawer file cabinet next to her desk. The key fit, and he quickly searched both drawers. No Tim Thomas file, though. Just some active cases and a few supplies. He made sure he relocked the cabinet when he was done. He checked the shelf on the wall of her office and opened the door to her closet.

"What are you doing in there?"

Ray jumped.

Clint Williams laughed. "Sorry, I couldn't resist," he said.

"You scared me." *He doesn't know how much.* "What brings you out this late?"

"Just dropping off a file. I had to wait on a jury in Georgetown. How about you?" he said.

"Just catching up on some of these foreclosures. How'd you do?"

"Not guilty," he said with a grin. "And isn't that murder case of yours about to come up on the roster?"

"I've got it ready. We go to trial week after next. I'm going to handle it, but I need someone to be second chair. Do you have time to help?"

"Why don't you find me sometime tomorrow or Wednesday and we'll discuss it. I'm ready to get home. I'll see you tomorrow."

"Tomorrow. I owe you one. I didn't hear the door."

"Only the front door chimes. I came in the back. What are you looking for?"

"Do you know where I can find a legal pad?"

"Not in there. I think I've got one in my office." Ray followed Clint out of Trish's office and took a legal pad from him. After Clint had left, he waited until his heart stopped racing before resuming the search. But there wasn't another file-cabinet key in her office.

There was one more place to look, though. Ray slid the door key into the lock of Nelson's office. It opened. He searched every drawer in the desk. He searched the credenza behind the desk and every cabinet under the bookshelves that lined the office. He couldn't find the key or the file. But he did discover a safe in the back of the small closet in Nelson's office.

Ray walked back to Nelson's desk and sat in his chair. He surveyed the desk. There were two neatly stacked files on top of a leather desk pad. Neither one was for Tim Thomas. Nelson's desktop held a pencil holder, a couple of pictures and a gavel with an engraved metal plate. Ray looked under the leather desk pad. Nothing. He dumped the pencil holder in the middle of the pad. And there it was. A file-cabinet key and two folded slips of paper were lying amid the pens and markers. One slip had Nelson's user name and password for the office computer system, and the other looked like a combination. Having learned about the back door, he peeked out Nelson's window at the parking lot before going back to the file room.

This key worked. Ray found the files with the supporting documentation for each contributor. He put the contents of the current year's file on the copier. He could more safely review the documents at home. He pulled out last year's file but didn't copy it. It was large and would take too long. In the bottom drawer of the cabinet were bank statements. He copied the statements for the current year, too. While the copier was working, he checked the cabinet for Tim Thomas's folder. No luck. He returned the campaign files to their place and locked the cabinet. He checked it twice. A large stack of paper went into his briefcase, so large that he had to push on the top with both hands to close the clasps with his thumbs.

It was getting dark when he dropped the key back into Nelson's pencil holder. The slip of paper with the combination was lying next to the pencil holder, and he picked it up. *I should leave. I found what I was looking for. Except for the church file.*

The black safe, about four feet high and three feet wide, filled the bottom half of the coat closet. Ray knelt and spun the combination into the dial in the middle of the door. It opened on the second try. On the right side of the safe was a handgun resting on top of stacks of hundred-dollar bills. The money was bound by rubber bands into bricks of ten thousand dollars. It looked to be a million dollars or more. No time to count. On the left were several manila file folders. The first two dealt with Nelson's divorces. The third one that Ray picked up had "Thomas, Timothy" handwritten on the tab.

The file contained fewer than twenty pages and a copy of a check from the firm's trust account. It was made out to Brittany Jackson. He had to read the name twice.

Ray's heart nearly stopped. The check was dated the same day she'd disappeared. *Oh my God. Oh my God. Brittany. What did you do?* He glanced through the file. Now he understood. His sister had taken the money and gone into hiding. Did Reverend Tim know where she was? Did Nelson?

Ray checked the time on his phone. *Shit, I'm taking too much time.* He hurriedly copied the contents of the folder and returned the file to Nelson's safe. He closed the safe and made sure it was locked. He refilled the pencil holder. He checked and double-checked to make sure that the desk and Nelson's office looked untouched. Then he locked the office and returned the key to Trish's desk. He straightened his desk and left. His briefcase was heavy. His heart was soaring.

34

The blue lights of an unmarked South Carolina Highway Patrol car were strobing in Ray's rearview mirror. He was sitting just outside the city limits of Conway, drumming his fingers on his steering wheel, waiting for the patrolman to finish writing the speeding ticket. Ray wasn't sorry he'd been speeding. He just wanted to get home so he could start on the contents of his bulging briefcase.

"Mr. Jackson," the nice highway patrolman said before handing the ticket to him, "I am giving you a ticket for doing sixty in a forty-five mile an hour zone. Please slow down."

Ray nodded, but he drove slower only until he was safely away from the patrolman.

When he got home, he marched straight to the kitchen table and grabbed the copy of Brittany's file from his briefcase. Whiskers jumped onto the table to help, and Ray pushed him out of the way. The first document was titled "Full and Final Release and Nondisclosure Agreement." Ray read it slowly, twice. The settlement documents required the confidentiality of all parties and provided a full and final release to the church and Tim Thomas for any and all causes of action that Brittany had or may have against the church and Tim Thomas as a result of the conduct of Tim Thomas upon the payment of two hundred fifty-thousand dollars and related medical expenses. It denied the paternity of Reverend Tim for Brittany's unborn child. Reverend Tim had signed the document. Attached to the back of the release was an appointment slip for an abortion at a clinic in North Carolina. The appointment was for a week after the date listed on the documents.

Ray pounded the table. Reverend Tim had gotten Brittany pregnant. *That bastard, that goddamned bastard.* And he'd wanted her to get an abortion. *An abortion.*

Ray stood up. He pulled his tie loose and undid his collar button. *Shit.* He kicked the refrigerator. "Whiskers, I'm gonna kill the son of a bitch." He kicked the appliance again. "After I find Brittany."

He fixed a bourbon and water and took a big swallow. The whiskey warmed his throat. He took a breath and returned to the file. He took off his coat and hung it on the back of a chair. Now he understood. *At least a little.* That's why Brittany had broken up with her boyfriend. She was seeing Reverend Tim. And when she got pregnant, she wouldn't talk to anybody. Then she aborted it. *No, she wouldn't do that.* Brittany believed in a child's right to life. That's why she took the job working for Reverend Tim. *That hypocritical bastard.*

The other document in the file was a duplicate of the release. There were also photocopies of two checks. One page showed the front and back of a check for two hundred fifty-thousand dollars from the church to the Patterson Law Firm Trust Account. The check was signed by Reverend Tim and Nelson. It had been endorsed by Nelson. The other page showed only the front of a check in the same amount and made to Brittany.

He looked again at the release. Brittany didn't sign it. Her signature was not on any document. *Why? Because she changed her mind about the abortion and ran.* That's what she did. She escaped with her baby if not the money.

At least she was alive. He had been looking in the wrong direction. She'd never gone back to Columbia. He spent the next couple of hours reviewing everything he had about her disappearance but found no new clues.

At some point, he came back to the money. A check for a quarter-million dollars had been deposited into the firm's trust account. It couldn't be there after all this time. There would be too many questions for Nelson to answer. Where was it now? He knew Brittany hadn't gotten it, because she hadn't signed the release. Was it part of the stash in Nelson's safe? Or was Nelson's money from somewhere else? Did Nelson know what had happened to Brittany? Ray dropped his head to the table. He still had as many questions about her as ever, if not more.

Around midnight, Ray got a new drink and turned to the campaign files. He started with the donation of Tonya Smalls. All the required documentation was in the copies. The donation had been made in cash, according to the records. There was a corresponding receipt and cash deposit in the bank account records. The same was true for donations by Royal McKenzie, Tony Evans, Jennifer and Annette. It would be impossible to trace the origins of the cash. Nothing to work with except that Tonya was dead when she made the contribution.

The corporations that were in the ownership line of Caroline, the shrimp boat, had all made contributions by wire transfer. The documentation lacked full addresses for the businesses, which was probably a minor violation of the election commission regulations if it was a violation at all. The information on the contributing corporate officers was the same as for the corporation for whom they allegedly work. Their contributions had come by wire transfer as well. All the transfers had originated from the same account at a bank in Reno, Nevada. A dead end.

Ray took a sip of his drink. The ice in his glass was long melted. The bourbon was warm. He added more bourbon and a piece of ice because it looked like this was going to be an all-nighter.

Searching the corporate officers still turned up nothing. The search of the corporations returned the same basic information as before. He searched the bank in Nevada. The state-chartered bank was owned by a bank in Switzerland. The Web site of the Swiss bank proudly displayed its worldwide presence, including a branch in the Cayman Islands with a vaguely familiar name. Jennifer's file was at the office, but Blue Water Trust could be one of the banks involved in the money laundering. He printed the page.

Tuesday morning after settling behind his work desk, Ray called Jarrett Brown and left a voice mail. "Captain Brown, I have a question about a different case. Please call me at your convenience. Thanks."

He retrieved Jennifer's file and looked at the names of the banks involved in the money laundering transfers. Blue Water Trust was the first bank in the alphabetical list of banks that received wire transfers from Orion's accounts. The SLED documents indicated that the money trail ended there. Swiss privacy laws.

Ray was totaling the amount transferred to Blue Water Trust when Nelson stomped through the door. Ray put the file down.

"Has anyone been in your office?" Nelson said.

"What?" Ray felt the blood drain from his face.

"Has anyone been in here? Someone's been through my office."

Shit. "Is anything missing?"

"No—well, I don't think so."

"Now that you mention it, a couple of the files on my desk were disturbed. Maybe it was the cleaning crew. They were here last night. They probably moved some things around."

"They didn't just move things. Someone went through every drawer in my desk. They were looking for something. Check your desk drawers."

"There's nothing worth anything in my desk. I've still got a bunch of stuff in my desk in the Myrtle Beach office."

"Trish thinks her office was searched, too. Would you check with the other guys? I've got to go to Columbia. They found the governor." The governor of South Carolina had been missing for three days. "The self-righteous prick has a girlfriend."

"I'll take care of it," Ray said.

"Good. Thank you."

As soon as Nelson had left for Columbia, Ray walked into Trish's office. "What was that all about?" he said. "I think Nelson's getting paranoid on us."

"Someone was in my desk last night."

"The cleaning crew was here."

"I keep my key to Nelson's office on the right side of my drawer here. It was on the left this morning. And some other stuff is out of place."

"But he said nothing was missing."

"Not that we know of. But that's not why he's so upset. Someone went into his safe."

"Nelson has a safe?" Ignorance was more than bliss. *At least I hope it is.*

"He keeps the dial set on zero. It wasn't on zero this morning."

"Really? Why does he need a safe?"

"I don't know. It's his personal safe. But he locked his door this morning while he checked it. Then he was on the phone for a while."

"Well, he asked that I check with everybody to see if anything is missing. This is weird." He turned to go.

"Ray, I'll be out of the office this afternoon. I've got my divorce hearing. After that a few friends are getting together at Murphy's Law to celebrate. Why don't you join us? About five thirty?"

"Yeah, I can do that. Congratulations."

Ray knew that no one was missing anything, but he checked with every attorney and staff member. He didn't want to make any more stupid mistakes.

35

Clint Williams was not impressed with Ray's plan to blame Royal McKenzie. They had been going over the case for the past hour in Clint's office. Most of the walls were decorated with football memorabilia from high school and Clemson. One wall was reserved for awards from law school, including one for winning the Moot Court competition and another for being assistant editor of the *Law Review*.

"I am not sure that I go after Royal McKenzie with all of the other girls. There's not enough substance to it. You don't have a motive, he's never been a suspect in any of the cases and one of them isn't even a murder. It's a distraction," Clint said, turning pages in the folder that Ray had prepared.

"But that creates some reasonable doubt, doesn't it?"

Clint grimaced. "It could, but you get enough of that just by putting Royal McKenzie at the Three Door and comparing your case with the Tameka Shelley case. I think you should push hard on the DNA and the alibi, especially if your forensics expert can expand the time. And I would spend a lot of time on the unknown person who left Sample B who may or may not be this Thomas Reed. That's your best shot."

"I need to check on that again. I still don't have anything from Illinois on that."

"Do you really need anything more on him? What if you find him and he's got a solid alibi? What if his DNA excludes him?"

"I know," Ray said with a shake of his head. "I know. But the loose end bothers me." His mother always said that the best way to take care of a client was to know the whole truth—good and bad.

"You could try the DMV. They might have an old driver's license on file. It's a long shot, but you could get a picture."

"Thanks. That's a good idea."

"And count on Harry to make a better offer, but not until you get to the courthouse. Ten years or less, your guy should take it. Prepare him now."

"Bo doesn't want a plea. He won't even consider it."

"He'll change his mind when he gets to court. They all do. And, Ray, relax a little. You've got a good case and you know it backwards and forwards. You'll do a good job if you have to try it. And I checked my calendar—I can be your second chair."

"Thanks."

Ray waited until he was out of the office running an errand to call Bubba McHenry. He needed a few private minutes with the attorney general on Saturday. No luck. He called the police officer in Illinois when he returned to work after lunch at a meat and three restaurant. Ray read and replied to four e-mails while he was on hold.

"Mr. Jackson, sorry to keep you waiting. We've been through the archives. I think that Reed file is lost or misfiled or something. We can't find it."

"Well, uh ... can you tell me anything about the case?"

"It must have been a sexual assault case, because it was assigned to Detective Daphne Moore. She investigated most of those."

"Can I talk to her?"

"No, sorry, she died of cancer about two years ago."

"What about a victim's name?"

"It wasn't listed in the directory. The victim must have been a minor. All we got is the file number."

Ray thanked the officer. Another dead end. He called the Illinois Department of Motor Vehicles. If he could get a copy of a driver's license, he might be able to locate Thomas Reed. Assuming Thomas Reed was from Illinois. The department required that a subpoena be mailed just to look, though. It wouldn't accept a fax. He prepared the subpoena himself because Trish was in court for her divorce and put it in the mail, return receipt requested. He wouldn't worry about what Thomas Reed might say until they found him—if they found him.

Ray stopped by Murphy's Law to congratulate Trish after leaving the office. Trish and four girlfriends were doing a shot called Sex on the Beach when he arrived. Ray ordered a drink but soon discovered that this was a girls night. He made his excuses when his first bourbon was gone. Trish gave him a big lingering hug when he got up to leave. If he wasn't the only guy in the group, he might have been tempted to stay.

At five thirty Saturday morning, Ray woke up. Trish was in his arms. What began as a Friday after-work drink had turned into dinner and more. It was no wonder that they fell asleep in her bed. Making love with a woman who hasn't had sex in over a year was ego-boosting and exhausting. But right now he had a problem. He was meeting Bubba McHenry early in Georgetown. He couldn't miss the thirty private minutes that he had finally arranged with Bubba. After a short debate with himself, he woke Trish.

"I've got to be in Georgetown at seven. I hate to leave."

"I know. You told me last night. It's all right. But"—she kissed his chest—"I'll feel better if you stay a little longer." She kissed him again, a little lower. She continued to tease him as she moved slowly down his torso. After a while, they made love again.

"I'll call you when we're done," he said after a quick shower and one last kiss.

"You'd better."

Despite drinking an entire vente coffee with a shot of espresso on the way, Ray was dragging when he arrived at Suzie's Restaurant in Georgetown. It was located at the bottom of the Highway 17 Bridge as you head south. Suzie's had a great view of the Intracoastal Waterway where it joined the Black River. From there it flowed into Winyah Bay and the Atlantic Ocean. Miss Suzie was known for her southern cooking. Her shrimp and grits, made with fresh-caught creek shrimp, was hard to beat, according to an old review in *The New Yorker* that was framed on the wall behind the register.

Bubba was already there and holding court at a large Formica-topped table with seven men of various ages. There was one place left and Bubba motioned him over. "Sissy, Ray looks like he could use a cup of coffee!" he yelled across the place.

Sissy, their waitress, already looked frazzled, but she was prompt with the coffee. Ray ordered while Bubba made the introductions. He knew about half the men. They were from all over the state and appeared to be more financially successful than Ray. They were all wearing hunting shirts or jackets with leather patches on their shooting shoulders. His blue jeans and polo shirt didn't quite match.

After the first round of shooting, the party was grabbing some beers at the clubhouse bar when Bubba tapped Ray on the shoulder. "Let's step over here and talk a minute before the next round." Half the guests were leaving, but Bubba was going to shoot another round of clays with the ones who remained. Ray didn't think his shoulder could take the punishment.

They walked outside.

"How can I help you?" Bubba said.

Ray explained to Bubba about the contributions to Nelson's campaign. "I think some of the laundered money from the bingo games goes to Nelson and his campaign fund. I've got copies of what I found in the car."

"Don't give it to me. I'm running for governor and he is, too. If I present your allegations, they will be dismissed as political. Give it to SLED."

"They already screwed up the investigation of the money laundering."

"I know she's a friend," Bubba said, pointing a finger at him, "but don't let that blind you to the facts."

"That's not it. I think she's involved. But when you tie it all together, the evidence points at John DeHaven."

"I understand that Nelson called in some favors to protect DeHaven. He was cleared before the case got to my office."

"Can't you do anything about that?"

"I'm not the director of SLED, just the AG."

"So what do I do about these donations?"

"Do you know anybody at SLED?"

"Just the agents on this investigation. Maroney and Thompson."

"Call Maroney, Monday. He's pissed off about missing DeHaven. If there's some substance to what you're telling me, they will find it and my office will prosecute."

"Won't Nelson call in some more favors?"

"He can try, but we'll be ready. Besides, I'll be sure Maroney keeps this investigation quiet." Bubba checked his wristwatch. "Are you sure you won't join us for another round?"

On the way home, Ray called Trish just as he had promised. He told her about shooting clays, and she bragged about staying in bed until ten. She invited him to join her for dinner at her house. They ordered some takeout and watched a pay-per-view movie. When he woke, he was still on Trish's couch and it was pitch black outside. He didn't know when he'd fallen asleep and didn't remember much of the movie. He didn't feel like getting in his car to drive home. *Besides, if she wanted me to leave, I wouldn't have a blanket and a pillow.* He pulled the blanket up and turned over. *I wonder what Trish is like in the morning.*

36

After waking to the smell of coffee, Ray walked to the kitchen, leaned against the door frame and watched Trish dance around the room. Her ponytail was bouncing to a tune he couldn't hear. Her lace-lined cream silk nightgown was opaque, revealing less but promising more, much more, than the wax paper covering the top of a hot Krispy Kreme doughnut.

"You sure know how to show a girl a good time," Trish said while pouring two cups.

"Are you talking about Friday or Saturday night?"

She walked over to him, wrapped her arms around his neck and gave him a kiss. Not a peck on the cheek but a breakfast-can-wait kiss. He nibbled her ear and began a slow course of kisses down her neckline to her breasts. They made love in the kitchen and then tried the bed. They never drank the coffee.

"Tell me about your boat," Trish said, stroking his chest.

"Would you like to take her out?"

"That sounds like fun as long as I'm back by five. I've got to be here for the kids."

Ray knew something was wrong before he stopped the car in front of his empty boat slip. Leaving Trish in the still-running car, he jogged over to the office.

"Where's my boat?" he said to the tanned college kid behind the counter of the waterside convenience store that was also the marina office.

"Who are you?" the attendant said.

"Ray Jackson."

The student pulled out the logbook. "It says here that you took it out Monday. You never brought it back."

"I didn't take my boat."

"According to this, you did."

After a useless phone conversation with the marina manager, Ray called the Sheriff's Department to report the theft of his boat. The officer on duty promised to send a deputy when she could. Disconsolate, Ray took Trish to meet Whiskers. She won the cat's approval with a thorough back scratch and then found a way to improve Ray's mood.

Following Bubba's advice, Ray phoned Agent Maroney at SLED before he left his condo Monday morning. He stopped at an office supply store and paid them to fax a few of the supporting documents to Maroney. He was only a few minutes late when he walked through the back door of the law firm. Trish followed him into his office, and he grabbed her and kissed her as if he hadn't seen her for a week.

"You shouldn't do that here," she said, grinning. She looked to be sure they weren't being watched and then kissed him. "Now stop. Captain Jarrett Brown is here to see you. He won't say what it's about, but it's probably your boat."

"No, he's not here about that. He's homicide. I'll see him in a minute. I've got a couple of calls to make."

"He was here when I got here. He seems pretty anxious."

Has he finally looked at Candi's file? "Tell him I'll be with him in just a minute." No harm in making him wait a little longer.

Before Ray could make his first call, the receptionist called. "Captain Brown asked me to say he needs to see you now. It's urgent."

She showed Captain Brown into Ray's office. "Good morning," Ray said standing. "Sorry to keep you waiting."

Brown ignored the proffered hand and grabbed the back of a chair like a bird of prey hitting its victim. "How well did you know Annette Smalls Murphy?"

Ray sank back in his chair. *Oh my God.*

"Do you own an eighteen-foot inboard/outboard with the registration of AG159762?"

"What does that have to do with Annette?"

"Is that your boat?"

"I think those are the numbers. I reported it stolen yesterday. But-"

"Mr. Jackson, I'd like you to come with me. I have some more questions."

"What's going on?"

"We can talk about it at the sheriff's office. Let's go." He motioned for Ray to move to the door.

"Captain Brown, tell me what happened to Annette."

Brown looked at the floor and then at Ray. "The Coast Guard found your boat. It looks like someone pulled the plugs trying to sink it. It was barely afloat. We need to talk about when you took the boat out last."

"Pulling the plugs won't sink my boat. Besides, that's not a crime."

"Ms. Murphy's body was in the boat tied to a seat with your ski rope. We are still working on a time and cause of death. That is a crime. Come with me."

"What?" A couple of tears began to slide down Ray's face. "We can ... we can talk right here."

"Mr. Jackson, I am giving you an opportunity to give a voluntary statement. Or I can arrest you right now." There was a shadow of sadness in his face.

Ray wiped his tears with the back of his hand. "You know I didn't kill Annette."

"I don't know any such thing. Let's go."

It was a basic legal tenet that a suspect didn't talk to the police without a lawyer, and Ray had two of the best lawyers in Horry County, Nelson and Clint, just down the hall. But he didn't call them. The two men walked to the Sheriff's Department without saying a word. Jarrett Brown left Ray in the same somber interrogation room he'd been in last week.

After nearly twenty minutes, Brown returned with his notes and slapped them on the table. "Tell me about your relationship with Ms. Murphy."

Ray told him almost everything. "We are still friends."

"When was the last time you saw Ms. Murphy?"

"At the jail, last Monday afternoon."

"I thought you said that relationship was over."

"I said we're still – shit…" He put his head in his hands. "We had become friends."

"What were you doing at the jail?"

"I have a client in jail. She is—was a friend of my client. She happened to be visiting him when I went to see my client. We talked for a while before she left and I went in to see my client."

"When did you see her after that?"

"I haven't seen her since."

"Where were you last Monday evening?"

"I was in this same room with you and Deputy Ross. Has he found anything?"

"Where did you go after you left here?"

"Back to my office."

"What were you doing there?"

"Uh, working." *I was searching Nelson's office, but I'm not sharing that.*

"Was anyone there with you?"

"No." Ray threw a hand in the air. "Wait, Clint Williams came in while I was there."

"What time was that?"

"Around seven. He didn't stay long. He left before I did."

"How long were you at your office?"

Ray paused. "Until eight or so."

"Where did you go once you left your office?"

"I went home. I was alone except for my cat."

"Did you stop for dinner?"

"Fast food from a drive-in window."

"What time did you get home?"

"Between eight-thirty and nine."

Brown let out a small sigh. "The attendant at Captain John's Marina has told us that you and Ms. Murphy got on your boat between seven thirty and eight o'clock on Monday. You had a bag from a fast-food chain and bought a six-pack of beer." He passed a photocopy of a charge slip from the Marina across the table. "Is that your signature?"

"The date's wrong. I bought the beer on Friday. I wasn't at the marina on Monday. I—"

"Is that your signature?"

"Captain Brown, I nearly forgot. I got a speeding ticket on Highway 501 on the way home Monday. I wasn't at the marina. I can prove it. The ticket is in my car."

"The attendant and another witness identified you from a photo line-up. The other witness says that you and Ms. Murphy were fighting."

"That's a bunch of bullshit. I wasn't there and we never fought. Let's go get the ticket from my car. Call the highway patrolman."

"And we know that you were at her apartment on Saturday."

"I told the deputy that I was checking on her."

Brown sat unmoving for what seemed to be ten minutes. Mute. Ray waited, trying to hang on to his emotions like a kid flying a kite in a storm. Brown looked to his left and then his right even though no one else was in the room. "The other witness is Royal McKenzie. He just moved his boat to your marina."

"Was Annette strangled?" A tear escaped and rode the slope of Ray's face.

"We don't know. The body has been sent for an autopsy. It wasn't in great shape when she was found … I am sorry for your loss."

Ray began to cry. Brown watched for a moment unabashed. Then Brown left the room and Ray had some time to himself. When Brown came back, he had two cups of coffee. A doughnut was riding on a napkin on top of each cup.

"Here. I hope you like it black."

"Thanks." The coffee tasted as if it had been warming in the pot for two hours. Ray took a bite of the doughnut. It was dry, but that actually helped the coffee. "So, what can you tell me?" Ray said after getting a piece of the pastry down.

Brown walked across the room and leaned against the wall with his hands in his pockets. "The boat has been washing around in the salt water for a few days. Whatever physical evidence that might have been left on the boat has probably been washed away. The marina has one security camera in the office. It is on a three-day loop and has been recorded over. You are our only suspect."

"Aren't you the least bit curious about Roy Mack's involvement?"

"I'll need to question him again."

"This is the third murder he's connected to, plus your daughter's death and maybe Bobby Jones."

"When will you let go of that?"

"When you look at the file. There are two sets of marks on your daughter's neck."

"You still haven't given me a motive."

"He's doing it for John DeHaven." Ray blew his nose with a paper napkin. "Somehow all of these girls became a threat to DeHaven. Did you know that Annette was a SLED informant in a money laundering case involving the bingo game at the church, Orion Management and DeHaven? Her identity had been discovered and SLED feared for her safety. Why do you think they arranged for one of your deputies, like the one that stopped me, to ride by her home regularly? She was supposed to be leaving town Monday and going to a safe house."

"Can you confirm that?"

Ray gave him Agent Maroney's name and number. Brown left the room for about twenty minutes. "How did you know she was the informant? Her name has not been released to the public."

"Maybe not to the public, but it was disclosed. Her name was in some discovery filed in SLED's case against Jennifer Jones last week."

"Who would have access to that?"

"The attorneys." Nelson could get it, and Jennifer had been told by her attorney. One of them told DeHaven.

———◆———

37

Captain Brown and Ray Jackson walked quietly back to the law office. Outside, they retrieved the ticket from the glove box of Ray's car, and Captain Brown examined Ray's alleged alibi as they walked inside.

Brown took the same chair he'd nearly strangled earlier while Ray copied the ticket. This time Brown sat. Not relaxed, he seemed lost in his thoughts. After taking the copy, Brown rose to leave. "I know this patrolman. His dad was in the department with me when I started. I can fix this for you."

"That would be great. But don't you think this is a little bigger than a speeding ticket?"

"Yeah, but ..."

"Annette Murphy, Tonya Smalls and Tameka Shelley somehow became a threat to John DeHaven. And now *I* have become a danger to him. I think Royal McKenzie killed these girls. I think the same thing happened to Cindy Martin and your daughter."

"You've got no proof."

"I think it's time that you looked at some photographs that I have over here." He pulled an envelope from his desk drawer.

Brown didn't respond except to straighten his back like a boxer readying for the bell. Ray slid the photographs from Candi's file across the desk and spread them apart. Brown bent over them but did not touch them. He made no sound as his eyes moved from frame to frame. "The marks on her"—he cleared his throat—"on her neck are curious. It could be that she was strangled before she was hung, but you would need a forensic pathologist to tell you that." He looked up at Ray and then back at the photographs. "I'll send them to SLED's guy today." He selected a picture from the near the corner of the desk and pushed it to Ray with one finger. "This is strange."

The photograph showed the rope hanging from the top rail of the staircase and the overturned table on which the investigating deputy surmised that Candi had stood to put the noose around her neck. Ray waited quietly for the explanation. No need to interrupt Brown now.

"Her pictures are still on the wall." Brown was beginning to regain his professional tone. "Death is not instantaneous when you hang yourself. There are"—he blinked his watery eyes—"involuntary body movements. People thrash around. At least some of the pictures should have fallen to the floor. And there should have been some marks or scratches on the wall from her shoes." He stood and pointed at one of the photograhs. Then he walked to the back of the office.

"Did you know that there was a beer bottle in the kitchen trash with Royal McKenzie's fingerprints on it?" Ray said. "He claims that she was upset the night before and he had been there to check on her. According to him, they drank a beer and talked. He said she felt better before he left. That's why he came back when she didn't show up for work. The investigator believed him."

Brown blew his nose and turned toward Ray. "What about Cindy Martin? Royal McKenzie wasn't on the boat."

"Tony Evans was. I think he killed Cindy Martin. And either Tony or Roy Mack killed Bobby Jones."

"Or both."

"True."

"Now all we have to do is prove it," Brown said. "Can I take those pictures? I need to send them to SLED." Brown took the envelope and extended his other hand across the desk. Ray took it with both of his. Brown kept the grip longer than required and met Ray's eyes. "Thanks." A tear welled in Brown's left eye and he wiped it away.

Brown began to leave but turned back. "It's going to take a few days for me to find this trooper," he said, pointing at Ray with the envelope. "You won't be officially cleared until then. OK?"

"That'll give us some time to put it all together."

"Yeah. I'll be in touch." Brown gave a nod and left.

Nelson stormed into Ray's office as soon as Brown had left. "What was that all about?"

"My boat was stolen and they found my ex-girlfriend in it. Dead. Jarrett Brown thinks I did it. He just doesn't have enough to arrest me."

"Did you give him a statement?"

"I did."

"Are you stupid? You know you shouldn't do that without an attorney."

"I know, but—"

"I would have sat with you, or Clint. Hell, where's Clint? Let's get him in here and talk about this. Goddamn it. Trish," Nelson yelled down the hall, "get Clint over here."

Clint joined them in less than five minutes. Nelson shut the door and said, "Now tell us what's going on."

"My former girlfriend, Annette Murphy, was found dead in my boat off the coast somewhere. The plugs had been pulled and the boat was barely afloat. There is a witness statement that I was seen fighting with her at the marina before we left for a ride last Monday."

"What did you tell Captain Brown?" Nelson said.

"That I was working. In fact, Clint came in and scared the shit out of me, remember?"

"Yeah, I stopped by here to drop off the file after winning that B and E in Georgetown. That was, what, about six thirty?" Clint looked to Ray.

"That's right, and I worked for another hour, hour and a half," Ray said.

"That was last Monday night? What were you working on so late?" Nelson stopped his pacing to lean on the back of a chair.

"I've got that murder trial coming up. Mostly I was reviewing that."

Nelson turned to pace, stopped and turned back to Ray. "That's the night someone went through my office."

"Aren't you being a little paranoid about that? Nothing is missing. Not from your office or from anyone else."

"Someone went through my office and got into my safe."

"It wasn't me, and Clint was the only other one here. Did you go into Nelson's safe?"

"What? Me? Hell no," Clint said, sitting up. He looked at Nelson and then back at Ray. "What time does the witness put you at the marina?"

"About an hour after you left."

"So Clint's not really an alibi for you," Nelson said, pacing again. "There's plenty of time to get to your boat from here."

"I guess so."

"So why didn't he arrest you?" Clint said.

"He, uh, might think that Clint was here later than that."

"Clint, are you sure about the time?" Nelson said.

"I … think … I was here for longer than Ray remembers. Seven fifteen?"

"Or seven thirty," Nelson said like a teacher correcting a student.

"Yeah," Clint said, nodding in agreement. "Seven thirty."

"Good," Nelson said, taking a seat. "Well, here's what we're going to do. From now on, I will represent you because Clint's your alibi. Do not talk to Captain Brown again. I think you should go home at least for the rest of the day. I'm afraid the press will be all over this because of my upcoming campaign. If they find you, don't talk to them either. Do you understand?"

"Yes, I do." Ray nodded.

"Are you sure, because you already talked to Captain Brown once?"

"I'm sure."

"Let me know if anything happens, like they come to arrest you," Nelson said, pointing at Ray.

"I will." Another nod.

"And don't say anything else to the police without me."

"Got it."

After Nelson and Clint left, Ray noted that they hadn't asked if he did it. Clint wouldn't want to know. Clint was more interested in winning and losing than in justice. *But does Nelson already know?*

On his way out, Ray stopped at Trish's desk. "I'm going home. You can reach me on my cell if you need me."

"What's going on?"

"There's a problem that will be cleared up soon. Don't worry. I didn't do it, but I am the suspect in the murder of an ex-girlfriend of mine."

"Oh-my-God-Ray. That's terrible. Is that why Nelson needed Clint? Is he going to represent you?"

"He's my alibi, but I won't need him. Captain Brown has to check on a couple of things I told him and then I'll be cleared. If he thought I did it, don't you think he would have arrested me?"

"I guess. How are you doing?"

"I will be all right, but Nelson is afraid that there will be some bad press and wants me to go home. It'll blow over very quickly."

She hugged Ray. She was shivering. "You're really going to be OK?"

"Yes, I promise. I've got to go. Did the subpoenas go out for Bo Heath's case?"

"Of course."

"I might have one more. I'll call you with the information." She pulled him tighter and rested her head on his shoulder. Her hair smelled like some kind of fresh fruit just after it's been cut. *Apple maybe?* He liked it. He gave her a reassuring kiss.

"Call me and let me know that you're OK," she said.

"I will."

Ray decided not to go home. There were two people he needed to see, Lillie Mae Smalls and Bo Heath.

38

There were half a dozen cars parked between the mailboxes and driveways along the road in front of Lillie Mae Smalls's house. Hattie Barcous was the sentry at Lillie Mae's door.

"What do you want?" she said as if he were a wife-beating husband returning home.

"I have come to share Ms. Smalls's sorrow and offer my condolences."

"They say you did it," Hattie said from behind the screen door. Her fists were on her hips. "Lillie Mae's done suffered enough. First Tonya and now her Nettie is killed, and then the sheriff bring out that subpoena from you to go to court next week. Ain't nobody here wants to see you."

"Let him in." Lillie Mae, her face tear-stained, had come near the door.

"Thank you, Mrs. Smalls, but I see that I might cause a disturbance. I wanted to tell you that Annette was very special to me and that I share in your loss. You are in my prayers and thoughts. And I am not Annette's murderer."

Lillie Mae stepped closer to the door. "Thank you, Mr. Jackson. I believe you. I don't think murder is in you."

"I'll leave now, but if there is anything I can do, here is my card, I've written my cell phone number on the back. Call—"

"Can you get them to give us her remains? We can't have a funeral until ..." She began to cry and turned from the door.

"I'll call the officer and see what I can do," Ray said to Hattie, who stood statue-like. The polar cap couldn't have been colder.

"Go away."

A cockroach scurried into the attorney's room under the door while he waited for Bo. It ran out between the guard's legs when his client was brought in. Bo, in his yellow county jumpsuit, slumped into a chair on the other side of the table. "Hello," he said to the floor.

"Bo, Annette Murphy is dead."

"I know." He gave Ray a hard eye-to-eye stare. "I heard you did it." News traveled fast in small-town South Carolina.

"I didn't." Ray took his seat at the table. "Who told you that?"

"One of the guards said I was going to get life and my lawyer was, too."

"He's wrong on both counts. What do you know about Roy Mack and Tony Evans smuggling drugs."

Bo tensed but did not respond. He began to study each finger on his hands.

"Bo." Ray leaned over the table and tried to look him in the eyes. "Bo, Roy Mack has falsely accused you and me of murder. I need your help to expose his lies."

Bo let out a deep breath. "I didn't mean to hurt her." He glanced up at Ray and then looked away. "She made me so mad."

"What? What did you say?"

"I didn't mean to hurt her, and then she was dead and I didn't know what to do."

Ray stared at Bo. "Why are you telling me this now?"

"They got you and now they're going to get me."

"Who?"

Bo gave him an "are you really that stupid?" look but didn't speak.

"OK. Tell me what happened." *Then I'll decide whether or not to believe you.*

Bo shifted in his chair and leaned forward over the table. He began in a voice just above a whisper. "Roy Mack called me on that Saturday afternoon and says he has a job for me."

"And?"

"I meet him at the Three Door and he gives me a rock. He tells me Tonya has to go and can I do it real quiet? I say sure I can."

"Roy Mack asked you to kill Tonya?"

"Yeah."

"Did he ever ask you to kill anyone before?"

"No."

"OK. I'm sorry, Roy Mack was telling you something?"

"Right. He says she's coming soon and he'll tell her to be nice to me and to let him know when it's done. He buys me a beer and I go wait in the back."

"What happened next?"

"I saw Tonya when she come in the Three Door and she talked to Roy Mack. I stopped her when she was leaving and asked her to come with me. I told her I had a rock and did she want to smoke it with me. She said yes. We took a cab to the Thunderbird Motel. I got a room and we smoked the rock and made love. Then she tells me she's pregnant. And I get mad. Next thing I remember she's dead and I got the rope from the blinds in my hand. They were around her neck."

"Why didn't you call nine-one-one? Maybe they could have saved her."

"I didn't want to save her. Roy Mack said she had to go, so I killed her. Anyway, I carried her out to the woods and walked as far from the motel as I could go. I left her there. I didn't like leaving her there, but I didn't know what to do. I didn't even know where I left her until the police told me."

"Did she say who the father was?"

"No, she wouldn't tell me. That pissed me off, too."

Ray paused. "Do you know what she talked to Roy Mack about?"

"No, he just sent her over to me."

"Did you talk to Roy Mack after?"

"Yeah, he called me Monday to ask if I knew where she was."

"What did you tell him?'

"I told him not to worry."

"Was he worried?"

"He didn't think I did it."

Ray sat back in his chair. He rubbed his forehead. "Shit," he muttered.

"You can still win my case, can't you?"

"Win? You just told me you killed her. We should make a plea agreement. Maybe I can get them to agree to a fifteen-year sentence. You—"

"No plea. If they find me guilty, that's all right. I have a right to a trial by a jury of my peers." It sounded like he had memorized that. "That's what Hampton told me. He said I shouldn't take a plea, because you got reasonable doubt. He says you're going to win. No plea."

"Who's Hampton?"

"Willie Hampton. He's in Block A with me. He's been reading up on the law on the computer."

"He's not a lawyer. You'll get at least forty years when we lose, maybe more. Don't forget you are charged with two murders and criminal sexual conduct." Harry Carson had added the charge for the death of Tonya's child, but at least he wasn't seeking the death penalty.

"Hampton says the most I'll do is twenty. They always let you serve concurrent."

"Twenty, thirty or forty—who cares if we can get a deal for less?"

"I'm not worried about that. I told him about how you is going to point the finger at Roy Mack and the DNA thing. Hampton thinks you'll win and I'll go home. I want justice."

"Bo, the last thing you want is justice. You need mercy. Justice puts you in jail for a long time. Mercy for less. I can get a good deal for you if you testify against Roy Mack."

"I'm not turning on Roy Mack."

"Your testimony and some other information I have will put him away for a long time." *And some others with him.*

"No way."

"Why not? He's testifying against you."

"Yeah, but he ain't trying to kill me. If I turn on him, he'll kill me."

"The police can protect you."

"Like they did Annette?"

For the next thirty minutes, Bo and Ray went back and forth over the merits of a guilty plea and the risks of a trial. Bo wouldn't budge.

39

The media were waiting for Ray when he drove into his condominium complex. The mob consisted of two local TV crews and three other press people dispersed along the sidewalk. He was almost disappointed. He walked quickly past the TV reporters, who were busy talking into their cameras, before being recognized. It was the reporter from the *Sun News* who barked the first question. "Did you kill Annette Murphy?"

"I am not guilty and will not make any further comment."

"According to my sources, the victim was your lover." Two microphones and three micro-recorders were shoved into Ray's face.

He decided to try to turn this to his advantage. "Ms. Murphy was working for SLED as an informant. While the sheriff's office is verifying my voluntary statement, they are also investigating a possible connection to the murder of Bobby Jones." He hoped DeHaven and Royal McKenzie would hear that.

"How is this connected to Bobby Jones?"

"I don't know, but investigators are seeking to question the witnesses again. It is possible that a witness is involved in the murder of both Annette Murphy and Bobby Jones. That's all, folks."

He ignored the other questions and went inside. Ray thought about a bourbon but opened the refrigerator instead. He stared at the beer for a minute and then, without taking one, walked to the couch and lay down. He didn't turn on the TV. He just lay there quietly. When Whiskers joined him, he began to weep. He didn't know if he was crying for Annette or Tonya or himself.

Sometime later, Ray got up and went to bed. He couldn't sleep. He had already begun to rework his plan for Bo's trial in his head. Bo's confession meant a change in his trial strategy. Ray could no longer argue that someone else murdered Tonya Smalls. He couldn't make an argument to a jury that he knew was not true. All he could do was make the solicitor prove the case. The U.S. Constitution required that. Ray could point out that the unknown person's DNA created reasonable doubt, but he could no longer argue that Royal McKenzie or Thomas Reed was Tonya's murderer. And he couldn't let Bo testify untruthfully. *Willie Hampton didn't know that.*

On Thursday morning, Jarrett Brown found Ray at the doughnut shop. He got a cup of coffee before he sat at the table.

"How ya doing?" he said.

He might actually be a good guy. "Don't worry about me. Have you heard from forensics?"

"Yeah, they're going to release the body to the family tomorrow. The cause of death was strangulation."

He was talking about Annette. Ray wanted to know about Candi. "That ties with Tameka Shelley's murder and leads to Roy Mack." *And Bo.*

"And Tonya Smalls's case, but I've got no evidence that Roy Mack is the murderer."

"You know Roy Mack and the marina attendant lied about seeing me."

"They'll claim it was just a case of mistaken identity. The guy looked a lot like you. I've seen it a hundred times. I got nothing on him. We're going to talk to Jennifer Jones. The victim was a key witness in SLED's case against her."

"She may not know anything. I believe that John DeHaven set her up to take the fall for the money laundering scheme, but I don't see her involved in murder."

"It's my best lead. According to Agent Maroney, the victim could testify that thousands of dollars were added to the bingo deposits every night. That is several million a year. It was all accounted for and covered with inflated costs submitted to the church by Jennifer Jones."

"There must be some way to implicate John DeHaven."

"I don't see how. Jennifer Jones originated and approved all of the transactions. DeHaven didn't know about it, or at least SLED can't prove that he did." He took a long sip of his coffee. "I see why you like this place. They do make a good cup of coffee."

"Yeah, but I come for the doughnuts." Ray feared he was addicted to that sugar glaze. "Have you heard from forensics on the other case?"

"He'll get to it. It's an old case. It's not urgent for him. I'll call him in a day or two. If he can get something before trial, I'll let you know. And you can use it in the trial if you need to."

"Really? You'll let me use it?"

"Yeah. Believe it or not, you convinced me. I don't think Mr. Heath committed the murder."

"Thank you." *Great.* Obviously, Ray couldn't tell him about Bo's confession. He couldn't tell anyone. "What are you going to do when you get the report from forensics?"

"If my daughter was murdered, I am going to reopen the case. Roy Mack was in her apartment the night before. We have his fingerprint on a beer bottle and he admits being there. You know that."

"Did Deputy Ross turn up anything on the drug smuggling?"

"He gave that to the DEA. We don't have any equipment to hunt submarines. They were very interested."

With nothing more to discuss, Brown rose to leave. "I've got to go. I'll call you when I hear from forensics on that other case. Have a good day."

"One more thing. Did you question Reverend Tim about my sister?"

"What?"

"When my sister disappeared, did you question Reverend Tim?"

"Sure," Brown said with a shrug.

"Did you get the impression he was hiding something?"

Brown sat. "What have you found?"

Ray glanced to the left to be sure no one was listening. "I think Brittany may have been pregnant with his child."

"What makes you think that?"

"I found some papers."

"I'll follow up on that. Can you send me copies?"

"Sure. Thanks."

Brown stood and gave Ray a pat on the shoulder. "No problem."

Jennifer called Ray's cell phone in the middle of the afternoon. He let it ring twice. *Do I really want to talk to her? Probably not.* But he answered anyway.

"I just heard about the death of your stripper. Are you doing all right?"

"I'm doing well, thank you."

"I heard that they think you did it."

"I didn't do anything. Everything will be fine."

"That's what I told you about *my* case. You didn't believe me. But now my attorney says that she expects the charges against me to be dropped."

"She may be right, but I wouldn't count on it. Besides, you've got other things to worry about. When I'm cleared, they will come to talk to you about Annette's death. DeHaven was trying to pin the money laundering to you—don't you think he'll do the same with this murder?"

"I don't have anything to do with it."

"Jennifer, you benefit directly from her death. Who else benefits? Who else has motive?"

"I don't know. You should know. You were sleeping with her."

Ray closed the document on his computer screen so he could focus. "Who do you think killed her?"

"I don't know. I haven't thought about it. Certainly you don't think that I would be a part of that? I don't know anyone who would."

Or you just want to ignore the fact that you do. "And you don't know anyone that would launder money either."

"That's not fair."

"Jennifer, give me a break. Annette was murdered to stop her from testifying against you about the money laundering at the church and Orion. You just said it. Without her testimony, SLED probably drops the case against you. Surely you can see that makes you a suspect. Why don't you come to my office and we'll go talk to Jarrett Brown, the investigating officer? Tell him what you know. It will be a start. They can protect you."

"Protect me from what? I don't know anything. I just called to check on you."

"Where did all that money come from and where did it go?"

"I don't have to take this shit."

"Jennifer, where did the money come from?"

She didn't answer. She was gone. One thing about cell phones was that they took all the drama out of being hung up on.

Before he left for the day, Ray was asked to be a pallbearer for Annette's funeral on Saturday and invited to attend the visitation on Friday. He was honored to accept.

He spent Friday making final preparations for the trial. Friday morning's mail brought copies of driver licenses for six Thomas Reeds from Illinois. He recognized the fourth one.

40

It has been said that many a mourner attending a wake has found solace in a glass of whiskey, but at southern visitations, mourners find their comfort in the intoxicating mixture of fried chicken and sweet tea. Dishes of food covered every available surface in Lillie Mae Smalls's kitchen, all jammed together like cars of tourists trying to get to the beach on the Fourth of July. Ray navigated a tricky path between mourners with overloaded paper plates and the desserts that were scattered throughout the house on every available space. Ray carried a lemon pound cake that he'd purchased at the bakery. His mother had taught him well.

Hattie Barcous confronted Ray at the kitchen door. "You shouldn't have come," she said as she took the cake from him. She created a place for it between some brownies and a lemon meringue pie.

Ray took one of the brownies. "I won't stay long. I don't want to be a distraction."

"People are already staring."

She was right. And those who weren't had turned their backs to Ray. It should have been difficult to walk from room to room, but the crowd shrank away from Ray like he was HIV-contagious. He had no trouble finding Lillie Mae. She alone seemed glad to see him.

Lillie Mae introduced Ray to her daughter, Annette's mother, and as he expressed his condolences, a well-dressed man entered the house. The broad-shouldered gentleman was wearing a navy-blue three-piece suit with a collarless white shirt fully buttoned. He took off his bowler, and his eyes seemed to look everywhere at once. He acknowledged many of the guests as he made his way to Annette's mother, the crowd yielding to him as if he were a minor celebrity.

After he had finished speaking to the mother, he took Lillie Mae's hands in his and whispered a few words that Ray couldn't hear.

"Thank you so much," Lillie said before releasing his hands and turning to Ray. "Do you know Ray Jackson?"

"We've met," Roy Mack said between the teeth of his big false smile that reminded Ray of a shark he'd met on a dive in Cozumel except that Roy Mack's teeth were the smoke-faded yellow of a dying daisy. Ray gave the shark plenty of room. His strategy was different today.

"Good to see you again. I hear you have a boat."

Roy Mack's smile narrowed. "You'll have to take a ride with me sometime."

"That sounds like fun," Ray said. "I still have something I need to talk to you about."

"Today's not a good day."

"It won't take long. Why don't we walk out back?"

"Why don't you leave?" Roy Mack said, standing taller and leaning toward Ray. "No one wants you here."

"I invited him," Lillie Mae said.

"Then don't stay long."

Not wishing to make a scene, Ray excused himself and found a paper plate. He was a southern boy and he loved fried chicken, macaroni and cheese and sweet tea as well as all the other homemade dishes he had to choose from. The selection process wasn't hard. He took a little of everything until his plate was full.

Plate in hand, he found a shady spot in the backyard. Standing where he could overhear a family friend telling an anecdote of Annette's childhood without intruding, Ray watched the back door until he saw Reverend Tim come out of the house. Somehow he had more on his plate than Ray had been able to fit on his. Ray stalked Reverend Tim like a wolf until he cornered him at the back fence. Here was a chance to ask about Brittany.

"Hi, Ray. I'm surprised to see you here."

"Lillie Mae invited me. She's a classy woman."

"It has been such a difficult time for her, losing two grandchildren in such a short time." Reverend Tim took a sip of his tea. "Some of the guests are disturbed that you are here. Maybe you shouldn't stay much longer."

"They'll get over it. I came to give my condolences to Annette's family. You remember I met Annette at bingo. She and I went out a few times."

"Yes, but I understood that you were no longer seeing each other."

"How did you know that?" *Stupid question. There are any number of ways he could know that.*

"I had been doing some … counseling with Annette. She liked you a lot. She blamed herself for your breakup."

"Counseling? Really?"

"Yes, she had a lot of guilt about the way she chose to live her life."

"Were you fucking her?"

Reverend Tim took half a step back. It was all the room he had. His head flipped from side to side, seeking an avenue of escape. "No, that's … that's ridiculous. I was counseling her. That's all."

"Did you counsel Tonya and Tameka Shelley, too?"

"What are you talking about?"

"Do you know that Annette was strangled, like Tonya?"

"No, but I heard that she was found on your boat. I'm surprised you're not in jail."

"I didn't kill her, but I think I know who did. I think they are involved in the deaths of several other women. I think that they are trying to frame me and place all of the blame for this on me, Bo Heath and Jennifer Jones."

"What do Bo and Jennifer have to do with Annette's death?"

"Nothing, it's just that Tonya was strangled and Annette was strangled. Tameka Shelley was strangled. All of them were strippers that had been sleeping with a certain prominent preacher who is covering up money laundering at his church."

"That's absurd." His voice was cool, but his face was pinched.

"You probably know that SLED matched some DNA on Tonya's jeans to Bo. But did you know that a business card with the name Thomas Reed was found in Tonya's pocket?"

Reverend Tim's eyes narrowed into those of a snake. "Who's that?"

"He's a suspect in a rape case in Illinois. I just got an old picture."

Reverend Tim's hand began to shake. He started to look around like a drowning swimmer looks for help. He tried to leave, but Ray blocked his way.

"Reverend Tim—or is it Thomas Reed?—I know you are the father of my sister's child. Where is she?"

Reverend Tim spilled his plate of food. "Fuck," he said, staring at the mess on the ground. "I don't know what you're talking about."

"Yes you do. I've seen the file. Tell me about Brittany."

"No, this conversation is over." He stooped to scrape the scattered food back onto his plate.

Ray squatted but didn't help. "I'll get you out of this if you tell me where my sister is."

Reverend Tim, his face gray and drawn, looked at Ray. "How would I know? She took the money and left."

"She didn't take the money." Nelson would never have released it without her signature. "She didn't get the abortion. She has your child."

Reverend Tim stared at Ray. "She didn't take the money?"

"No."

"Well, where did it go? Nelson said she took it."

"That doesn't matter right now." *I'll bet it's in Nelson's safe.* "Have you heard from her?"

Reverend Tim shook his head and stared at the food on the ground. "No, never."

"Any ideas about where she might have gone?"

Reverend Tim's eyes were wide and his face pale. "I don't know. I've got to go." He dropped his plate to the ground and stood to walk away.

Ray grabbed him by the shoulder. "What? What aren't you telling me?"

"Let me go." Reverend Tim pushed Ray's hand away.

Ray stepped in front of him. "Tell me what you know."

Reverend Tim dropped his head.

"Tell me where she is."

Reverend Tim looked up slowly. "I'm sorry, but if she didn't take the money, she didn't go anywhere." He stepped to the side and walked away. This time Ray let him go.

Ray put one hand on the fence to keep his balance. *He's wrong. She got away.* Then he began to cry quietly. No one bothered him.

Ray took his half-empty plate to the kitchen. The crowd was thinning, and a few of the ladies were already washing dishes and storing food in the kitchen. As Ray gathered a few of the empty platters and casseroles, no one spoke to him, but no one objected either. He added the plates to the pile of dirty dishes on the counter near the sink. He continued the search and rescue for dishes and dinnerware until every dish had been washed or covered. Lillie pressed a paper plate of chicken, macaroni and squash casserole into Ray's hands before he left. A true southern lady never lets an unmarried man go home without food.

Royal McKenzie was leaning on the driver's door of Ray's car. He stood as Ray approached.

Ray stopped a few feet short. "Can I help you?"

"I hope you have a good lawyer," Royal McKenzie said, a wolf's grin spreading across his face. "You're going to need one."

"You will, too. I'll see you in court Tuesday."

They stood silently staring at each other like gunfighters in an old western until a couple of women came out of Lillie Mae's house. Roy Mack waved at them and opened Ray's car door like a valet. Ray had locked it. He always locked his car.

"Have a good night," a still-grinning Roy Mack said when Ray was seated. "Don't forget to buckle up." He closed the door and walked away.

Ray put his food in the passenger seat and looked under the dash. Then he looked under his seat. Finally, he put the key in the ignition, took a deep breath and turned it.

41

Half the graveside crowd was already crying, and Reverend Tim continued to punch the emotional buttons with practiced ease. *They'll all be crying before he's done. Everyone except me.* Ray knew Tim's secrets, and that robbed him of any authenticity.

"Our God, Annette's God, is a God of justice," he said as he stared pointedly at Ray, who was sitting in the front row with the other pallbearers. "Annette will see justice done. Justice is what we all want, and we can have faith that justice is part of God's plan."

The people near Ray began to stare at him. Reverend Tim tried to hide a smile as he seemed to enjoy Ray's discomfort for a moment before resuming his battering of the congregation's emotions. When a tear escaped Reverend Tim's right eye, he let it roll down his cheek without wiping it. Ray doubted that the tear had come from any real emotion. Reverend Tim was just trying to be the Brad Pitt of the pulpit.

Ray didn't talk to Reverend Tim after the funeral, but he wanted to keep the pressure on him. That's why he was standing in line at the door of the church after morning worship the next day.

"Ray," Reverend Tim said loudly and grabbed his hand as if he were an old college buddy, "glad to see you this morning."

"We need—"

Reverend Tim discarded the hand and turned his back to Ray. "Mrs. Mason, how is your son?" he said and gave Mrs. Mason a fatherly hug.

Monday, Nelson walked into Ray's office. He unbuttoned his jacket as he took a chair. His tie was cinched tight in a perfect Windsor knot. "Are you ready?"

Ray glanced up from Bo's file. "Good morning. Yes, just waiting for Clint."

"You're not asking for a continuance?"

"No, I don't need one." He turned a page in his file.

"You're under investigation for murder."

"That has nothing to do with Bo's case."

"Really? I heard that Roy Mack is one of the witnesses who identified you at the marina."

Ray looked up. "So?"

"I don't think you should be trying this case under these circumstances."

"I'll be fine."

"I took Clint's file home with me and worked on it all weekend. We're going to ask Judge King to substitute me as counsel."

"No, we're not," Ray said leaning forward in his chair. "This is my case and I'm going to draw a jury today and try it tomorrow."

"Ray"—Nelson leaned back in his chair and spread his hands—"be reasonable. You're under a lot of stress with this girl's death and the sheriff's office breathing down your neck. You can't try this case."

"Trust me. I can."

"I have an obligation as an officer of the court to bring this to the judge's attention."

"Then let's go do that." Ray stood.

"Wait a minute," Nelson said, holding up a hand. "I can see that you think you can handle this. I hoped you would see that your judgment is impaired but didn't really expect it. I'm not going to Judge King with this—yet. But I am going to be your second chair."

"Clint—"

"Clint understands. I'm your second chair. I want to be there to protect you if you're wrong."

"Protect me?"

"From yourself."

"But—"

"You don't have a choice. Get your file. It's time to go."

The main courtroom in the Horry County Courthouse reminded Ray of his old grade-school auditorium. There were three sections of wooden chairs with seats that folded up separated by two aisles. They were not as comfortable as they looked. The middle section was filled by 127 randomly selected voters and drivers of Horry County. They would be vetted by the judge and scrutinized by the lawyers. They were, allegedly, Bo's peers, and twelve of these people would be chosen to decide his case.

Ray and Nelson took seats in the jury box with other attorneys who had cases scheduled for the week. Everyone rose when Judge King entered and took his place on the bench.

"Madam Clerk," Judge King said, "we're going to select juries for the first two cases. Are the attorneys here and ready to proceed?"

Harry jumped up from his seat at the solicitor's table like a jack in the box. "Harry Carson for the solicitor's office. The attorneys are here and we are ready."

The clerk called the first case for trial. It was an assault and battery. Veteran defense attorney Lyle Dewitt was defending a young woman accused of attacking her boyfriend's lover in a bar.

Then Judge King called Bo's case. The clerk placed slips of paper naming all the potential jurors in a bin and spun it. It looked like an old-fashioned bingo tumbler. A slip of paper was pulled from it and the juror named on it came to the front and stood in front of Judge King. The solicitor went first.

"Please seat this juror," Harry Carson said.

Nelson leaned over to Ray. "Strike this one," he whispered. "He's a pro-death penalty Republican."

Ray stood. "Please excuse this juror."

And so it went until there were twelve jurors in their box along with an alternate. Judge King announced that the trial would begin the next day and excused everyone in the jury pool except the jury chosen for the first case until ten the next morning.

"Gentlemen," Judge King said to Ray and Nelson, "I'll see you at nine tomorrow to hear any preliminary matters."

Harry Carson motioned Ray over to him. "Say, Ray, who is this highway patrolman you subpoenaed? I might have to move to have him excluded. I talked to him—he doesn't know anything about this case. He doesn't know Royal McKenzie. He doesn't know why you subpoenaed him. The reason you listed doesn't appear relevant."

"I disclosed it." Trish had sent Harry an updated witness list on Friday. "He's a potential rebuttal witness to the testimony of Royal McKenzie."

"What's he going to rebut?"

"It goes to the veracity of Mr. McKenzie and statements he made in another case."

"All right. Your guy doesn't want to discuss a plea?"

"He wants his trial."

"See you in the morning," Harry said with a shrug.

Tuesday morning, Ray was at the office by eight. He felt ready. He stopped by Nelson's open door on the way to his office. Nelson's tie was already loosened at the neck and his desk was covered by the contents of a file.

"Ray. Come in and push the door closed if you would."

"Sure," Ray said.

"Come on. Sit down. It's nothing bad," Nelson said, pulling his tie into place. "In fact, I've got to say you have prepared a great case."

Ray sat. He put his briefcase in his lap. "Thanks."

"No, really. I didn't know how well you had done until I went to see our client yesterday afternoon."

"You went to see Bo?"

"Of course. I want to be ready for today."

"Well, good."

"That's why we need to talk a little strategy this morning before we head over to the courthouse."

Ray stiffened. "Like what?"

"We won't mention Thomas Reed."

"I can't do that."

"Think of it as a favor for a client like that Bobby Jones thing." Nelson's eyes, cold like a dead fish, met Ray's.

Ray felt a hard chill run through his body. "No, it would be too obvious and, um, probably grounds for an appeal."

"Could be." Nelson nodded. "But there won't be an appeal. And I'm going to cross-examine Royal McKenzie."

"Thanks, but I've already got that mapped out."

"I think it would be best if I did it, since Roy Mack's a witness against you in an ongoing case."

"That doesn't matter."

"I've heard that he might change his statement after Bo's trial. It was a simple case of confusion. The guy looked like you." Nelson paused to be sure Ray understood. "I'm doing the cross."

"You want Bo to lose."

"I want him to get justice. We both know he killed her."

Ray dropped his chin to his chest but didn't have anything to say.

"Good," Nelson said, rising, "that's settled. I need a cup of joe before we head over. Would you like one?"

Ray stood. "No, not right now."

Nelson walked over and put his hand on Ray's back as they walked toward the door. "You're doing the right thing. You'll find that there are lots of rewards for team players."

42

At nine a.m. Tuesday, a guard from the jail brought Bo into the courtroom. He had on a white button-down shirt with the sleeves rolled up and clean blue jeans. The shirt was new. Ray had bought it.

Bo's jury was not in the courtroom. "Gentlemen," Judge King said to Harry, Nelson and Ray, "I expect to begin this trial around eleven. Can we get opening statements and maybe a witness before lunch? I want to move this along. I've got a full docket this week."

Harry checked with Ray and replied, "I think we can your honor."

"Good. Mr. Jackson, you're not holding out for a better deal for your client, are you?"

"No, sir. My client insists upon his day in court."

"He'll have it. I want you back and ready to go at eleven."

Jarrett Brown followed Ray out of the courthouse. "How about a cup of coffee?" he said. "I've got something for you."

They found a booth at the meat and three restaurant on the corner across from the courthouse. "Here's a copy of the report from SLED on my daughter. She was strangled and then hung. The case is being reopened. Royal McKenzie is the suspect. I wish the sheriff would let me arrest him."

"I bet you do. Thanks," Ray said, indicating the brown envelope. "I think this has brought you some comfort about her death."

"It has, and for my wife." The coffee came. "If you ask, I can testify that Mr. McKenzie is the suspect in another murder. That should help your case," Brown said as soon as the waitress left.

"Thanks," Ray said. *But I can't use it now.* He tried the tepid coffee and made a face. "I hate to run, but I want to review my notes one more time before the trial begins."

"Speaking of notes, I looked at mine and I spoke with Reverend Thomas once about your sister. Now we know he lied about their relationship. I called him yesterday, but he hasn't returned my call. I will be talking to him soon."

"I appreciate that. I'll get you copies of what I have after the trial is over." *And it's more than you think.* It hurt that he couldn't give him Thomas Reed's driver's license until then because it could compromise Bo's case. *Reverend Tim, or whatever his name is, knows something.*

Ray reviewed the file again at the office with a better cup of coffee. Trish had left to meet Dr. Green at the airport. Briefcase in hand, Ray walked with Nelson across the street to the courthouse. They didn't speak. They were ready for trial.

At ten minutes after eleven, Judge King invited Harry Carson to address the jury. Twenty-five minutes later, it was Ray's turn.

"Ladies and gentlemen of the jury, if I were you I would be ready to convict Michael Heath right now. But I caution you to beware of half-truths because they are unreliable. They point us in the wrong direction. Half-truths are not lies, but like lies they hide the whole truth. It is true that Michael Heath was a friend and lover of the victim. It is true that he was at a place called the Three Door on the night the victim was last seen alive. It is true that DNA evidence was found on the victim's clothing that matches Michael Heath." Ray put quotations around the word *matches* with his fingers—corny but it made the point. "It is your job today to determine whether these are whole truths or merely half-truths. Can you trust the witness who will testify that he saw the defendant and the victim leave the Three Door together? Can you trust the testimony that is based on testing of degraded DNA? Is the test accurate? Does it provide the whole truth or is it merely a half-truth?

"You all know that the solicitor has a duty to prove Bo—that's Michael's nickname—guilty beyond a reasonable doubt. Judge King will tell you later that reasonable doubt is simply a doubt that is based in reason, not speculation or whimsy. You are going to hear testimony about

DNA. You will learn that DNA testing brings a mathematical answer. The solicitor will bring a technician from SLED who will testify that DNA found on the victim most likely belongs to the defendant. But he will not testify that the DNA absolutely, positively is the DNA of the defendant." Ray walked slowly to the end of the jury box and turned. "Our witness, Dr. Norman Green, a Ph.D. from a major university, will testify that the DNA is at best a poor match to the defendant and that the DNA could be just as good a match for any number of people. As you listen to the testimony of the DNA experts, use your common sense to decide what evidence to believe.

"You will hear about more DNA evidence. The police found two samples on the victim from which DNA was extracted and tested. The second sample of DNA does not match Bo Heath. SLED's technician will say that there are similarities to the DNA of the defendant, but Dr. Green will testify that it is the DNA of another person.

"Could it be the DNA of Thomas Reed? His name was found on the back of a business card in the victim's pocket, but you won't hear from Thomas Reed. The police can't find him. Did the missing and mysterious Thomas Reed commit this crime?"

Harry jumped to his feet. "Objection. Argument."

Ray walked to his table to hide his smile. Harry had just underlined his point. Ray took a sip of water.

"Mr. Jackson, please confine your remarks to the purpose of opening," Judge King said.

"Thank you, Your Honor," Ray said and turned back to the jury. "That brings me to another area of concern about this case, the investigation. Not only have the police not found Thomas Reed, they haven't found the murder weapon or even the place where the murder was committed. Tonya Smalls was not murdered where her body was found. All the witnesses agree on that. And the police haven't talked to any of Bo's co-workers, the men that were with him when he was arrested. They are just another on the list of things they can't find in this case."

Ray approached the center of the jury box.

"Ladies and gentlemen, you will hear the coroner testify about the time of death. After all of his investigating and scientific testing, he will tell you that Ms. Smalls died after she was last seen at the Three Door on Saturday night between 3 a.m. Sunday morning"—Ray extended his left arm to his side—"and 3 p.m. Sunday afternoon"—he extended his right arm to his other side. He looked from his left hand to his right, swiveling his head slowly. "Twelve hours. No kidding. He knows that she died during these twelve hours even though her body was not discovered until the following Thursday. This is important because you will hear testimony from the police that Mr. Heath was arrested in Charleston on Thursday afternoon where he was working and testimony that he went to work on Sunday"—he paused for effect—"morning." He saw that all the jurors were giving him their full attention. "He stayed in Charleston until his arrest. There will be no testimony that Bo Heath returned from Charleston after leaving on Sunday morning. You will hear testimony from two ladies who found the victim's body." Ray gestured toward the two witnesses sitting in the gallery. "They will tell you that they walked around the field for exercise every morning that week and didn't see the body until Thursday. When they found the body on that morning, they saw it from across the field. They will testify that they didn't see the body before Thursday even though they walked within fifty feet of the place where the body was found on Monday, Tuesday and Wednesday. You will hear that evidence.

"And"—Ray took a few steps along the jury box—"you will hear from Martha Sturn, a forensic pathologist. She will offer expert testimony that questions the findings of the coroner. You will have to weigh her testimony and that of the coroner along with all of the other evidence presented to you from this stand"—he pointed to the witness stand—"to find the truth.

"In the same way, you must test the truthfulness of every witness. For instance, the testimony will show that Bo Heath was at the Three Door with the victim. Who else was at the Three Door at the same time? The witness who brings that testimony: Royal McKenzie. And Royal McKenzie was at the scene when the body was found. I just think that's curious."

Harry began to rise to an objection, but Judge King cut him off with a wave. "Mr. Jackson, please confine yourself to the facts."

Ray turned to the judge. "Thank you, Your Honor." He faced the jury again and took a breath. "Let me address one more thing. Bo Heath will probably not testify in this trial. The judge will tell you that he is not required to testify and that you cannot take that as evidence of his guilt or innocence." He walked back to the table with a smile for Nelson.

"Ladies and gentlemen," he said as he turned again, "let me finish by urging you to test the evidence, for that is how you will discover the whole and half-truths. If you do that, Michael Heath will trust you to find a fair and truthful verdict. Thank you." Ray started toward his seat.

"Mr. Carson, please call your first witness," Judge King said.

"The state calls Captain Jarrett Brown of the Horry County sheriff's office."

Under Harry's questioning, Brown gave the jury an overview of the case. He told them about the investigation and the arrest of Bo. He testified about the scratches on Bo's arms.

When it was Ray's turn, Judge King called the attorneys to the bench. "Mr. Jackson, is your cross going to be long? It is almost time for lunch. The jurors are beginning to fidget."

"Fifteen minutes, maybe twenty?" Ray said.

The judge looked at his watch. "Make it fifteen."

Ray nodded and returned to the defense table. He flipped a page on his legal pad and turned to face Brown. Brown shifted in the witness chair as if he were trying to get more comfortable and was not succeeding.

"Isn't it true, Captain Brown, that the defendant was arrested in Charles—"

"Yes, that's correct."

"And the defendant, according to your investigation, had been in Charleston—"

"He left Myrtle Beach on Sunday morning around 10 a.m."

"Captain Brown," Judge King said, "please allow counsel to complete his question before answering."

"Yes, sir. Sorry, sir."

"And you don't have any evidence that the defendant returned to Myrtle Beach from the 10 a.m. on Sunday morning until the time of his arrest in Charleston on Thursday afternoon, do you?"

"No, sir."

"The victim's body was found on Thursday morning, right?"

"That's correct."

"So, if I understand your testimony, if Bo—I mean Michael Heath—committed this crime, the murder would have had to have been committed before 10 a.m. Sunday morning, isn't that correct?"

"Yes."

"And that would mean that the victim's body was left where it was found behind Palmetto field undiscovered for nearly four days, isn't that correct?"

"That's correct."

"One of the witnesses you questioned at the murder scene was Royal McKenzie, right?"

Brown sat up straighter in the witness chair. "Yes, sir."

"You also questioned Mr. McKenzie at the murder scene of another woman, Tameka Shelley, about three years ago, didn't you?"

"Objection," Harry shouted as he leaped to his feet. "Relevance."

"Your Honor," Ray said, facing the judge, "this goes to the reliability of the testimony of Mr. McKenzie, who is expected to testify later."

"Approach the bench."

When the three attorneys were huddled in front of him, Judge King looked at Ray. "Well?"

"Your Honor, Mr. McKenzie found the body of Tameka Shelley. That case is unsolved. He is connected to the suspicious deaths of several other women. I am simply trying to impeach his testimony."

"Is he a suspect in those cases?" the judge said.

"No," Harry said. "He's not even a person of interest."

"So how does this impeach his testimony?" the judge said.

"Your Honor," Nelson said, "I think there's a deeper issue here."

"Really? You want to tell me what's going on?"

"Why don't we let the jury go to lunch so we have time to discuss this," Nelson said.

Judge King sat back and crossed his arms. Still looking at the attorneys in front of him, he said, "Ladies and gentlemen, something has come up that I need to address with these fine attorneys before we can continue." He sat up and turned to the jury with a smile. "This happens from time to time in a trial. So we're going to take this opportunity to allow you to break for lunch. Do not discuss this case among yourselves or with anyone. Please be back in your jury room by"—he consulted his Rolex—"2 p.m. I hope we can begin again then."

The attorneys waited where they were until the jury had left and the door to the jury room had been closed. "Captain Brown you are excused until two," Judge King said and then turned to the attorneys with a glare. "In my chambers, now!"

Harry began as soon as they'd entered the judge's office. "Your Honor, if they think they can pull some trick and get a new trial—"

"Sit down, Harry, and be quiet," Judge King said. "Explain yourself, Nelson." Ray started to speak, but the judge held up his hand. "You'll get your turn."

"I think that you will agree, Leon, that it is highly unusual for me to sit second chair for a case, particularly an appointed one," Nelson said.

Judge King nodded. It was no secret that Nelson liked to get paid.

"It was all that Ray would let me do. I urged him to ask for a continuance or to allow me or Clint Williams—you know Clint—to try the case because of the personal stress Ray's been under. Ray is under investigation for the murder of Annette Murphy."

"I saw something about that. I would have granted a continuance if asked," the judge said to Ray.

"Ray refused to ask. I was afraid that I knew why. He just confirmed it. The witness in question, Royal McKenzie, has given a statement in the case against Ray that is rather damning. Ray agreed to allow me to examine

Mr. McKenzie. I'm sorry, I didn't think he'd bring it up with a different witness." Nelson lowered his head slightly. "Your Honor, it is with regret that I ask that you relieve Ray. As a friend and attorney, I must stop him before he harms himself further. You know that he has already been punished by the ethics panel in a different matter. I am prepared to finish the case if you desire."

"Why didn't you come to me before the trial began?" Judge King said to Nelson.

"We discussed it at the office and I didn't think there would be problem. Ray has tried a good case to this point."

Harry's mouth hung open.

"Mr. Jackson, were you asking the witness about your case?" Judge King said.

"I didn't kill Annette. And as soon as Captain Brown verifies my alibi, I won't be a suspect. But, Your Honor, this witness gave a false statement to the sheriff's office in a recent murder investigation. The fact that it concerns me is irrelevant. He made a similar statement against Michael Heath in this case. If his most recent statement is false, then the credibility of his statement in the Heath case is questionable. This has nothing to do with me. It concerns the credibility of the witness. A key prosecution witness."

"Clint's statement?" Nelson said.

"He got a speeding ticket," Harry said.

"That's right. I was ten miles inland fifteen to thirty minutes after Mr. McKenzie says he saw me leave Captain John's Marina on my boat with the victim in that case."

"I am going to object to this line of questioning," Harry said. "The introduction of evidence from another, unrelated murder case could lead to confusion among the jurors."

"Your Honor, the witness gave similar statements in both cases identifying a suspect. He misidentified me. He could have misidentified Mr. Heath. It is an important part of the defense."

"Leon," Nelson said, "I think that this is an indication that Ray is not functioning at his best. He is fixating on this particular witness in a manner that appears to be detrimental to the rest of his case and his client. With regret, I renew my request to relieve Mr. Jackson."

"Do you need to be relieved, Mr. Jackson?" Judge King said.

"No, sir."

The judge shook his head and rubbed his face with his hand. "Harry, have you got anything you want to say?"

"No, Your Honor. I just don't want a mistrial."

"There will be no mistrial." He glared at Ray and then at Nelson. "Understood?"

They both nodded.

"Give me a few minutes to consider this and I will rule from the bench on the record. Oh, and gentlemen, since I'm not getting a lunch break, neither are you. Wait for me in the courtroom."

43

Judge King resumed his place on the bench after nearly fifteen minutes. The jury was still at lunch. "Mr. Patterson and Mr. Jackson, will you approach? You can come, too, Harry." They all stood in front of him again. "Nelson, I am not going to grant your request or motion or whatever it is. Like you said, Mr. Jackson has tried a good case so far and we don't want a mistrial. I am not inclined to put it on the record unless you insist."

"There's no need to do that, Your Honor," Nelson said.

"I might be persuaded to revisit the issue if you continue that line of questioning or if Nelson does not continue as co-counsel. Do you understand, Mr. Jackson?"

"I value his input, Your Honor."

"Good." Judge King turned to the court reporter. "Let's go on the record. After an interesting discussion with counsel in chambers, I am going to sustain Mr. Carson's objection to the line of questioning regarding Mr. McKenzie's connection to any other murders or investigations. Mr. Jackson, do you have any further questions for this witness?"

"Yes, sir."

"We'll finish the testimony of Captain Brown when the jury returns. We will resume at two o'clock." He rapped his gavel and strode out of the courtroom.

Shortly after two, Judge King returned to the bench and the jury was brought back. "Ladies and gentlemen," the judge said, addressing the panel, "we are ready to continue with this trial, but I must instruct you to ignore the last question asked of Captain Brown. It has no relevance to this case. Is there anyone who cannot do that?" He paused for a moment and then turned to Ray. "Mr. Jackson, you may continue. Captain Brown, you are still under oath."

"You testified earlier about the photographs on Mr. Heath's arms, right?"

"They had a lot of scratches on them."

"Yes they did. You asked him to explain those scratches didn't you?"

"He said they were from his work and from a mixed martial arts fight he had."

"He denied that they came from the victim, didn't he?"

"Yes."

Ray flipped a page of his notes. "Captain Brown, have you found Thomas Reed?"

"No, we haven't. There wasn't much to go on. The number on the card is no longer a business. The individual who answered didn't know Thomas Reed."

"You would still like to find him, wouldn't you?"

"But we can't. We don't have anything to go on."

"You would like to question him about the murder of Tonya Smalls, wouldn't you?"

"We don't know why she had his name on a card."

"You haven't found any of Mr. Heath's co-workers either, have you?"

"No."

"You would still like to find them, wouldn't you?'

"We tried, but they were probably undocumented workers."

"You would like to question them about this case, right?"

"It might incriminate your client."

"But it might exonerate my client and the point is you don't know, isn't that correct?"

Harry jumped to his feet. "Your Honor, he's—"

"Overruled. The witness will answer."

"What was the question?"

"You don't know what the construction workers would say, do you?"

"No, sir."

"And you haven't found the murder weapon, have you?"

"She was strangled with a small rope."

"But you haven't found that rope, have you?'

"No, sir."

"Or any evidence attached to it?"

"No, sir."

"Or the murder scene?"

"No."

"No further questions, Your Honor."

A bartender from the Three Door was Harry's next witness. He testified that he saw Bo and Tonya at the bar that night and remembered seeing them leave together. Upon cross-examination, he testified that he saw Royal McKenzie that night, that Tonya Smalls was alive when they left and that he didn't know anything about what they did after they walked out the door.

The coroner followed the bartender to the stand.

"Were you able to establish a time of death?" Harry asked after qualifying the witness.

"Yes, the victim died between 3 a.m. on Sunday morning and 3 p.m. on Sunday afternoon."

"Wow, that's a big window."

"Yes it is, but the weather conditions that week prevent us from narrowing it any further."

Harry let the coroner explain how the weather had hampered his determination. Then Harry introduced his best evidence.

"When you examined the body of Ms. Smalls, did you find anything that needed further testing?"

"Yes, I found some tissue underneath her fingernails that appeared to be human skin and some fluid residue on Ms. Smalls's clothing."

"Do you know how they got there?"

"Objection," Ray said, standing. "The question calls for speculation."

"I'm going to overrule that. You may answer the question."

"Tissue of this type when found under the victim's fingernails is usually the result of defensive action by the victim."

"Defensive action?"

"Yes, in trying to defend herself from her attacker, she scratched him, and some of the attacker's skin was left."

"Did you send those samples to SLED?"

The question was leading but harmless, so Ray let it go. The remainder of the coroner's testimony covered the chain of custody for the DNA evidence.

Ray glanced at his notepad as he rose to cross-examine the coroner. He smiled and walked deliberately across the courtroom. "That skin you found under the fingernail, when was it left on the victim?"

"I am not able to determine that."

"And you don't know when the sample on her blouse was left, do you?"

"No, sir, I don't."

"And you don't know what time the victim died, do you?"

"She died between 3 a.m. and 3 p.m. on Sunday."

"You can't testify that the defendant died beyond a reasonable doubt on Sunday morning, can you?"

"She died between 3 a.m. and 3 p.m. on Sunday."

"You can't testify that the defendant died beyond a reasonable doubt on Sunday afternoon, can you?"

"She died between 3 a.m. and 3 p.m. on Sunday."

"Isn't it true that the reason you are giving a range of time is that you don't know when she died?"

"Objection." Harry was on his feet. "Asked and answered."

"I think you've made your point, Mr. Jackson. Sustained."

"Thank you, Your Honor." Ray walked back to the defense table. "One more question. When you examined all of the evidence you received and performed all of the tests that you performed, you didn't find any evidence linking Michael Heath to this murder, did you?"

"I found the DNA samples."

"What tests did you perform on the DNA?"

"I didn't test the DNA. SLED does that."

"I see. So, one more time—none of the tests *you* performed connect Michael Heath to this murder, do they?"

"They don't."

Ray sat down. Nelson was wearing a frown. Harry tried to limit the damage with a few additional questions for the coroner. Then he called his next witness.

The SLED DNA technician looked like a sloppily dressed Harry Potter without the self-confidence. The neck of his dress shirt hung loose like a shirt a boy has borrowed from his father. His suit coat was crumpled and he was wearing tennis shoes beneath unpressed kakis. He stumbled while getting into the witness chair, and a nervous giggle traveled the courtroom. During the course of his direct testimony, Judge King twice asked him to speak up. Harry was not flustered, though. He'd been there before. He covered the two DNA samples, and he didn't sit down until he was sure the members of the jury understood that the DNA from under the fingernails strongly matched Michael Heath and that they understood the similarities to the second sample. Then it was Ray's turn.

"Isn't it true that you tested two DNA samples in this case?"

"Yes, sir"

"Speak up so that the jury can hear you. That was a yes?"

"Yes."

"You have already testified that the defendant matched one sample, isn't that true?"

"Yes, sir." He was louder this time.

"But you can't say that he matches the second sample, can you?"

"There are strong similarities."

"But not a match like to the first sample, right?"

"The second sample has some concurrent points."

"But that's not what you can call a match, is it?"

"No, sir. But they are similar."

"Isn't it likely that the DNA from the second sample belongs to some-one other than the defendant?"

"No, sir."

"But it's not a match to the defendant, is it?"

"I really can't tell. It is similar to the defendant."

"So it could be someone else?"

"I guess so."

Ray walked slowly to the defense table just to let the jury think about that answer. He turned when he got to the table. "What day was the sample that you say matches the defendant left?"

"I'm sorry?"

"Please tell us, if you can, the day that the first sample was left."

"I don't know."

"Can you tell us, like the coroner, that it happened sometime between 3 a.m. and 3 p.m. Sunday?"

"No, that's not what we test."

"So your testimony is that you don't know when the DNA was left on the victim, is that correct?"

"Yes, that's correct."

"Can you tell us which of the men that left the DNA samples on the victim's jeans committed this crime?"

"Objection!" Harry was overloud. "The defense attorney is assuming facts not in evidence."

"Your Honor, the witness just testified that the second sample could belong to someone else."

"I'm going to allow you to ask the substance of the question, but please rephrase it," Judge King said.

"Thank you, Your Honor," Ray, said meaning it this time.

"You can't you tell who murdered the victim from these samples, can you?"

"No, sir. That's not what—"

"You can't even tell us if whoever left these samples committed the crime, can you?"

"No, sir."

"Or if the samples were left at the time the crime was committed?"

"No, sir."

"DNA doesn't do that, does it?"

"No, sir."

"Not bad," Nelson said when Ray returned to his seat. "Your mother would be proud."

Royal McKenzie was sworn in as a witness shortly after three. He had on a tailored teal-blue business suit with a starched white shirt and a conservative striped tie. He looked like a funeral director. The SLED technician could have taken a lesson.

The direct examination of Royal McKenzie was short. Harry elicited little more than a history of the relationship between Bo and Tonya and that Roy Mack saw them leave the Three Door together.

"Your witness," Harry said.

Ray and Nelson both rose. Judge King noticed and glared.

Nelson stared Ray back into his seat. Then, with a big smile, he stepped to the podium. "Mr. McKenzie, you've known both the victim and Mr. Heath for a number of years, isn't that correct?"

"Yes, we work for the same employer."

"But you never worked together, did you?"

"I briefly managed Mr. Heath."

"Oh, where was that?"

"He is a mixed martial arts fighter. I helped him get some fights."

"Good. You said in your testimony that the victim and the defendant were in a relationship, but isn't it true that the relationship was over?"

"Yes, but Bo still had a thing for her."

"But it was over, right?"

"Tonya, thought so."

"And you didn't follow them out of the club, did you?"

"No."

"So you don't know where they went or what they did, do you?"

"No, not until I found Tonya."

"But you didn't see the defendant harm the victim that night, did you?'

"No, but I know he beat her before."

"Please just answer the question."

"I did."

"Ms. Smalls was fine the last time you saw her, right?"

"No, she was dead."

"I mean on Saturday night, when you saw her leave with the defendant, she was fine, wasn't she?"

"Yes, she was still alive then."

"Thank you, Mr. McKenzie, that's all I have." Nelson walked back to the table with a big grin. Ray hung his head.

"I have a few more questions for this witness," Harry said. He asked what Royal McKenzie knew about any physical abuse the victim suffered at Bo's hands. Questions he couldn't have asked without Nelson opening the door because there were no police reports.

Nelson rose to re-cross-examine, and Ray grabbed him by the arm. "Leave it alone," he whispered. "You'll only make it worse."

Nelson shook off the hand and approached the witness. "Ms. Smalls wasn't injured enough to seek medical treatment after any of these alleged incidents of abuse, was she?"

"I don't know. I wouldn't know about them till she come to work with a black eye or something."

"Ms. Smalls never filed a police report about these alleged incidents, did she?"

"No, man, she was too scared of Bo to do that."

"Just one minute, Your Honor," Nelson said as he walked back to the defense table. He leaned over and whispered to Ray, "Any other questions you think I should ask?"

"No, you've done enough."

"I think so, too." Nelson turned to the judge. "That's all I have for this witness."

"Do you have another witness, Mr. Carson?" the judge said.

"The state rests," Harry said.

"Gentlemen, if you will approach the bench. Mr. Jackson, do you want to argue any motions or proceed with your defense?"

"I would move to dismiss all the charges."

"I want to finish this case today, so I'm inclined to dismiss the criminal sexual conduct charge—"

"Your Hon—"

"Be quiet, Harry. You haven't presented any evidence of criminal sexual conduct. But I'm not going to dismiss the murder charges. I'll allow you both to argue any motions once the case is concluded. We're going to take a ten-minute break for the jury. But be ready to go when we get back."

44

As soon as the jury had left the courtroom, Nelson turned to Bo. "Are you ready to testify?"

"We've been over this," Ray said. "He's not testifying."

"Are you sure that's wise?" Nelson said. "I don't think it's going so well. I'll do the direct."

Ray leaned forward to see around Nelson. "Bo, if you testify, you lose. It's that simple."

"I think you need to tell the jury your side of the story," Nelson said.

"Bo, if I think that you aren't going to be truthful, I am required to tell the court of my concern. You don't want that."

"I'm sure Bo will be truthful, won't you?"

Bo looked at Ray and then at Nelson. He started to speak.

"Hang on," Nelson said, holding up a hand. "Rather than making a decision now, why don't we wait and see how it's going?"

"He's not going to testify," Ray said.

"We'll decide that at the appropriate time. We may need him."

"Nelson, there's a problem—"

"Save it. We don't need to do this in the courtroom."

Nelson was right about that. Harry was trying to overhear the conversation while looking busy with his notes.

Judge King returned and then the jury. Ray's first witness was Hattie Barcous.

"Mrs. Barcous, where do you live?"

"Two fifteen West Oak Street, in Conway."

"Where is that in relation to Palmetto field?"

"It's across the street from my house."

"Would you tell us what happened on the morning of October third?"

"That's when me and Lucille, Lucille Johnson, my neighbor, found Tonya Smalls."

"Yes, ma'am. Tell us about that." Ray walked to the far end of the jury box, encouraging Mrs. Barcous to address the jury.

"Well, me and Lucille were on the front steps of my house getting ready for our walk and we seen her."

"You saw the body of the victim?"

"Yes, sir."

"From the front steps of your house across the street—"

"Objection. Leading," Harry said.

"Direct questions, please, Mr. Jackson."

"Thank you, Your Honor."

"What day of the week was this?"

"It was on Thursday."

"How far away from the victim were you?"

"Oh, a long way. We was still on my front steps and she was out in the bushes behind the outfield fence."

"Did you see her body before Thursday?"

"No, sir. It wasn't there."

"How do you know that?"

"Me and Lucille, we walked around the inside of the fence every morning five times for exercise."

"What days did you walk that week?"

"We walked on Monday, Tuesday and Wednesday."

"Did your walk take you near the place where the body was found?"

"Every day."

"And where were you when you first saw the body?"

"Over on my front steps."

"And that's across the street from Palmetto field, right?"

"Objection. Leading," Harry said.

"I'll withdraw. Thank you, Mrs. Barcous. Please answer any questions Mr. Carson has."

"Mrs. Barcous, you and Mrs. Johnson walk inside the fence because the bushes and thorns outside the fence are so thick, right?" Harry said.

"Yes, sir."

"And the victim's body was found behind the right-field fence, correct."

"I think so."

"That would be at the end of the field furthest from your home."

"Yes, that's right."

"And that area behind the right-field fence has a thicket of blackberry bushes that you pick and eat, right?"

"Not anymore."

"Mrs. Barcous, isn't there a large, dense, almost impenetrable growth of blackberry bushes behind the right-field fence?"

"Yes, sir, but we don't eat them anymore."

"And wouldn't you agree that it is a very thick, thorny bunch of bushes?"

"Yes, sir."

"And there are other thorns, weeds and bushes growing up in that area, aren't there?"

"Yes, sir."

"If you think about the fence itself, aren't there some vines growing on the outfield fence?"

"Yes, sir."

"And these vines have leaves and all so that you can't always see what's behind the fence, right?"

"Yes, sir."

"So, isn't it true, Mrs. Barcous, that considering the thickness of the bushes and the thorns and the vines on the fence, Tonya Smalls's body could have been laid in the thick brush behind the field on Saturday night or Sunday without being seen until Thursday?"

"I would have seen it. It wasn't there before Thursday."

Lucille Johnson testified next, and her testimony was nearly the same as Hattie Barcous's.

"The defense calls Dr. Norman Green."

Dr. Norman Green was Ray's DNA expert. Ray gave him a tablet and a marker to use while he explained DNA testing and what he had found. The tablet screen was displayed on a large video screen for the jury. It was also on the judge's computer and two other monitors in the courtroom.

Dr. Green was sixtyish and wore a summer gray suit with a black patterned tie over a starched shirt. His full head of white hair gave him an air of authority. The first step in presenting a scientific witness like Dr. Green is to get the court to recognize him as an expert, so Ray began with a series of questions about Dr. Green's education and experience.

When Ray offered his witness as an expert, Harry stood. "I'd like to ask the witness a few questions regarding his qualifications," he said.

Judge King nodded his consent. Harry approached the witness stand like a bantam rooster entering the fighting circle. "Dr. Green, your resume is impressive. You've written two books and multiple papers about DNA and DNA testing, right?

"Yes, sir."

"You've lectured all over the world, right?"

"Yes, sir."

"And you've provided expert testimony in over fifty murder cases all across the country, right?"

"Yes, that's true."

"And isn't it also true that in every one of these cases"—Harry turned to the jury box—"you testified for the defendant?"

"Yes, it is."

"In fact, you have never testified for the state in any murder case, right?"

"That's correct. They can't afford my fees."

"So, isn't it true that you're being paid for your testimony?"

"No, sir. I'm being paid for my time."

Harry turned toward the jury and paused. "Your Honor," he said without looking at Judge King, "I object to this witness as being biased."

"Objection overruled," Judge King said, looking up from something in front of him. "We will recognize Dr. Green as an expert witness in the area of DNA and DNA testing. Mr. Jackson, you may proceed."

"Thank you, Your Honor," Ray said, standing. He took a look at his notes and stepped toward the witness. "Dr. Green, earlier the jury heard testimony from a SLED technician who examined two samples taken from the victim. Did you study the same material?"

"I believe I did. The samples I received came from SLED."

"Did you receive anything else from SLED?"

"A copy of their findings."

"Did you test the samples?"

"First, the DNA samples you asked me to examine seem to have been degraded. That has a negative effect upon the test results."

"What would cause the material you tested to be degraded?"

"In this case, it appears that the samples were exposed to the weather for several days. Cold, water and exposure to sunlight can impact the integrity of the sample."

"How does that affect the results of the test?"

"DNA testing is, in its most basic form, a comparison test. One maps the DNA strands from one sample and compares them to the map of another sample. A DNA sample looks something like this." He drew on the tablet. "In this instance, the DNA samples taken from the victim provide an incomplete map. We are missing part of the DNA chain. Like this." Another quick illustration. "That renders this test less reliable."

"In what way?"

"It is important to understand"—Dr. Green looked at the jury—"that there are two parts to DNA testing. The first part would be to determine if the samples match in any significant manner. We do that simply by putting the DNA chain of the sample next to the chain of the person we're comparing it to." He turned to Ray. "Do we have those slides?"

"State's exhibit four," said Ray, putting it on the screen for the court.

"Thank you. May I stand?"

"Certainly," Judge King said.

Dr. Green walked to one of the screens and began to teach. "This is a sample from the defendant, Michael Heath, and below it is the sample from under the fingernail of the victim."

A couple of the jurors nodded. They had seen the exhibit earlier.

"You can see by a quick comparison that the sample on the bottom is not as long as the top sample. That is where"—he pointed—"the missing markers would be. Obviously, it would be easier to make a comparison if we had the entire chain."

"Dr. Green," Ray said, "does this sample match the defendant's DNA?"

"As you can see, in the parts of the chain that we have, the strands match at most points." He touched a few of the matches.

"So, is the sample DNA the same DNA as the defendant's?"

"Well, we haven't finished our test."

"There's more?"

"The primary part of the test is not the match but how reliable it is in identifying a person. Let me explain. Many people have a DNA strand that would match the sample from the victim that we have."

"How is that possible? I thought everyone's DNA was different."

"It is, but they are also similar in many places. Since we don't have a complete map to compare, this sample will match other samples. Suppose you asked your GPS for directions to Atlanta and to Chattanooga. From here the first half of the route would be the same, but at some point the routes would diverge and be very different."

"Yes?"

"We don't know whether or not the sample from the victim continues to match the defendant or not."

"So what do we do?"

"We should be concerned with how often a person selected at random from the general population would match Sample A."

"The general population? Isn't this about whether it matches the defendant?"

"No, and that's where many people get lost. If we had a complete strand, we could say definitely that this is the defendant. But with the limited amount of material that we have, we can only say it *could* be the defendant. So we need to ask if it could belong to anyone else."

"I think I understand."

"Think of it like this. Let's say we're looking for a particular green convertible and you own a green convertible. But your green convertible may not be the one we want. Lots of people have green convertibles like many people may have a DNA strand that matches the part we have."

"So what do we do?"

"We need to determine how many other potential matches there are and that will let us compute how likely it is that this sample came from the defendant."

"How did you do that?"

"I compared the sample to the rest of the world. The results of this part of a DNA identification test are reported as a fraction. In regard to the defendant"—Dr. Green turned to the white board and wrote a number—"SLED found that fraction to be one per two hundred fifty-thousand."

"What does that mean?"

"In other words, there is only one match to this sample in every two hundred fifty-thousand people. If this is correct, there is a strong likelihood that the material that was taken from under the fingernail belongs to Michael Heath."

"Is it correct?"

With a smile that made Ray feel like a good student, Dr. Green turned to the jury. "I don't think so. The methodology SLED uses ignores the missing chromosomes at the end of the sample and matches only those that were present." He pointed again. "This failure results in a report that far overstates the likelihood of a match. The formula that I employ, and that is supported by research across the world, accounts in a reasonable manner for the missing part of the sample and provides a far more accurate result."

"In your opinion, what is the likelihood that the DNA sample from the victim's fingernails matches the DNA from Bo Heath?"

"Conservatively, one match would be found in every twelve hundred sixty people." He wrote the number on the board.

"One thousand two hundred and sixty?" Ray said.

"Objection," Harry said, leaping to his feet. "Argumentative."

"Sustained," Judge King said.

"In your expert opinion, Dr. Green, is that a strong match?"

"No. In my opinion"—he turned to the jury—"it is an unreliable match."

Ray walked back to the defense table. He wanted the jury to linger on that answer.

"Now, how well does the other sample match Bo?"

"Even SLED doesn't call that a match." He tapped a link on his tablet and a page appeared on all the screens.

"State's three," Ray said.

Dr. Green looked up and, after a nod from Ray, continued. "Their report says that there are some similarities between your client's DNA and the DNA in Sample B."

"What do you think?"

"SLED is overstating the results again. There are no important similarities. I believe that this is DNA from another person."

"Not Bo Heath?"

"Not Mr. Heath."

"Can you say who?"

"I can only say that the person is a male. The sample is so poorly populated, a comparison search of any database would generate too many matches to make such a search useful."

"Is the person who left Sample B the father of the victim's child?"

"I don't think we can determine that from this sample," Dr. Green said with a shake of his head.

"But we know my client is not the father, right?"

"Right, Mr. Heath is not the father. That is clear."

"Thank you, Dr. Green. Please answer any questions Mr. Carson might have."

Harry approached the witness slowly, holding his clasped hands under his chin. He pointed to Dr. Green with both index fingers. "Isn't it true that after all of your tinkering with the DNA evidence, the formulas and such"—he glanced at the jury—"that the DNA sample found under the victim's fingernail matches the defendant?"

"Yes, it does. It is not a strong match, in my opinion."

"But it is a match."

"It is."

Harry stood still for a second. "Thank you," he said. "That's all I have for this witness."

"Why don't we take a fifteen-minute break so that everyone can stretch their legs?" Judge King said.

45

When the jury had been reseated, Ray called Martha Sturn to the stand. She was dressed in a black business suit with a frilly white blouse over sensible shoes. Her graying hair was cut short in an almost boyish style.

First Ray asked about her qualifications, and after the court accepted her as an expert, he said, "What have you done to prepare for your testimony today?"

"I reviewed the reports of the coroner and the police."

"Did you examine the body of the victim?"

"I wasn't able to do that."

"I see. Do you agree with the coroner's findings?"

"I do not."

"Can you tell us why?"

"He relies primarily on body temperature to determine the time of death. The core body temperature was somewhat cooler than the ambient temperature."

"Ambient temperature?"

"The temperature of the air."

"How could that happen?"

"One way is that the body could have been outside in colder weather for several days, like the coroner says in his report."

"Is there another explanation?"

"Yes, the—"

"Objection," Harry said, rising, "The question calls for speculation."

"Your Honor, the question is based upon the *fact* that no one knows when the body was placed where it was found. There is testimony that the body was not where it was found for several days after the victim went missing."

"I'm going to overrule the objection," the judge said.

"Thank you, Your Honor," Ray and Harry said in near unison.

"Ms. Sturn, what other explanation could there be for the temperature the coroner found?"

"The body could have been stored in a freezer for a time before it was deposited behind the ball field."

"Is there any evidence that the victim's body was stored in a freezer?"

"There are some postmortem temperature burns on her lower legs."

"How would those happen?"

"They could be induced by a freezer but also by being exposed to cold weather."

"So, were you able to determine a time of death?"

"I could not. There are just too many variables."

"Thank you." Ray turned to Harry. "Your witness."

Harry rose but didn't leave his table. "You aren't testifying that the victim's body was stored in a freezer, are you?"

"No, sir, just that—"

"Answer the question. I don't need an explanation. And you're not saying that the victim wasn't killed when the coroner said she was, are you?"

"No, sir, it's—"

"You're not saying the coroner did anything wrong, are you?"

"No, sir."

"You aren't testifying that his data is wrong, are you?"

"No, sir."

Harry's "Thank you, that's all I have" drowned out her final response.

"Please call your next witness," Judge King said as Harry walked back to his seat.

Ray stood. "The defense rests, Your—"

Nelson jumped to his feet. "Could we approach?"

Judge King glared at Nelson and then at Ray. He waved them forward and Harry joined them at the bench.

"What is it this time?" Judge King said with his hand over his microphone.

"Your Honor," Nelson said, "could we get a short recess? I think we need a few minutes to discuss whether or not Mr. Heath is going to testify."

Ray turned his head to Nelson but did not speak.

"You haven't decided this?" the judge said.

"Your Honor," Nelson said, "we did discuss it but delayed our final decision. We only need a few minutes. I am prepared to examine the witness if he testifies."

"Very well," the judge said. "I'll give you fifteen minutes. I assume this is your last witness, so we'll go straight into closing unless Harry is going to offer any rebuttal witnesses."

"None, Your Honor," Harry said.

"Let me excuse the jury. Then you can use my conference room."

"Thank you," all three lawyers said.

The conference room was huge. It had long dark wood table with eighteen chairs around it. On the wall behind the head chair was a framed state flag. Behind the other end chair was a mirror in a gold filigree frame. Nelson took the head chair. Bo and Ray took seats on either side.

"Bo," Nelson said, "You need to testify. It will—"

"He can't testify," Ray said.

"Sure he can."

"Then we can't examine him."

"I can," Nelson said, leaning toward Ray.

"Not if he's going to lie."

"Bo, would you lie under oath?"

"Well, no, sir."

"Yes, he will. Unless he wants to be found guilty."

"Stop right there. I can examine him if I believe he's telling the truth." Nelson said.

"But you know he's not," Ray said.

"Bo"—Nelson grabbed his client's hand—"you need to testify. I can get you through this."

"Nelson, you know the ethics rules won't allow me to watch you solicit perjured testimony. I'll have to inform the judge," Ray said.

"When did you become such a stickler for the rules?"

"Bo." Ray leaned across the table. "It is something that I would be required to do. And if I have to inform the judge, both he and the solicitor will know you are guilty. You don't want that."

There was a knock at the door. "The judge is ready," someone said.

"He's not testifying," Ray said and stood.

"You might want to reconsider that."

"What?"

"The decisions you make in this case, like this one, may have a major impact on your future."

"Is that a threat?"

"A threat?" Nelson said. "No, it's a reminder about what's a stake. I'm just thinking about Bo here." He turned to Bo again. "You need to testify. Ray won't say a thing."

"Damn it, Nelson, he might as well admit his guilt. Bo, you want to be quiet. We've got a chance to win this thing." *And I want to win it*. It didn't matter that Bo was guilty—justice under the Constitution required that the solicitor prove it.

"Bo," Nelson said, "I'm only thinking of you. The jury will know something is up if you don't testify."

Bo looked first at Ray then back at Nelson. He laid his head on his hands on the table.

There was another knock. "The judge is on the bench. He wants you in the courtroom now."

"He's not going to testify and that's final," Ray said. "Let's go."

"Well?" Judge King said as they walked to the defense table. The jury was not in the courtroom.

"Your Honor, thank you for your patience," Ray said. "Mr. Heath is not going to testify. We are ready for closing."

Harry stood. "Your Honor, could you inquire of the defendant regarding his testimony. We need to be sure this is his decision in case of any appeal."

"Certainly, Mr. Carson. Mr. Heath, would you please stand? I am going to ask you some questions about your decision. Madam Clerk, please swear the witness."

Bo stood at the defense table, raised his right hand and swore to tell the truth.

"Mr. Heath, I understand from your attorneys that you do not wish to testify on your own behalf. Is that correct?"

"Yes, sir."

"You understand that you have the right to testify?"

"Yes, sir."

"Are you under the influence of alcohol or any drugs, legal or illegal, at this time?"

"No, sir."

"Has anyone made you promises or coerced you into this decision?"

"No, sir."

"And you realize that this is your only chance to tell your side of the story, to tell the jurors who will decide your guilt or innocence what really happened?"

"Yes, sir."

"Mr. Heath, I don't want any fear that your lawyers aren't prepared for your testimony to influence you. I will recess this trial until tomorrow if you want that time to prepare. Do you understand?"

"Yes, sir."

"Mr. Heath, do you want to testify on your behalf?"

Bo looked down at the table. He looked at his attorneys. Then he raised his head. "No, sir."

"Anything I overlooked, Mr. Carson?" Judge King said.

"No, sir."

"Very good. Mr. Carson, will you open?" The solicitor had the right to begin the closing arguments and to close after Ray's argument, but his second turn was limited to rebutting anything Ray said if he also went first.

"No, sir. We'll waive opening."

"Bailiff, please bring the jury in."

When the jury was seated, Judge King asked Ray to begin. He took the floor, took a breath and began by thanking the jury members for their service and the decision that they were about to make.

"You must decide whether or not the state has proved its case against Mr. Heath beyond a reasonable doubt." Ray began a deliberate walk down the length of the jury box. "The judge will tell you that reasonable doubt is simply doubt for which you can give a reason. You may doubt the guilt of Mr. Heath for the reason that he was not in town for most of the time Ms. Smalls was missing. You may doubt the state's contention that the murder occurred between 3 a.m. Sunday morning and 3 p.m. Sunday afternoon for the reason that the body wasn't found until Thursday and for the reason that Mrs. Hattie Barcous and Mrs. Johnson testified that they walked that field right past the place the body was found on Monday, Tuesday and Wednesday morning without seeing the victim's body. And you recall their testimony that on the morning the body was found, they saw it not from the field but from Mrs. Barcous's front steps. You may doubt the DNA is a reliable match for the reasons given by Dr. Green. You may discount the testimony of Mr. Royal McKenzie because he saw the defendant and the victim together sometime before her death but adds nothing else to the solicitor's case. Ladies and gentlemen, if you have any one of these reasonable doubts, then the state has failed to prove its case and you must acquit Mr. Michael Heath." He reached the end of the jury box and did an about-face.

"Ladies and gentlemen, the state will ask you to convict Michael Heath because he had the opportunity to commit the crime. But what does the state say about the second sample of DNA? Who does it belong to? The SLED technician could not testify that it belonged to Michael Heath. Did that person meet the victim after she left the Three Door? We don't know, because the evidence can't tell us. All that the evidence tells us is that person had the same opportunity to commit this crime as Michael Heath. Was that person Thomas Reed? Was Thomas Reed at the Three Door that

Saturday night? We don't know. When you review the testimony, you'll see that there's still a lot we don't know about this tragic murder." He started to walk again.

"We don't know where Ms. Smalls died. When you listen to the testimony of Hattie Barcous and Dr. Sturn, we don't know when Ms. Smalls died. We don't who left the second sample of DNA. If you believe the testimony of Dr. Green, we don't know if either sample matches Michael Heath. All the state has shown is that Mr. Heath saw Ms. Smalls at a club on the Saturday night sometime before she died. That's all And, I don't think that's enough."

He walked to the defense table and took a sip of water before he continued, "Ladies and gentlemen, I want to thank you for your service today. Please take your time. Consider all of the evidence and I am confident that you will return a fair and just verdict of not guilty."

After Ray had sat down at the defense table, Harry rose slowly, almost reluctantly. Empty-handed, he walked to the jury box. "Common sense. Experience. Ladies and gentlemen, you sit in this box today so that you can bring your common sense and experience to the facts of this case and find the truth. It boils down to this: Michael Heath was seen leaving the Three Door with Tonya Smalls. It was the last time she was seen alive by anyone other than her killer. Michael Heath was a former boyfriend and sexual partner of the victim. He has a history of jealous violence and of abusing the victim. We found his DNA on the victim's clothing. Although the experts disagree on the strength of the match, both experts agree that the DNA matches. Tonya Smalls was pregnant with a child, and Michael Heath was not the father. I believe that Michael Heath discovered the pregnancy and killed Tonya Smalls and her baby in a jealous rage. Your common sense and experience will bring you to the same conclusion."

Ray looked at Bo. He sat at the end of the table nearest the jury and examined his fingernails.

"The defense did the best they could. Michael Heath was out of town for most of the time, they argue, but it was not the entire time. They argue that the body being found on Thursday is somehow proof that Michael Heath didn't commit this crime. But the body lay for days in a thicket of blackberry bushes behind a vine-covered fence. That's why the DNA samples were degraded. And the defense points a finger at Thomas Reed. Maybe Thomas Reed committed this crime. Why does the defense suspect Mr. Reed? Because his name was on a business card found on the victim. That's it. Unfortunately, the victim was not a perfect citizen, but no one saw the victim after 11 p.m. on Saturday with anyone other than Michael Heath. The evidence is that she left with Michael Heath, not Thomas Reed or anyone else. Michael Heath. Ladies and gentlemen, apply your common sense to the facts and you will have no choice but to return a verdict of guilty. Thank you."

Judge King sent the jury out with strict instructions not to begin deliberations until he finished some business with the lawyers. "Gentlemen," he said as soon as the bailiff had closed the door behind the last juror, "I will listen to your motions if you want, but I've heard them before. I'm going to dismiss the criminal sexual conduct charge. Mr. Carson, you just didn't present any evidence to support it beyond the victim's being half naked. And I'm not going to direct a verdict of not guilty, Mr. Jackson. I'm going to let the jury decide this case. That said, do either one of you want to be heard?"

"No, sir," Harry and Ray both said and returned to their seats.

The jury began deliberations at 5:22.

Nelson turned to Ray. One of his huge campaign smiles was fixed to his face. "You did a great job," he said, clearly for the benefit of those nearby. "The jury won't be out long."

"Thanks. I hope you're right."

Nelson walked to the back of the courtroom and made a call. Ray put everything into his briefcase except a legal pad and sat down to wait.

Jarrett Brown tapped him on the shoulder. "It's a shame you couldn't use any of the evidence from the other murders."

"Well, I've got something that you need." Ray reached into his briefcase and retrieved a photocopy of Thomas Reed's driver's license and the phone number of the Illinois police officer. "Here. Call this guy and tell him you found Thomas Reed."

Brown stared at the document. "Reverend Tim is Thomas Reed?"

Ray nodded.

"I'm going to pick him up, now." Brown gave Ray a pat on the shoulder and left.

46

———◆———

After thirty minutes, Ray began to mentally rehearse the motions he would need to make if Bo were found guilty. At the hour mark, he got a cup of coffee from the machine in the judge's office. He got his third at the two-hour mark. The jury finally reached a verdict at 7:43. Not guilty.

After the jury was allowed to leave, Judge King adjourned court for the day. Bo turned to Ray with a grin. "I knew you'd get me off." The guard took Bo without handcuffs to the jail to get his belongings.

Harry met Ray between the attorneys' tables and extended his hand. "I hope you can sleep now that you let a murderer go."

I hope so, too.

As Ray left the courtroom with Nelson for their walk to the office, he turned his phone back on. There were several missed calls and messages. The last two were from Jarrett Brown. Ray tapped the one that had been left just five minutes earlier.

"I've got Thomas Reed and I need to talk to you," Jarrett Brown said in the recording.

Ray looked at Nelson. He couldn't call Jarrett with Nelson standing next to him.

"Anything urgent?" Nelson said.

"No, nothing that can't wait until tomorrow." Ray put his phone in his coat pocket. *I'll call as soon as I get rid of Nelson.*

When they returned to the office, Nelson took a seat behind his desk. "Ray, we tried one hell of a case. Let's go get a drink and savor your victory."

"We?" Ray said, standing next to one of the client armchairs. "You tried to sabotage it."

"I misspoke, opened a door I didn't mean to. But you won."

"Yeah, well, I …" Ray motioned toward the door.

"Besides, we both know he's guilty."

"Not under the law."

"You helped him get away with murder."

"He got justice. The state couldn't prove their case, so he's not guilty."

"Doesn't change the facts."

"What facts are those?"

"Never mind about that," Nelson said with a wave of his hand. "It's over. We should take a minute and enjoy your victory. You've earned it. Your mother would be so proud of you. I've got a bottle of Champagne in the refrigerator on my boat. Why don't we start with that?"

"That sounds great, but I've got a hearing in the morning. I'm going to grab that file and go home." Ray wanted to celebrate. *Winning feels good.* But he wanted to be rid of Nelson so he could call Brown more.

"Bullshit. You don't need five minutes to prepare for a foreclosure hearing."

"Nelson, I appreciate the offer, but I'm going home. I'm tired."

"At least let me buy you dinner."

"Thanks, really, but I'll grab a burger or something."

"Nonsense, Ray. We need to discuss—"

Jennifer walked into the office. Tony Evans, Royal McKenzie and Bo Heath were behind her. Nelson began to stand. "Sit down, Nelson," she said with a wave of her hand.

He dropped into his chair. Jennifer walked over to Ray. Roy Mack took a place behind him.

"You are a pain in the ass," Jennifer said.

Ray wasn't sure how to respond, so he said nothing.

"How did you find out about your sister? And you scared the shit out of Reverend Tim, by the way."

"I was just looking through a file cabinet and there it was." The truth wasn't going to impress her.

"No, you searched Nelson's office, didn't you?"

"Is she alive?"

"Well?" Jennifer turned toward Nelson. "Is she?"

Nelson looked at his lap and didn't respond.

"Did you kill her?" Ray took a step toward Nelson, but Roy Mack grabbed his arm.

"Nelson wouldn't kill anyone," Jennifer said. "So who was it?"

"Tony?" Ray said, straining against Roy Mack's hold.

Tony grinned. "Like I said, it's a big ocean."

"You son of a—" Ray went down. Roy Mack had hit him in the kidney.

"That's when you got the idea to run the money through the church, isn't it?" Jennifer said to Nelson. "You blackmailed Reverend Tim."

Nelson just stared at her.

"Yeah, that's it, and you fed the horny bastard all the girls he wanted."

"We needed him," Nelson said.

"And his reputation," Ray said, getting to his knees.

"Yes."

"That's why Tonya Smalls was killed. She was carrying Tim's baby."

"The stupid bitch thought she could make some money by keeping it." Roy Mack said.

"And that would ruin everything," Jennifer said. "The only reason they didn't kill me is that they didn't know what I had hidden." She nodded at Bo, who tossed a stack of papers onto the floor. "Can't say the same for you, Ray. Are those the only copies you made? Maybe you should think about investing in a safe. But you already know that those aren't foolproof, don't you?" She stared at him for a moment and turned to Nelson. "OK. Here's what we're going to do. Nelson, open your safe and get me the money."

"What?" Nelson said. "I, uh, I ..."

"Open your safe. And give me all the money."

"I don't have—"

Jennifer pulled a gun from her purse. It was small but it shut Nelson up. "John told us about your safe, Nelson, and what's in it. So I want my money."

"There's no money in there."

She turned to Ray, casually pointing the gun. "How much money did you find in the safe?"

"About a million, maybe more."

She turned back to Nelson. "Don't lie to me. I know that you and John didn't like sharing with me. You see, Ray, when I found out what John and Nelson were up to, I asked them to share."

"Or you'd go to the police," Nelson said.

"Shut up," she said with a fast glance at Nelson. "Ray, I made them so much money. I improved the systems. I protected their asses. And what did I get?"

"You got well paid," Nelson said.

She stepped to the desk and leaned over it. "A pittance, Nelson, a pittance. Anyway, Tony and I spent some time with John this afternoon and he told us how the two of you were setting me up." She turned and sat on the desk. "You see, they knew that your girl, Annette, was an informant the whole time. But they let her in so SLED could take me out. Isn't that right, Nelson?"

"You don't know what the fuck you're talking about," Nelson said.

"Really? According to John, I made running the money through bingo much more profitable than when you were doing it yourselves or when you used the casino boat or strip clubs. Then you moved me to the church because it was making so much money that we needed someone on site. That was the excuse, but it was just to set me up. If I was at the church, you wouldn't implicate the other operations. Sure, you'd have to shut down bingo for a while, but you could start over later."

"Jennifer, we can put this all back together. Equal partners."

"Wow, that's a really nice offer. I'll think about it. I do still need your contacts. But right now I want my money. So will you open the safe or do you want Tony to help you?" She motioned to the grinning goon.

Nelson stood. "Jennifer, we can still save this."

She motioned to the closet with her gun.

Nelson took a step. "Really, we can pin it on John."

"Tony," Jennifer said.

Nelson walked to the closet. "Let me give you some of this money and we'll talk about it."

"Sure."

"We can figure this out," Nelson said, kneeling on one knee in front of the safe.

"Open it."

He fiddled with the dial. Tony stood behind him. Ray couldn't see the safe but he could hear the dial turning. Nelson grunted as he pulled the handle, but it didn't open. A second attempt failed. Tony placed his long hands on Nelson's shoulders, touching his neck. Nelson tried a third time.

"Maybe Ray here remembers the combination," Jennifer said.

Ray shook his head. He heard the clunk as the lock released. "Shit," Tony said as he began to wrestle with Nelson.

"You stupid fuck," Tony said, "give—me—that—gun."

It fired. Everyone in the room flinched. It was quiet for a moment as the acrid smell of the powder filled the office.

Then Tony pushed Nelson aside and stood up holding a handgun. "Dumb shit had this on top of his cash."

"Did you kill him?" Jennifer said.

"Hell, no," said Nelson, rolling over. "He shot my prosthetic foot." He crawled out of the closet. His false foot had a hole torn in it just above where the pinkie toe would have been.

"Over here," Jennifer said as she motioned Nelson to his desk with her gun. He had to hop over because the blast had loosened the prosthesis so that it flopped on the end of his leg.

"Bo," Jennifer said, "watch Ray while Roy Mack helps Tony."

Roy Mack had a cloth bag like one for dirty laundry. Tony gave him Nelson's gun, which he put in the back of his pants. Tony started tossing bundles of money into the bag.

"Bo?" Ray said when his client came to a stop behind him.

Bo shrugged. "It's what I do. You know that."

Jennifer looked back at Bo and he shut his mouth. "Nelson," she said, "I need a suicide note for Ray. Type something up. Include how broken up he is about Bobby Jones." She turned to Ray. "Sorry, but someone has to take the fall for this and I told you it wouldn't be me."

"Jarrett Brown and SLED already suspect you in the murder of Annette Murphy." Ray said.

Jennifer looked at Ray. "You know I never liked that little bitch, but they won't tie me to her or your boat. Besides, I thought I set you up pretty well. How did you get out of it?"

"A lucky alibi," Nelson said.

"And Brown also knows that Reverend Tim is Thomas Reed," Ray said.

"Really? Well, that's too bad for Reverend Tim. But we're already out of the bingo business because of the SLED investigation, so that won't matter. And that investigation will end with Reverend Tim's arrest and your disappearance tonight. I'm sorry to tell you that you, Nelson and John DeHaven will get a lot of the blame. Poor John, he was so worried about this he committed suicide just a little while ago. Isn't that right, Tony?"

Tony nodded. "Yeah," he said. "Hung himself."

"And Ray, you've been the bingo attorney all these years. Some of this money will be found in your condo. There's even going to be an account in the Caymans that is connected to you. You helped me see that John and Nelson were setting me up. You were so worried about me. You're so sweet."

"Fuck you," Ray said. *Very original.*

"Never again, Ray. You'll never do that again," she said, patting his cheek. "I am going to miss you. You weren't half-bad." She turned to Nelson. "Let me see that note." She walked around the desk and looked at the screen. "Sit over there." She directed Nelson to a chair on the other side of the desk. Tony walked over to stand behind him while Roy Mack tied the bag of money. "Pathetic." She began to type. She printed a page and placed it on the desk in front of Nelson. "Sign it," she said.

"I—I thought it was for ... for ..."

"Ray," Jennifer said. "I know. I changed my mind. You're the one committing suicide. I think Ray's going fishing." She looked across the desk. "Like his sister."

"Wait, I—" Nelson's words were choked by the rope Tony had whipped around his neck. His eyes bulged.

Jennifer walked around the desk and sat on the edge in front of a gasping Nelson. She leaned into his face. "I told you a long time ago don't fuck with me. But you boys didn't listen." She stood and, with a last look at Nelson, turned toward the door. "Bo, Roy Mack, let's go," she said as she put the gun back in her purse. Bo directed Ray to the door. Ray walked ahead of the men, and Jennifer fell in beside him.

A full moon illuminated the large white Yukon XL that sat in the middle of the parking lot just behind Nelson's Escalade. When Ray stopped, Roy Mack shoved him hard. Having gained a little space, Ray backhanded Jennifer across the face and snatched her purse, hoping to get the gun. Jennifer fell to her knees. Roy Mack swung the bag of money, hitting Ray and knocking him to the ground. The purse skittered away and came to rest under Nelson's car. Roy Mack stepped toward Ray, but Bo tripped him. The big man caught his fall with his hands and sprang to his feet in a boxer's stance. He turned to face Bo.

"Bo, what you doin'?" he said. "You don't want none o' me."

Bo grinned and circled to his right. Roy Mack matched his move. Ray rescued the gun from Jennifer's purse. She was standing beside him with the bag of money when he slid out from under the car.

"Don't move," Ray said as he trained the gun on her.

Jennifer glanced down and then returned her gaze to the two fighters. "You won't shoot me."

Bo faked a jab, and when Roy Mack missed with his roundhouse, Bo kicked Roy Mack in the groin. With the big man bent over in pain, Bo finished him with a left-handed roundhouse and a solid right-handed uppercut. Roy Mack collapsed like one of the twin towers.

Jennifer shrugged and started for the Yukon, dragging the bag.

"Stop," Ray said as he got to his feet. "Jennifer, stop now."

She rounded the vehicle and put the money in the backseat.

"Jenn-i-fer," Ray said, "stop now."

She flipped him the bird and got into the Yukon and drove off. Ray followed the truck with the gun as it left the parking lot. He didn't shoot.

Just then Tony Evans exited the building. "Hey," he shouted at the Yukon. "Wait."

"Stop right there," Ray said, pointing the gun at him.

Tony put his hands up. Bo did the same. Roy Mack, still on the ground, moaned.

"You can't take us both, Ray," Tony said, taking a step closer.

Ray fired. He hit a window behind and to the left of Tony. *Shit, that's my office.* "That, uh, that was a warning," Ray said. "On your knees."

Tony obeyed.

"Bo, come here. Take this," Ray said, indicating the gun. "And get the gun from Roy Mack."

Bo trained the gun on Tony and retrieved the other weapon from Roy Mack while Ray pulled out his phone and called Jarrett Brown.

About the Author

Ben Matthews is a native of South Carolina. He is a graduate of the University Of South Carolina School Of Law and is admitted to the South Carolina Bar. He maintains a law practice in South Carolina. His practice has allowed him to appear in the Horry County Courtrooms on many occasions.

Although he is not a resident of Myrtle Beach, he spent many weeks of summer, multiple spring breaks and a host of weekends along the Grand Strand where he learned to water ski, fish, crab, shrimp, scuba dive and party. It is still the number one getaway for him and his wife.

Mr. Matthews is also the co-author of <u>Blended Family Bliss</u>, a nonfiction work.

56797954R00173

Made in the USA
Lexington, KY
30 October 2016